T5-AGO-854

The Reenchantment of Nineteenth-Century Fiction

Palgrave Studies in Nineteenth-Century Writing and Culture

Palgrave Studies in Nineteenth-Century Writing and Culture is a new monograph series that aims to represent the most innovative research on literary works that were produced in the English-speaking world from the time of the Napoleonic Wars to the *fin de siècle*. Attentive to the historical continuities between "Romantic" and "Victorian", the series will feature studies that help scholarship to reassess the meaning of these terms during a century marked by diverse cultural, literary, and political movements. The main aim of the series is to look at the increasing influence of types of historicism on our understanding of literary forms and genres. It reflects the shift from critical theory to cultural history that has affected not only the period 1800–1900 but also every field within the discipline of English literature. All titles in the series seek to offer fresh critical perspectives and challenging readings of both canonical and non-canonical writings of this era.

Titles include:

Laurel Brake and Julie F. Codell (*editors*)
ENCOUNTERS IN THE VICTORIAN PRESS
Editors, Authors, Readers

Dennis Denisoff
SEXUAL VISUALITY FROM LITERATURE TO FILM, 1850–1950

Laura E. Franey
VICTORIAN TRAVEL WRITING AND IMPERIAL VIOLENCE

Lawrence Frank
VICTORIAN DETECTIVE FICTION AND THE NATURE OF EVIDENCE
The Scientific Investigations of Poe, Dickens and Doyle

David Payne
THE REENCHANTMENT OF NINETEENTH CENTURY FICTION
Dickens, Thackeray, George Eliot and Serialization

Palgrave Studies in Nineteenth Century Writing and Culture
Series Standing Order ISBN 0–333–97700–9 (hardback)
(*outside North America only*)

You can receive future titles in this series as they are published by placing a standing order. Please contact your bookseller or, in case of difficulty, write to us at the address below with your name and address, the title of the series and the ISBN quoted above.

Customer Services Department, Macmillan Distribution Ltd, Houndmills, Basingstoke, Hampshire RG21 6XS, England

The Reenchantment of Nineteenth-Century Fiction

Dickens, Thackeray, George Eliot, and Serialization

David Payne

First published 2005 by
PALGRAVE MACMILLAN
Houndmills, Basingstoke, Hampshire RG21 6XS and
175 Fifth Avenue, New York, N.Y. 10010
Companies and representatives throughout the world

PALGRAVE MACMILLAN is the global academic imprint of the Palgrave Macmillan division of St. Martin's Press, LLC and of Palgrave Macmillan Ltd. Macmillan® is a registered trademark in the United States, United Kingdom and other countries. Palgrave is a registered trademark in the European Union and other countries.

ISBN-13: 978–1–4039–4774–1
ISBN-10: 1–4039–4774–0

This book is printed on paper suitable for recycling and made from fully managed and sustained forest sources.

A catalogue record for this book is available from the British Library.

Library of Congress Cataloging-in-Publication Data
Payne, David, 1961–
The reenchantment of nineteenth-century fiction : Dickens, Thackeray, George Eliot, and serialization / David Payne.
p. cm. – (Palgrave studies in nineteenth-century writing and culture)
Includes bibliographical references and index.
ISBN 1–4039–4774–0 (cloth)
1. English fiction – 19th century – History and criticism.
2. Literature publishing – Great Britain – History – 19th century.
3. Literature and society – Great Britain – History – 19th century.
4. Serialized fiction – Great Britain – History and criticism.
5. Thackeray, William Makepeace, 1811–1863 – Criticism and interpretation. 6. Dickens, Charles, 1812–1870 – Criticism and interpretation. 7. Eliot, George, 1819–1880 – Criticism and interpretation. 8. Social problems in literature. I. Title. II. Series.
PR868.P78P39 2005
823'.809 – dc22 2004056954

10 9 8 7 6 5 4 3 2 1
14 13 12 11 10 09 08 07 06 05

For Audrey

"Behold this gateway. . . . Two paths meet here; no one has yet followed either to its end. This long lane stretches back for an eternity. And the long lane out there, that is another eternity. They contradict each other, these paths; they offend each other face to face; and it is here at this gateway that they come together. The name of the gateway is inscribed above: 'Moment.'"

Nietzsche, Thus Spake Zarathustra

Contents

Illustrations

Preface and Acknowledgements

From Elie Halévy to Boyd Hilton, historians have puzzled over nineteenth-century Britain's respectable religiosity and fervent worldliness. This book shows how Charles Dickens, William Makepeace Thackeray, and George Eliot reenchanted the Victorian world when they delivered their gospel of disenchantment in the symbolic vessels of Christianity, still the primary source for their society's ordeals of development, and in the literary form of the serial, a potent sign of the commodification of culture.

As Linda Colley has suggested for the period 1707–1837, and as Hilton has shown in detail for 1785–1865, the course of nineteenth-century modernization is most visible in the secularization of British political economy and social theory, one example of the phenomenon Max Weber would call "the disenchantment of the world." With the periodical press from which they sprang, Victorian serial novels served as their age's principal source of information about and defense against this development. I entwine the ideological history of theology and political economy, the literary history of the novel, and the commodity history of the serial into a single sociological narrative of developments in religion, social theory, and literary culture.

With their national literary ancestors, Victorian serial novelists shared a disposition to deny the very modernity that had elevated them to positions of unprecedented cultural influence. In its pursuit of categories usually inherited from the Marxian tradition (including capital, the commodity, and the everyday, but sometimes taking up Durkheimian anomie and Weberian spirit as well), recent literary criticism has virtually ignored Victorian literary culture as a compromise-formation between a Protestant past and a commodified present. I too set sketches, stories, melodramas, and serials written between 1836 and 1873 in a sociological context. But I analyze them along lines sketched out by Weber and Bourdieu as well as Marx: as negotiations with modernization on behalf of a society long hostile to social theory; as products of struggle within a field of cultural production; and, most important, as expressions of the religion of benevolence appropriate to a society of commodity producers.

My first chapter shows how ideological, literary, and commodity history come together in the Dickens phenomenon of 1836–7. In his

1836 sketches, written just as *Pickwick Papers* was getting underway, Dickens became the world-capital's leading sociologist of disenchantment when he perceived a common alienation in starving children and dying prostitutes, riverboat revelers and embittered testators. His own mythic response to this modern poetics attached a devoted Cockney to a benevolent capitalist, though the secrets of capital are preserved in Sam Weller's wordplay and Mr. Pickwick's silence. Only a few months afterwards, however, and at the very moment he became the first novelist to wrest away a copyright share from the publisher Richard Bentley, Dickens spoke the dark side of Victorian benevolence when he transformed *Oliver Twist*'s Nancy from insignificant criminal accomplice to significant atoning victim.

I have always been most interested in those moments in Victorian literary history where levels of ideological and generic order change dramatically. The reduction of semiotic complexity between Bulwer's *Paul Clifford* and Dickens's *Oliver Twist* and the prohibition on transfers of capital in the otherwise capacious *Middlemarch* are two such moments in this book. When Dickens reduced the modern city's profusion of signs by means of the generic conventions of the Christian "progress," and when George Eliot restored Dorothea Brooke to her original economic condition, both novelists were conforming to the ideology of restoration that ruled English cultural as well as political life from the Glorious Revolution to the First Reform Bill and beyond. Thus my account of Thackeray's struggle to transform himself from the rejected *Pickwick* illustrator of 1836 to the successful serial novelist of 1847 spends as much time on nearly forgotten serials like *The Yellowplush Correspondence, From Cornhill to Grand Cairo,* and *The Book of Snobs* as on *Vanity Fair* itself. Just as Thackeray secured his distance from the Dickens phenomenon, he innovated the multiplotted serial novel, becoming Dickens's best critic and most serious rival at once.

By contrast, my third chapter approaches another key phase of Dickens's life and career from within the pages of what is perhaps his greatest novel. Between 1856 and 1858, Dickens went through what is now agreed to be the most significant series of personal and professional transformations since his rise to fame nearly twenty years before: his separation from his wife Catherine and her replacement by Ellen Ternan; the conclusion of *Household Words* and the start-up of *All the Year Round*; and the subsumption of Dickens the charitable reader, the melodramatic actor, and the ruthless entrepreneur by the public reader for profit. Such changes appear all the more inevitable when approached from the text of *Little Dorrit*. Burrowing his way to the insight that no sign system, including his own, could represent Victorian modernity's disordered totality, Dickens threw off an astonishing profusion of new literary forms in this work. As he did so, he proved once again that literary culture can sometimes attain truths that the social sciences, for all their ambition, can never quite grasp.

My treatment of George Eliot begins with her early imagination of a genre called "incarnate history," a critical narrative of historical development still illuminated by the presence of the transcendent. The contradictions inherent in this idea would always define George Eliot's vocation as a writer of fiction, just as her production would perennially split the difference between marketed monthly serial and fashioned prewritten volume. Only months after imagining this category, however, "Janet's Repentance," her last "scene of clerical life," turns the dream of sanctifying Victorian modernity into a nightmare of carnality. Only in *Silas Marner* were these extreme representations of "incarnate history" put to their ultimate ideological work. When George Eliot provided a diagnosis and cure for Silas's seizures, she was producing a contented working-class subjectivity, the same fantastically functional object *Pickwick* had imagined a generation before.

The Reenchantment of Victorian Fiction concludes with an examination of the means by which, within and beyond the pages of *Middlemarch*, Eliot ordained herself the high priestess of Victorian sympathy. The circumstances surrounding this first bimonthly serial in Victorian publishing history suggest how essential it had become to supplement the austerities of an intellectualized imagination. As she labored over her masterpiece of disenchantment, Eliot began to practice a sympathetic theatricality from the gardens of Cambridge to the parlor of her London home, while canny publishers, ardent fans, and intellectual disciples all sought out the novelist become "Great Teacher." In this late turn to performance, she was surpassed only by the dying Dickens, the subject of my epilogue, who could not abandon his immensely profitable readings of Scrooge's conversion and Nancy's murder in time to save his own life.

All three novelists, then, succeeded in sacralizing Victorian modernity by incarnating their age as a moment of transcendent fulfillment, or, when that failed, by reenacting bloody rituals of sacrifice from a fading cultural past. Both the magnitude of their success and its historical brevity – the span of a single working lifetime – make these works exemplary for our own era of uneven cultural development, caught as we remain between the familiar but archaic gods of traditional religion and the still mysterious ones of market society.

Though my interest in nineteenth-century British culture dates at least from Frank Turner's 1981 Yale seminar in Victorian intellectual history, this book had its genesis years later as a dissertation under the direction of Steven Marcus and Franco Moretti at Columbia University. The high ambitions and rigorous methods of these two distinguished scholars have been a constant inspiration to me. Though they are not responsible for the failings and excesses that remain, I hope that they will accept my heartfelt thanks.

I have received essential help and invigorating criticism from many friends and collegues over the years. I owe particular debts of gratitude to David Cannadine, who confirmed the importance of Boyd Hilton's work for my own; Professor Hilton himself, for his encouraging response to my early efforts; Martin Hewitt, for helping me reach a wider audience; Regenia Gagnier, for her steadfast support; and John Bowen, for his expert advice and good fellowship. I will always be grateful to John Jordan and Hilary Schor for making me welcome at Santa Cruz, and would also like to thank Jim Adams, Gillian Beer, Rosemarie Bodenheimer, Robert Ferguson, Catherine Gallagher, Edgar Harden, Christopher Lane, James Olney, Bob Patten, John Rogers, Peter Shillingsburg, David Simpson, and Jane Yates, all of whom made important contributions to my thinking. I am grateful also to the Mrs. Giles Whiting Foundation for its financial support at a critical stage.

At Georgia State, Robert Sattelmeyer and Matthew Roudané allowed me time for new drafting and extensive revisions; James and Kathleen Hirsh provided support and friendship throughout. At the end of the project, I found the ideal editor in Joseph Bristow; Paula Kennedy made the production process a pleasure from beginning to end.

Earlier versions of Chapters 1 and 5 appeared in the *Journal of Victorian Culture* and *Novel* respectively; I am grateful to the editors of these journals for the opportunity to present revised versions here. For permission to reproduce visual materials, thanks are due to the New York Public Library, where I spent many happy hours in the early stages of the project, and especially to the curators of the Arents and Berg Collections; to Andrew Mealey at Coventry Libraries and Information Services; and to the Fine Arts Library of Harvard College Library.

Finally, I thank my friends and family for their love and support. Without Audrey Goodman, this book would never have been completed.

Abbreviations

S	*Sketches by Boz*, ed. Dennis Walder
PP	*The Pickwick Papers*, ed. James Kingsley
OT	*Oliver Twist*, ed. Kathleen Tillotson
LD	*Little Dorrit*, ed. John Holloway
PR	*Charles Dickens: the Public Readings*, ed. Philip Collins
PL	*The Letters of Charles Dickens* [Pilgrim Edition]
DP	Robert L. Patten, *Dickens and His Publishers*
CGC	*Notes of a Journey from Cornhill to Grand Cairo*
VF	*Vanity Fair*, ed. Peter L. Shillingsburg
LPP	*Letters and Private Papers of William Makepeace Thackeray*, ed. Gordon N. Ray
SE	*The Standard Edition of the Complete Psychological Works of Sigmund Freud*, trans. and ed. James Strachey
Essays	George Eliot, *Selected Essays, Poems and Other Writings*, ed. A. S. Byatt
SCL	*Scenes of Clerical Life*, ed. David Lodge
SM	*Silas Marner*, ed. Q. D. Leavis
M	*Middlemarch*, ed. David Carroll
L	*The Letters of George Eliot*, ed. Gordon S. Haight
J	*The Journals of George Eliot*, ed. Harris and Johnston
FMW	*From Max Weber*, ed. Gerth and Mills

Introduction

> [D]id the novel replace devotional literature because it was a *fundamentally secular form* – or because it was *religion under a new guise*? If the former, we have a genuine opposition, and the novel opens a truly new phase in European culture; if the latter, we have a case of historical transformism, where the novel supports the long duration of symbolic conventions. . . . This is a task for morphological analysis, and the literary history of the future.
>
> Franco Moretti, *Atlas of the European Novel* (1998)

To the young Charles Dickens, what was distinctive about his London was not only its state of ceaseless change but also its atmosphere of pervasive loss. Making a profit there takes nearly magical powers, as his 1836 account of a fading city nightspot suggests:

> There was a time when if a man ventured to wonder how Vauxhall-gardens would look by day, he was hailed with a shout of derision at the absurdity of the idea. Vauxhall by daylight! A porter-pot without porter, the House of Commons without the Speaker, a gas-lamp without the gas – pooh, nonsense, the thing was not be thought of. It was rumoured, too, in those times, that Vauxhall-gardens by day, were the scene of secret and hidden experiments; that there, carvers were exercised in the mystic art of cutting a moderate-sized ham into slices thin enough to pave the whole of the grounds; that beneath the shade of the tall trees, studious men were constantly engaged in chemical experiments, with the view of discovering how much water a bowl of negus could possibly bear; and that in some retired nooks, appropriated to the study of ornithology, other sage

> and learned men were, by a process known only to themselves, incessantly employed in reducing fowls to a mere combination of skin and bone. (*S* 153)[1]

From ham-shaving to punch-watering to chicken-thinning, Dickens is suggesting that a single process the economic historian Joseph Schumpeter would later name "creative destruction" – technical innovation, market expansion, and capital accumulation, haunted by competition, contraction, and loss – has long been at work behind the scenes at Vauxhall Gardens.[2]

Throughout the age of Dickens, economic activity was the province of "political economy," not yet separated into the modern disciplines of political science, economics, and sociology. Among the great writers in this tradition are John Stuart Mill and Karl Marx, both of whom spent much of their lives in Dickens's London, as well as their predecessor Adam Smith, whose *Wealth of Nations* appeared in 1776. For all three, as for Dickens's narrator, making money is a Faustian enterprise. Even if Smith's ambitious man, beginning life neither desperately poor nor comfortably rich, is successful in his pursuit of economic and social power, he will regret having spent his life in that pursuit; likewise, Smith's progressive division of labor, even as it creates unprecedented wealth, is sure to degrade the lives of most people. Mill also included unequal distributions of wealth and labor in his description of modern capitalism, though its apparently limitless expansion should, he argued, give way to a phase of human progress featuring an improvement in "the art of living."[3] Finally, Marx broadly extended and intensified Mill's critique when he imagined market society as a Faustian drama with commodity exchange as its originating deed, capital as its "animated monster," and the capitalist as its conflicted hero, torn between the old virtues of accumulation and the novel pleasures of consumption.[4]

The scholars of "Vauxhall-Gardens by Day" are commonplace Fausts, well-practiced in the black art of profit maximization. As long as the Gardens were open only at night, the question of how their owners made money from the food and drink they served cast "an air of deep mystery" over the place. But the magic is fading. The most dramatic moment in this sketch is the one in which, having put off his daytime visit – whether from "a morbid consciousness of approaching disappointment" or the weather, he refuses to decide – Boz penetrates the mystery, and consigns his Fausts to the realm of the imaginary: "We paid our shilling at the gate, and then we saw for the first time, that the entrance, if there had ever been any magic about it at all, was now decidedly *disenchanted*, being, in fact, nothing more nor less than a combination of very roughly-painted boards and sawdust" (*S* 155). Even for this twenty-four-year-old, the light of day is harsh, and the enlightenment it brings painful.

Marx was not only the true heir and most devastating critic of classical political economy, but also the founder, with Auguste Comte, of modern sociology. Among Marx's successors, Max Weber too would devote his working life to understanding the phenomena of modern capitalism, concluding that nineteenth-century European humanity deserved the species name "Economic Man." But unlike Marx, Weber pursued this insight far into the realm of culture: in the course of his life, he attempted not only a massive and finally unfinished sociology of world religions, but also an account of the development of music from elemental clang to modern symphony. Being eternally subject to processes of "rationalization and intellectualization" – with results that are often anything but rational – Weber's Economic Man had become a mere pawn in a titanic struggle between the familiar gods of Christianity and the unfamiliar ones of modernity, such that, as Weber intoned to a group of German graduate students in 1918, "the fate of our times" amounted to the "disenchantment" or "demagification [*Entzauberung*] of the world."[5]

The Protestant Ethic and the Spirit of Capitalism's brevity and rhetorical force have made this unrepresentative work the best-known of Weber's massive output, with the result that many readers underestimate both the fundamental importance of historical materialism for Weber's thought and the variety and complexity of his own views.[6] Shortly before his death in 1920, for example, as he labored over the massive work posthumously published as *Economy and Society*, Weber was still revising a classic essay on the sociology of world religions, emphasizing anew the irreducible importance of material factors in any so-called "intellectual history":

> Not ideas, but material and ideal interests, directly govern men's conduct. Yet very frequently the "world images" that have been created by "ideas" have, like switchmen, determined the tracks along which action has been pushed by the dynamic of interest. "From what" and "for what" one wished to be redeemed and, let us not forget, "could be" redeemed, depended upon one's image of the world. There have been very different possibilities in this connection[.][7]

Though Marx believed that class conflict was the fundamental dynamic of a progressive, if tragic, history, and though Weber critiqued the very notion of such a "developmental law," Weber borrowed his metaphors for the interplay of material and ideal interests from Marx and Trotsky respectively. In Weber's hands, however, they remain fundamentally ambiguous: the locomotive of material life is driven by a process that remains unidentified, like the identity of the "switchmen" who redirect it, while the lever wielded is an ancient rather than modern machine. As he acknowledged shortly before his death, then, Weber's debt to Marx was greater than to any other thinker besides Nietzsche, just as Pierre Bourdieu would later locate common "principles of social knowledge" in all three of these predecessors.[8]

To Matthew Arnold, like Dickens, living and thinking meant coping with the constant sensation of an historical uncanny, "wandering between two worlds, one dead, / The other powerless to be born."[9] The same could also be said of the founders of the sociological tradition. At some rare moment, as Marx wrote in *The Eighteenth Brumaire of Louis Bonaparte* (1852), a genuinely new historical event might occur; yet those involved in such events seem invariably to "conjure up the spirits of the past to their service, and borrow from them names, battle cries, and costumes in order to present the new scene of world history in this time-honored disguise and this borrowed language." Marx was speaking, of course, of the French revolutions of 1789, 1793–5, and 1848–51, but his point also applies as much to England's own seventeenth-century revolutionaries, whose theory of the "ancient constitution" had denied the sovereignty of the Stuart monarchy, as to British radicals of the 1790s and 1830s, nearly all of whom invoked the same idea in the name of change.[10] Weber also believed that the old gods were still, somehow, at work: even if they were now cast "in the form of impersonal forces," they nonetheless "strive to gain power over our lives," and again "resume their eternal struggle with one another," with the result that working life becomes more demanding than ever before, and private life more and more pressed to relieve objective meaninglessness and subjective ennui.[11]

"Vauxhall-Gardens by Day" too evokes this tendency to drag along the past on the way to the future. What drew the young Dickens to the place was a race between the balloonist Charles Green and his wife against Green's son and *his* wife: as they will go "'twenty or thirty mile in three hours or so,'" and then return to town by carriage, an observer murmurs that "'I don't know where this here science is to stop, mind you; that's what bothers me'" (*S* 157–8). But Dickens has noted that each balloon will also contain an aristocrat, the sole function of whom is to attract the middle-class audience with the spectacle of "a Lord . . . 'going up'" (157). Being useless, and like Marx's tricked-up historical actors, the Lord's only use is to decorate this race to nowhere with the semblance of meaning.

The English novel had long thrived on the contradiction between the needs to represent the phenomena of capitalist development, and especially its speed, and to assign some intelligible meaning to those phenomena – a contradiction longstanding enough to have already generated Defoe's *Robinson Crusoe,* featuring its title's moral accountant; Richardson's *Pamela,* a conduct-book on seduction; and Fielding's *Tom Jones,* a desacralized epic.[12] This book investigates how Charles Dickens, W. M. Thackeray, and George Eliot each puzzled over the difference between "creative" and "destructive" economic activity, as between "religious" and "secular" culture. As exemplary products of a society now requiring the imagination of some unitary past, but born into the conviction that the society for which they performed such strenuous work was fundamentally disordered, Victorian serial novels diffused their composites of archaic and modern cultural materials – the literary equivalents of a cross riveted onto a steam engine, or a virgin stenciled onto a dynamo – across the first industrial nation.[13]

Dickens and his successors achieved their distinctive positions when they produced their own characteristic variations on two Victorian world-views recently made available to us in all their rich and contradictory profusion by Boyd Hilton. The first of these is the Incarnation, the theological doctrine asserting the immanent sanctity of life; the second is the Atonement, the Incarnation's dark counterpart, just as the Passion's sacrificial meal has always followed, and contradicted, the Christmas feast.[14] By these means each writer I consider here oscillates between two contradictory dispositions: that Victorian social life, however disenchanted it may seem, must contain some hidden, sacred, and lively essence; and that only the suffering palpable in that life could atone for a fall into modernity. But I am also concerned with showing how this oscillation was worked out under the spell of the monthly serial, and especially the Dickensian monthly "part," perhaps the most distinctive hieroglyph for the commodification of Victorian literary culture.

In 1833, a tourist on the Isle of Wight spotted a certain fourteen-year-old girl sitting on a grave and reading to her mother. The girl was the Princess Victoria, the book *The Dairyman's Daughter* (1810), and the book's author Legh Richmond, father of Victoria's chaplain. Richmond's heroine, a "pure and simple" dairymaid taken from "real life and circumstance," urges the villagers around her to obey their clergyman and to repent their sins before she expires from consumption; the slim volume would sell two million copies by the end of the century.[15]

The twin imperatives animating now-forgotten works like *The Dairyman's Daughter* – not only to apprehend reality, but to pass judgment on it – also invigorated Victorian religious periodicals. In its first issue of January 1834, for example, only a few weeks after the appearance of Dickens's first published sketch, Charlotte Elizabeth Tonna committed her new venture, the *Christian Lady's Magazine*, to "articles on subjects deeply *practical*, affecting our Christian ladies in their various and important domestic relationships."[16] In doing so, she was recalling the title and mission of Wilberforce's *A Practical View of Christianity* (1798). To Wesleyan Methodism's "religion of the heart," requiring a personal and emotional conviction of sin, Wilberforce had added a nationalist dimension: even the victor of Waterloo and Trafalgar must make propitiation for its persistently sinful way of life.[17]

Perhaps no figure better embodies this evangelical world-view's fusion of theology, economics, and politics, than the ordained political economist Thomas Chalmers (1780–1847). Chalmers's efforts in the slum parishes of Glasgow, begun against the will of the church establishment there in 1819, were intended to prove that morality could enable economic success without the aid of philanthropy.[18] Even in the face of the Glasgow experiment's dubious results, and soon ensconced in a chair at St. Andrews University, Edinburgh, Chalmers remained the leading national spokesman for laissez-faire economics featuring moral instruction as the only acceptable form for poor relief: "I should count the salvation of a single soul of more value than the deliverance of a whole empire from pauperism," as he wrote in the Peterloo year 1819.[19] His series of analogies between profit and election, debt and sin, the speculator and the devil, and the poor man and the crucified Christ would remain in wide circulation through the 1830s.

This ideology of Atonement began to come under sustained attack only after 1826, the year of the same economic crash that brought down Walter Scott and his publisher Archibald Constable. Up to that time,

Figure 1: Princess Victoria's graveside reading: title page, Legh Richmond's *The Dairyman's Daughter* (1810).

No. 118.

THE DAIRYMAN'S DAUGHTER;

AN

AUTHENTIC NARRATIVE:

BY THE LATE REV. LEGH RICHMOND, A. M. RECTOR OF TURVEY.

PART I.

IT is a delightful employment to discover and trace the operations of divine grace, as they are manifested in the dispositions and lives of God's real children. It is peculiarly gratifying to observe how frequently, among the poorer classes of mankind, the sunshine of mercy beams upon the heart, and bears witness to the image of Christ which the Spirit of God has impressed thereupon. Among such, the sincerity and simplicity of the Christian character appear unencumbered by those obstacles to spirituality of mind and conversation, which too often prove a great hinderance to those who live in the higher ranks. Many are the difficulties which riches, worldly consequence, high connections, and the luxurious refinements of polished society, throw in the way of religious profession. Happy indeed it is, (and some such happy instances I know,) where grace has so strikingly supported its conflict with natural pride, self-importance, the allurements of luxury, ease, and worldly opinion, that the noble and mighty appear adorned with genuine poverty of spirit, self-denial, humble-mindedness, and deep spirituality of heart.

THE RELIGIOUS TRACT SOCIETY, INSTITUTED 1799;
DEPOSITORY, 56, PATERNOSTER-ROW.

the majority of literate Britons believed that there was a link between divine justice and worldly prosperity. William Cobbett thought the crash of 1826 undeniable proof of the existence of a just and retributive God, while Anthony Ashley Cooper, the future evangelical leader and Lord Shaftesbury, underwent a conversion from carefree dissipation to driven philanthropy at the same time.[20] By the early 1830s, however, the longstanding evangelical consensus that private charity was the only proper means of redressing economic injustice was splintering under the weight of events – Catholic Emancipation, regime change in France, the "Swing" riots, the reappearance of cholera – seeming to signal divine disapproval of current political and economic arrangements. To Charlotte Elizabeth Tonna, for example, the emergence of an urban proletariat in the mills of Manchester, Leeds, and Bradford was a "scourge that our own hands are twisting, for the purposes of severe chastisement," as she wrote in 1843.[21]

Other evangelicals, however, having linked popular distress to Chalmers's theology and economics of Atonement, finally condemned both. Having seen his father-in-law ruined by speculation, and now arguing that God must have increased the postwar national debt in order to "wound us in the part we deem most invulnerable," the Scottish clergyman Edward Irving launched an 1827 attack on Chalmersian "stock-jobbing theology" as an elaborate justification for greed and oppression.[22] In theological terms, this meant arguing that Atonement beliefs "oppose and outrage the conscience," and that "the incarnation was the root of the atonement," as F. D. Maurice would put the matter in 1853. Though this emergent incarnationalism would not become the majority theology of the Church of England for some years to come, it permeated the discourse of 1830s Reform.[23]

Applied internationally, the incarnational metaphor became utopian, as in Marx's conclusion to the preface of *Capital*'s first German edition (1867): "[W]ithin the ruling-classes themselves, the foreboding is emerging that the present society is no solid crystal, but an organism capable of change, and constantly engaged in a process of change."[24] Within England, however, as Mary Poovey has shown, the metaphor of the social body as sublime organism was ambiguous enough to demand sustained interpretative effort. James Phillips Kay's 1832 report on working conditions in Manchester can only insist what the nation is *not*:

> The social body cannot be constructed like a machine, on abstract principles which merely include physical motions, and their numerical results in the production of wealth. The mutual relation of men

> is not merely dynamical, nor can the composition of their forces be subjected to a purely mathematical calculation.[25]

To be intelligible, this imaginary entity requires not only statistical description and classification by a class of experts like Kay, but also the supplemental metaphor known as "sympathy."[26] Thus Edwin Chadwick sent his 1842 *Sanitary Report*, an innovative blend of numerical and written representation, to Carlyle, Mill, Dickens, and other literary figures: without their help, the sanitary reform movement would likely have languished in the House of Lords.[27]

My other principal subject is the literary and commodity form in which the leading novelists of the age produced most of their variations on these themes of immanence and sacrifice. As Norman Feltes has noted, the serial is a form of literary production peculiarly appropriate to middle-class society not only because it delivers culture on the installment plan, with the advantages of part payment for consumers and increased profit for publishers, but also because its capacity for specification and expansion mirrors the capitalist economy of which it is a part.[28] Likewise, as Michael Lund and Linda Hughes have suggested, the serial is an especially appropriate form in which to explore anxieties about historical change and periodicity. James Chandler has argued for the "case," a categorization of social action through historical analogy, as the prose mode in which these anxieties could be explored most fully.[29] And each of the authors I consider at length began their fiction-writing careers in this generic location. The characters in Dickens's "Passage in the Life of Mr. Watkins Tottle" (1835), a tale featuring a precursor of *Bardell v. Pickwick*, describe themselves as "cases"; Thackeray's "The Professor" (1835) embroiders the criminal history of a seducer, oyster-eater, and bill-avoider named Dando; and George Eliot's "The Sad Fortunes of the Reverend Amos Barton" (1856) examines "the problem presented" by its subject within an elaborate historicist frame.[30]

Of course, Dickens and his successors had a more concrete reason to publish serially: it could pay handsomely to do so. Scholars working in the tradition of Richard Altick's *The English Common Reader* (1957) have by now rendered the prehistory of the Dickens phenomenon, and thus of Victorian serial fiction, in considerable detail: not only the author-centered studies pioneered by Robert L. Patten in *Charles Dickens and his Publishers* (1976), now including Kathryn Chittick on early Dickens, Peter L. Shillingsburg and Edgar F. Harden on Thackeray, and Carol Martin on George Eliot, but also John Sutherland's landmark *Victorian*

Novelists and Publishers (1976), the fountainhead for recent work by Laurel Brake, Graham Law, and Deborah Wynne.[31]

Perhaps Sutherland's most significant point for our purposes, elaborated by Law and Brake, is that after an early efflorescence lasting only a few years, the Dickensian monthly "part" was the sought-after exception rather than the workaday rule in Victorian serial publishing. An aspect of a journalistic practice dating back to the early eighteenth century, and made more attractive by the exemption of monthly publications from the Newspaper Stamp Act of 1819, the Pickwickian monthly part became the gold standard for a generation and more of Victorian novelists. But the format of a single literary text with a customized cover and illustrations was far more expensive to produce and advertise than magazine serialization, and thus suited only the hottest topics and writers: Harriet Martineau's *Illustrations of Political Economy* (1832) and Mrs. Trollope's *Michael Armstrong, the Factory Boy* (1839–40); Thackeray's *Vanity Fair* (1847–8), which almost expired at first in what had become a fiercely competitive parts market; Dickens, who returned to monthly part publication "as of old" in *Our Mutual Friend* (1864–5) even after successful serialization of his two previous novels in *All the Year Round*; and George Eliot, whose bimonthly experiment *Middlemarch* (1871–2) would prove so expensive that her publisher declared the copyrights worthless in 1879.[32] Thus the Victorian market's rule of two alternatives after 1840 (for new fiction not by Dickens, that is): either serialization in a magazine (available from the local bookseller or railway stall) or the resulting three-decker novel, still priced at the luxurious 31*s.* 6*d.* of Scott's *Kenilworth* (1821), but more likely to come from Mudie's or another lending library, which had already extracted a substantial discount from the publisher.[33]

With my emphasis on the contradictory symbolisms of my three canonical novelists, then, must also come the point that nearly all the serial novels I consider appeared in monthly parts, a commodity form already exceptional by 1847, and positively archaic by 1860. Chapter 1 begins at the very exceptional beginning that set the rules of the game for a generation to come: Dickens's *Sketches by Boz*, and particularly the late sketches of 1836, which articulate a sociology of disenchantment with unprecedented power. In *Pickwick Papers* (1836–7) and *Oliver Twist* (1837–8), Dickens produced an astonishing cluster of solutions to this disenchantment: not merely a distinctive incarnation of the ethic of benevolence in Mr. Pickwick and Sam Weller, nor even the conquest of a new market for new fiction, but also, and just as he was preparing what would always be his most famous public sacrifice, the establishment of his identity as a professional novelist.

Thackeray's symbolizations of immanence and sacrifice could only have come from under the massive economic and symbolic weight of the Dickens phenomenon. Chapter 2 pays more attention than has been customary, then, to his odyssey through the Victorian literary marketplace, from the rejected illustrator of 1836 to the journeyman writer of the mid-1840s to the true Dickens competitor of 1847–8. Through most of this period, Thackeray published his work in periodicals edited by others, and containing a variety of literary and journalistic materials as well as advertisements. Only after developing his own ironized versions of benevolence and sacrifice – at a virtually Nietzschean distance from the literary culture of which Dickens was the idol – could Thackeray himself ascend on the wrappers of *Vanity Fair* to the literary and economic heights.

Dickens's own most profound insights into the structure of market society, and especially the position of literary culture in and for that society, come in symbolic, not expository, form; in this limited sense, as Henry James would say, Dickens has always been "nothing but figure."[34] Chapter 3 investigates how the work of Dickens most preoccupied with economics and religion – *Little Dorrit* (1855–7) – is also the one containing the greatest profusion of literary innovations. Dickens's rejection of the Victorian world is never expressed as convincingly as in this most inward and literary of all his novels. In the course of exploding not only the corrupt Merdle and his cronies in capitalism, but also the symbols of benevolence and sacrifice that had long provided Dickens with his occult moral poles, the massive detonation that is *Little Dorrit* throws off an astonishing and prophetic variety of literary forms. In the same way, though *Little Dorrit* appeared in the same monthly parts as its predecessors, Dickens's recognition of this commodity form's archaism is best seen in his decisive personal transformation into the theatrical public reader in pursuit of profit, one that accelerated during and just after this novel's appearance.

By contrast to the strictly symbolic language in which Dickens's insights are encoded, the works of George Eliot always intertwine intellectual "theory" and figural "practice." In a well-known early essay written before her first piece of fiction, Marian Evans was already proposing a new kind of prose form: "incarnate history," the representation of historical change in a register with biological and theological overtones. But she worried from the outset that writing "incarnate history" would be more difficult in Victorian Britain than in any other European state – for the most Weberian of reasons:

> The nature of European men has its roots intertwined with the past, and can only be developed by allowing those roots to remain undisturbed while the process of development is going on, until that perfect ripeness of the seed which carries with it a life independent of the root. This vital connexion with the past is much more vividly felt on the Continent than in England, where we have to recall it by an effort of memory and reflection; for though our English life is in its core intensely traditional, *Protestantism and commerce have modernized the face of the land and aspects of society to a far greater degree than in any continental country.*[35]

"Protestantism and commerce": the two leading factors in Victorian "modernization" are the same as those highlighted not only by the evangelical political economist Thomas Chalmers and his humanist successor John Stuart Mill, but also by social theorists from Schiller to Weber and historians from Halévy to Hilton.[36]

For the new novelist, as I explain in Chapter 4, the difficulties of writing "incarnate history" in the context of what she called "the nightmare of the serial" emerged almost immediately, as in "Janet's Repentance" (1857), which discloses sympathetic connection as a matter of carnality, pathology, and madness. Only in the unserialized *Silas Marner* (1861) did Eliot succeed in aligning her vocation to write "incarnate history" with a happy philosophical and sociological ending. Her later career, indeed, can be seen as a sublimation of her earlier, more overt passions for incarnational ideology and against serialization. By the early 1870s, as Chapter 5 argues, she had not only found it necessary to supplement the austerities of what had become an exceedingly mindful imagination with a new brand of theatrical sympathy, but had also found it possible to fashion a distinctive commodity form of escape from the Dickensian serial nightmare.[37] This turn away from the serial and to the theatrical also characterizes the late Dickens, the subject of my epilogue. His favorite program in the public readings given in the last year of his life paired the oldest, "A Christmas Carol," with the newest, "Sikes and Nancy" – another repetition of the incarnate benevolence and atoning violence which had assembled his massive audience thirty-five years before, but in a new format so profitable that it created, in a few years, nearly half the estate Dickens left at his death.

In some ways, my canvas is small: limited to the period of Dickens's literary production, from just before 1836 to just after 1870. But my method within this brief period is broadly synthetic: to show how the *literary* forms of each of these three novelists correlate not only to the religious and economic *ideologies* whose attenuation from each other is a leading feature of the place and time, but also, and sometimes virtually simultaneously, to changes in the serial novel's status as literary *commodity*.

This rich symbolic and material matrix is not available for all novels of the period. The Brontës are the obvious first example: however much *Agnes Grey*, *Jane Eyre*, and *Wuthering Heights* rely on ideologemes of benevolence and sacrifice, they were never serialized, and thus could not participate in the strand of material history I pursue here. Charlotte Elizabeth Tonna's *Helen Fleetwood*, the first novel to describe the Manchester textile mills that so fascinated Friedrich Engels, did appear serially in *The Christian Lady's Magazine*. But Tonna responds to the phenomena of the new by relatively simple symbolic means: cast out of her seaside home into the den of the Manchester textile mills, its saintly heroine finds scant relief in hymns to the Blood of the Lamb before expiring at last on the mill floor, surrounded by a jeering female mob.[38]

For his part, Anthony Trollope was one of the most successful, and certainly the most efficient, of the Victorian serial novelists. But Trollope's ascent to literary success, and even (or especially) the breakthrough of his first serialized novel, was more a rapprochement with an existing set of circumstances in "small increment[s] of success and remuneration" than a transformation of them.[39] The way had been prepared by the modest lending-library success of the first two Barsetshire novels, *The Warden* (1855) and *Barchester Towers* (1857). Next was the decisive 1859 move to London, George Smith, his editor Thackeray, and their new *Cornhill Magazine*. Smith rejected *Castle Richmond*, the political novel Trollope had nearly finished; mindful, perhaps, of a momentary vogue (including *Blackwood's* "The Sad Fortunes of the Reverend Amos Barton" by a still-mysterious author named George Eliot), he asked for another "clerical novel" instead. The result, *Framley Parsonage*, catapulted the *Cornhill* to unprecedented (though shortlived) success for a new monthly.[40]

When George Smith rejected the tumultuous Irish setting of *Castle Richmond*, both men understood that he was asking for the cluster of norms encapsulated in the imaginary county of Barsetshire – "as true blue a county as any in England."[41] As this line from the second chapter suggests, the formula was clear to Trollope from the start: avoid political topics and Gothic extravagances for a familiar Austenian setting; include characters "with not more of excellence, nor with exaggerated baseness, so that my readers might recognize human beings like themselves"; and embrace a vocation as both entertainer and "preacher of sermons." But Smith's money also overcame both Trollope's long-standing "principle" never to begin a serial run without a complete manuscript in hand and his fear that the "rushing mode of publication" would be "injurious to the work done." The result was a literary and commodity triumph: as uniformly entertaining as any novel he would ever write, with "no very weak part," "no long succession of dull pages," "no bathos of dulness" – and all because writing for immediate serialization had "forced upon me the conviction that I should not allow myself to be tedious in any single part."[42] All that remained was to repeat the formula, with the necessary modicum of variation, again and again. Though his yearly income would hover around a hefty £4500 throughout the 1860s, earnings and sales of each individual work always remained well below those of Dickens.

As John Sutherland thus concludes, it was Trollope's submission to and mastery of publishing norms already in place, a congruence best represented in his unprecedented *rate* of literary production, which characterize his success.[43] With the lending libraries steadily losing ground, and the provinces colonized for literature by the syndicates of W. F. Tillotson and his competitors, the Royal Commission of 1877–8 upheld existing arrangements even against Matthew Arnold's plea to encourage cheap literature by limiting copyright to a single year.[44] The monthly magazines' combination of new fiction with non-fiction, illustrations, and advertisements would keep presses humming at home and abroad for years to come, while even the most successful of these would pale before the rising tide of the weeklies. Dickens's weekly *All the Year Round*, priced at just twopence, dominated from the start with *A Tale of Two Cities* (1859), and consolidated its hold with *Great Expectations* (1860–1), *The Woman in White* (1859–60), and *No Name* (1862–3).[45] *Harper's Magazine* abandoned its policy of excluding British works soon after its founding in 1850; over George Eliot's objection to weekly publication, and her publisher John Blackwood's distaste for its "confounded trading look," *Middlemarch* would run in the same firm's *Weekly* – splintered and accelerated, but reaching American readers by the millions.[46] And fresh from the triumph of *Daisy Miller* (1878), Henry James's *Portrait of a Lady* – was it the work he imagined George Eliot should have written? – ran simultaneously in the *Atlantic Monthly* and *Macmillan's* from the fall of 1880.[47]

When Marx wrote that "the value of labour-power is the value of the means of subsistence necessary for the maintenance of the owner," he was being substantially less pithy than Trollope on the same topic: "A labourer must measure his work by his pay or he cannot live."[48] What Marx did see more clearly than any other writer of the 1860s was that culture's work for market society was the consecration of capital accumulation as a religion, and the elevation of the commodity as sublime object of the new cult.[49]

Before we join Marx in condemning this task or its results, however, it is worth recalling the confusion prevailing in the literary field around 1830. With Walter Scott counting his debts in the just-completed Abbotsford, publishers left standing did the prudent thing: they sold known works in new forms like Bentley's *Standard Novels*, launched in 1831, often losing money before making some. The first new novel to succeed in this hostile environment was Edward Bulwer-Lytton's *Pelham* (1827), the philosophical trappings of which counted for little compared to its specification of material and linguistic fashion: not only black evening dress for men, but epigraphs, allusions, footnotes, and quotations in three languages. Bulwer's next success, *Paul Clifford* (1830), simply extended this work of specification down the social scale, founding the subgenre of the "Newgate novel" in the process. And Hilary Schor has shown that Dickens captured and expanded Bulwer's audience not just by delivering the city in all its apparent complexity, but by *reducing* the number of sign systems necessary to make sense of it.[50]

One of the principal sources of Dickens's humor would always be specifying materiality to a point of manifest and hilarious absurdity, as in asking whether Mr. Jack Hopkins's baked shoulder of mutton has potatoes under it or not (*PP* 483). Such details, strung into paratactic chains, deny that meaning can reach some metaphorical or metaphysical conclusion: what one most often finds beneath or behind a thing (a shoulder of mutton) is simply another thing (potatoes).[51] To be sure, the fictional order to which this metonymic chain belongs is also large enough to include not only Bulwer's profusion of signs, but also Balzac's, as when readers of *Lost Illusions* (1837–43) are told that the sconce lighting Mme. de Bargeton's card table has two candles, not just one (ch. 2). What distinguishes Dickensian prose from both its English predecessor and its French counterpart is its delivery of its claim to know the modern city in all its complexity in a rhetoric of transcendence which is primitive rather than metaphysical (like Bulwer's) or systematic (like Balzac's).

For an example of this feat, we need not look further than Mr. Pickwick's first speech, as transcribed by the narrator-copyist:

> He (Mr. Pickwick) would not deny, that he was influenced by human passions, and human feelings, (cheers) – possibly by human weaknesses – (loud cries of "No"); but this he would say, that if ever the fire of self-importance broke out in his bosom the desire to benefit the human race in preference, effectually quenched it. The praise of mankind was his Swing; philanthropy was his insurance office. (Vehement cheering.)

First comes the projection of the vanity and philanthropy struggling within Mr. Pickwick on to a social landscape (self-love inflames and destroys, while philanthropy quenches and saves); next, the intensification of the metaphor through hyperbole: "The praise of mankind was his Swing; philanthropy was his insurance office." But even the few farmers prudent enough to have insured themselves before the Swing riots of 1830 collected well below their real losses, with other remedies, including actions for damages, government relief, and private subscription, yielding even less.[52] From the start, then, Pickwickian language inserts the losses of modernization, encoded but intact, into a character studded with signs of being and saying the Word.[53]

But *Pickwick Papers* and its successors also evoke an ethics and aesthetics based on an innocent individual's Christlike assumption of others' suffering, beyond what God requires of them personally, for the sake of the common good.[54] The theological term for this kind of supplemental suffering is "supererogatory" – a word which, appropriately enough, supplies one of the first jokes in George Eliot's first work of fiction (Amos Barton, being bald, washes his head with "supererogatory soap" [*SCL* 7]). *Pickwick*'s first illustration already evokes this inescapable countertheme when it puts Mr. Pickwick at the head of a Last Supper of sorts, including a glowering Mr. Blotton, the Judas haberdasher whose name also evokes the mark of Cain, in the lower left-hand corner.[55]

Dickensian seriality thus encompasses not only the meat-and-potatoes operation of metonymic representation, as well as the period's two contradictory varieties of transcendence, but finally projects these

Figure 2: The first supper: *Pickwick*, plate 1 (1836).

literary and ideological operations into its own distinctive commodity form: the "ephemeral" monthly part culminating in, and replaced by, the "permanent" three-decker novel. Thus constituted by the contradiction between the familiar rituals of Christianity and the unfamiliar ones of capital, the Dickensian serial novel was sufficiently explosive to throw off a profusion of objects – "coats, canes, cigars and chintzes," the handkerchief fluttering over the dying Nancy, its own bright yellow wrappers and freshly printed illustrations – all of which glimmer with kitsch as they burn out their brief half-lives of transcendence.[56]

Even a sober reader might reasonably ask what more Victorian literary culture could accomplish, apart from mere variations on a theme, after the Pickwickian incarnation. I find the beginnings of an answer in Durkheim's *The Elementary Forms of Religious Life* (1912), and especially its twin conceptions of worship. When one heeds the command "to flee the profane world," and economic activity in particular, one can "draw closer to the sacred world" in two ways: through what Durkheim calls "the positive cult" of ritual violence, or sacrifice; and through the worship of totems, the sacred objects which both incarnate the diffuse force Durkheim called *mana* (and the Victorians "sympathy") and also express a clan's distinctiveness.[57] Durkheim continues:

> A society is to its members what a god is to the faithful. . . . Society requires us to make ourselves its servants, forgetful of our own interests. And it subjects us to all sorts of restraints, privations, and sacrifices without which social life would be impossible.

As Raymond Aron has pointed out, the extraordinary quality of passages like this one comes from the profound tension between its two contradictory imperatives: to bring the phenomena of religion under the discursive control of social science; and to imagine "society" itself as a magical entity, one with the power to transfigure reality.[58]

Victorian incarnationalism should be seen in this context: as a compromise-formation *between* an earlier, overtly sacrificial Protestantism and a later, "functional" sociology which, though it aspires to the status of science, continues to sound the ancient notes of immanence and sacrifice nonetheless. When they emphasize the overwhelming nature of historical change, like the classical sociology to follow, works like *Little Dorrit* and *Middlemarch* deliver "a hauntingly stilled world, one that can withstand the inevitable transition from enchantment to disenchantment."[59] But it would not be or feel easy. Dickens, *Little Dorrit*:

> "My course," said Clennam, brushing away some tears that had been silently dropping down his face, "must be taken at once. What wretched amends I can make must be made. . . . I must work out as much of my fault – or crime – as is susceptible of being worked out in the rest of my days." (*LD* 779)

And, at practically the same moment, George Eliot, *Scenes of Clerical Life*:

> While we are coldly discussing a man's career, sneering at his mistakes, blaming his rashness, and labelling his opinions – "Evangelical and narrow," or "Latitudinarian and Pantheistic," or "Anglican or supercilious" – that man, in his solitude, is perhaps shedding hot tears because his sacrifice is a hard one, because strength and patience are failing him to speak the difficult word, and do the difficult deed. (*SCL* 312)

For these two greatest Victorian novelists, the task of atoning for modernity always seemed to loom just as that of incarnating its social world and life appeared to fail. Doing justice to such things must begin by approaching Victorian serial fiction as one passing attempt to mediate questions of immanent and transcendent value, not as some origin or terminus of a history of commodification. Even if Marcel Gauchet is correct that "we are at the point where religion has been systematically exhausted and its legacy has gradually disappeared," in other words, this state of affairs may well be "one from which we have barely begun to recover."[60] In this, perhaps, the central contradiction of Victorian culture remains our own.

1
The Cockney and the Prostitute: Dickens from *Sketches by Boz* to *Oliver Twist*

> [I]f I knew where there was such a knight of faith, I would make a pilgrimage to him on foot, for this prodigy interests me absolutely.... [O]ne might suppose that he was a clerk who had lost his soul in an intricate system of book-keeping.... [H]e is not a poet, and I have sought in vain to detect in him the poetic incommensurability. Toward evening he walks home, and his gait is as indefatigable as that of the postman.
>
> Kierkegaard, *Fear and Trembling* (1843)

Early Victorians generally agreed that the northern industrial city of the 1830s and 1840s – Leeds, Bradford, Birmingham, and especially Manchester – was a phenomenon of modernity, "the type of a new power on the earth," as the London *People's Journal* exclaimed in 1847.[1] The pressing question concerning this new city was whether the mysterious and powerful processes at work in and on it were constructive or destructive. Such was the implicit topic, for example, at an October 1843 meeting of literary luminaries at the just-completed Free Trade Hall, Manchester, with speeches by Richard Cobden and Benjamin Disraeli among others, several thousand in the audience, and Charles Dickens presiding. The purpose of the occasion's "brilliant assemblage of beauty and fashion" was the raising of funds for the Athenaeum, a philanthropic and educational organization conceived by Cobden and others in 1835 as the middle-class counterpart to the fashionable Royal Manchester Institution and the working-class Mechanics Institution, but struggling by 1842 with lackluster membership and attendance as well as a heavy mortgage on its recently completed headquarters.[2] Class conciliation was the common goal of all three of these organizations: in the words of the Mechanics Institution's Annual Report for 1836, though it and the Athenaeum each "has its separate sphere of action, the interests of both will ever be promoted by the mutual cooperation and friendly intercourse which the Directors trust will always subsist between the two Institutions."[3] Dickens's opening remarks from the chair at the Athenaeum benefit of 1843 recalled this goal, pressing enough to bring the Conservative and protectionist Disraeli and the Anti-Corn Law Leaguer and free-trader Cobden onto the platform with him. Assuming, as Dickens argued, that the Free Trade Hall was indeed "neutral ground, where we have no more knowledge of party differences, or public animosities . . . than if we were at a public meeting in the commonwealth of Utopia," then on such ground, and while Manchester's nearby factories "re-echo with the clanking of stupendous engines and the whirl and rattle of machinery," it would surely be possible to raise funds to save the Athenaeum, and to show thereby that "the immortal mechanism of God's own hand, the mind, is not forgotten in the din and uproar, but is lodged and tended in a palace of its own" (*Speeches* 45–6).

Early Victorian writers had few English-language precedents for a systematic description of the human costs of early industrial capitalism. It is true that as early as 1776, at the conclusion of *The Wealth of Nations*, Adam Smith had speculated on the deleterious effects of the historical tendency towards industrial specialization, or "the division of labor," with which he had begun his discussion. With the "progress" of that tendency, we learn hundreds of pages later, comes a regress of the worker's worth in other respects: as a result of the repetitiveness of modern work, "dexterity at his own particular trade" will be "acquired at the expense of his intellectual, social, and martial virtues."[4] But qualifying comments like these, buried at the back of Smith's treatise, are an exception to the British rule of "political economy" after 1789. Though radical writers of the 1790s such as Cobbett and Blake inveighed against what the latter called the "dark Satanic Mills," they were no less affected than their counterparts on the center and right by a nationalist political idiom, mastered by Burke, which deplored social theory in general, and its systematic and critical (meaning French and Revolutionary) varieties in particular.[5] Byron, too, writing in 1817, could condemn himself, along with other poets of his generation, for laboring over "a wrong revolutionary poetical system – or systems – not worth a damn in itself."[6] More immediately, Dickens's description in the Athenaeum address of the mind of the worker as a "mechanism of God's own hand" suggests that even three years after their first meeting in 1840, he had not yet absorbed Carlyle's critique of a mechanical modernity, symbolized by the steam engine, in *Sartor Resartus* (1833–4).[7]

As a result of this "revolt against theory" in the British generation after 1793, the spectacle of early industrial capitalism evoked two related but distinct responses from Europe's two leading Protestant cultures: a British Romantic tradition of aesthetic critique, epitomized by Shelley's poet-legislator, taken up in the Victorian period by Arnold and Morris in particular; and the German philosophical tradition that Marx inherited and transformed.[8] In his *Letters on the Aesthetic Education of Man* (1795), Friedrich Schiller speculated that "a more rigorous separation of ranks and occupations," as assisted by the "ingenious clockwork" of the modern state, was inflicting some deep "wound" on European humanity. The injury therefrom extended to intellectuals as much as other kinds of workers: while on the one hand "a riotous imagination ravages the hard-won fruits of the intellect," on the other "the spirit of abstraction stifles the fire at which the heart should have warmed itself and the imagination been kindled."[9] Hegel too was preoccupied with the quality of modern work, although his slave, who begins in a position of fear and powerlessness, may negate that unfreedom by producing an object, "something that is permanent and remains."[10] To the young Marx and Engels of the mid-1840s, Manchester's Anti-Corn Law League was the harbinger of a class whose revolutionary program of specialization, urbanization, and universal competition would inevitably subjugate science, family, and culture to its imperatives of relentless change and endless profit.[11] The opening pages of *The German Ideology*, drafted in 1843, rearticulate the question Schiller and Hegel had asked decades before: whether an "active" working consciousness could possibly survive in a rationalized sphere of production, epitomized for Marx by Manchester's capitalist enterprise.[12] Both *Either/Or* and *Fear and Trembling*, published the same year, consider the bourgeois side of the same question: might the English tourist, that "heavy, inert woodchuck" in whom "admiration and indifference have become undifferentiated in the unity of boredom," be indistinguishable from a modern "knight of faith," his gait "as indefatigable as that of the postman," who somehow "has made and every instant is making the movements of infinity"?[13]

Dickens began 1836, the first full year of the Athenaeum's existence and the year of the economic collapse which would quickly impoverish it, a still obscure piece-writer of twenty-four. Like Marx, who would produce the *German Ideology* in his mid-twenties, the young Dickens had an acute sense of the immense forces, both creative and destructive, unleashed by and for bourgeois society; like Kierkegaard, he would express this sense in forms more figurative than expository. For the author of the handful of sketches written in 1836, and included in the Second Series of *Sketches by Boz*, published that December, the question would be whether a consciousness constituted by the thronged streets of the world capital could respond to its frenetic rate of material and social change with anything else than some form of psychic disintegration – or, as Hillis Miller has posed it, whether the Londoner of the 1830s might "break the iron chain of metonymy whereby a person is inevitably like his environment."[14]

Describing the *Sketches'* revision, rearrangement and republication only begins a larger narrative of Dickens's effort, sustained throughout his career, to provide a satisfactory symbolic answer to such questions. Dickens's first two longer works of fiction, *Pickwick Papers* and *Oliver Twist*, inaugurate a literary and commodity form in which the incarnation of a lively and loving rule of capital in the Cockney and his master is followed, only a few months later, by a nameless prostitute's violent atonement. The moments at which these two ideologemes appear are landmarks on Dickens's journey to fame and wealth, from July 1836, when Sam Weller's appearance suddenly made *Pickwick Papers* a winning proposition, to November 1837, by which time Dickens had wound up Pickwick's serial run a successful writer at only twenty-five, and forced Richard Bentley to accept the miscellany piece "Oliver Twist" as one of the novels he had agreed to write for the powerful publisher. Taken as a pair, these two moments make for a striking demonstration of the vexed relation of early Victorian society to its culture: that place and time where, as Marian Evans wrote in 1856, "Protestantism and commerce have modernized the face of the land and aspects of society to a far greater degree than in any continental country";[15] but whose literary commodities, determined by new technologies of production, expressed a nostalgia for precisely the traditional Christian culture being steadily and irrevocably undone. This is the phenomenon of Dickensian seriality: a literary form determined, more than any of its predecessors, by the production deadline; and a commodity form invoking a premodern cultural inheritance.

A prose poetics of disenchantment: the sketches of 1836

Despite the generally comic tone of *Sketches by Boz* as a whole, consisting as it does of pieces written over a period of three years, death is the common narrative destination of the mere eight sketches Dickens produced after February 1836, when *Pickwick Papers* began its tumultuous course. Philip Collins has described Dickens's excitement over "A Visit to Newgate," written that very month, his first treatment of the psychology of the condemned prisoner that *Oliver Twist* would soon take up.[16] The Newgate sketch concludes with the doomed man awakening, after a dreamy night of freedom, to death in the present tense: "[h]e is the condemned felon again, guilty and despairing; and in two hours more he is a corpse." There was nothing new about an association between death and Newgate, the familiar setting of executions throughout the nineteenth century. But this kind of despair is no longer confined to the legally or morally guilty: both exhausted workers and embittered bourgeois voice it on their deathbeds. The expiring boy of "Our Next-Door Neighbors," who begs his mother to bury him "in the open fields – any where but in these dreadful streets"; the testators of "Doctors' Commons," who pile up "silent evidence of animosity and bitterness" as they lie "speechless and helpless on the bed of death"; the decrepit old man of "Scotland-yard," who holds "no converse with human kind," and who will sit "brooding" in the midst of the transformed thoroughfare until "his eyes have closed" upon the world; the abandoned mother of "Meditations in Monmouth-Street," who dies in a workhouse "with no child to clasp her hand, and no pure air from heaven to fan her brow" – all these have met their doom in the mysterious forces at work in the London of the mid-1830s.[17]

The simple ordering device of the first two volumes of *Sketches by Boz*, published by Macrone in February 1836, is the gathering together of individuals in political or social combination. Volume One opens with a selection from the 1835 *Evening Chronicle* "Sketches of London" series entitled "The Parish," featuring characters like "The Beadle," "The Schoolmaster," "The Curate," "The Old Lady," and "The Broker's Man." But the urban parish can no longer provide even the most basic services for its parishioners, as the opening paragraph makes clear (*S* 17): this obsolete political unit can hardly become the humane social unit of the future. Rather, the term in use by the end of Macrone's Volume One is the sociological category of "class" (133, 135) – the fashionable audience and hangers-on in "Astley's," the fallen women of "The Prisoner's Van," the fragile lower middle-class family of "A Christmas Dinner." The last five sketches of Volume Two, all of which were finally categorized as "Tales" in the Chapman and Hall serial, make an implicit argument that such intraclass London life is not all isolation or desolation by ending with sketches of larger social groups, having farce as their subject, method, or both.[18]

Assembled in the frantic fall of 1836, and published on 17 December, the one-volume Second Series is a mélange of Dickens's earliest and latest pieces – those rejected as inadequate for the first two volumes in February, and those written in the few months afterwards. It leads with the lightly revised "The Streets by Morning" (first published July 1834), followed immediately by its darker and later counterpart, "The Streets by Night" (first published January 1836); includes a heavily revised version of Dickens's very first *Monthly* magazine tale ("Mr. Minns and his Cousin," previously "A Dinner at Poplar Walk"); and concludes with the most melodramatic of all the tales of "degradation" (*S* 555), "The Drunkard's Death," written especially for this winding up of the *Sketches* project. With the exception of "A Visit to Newgate" (already published in February), all of Dickens's remaining 1836 sketches were included in this volume. Four of these document downward mobility, whether individual (the young criminal in "Meditations in Monmouth-Street," the battered woman in "The Hospital Patient") or social (the denizens of "Scotland-yard," the tenants in "Our Next-Door Neighbours"). The remaining two explore a wills office and a pleasure garden as settings for petty dramas of "wealth, and penury, and avarice," or moments of comic relief in "a bowl or two of reeking punch" ("Doctors' Commons," *S* 114; "Vauxhall-Gardens by Day," *S* 155).

Eleven months later, the Chapman and Hall serial reprint (begun November 1837) uses the weak ordering principles of each predecessor collection. It reproduces the opening device of "The Parish" from the First Series, now including seven sketches. The remaining forty-nine are divided along a spectrum of ever-increasing socialization, finally made explicit as the three categories of "Scenes," "Characters," and "Tales" in the one-volume edition of 1839. The generic category of the urban street "scene," featuring the demonic energy of the dancing clothes in "Meditations in Monmouth-Street," has won out in one clear sense: its twenty-five pieces are as many as the other two categories combined. The twelve sketches gathered as "Characters" make the pathological individual their determining narrative unit. Nine of the thirteen concluding "Tales" were written before February 1835, giving the final section the farcical tone Dickens had already outgrown. But despite his decision to end the volume with these lighter pieces, Dickens apparently could not resist giving despair the last word in the Chapman and Hall serialization, ending its final number with "The Drunkard's Death." The problem of 1836 is not solved but restated: how to represent both the intensity of the urban experience and some hope of escape from its apparently deathly destination?

Dickens's illustrator, George Cruikshank, solved this problem by reversing the younger writer's dialectical distinction between demonically active objects and lifeless human subjects: his illustration for "Meditations in Monmouth-Street" teems with human figures, while a few clothes hang limply on the storefronts behind them.[19] As to Dickens himself, the beginnings of an answer are visible to Kathryn Chittick, to whom we owe much of the picture we have of the London literary field of the thirties. Chittick singles out two fundamental symbolizations already present in Dickens's early "Street Sketches" of 1834. The first is the comedy of class struggle, played out between the working-class conductors and their middle-class passengers in "Omnibuses" (Sept. 1834). The second is the melodrama of that same struggle, in which the stationer's daughter of "Shops and Their Tenants" (Oct. 1834) is likely to be driven from the "miserable market" in "elegant little trifles" into prostitution (*S* 82–3).[20] In other words, Dickens has already distinguished comedy from melodrama by means of gender: the omnibus conductors or "cads" are the tyrants of the London streets, whereas the stationer's daughter is those same streets' victim, an icon of the human misery that market economies both create and allay. What I pursue here is how Dickens's first two longer works of fiction, *Pickwick Papers* and *Oliver Twist*, develop these two gendered ideologemes of the triumphant Cockney and the victimized prostitute. In the very summer Dickens incarnated a rule of capital in the masterful and devoted Sam Weller and his hapless but lovable master, he was also completing a sketch featuring a nameless prostitute's violent atonement – a scene he would begin to repeat in the fall of 1837, as he transformed Nancy from insignificant accessory to significant victim, and as he forced the publisher Richard Bentley to accept the miscellany piece "Oliver Twist" as the novel the two had bargained over the previous year.

Literary evolution (1): the Cockney meets his master

"Aggerawatin' Bill" Barker is the second principal subject of a sketch whose third and final version bore the title of "The Last Cab-driver, and the First Omnibus Cad."[21] The Cockney character of the omnibus cad, or conductor, is motivated by a single ruthless rule:

> If Mr. Barker can be fairly said to have had any weakness in his earlier years, it was an amiable one – love; love in its most comprehensive form – a love of ladies, liquids, and pocket-handkerchiefs. It was no selfish feeling; it was not confined to his own possessions, which but

> too many men regard with exclusive complacency. No; it was a nobler love – a general principle. It extended itself with equal force to the property of other people. (*S* 177–8).

Dickens here turns the "love" or "sympathy" preached by bourgeois philosophers from Hume and Adam Smith to Hegel and George Eliot into one rather large joke.[22] But if not this kind of moral abstraction, what idea or force can possibly limit the action of Bill Barker's greedy "general principle" on the London streets? One solution is D. A. Miller's "police," represented by the new prison at Coldbath Fields, Clerkenwell, which the narrator of this sketch takes pains to show he has visited. The last paragraph of the first published version has Bill Barker springing back from a prison term "with an ardour which persecution and involuntary abstinence have in no wise diminished."[23] By the final version of a year later, however, the "improvements" of Peel's police have had their effect:

> We have spoken of Mr. Barker and of the red-cab driver, in the past tense. Alas! Mr. Barker has again become an absentee; and the class of men to which they both belonged are fast disappearing. Improvement has peered beneath the aprons of our cabs, and penetrated to the very innermost recesses of our omnibuses. Dirt and fustian will vanish before cleanliness and livery. Slang will be forgotten when civility becomes general: and that enlightened, eloquent, sage, and profound body, the Magistracy of London, will be deprived of half their amusement, and half their occupation. (*S* 181)

This trope of improvement involves voyeurism and violation: the twenty-three-year-old Dickens still identifies as much with Cockney "slang," "dirt," and "fustian" as with any discourse of hygienic vision.[24] What Jonathan Arac calls the "spirit of overview" will only begin to emerge years later in characters like *Martin Chuzzlewit*'s Nadgett, reaching its climax atop Mr. Bucket's mental tower in *Bleak House*.[25] Even in the final draft of "The Last Cab-driver, and the First Omnibus Cad," then, bourgeois "improvements" threaten to efface Dickens's Cockney subject and discourse.

The first substantial solution to the late *Sketches*' problem of narrative destination thus took shape not in the much-revised Bill Barker sketch, but in *Pickwick*'s fourth number, written in June 1836. Though Sam Weller's "general principle" is, like his Cockney cousin's, economic self-interest, Sam implements that principle not through theft or violence, but through his own linguistic calculus of class, status, and power. Tony Weller is consistently taken in by the magic of linguistic elision, with deplorable results, as when he mistakes a first wife's bequest for a second wife's windfall, or confuses the names of a parish and a public house (*PP* 139–40). His son, on the other hand, is a master of metonymy, the first of Roman Jakobson's "two aspects of language," and the trope of substitution and juxtaposition driving all emplotted narrative.[26] We first see him refusing to polish one pair of boots before the others because that pair, and the tipping customer for which it is the synecdoche, is indistinguishable from those others: " 'Who's number twenty-two, that's to put all the others out?' " A better room means better service: when Rachel Wardel's shoes and Alfred Jingle's boots fly down into the yard, they displace all the others, because Jingle, having taken a private sitting room, is " 'vurth a shillin' a day, let alone the arrands' " (*PP* 138). And when Sam mistakes the legal authority whose name Mr. Perker is dropping so heavily for a legendary criminal, his metonymic substitution of the popular for the professional strikes a bargain with Mr. Pickwick in those modes of expression, one verbal, the other mute, each one will henceforth prefer: " 'You want me to except of half a guinea. Werry well, I'm agreeable: I can't say no fairer than that, can I, sir?' (Mr. Pickwick smiled.)" (145).[27] By a miraculous substitution, a young Cockney can suddenly gratify the elderly capitalist's need for both service and affection, just as the demonic and inhuman energy of Monmouth-Street's dancing clothes has been transformed into Sam's personal charm, social capability, and linguistic energy.

But perhaps the decisive element in the formula of Pickwickian success is Sam's ability to complement his skill at making metonymic connections with highly condensed and analytical metaphors of power, to show mastery in Jakobson's other aspect of language. Both Wellers have a deep distrust of metaphor. As the father warns the son working on his valentine, " 'Poetry's unnat'ral; no man ever talked in poetry, 'cept a beadle on boxin' day, or Warren's blackin', or Rowland's oil, or some of them low fellows' " (*PP* 540): those who abuse power for personal gain, like the beadle, the capitalist, and the advertiser, often do so with this kind of language.[28] But from the start, Sam uses metaphor to expose such abuses: " 'Who's number twenty-two, that's to put all the others out? No, no, regular rotation, as Jack Ketch said, wen he tied the men up' " (138). Sam complements his metonym of the shoes as the signs of their wearers' social status with a self-comparison to Jack Ketch, instantaneously imagining dominance over the very clients whose shoes he is polishing by repeating the name of the public hangman, still in use in Dickens's time, but dating from a century before, when few doubted the moral or political efficacy of public execution. A monopoly on the use of such violence is, as Trotsky and Weber would later assert, a fundamental feature of the bourgeois state; the removal of such displays of power from public view, as recommended by both Dickens and Thackeray in the 1840s, would provide Foucault with a point of departure for his critique of that state.[29] August's fifth number finds Sam again speaking a symbolized sociological truth to power. When Mr. Pickwick hints at hiring him, Sam urges him on: "'out vith it, as the father said to the child, ven he swallowed a farden'" (176). This time, Sam's metaphor transforms a relation between servant and master into one between father and son, while at the same time preserving the violence with which, as Marx would argue in the manuscripts of 1844, capital contaminates all relationships, including the most intimate.[30]

In the end, there seems to be no more convincing explanation for the breakthrough of these two numbers, when *Pickwick* circulation began its geometric growth, than this: Bill Barker's "general principle" of economic self-interest has met its literary negation when Sam Weller devotes himself to Mr. Pickwick, whose "general benevolence" is "one of the leading features of the Pickwickian theory" (*PP* 85). Having burst into the world in "all his might and glory" (*PL* 1: 132) wearing the "abstracted gaze" of the religious icon (*PP* 84), his tights and gaiters inspiring "involuntary awe and respect" from his companions (69), Mr. Pickwick quickly took his place at the center of just the kind of "cult of man in the abstract, more particularly in its bourgeois development, [such as] Protestantism, Deism, etc." that Marx would later call "the most fitting form of religion" for "a society of commodity producers."[31] Sam is a representation of labor reduced to a position of dependency and marginality in such a society, as symbolized in the valet – what Dickens calls a "faithful" even if "eccentric functionary" (*PP* 877, 151). And between these two literary incarnations must remain, as the serial's closing sentence fervently proclaims, "a steady and reciprocal attachment, which nothing but death will sever" (877). Even after all this effort and enjoyment, it seems, Death is still getting the last word. Sam's jokes, spreading like wildfire all over London, are the highly compressed forms in which the imaginary status of this entire Pickwickian *Verneinung* appears most clearly, the "veiled revelations" of the kinds of unbearable truths formulated in the sociological imagination of the next century and more.[32]

Dickens signals the generic importance of this ideologeme of transcendent fellow-feeling, which sublimates impersonal bourgeois capital into Mr. Pickwick's childlike helplessness, and brute working-class dependence into Sam's fatherly control, when the latter rescues the former under the sign of Dickens's primordial literary ancestor, Cervantes. Pickwick/Quixote is "a philosopher, but philosophers are only men in armour, after all"; and Alfred Jingle's parting insults at the conclusion of the Rachel Wardle episode "penetrated through his philosophical harness, to his very heart" (*PP* 151). Mr. Pickwick throws first an inkstand and then himself at his tormentor; but Jingle has disappeared, and Mr. Pickwick finds himself "caught in the arms of Sam," who tries to explain to his master the difference between Quixotic principle and Cockney reality: "furniter's cheap where you come from, sir . . . wot's the use o' running arter a man as has made his lucky, and got to t'other end of the Borough by this time" (151). Deviance from this pattern in the fifth number – when Mr. Pickwick finds economic self-interest in his arms, in the form of Mrs. Bardell – provides the kernel of reversal from which the plot of the rest of the serial will germinate. With this new generic pattern established, Dickens felt free to abandon the original scheme of Pickwick Club transcription for good (177–8), moving on to the Eatanswill election, his most pointed political satire to date, excerpted in seven different London papers between 10 and 21 August.[33]

But the very success of the *Pickwick* mutation would create its own species of problems in the unstable London literary field of the late 1830s. Throughout the decade, the Victorian literary market was determined by the costly three-decker (31*s.* 6*d.*) at its summit. The *Athenaeum*'s inaugural issue of 1828 justified its plans to review novels on the ground that "no Englishman in the middle class of life buys a book," an incapacity the periodicals, with the help of an 1819 tax break, were happy to remedy.[34] At the top of the periodical heap were the Whig *Edinburgh Review* (founded 1802) and the Tory *Quarterly Review* (1809), accompanied by the *Monthly* (1814) and *Blackwood's* (1817) as well as the newer *Fraser's* (1830) and *Metropolitan* (1831) magazines. In December 1833, Dickens published his first piece in the *Monthly*, priced at a gentlemanly 3*s.* 6*d.* per issue, but received neither credit nor pay for pieces on a *flâneur* class he knew little of.[35] So even as he continued to present pieces to the *Monthly*, he also moved decisively down-market to the middle-class weeklies and dailies. The *Morning Chronicle*, costing sixpence, paid Dickens a reporter's salary of five guineas a week from August 1834, raised to seven guineas in January 1835, making further submissions to the *Monthly* unnecessary.[36] The more fashionable *Bell's Weekly* and *Bell's Life in London and Sporting Chronicle* cost a little more too: at sevenpence, the latter may have paid Dickens even more for the

"Scenes and Characters" series begun in September 1835.[37] Below all of these, but not below Chapman and Hall's notice, was the "penny press" of Chambers's *Edinburgh Journal* and Charles Knight's *Penny Magazine* (founded 1832), the latter making unprecedented sums by featuring woodcut illustrations, but required by its backer, the Society for the Diffusion of Useful Knowledge, to eschew fiction and criticism in favor of subjects of "direct utility."[38]

The *Pickwick* of July 1836 found itself in the spacious, profitable and heretofore invisible middle of this field.[39] After the fifth number of August 1836, however, it was visible to others besides Dickens or Chapman and Hall. On 22 August, Richard Bentley, whose Standard Novels had succeeded at the cut rate of six shillings only by offering reprints of proven writers like Scott, Cooper, and Austen,[40] signed the first of what would eventually become nine written agreements with Dickens, under which Dickens would provide two novels and their copyrights in exchange for £500 and a bonus contingent on sales. By the end of November, Dickens was suffering from acute success, juggling Macrone's *Sketches*, Second Series; Chapman and Hall's *Pickwick*; not one but two Bentley contracts (the second, of 4 November, naming him the manager and leading contributor of a new magazine to be called *Bentley's Miscellany*); and the run and reprints of his first operetta (*The Strange Gentleman*, premiered 29 September), as well as the production of his second (*The Village Coquettes*, premiered 6 December). Though it took years to extricate himself from Bentley, Dickens did what else he could: he resigned from the *Morning Chronicle*, truncated the Second Series of *Sketches by Boz*, and temporarily abandoned the role of theatrical impresario. Moreover, he consolidated *Pickwick*'s generic structure along the lines first laid out in the summer. The December number's adventures with Nupkins of Ipswich make up the last significant Jingle episode until the Fleet. The first line of its final chapter points to a more daunting prospect for Mr. Pickwick: "to London, with the view of becoming acquainted with the proceedings which had been taken against him, in the mean time" (*PP* 391).

In the course of 1836, then, Dickens was working simultaneously in two very different directions. In the eight sketches published throughout the year, he stated a prose poetics of urban alienation more unequivocally than ever before. But in *Pickwick*'s July and August numbers, he took the *Sketches*' personification of urban society, the Cockney "specimen of London Life," and, with a bow to Cervantes, submitted it to the negation of capital become benevolent and labor become devoted. In December, he set in motion the serial's central confrontation between these incarnate abstractions, already the objects of a popular cult, and Dodson and Fogg's forces of obfuscation and darkness. Before a year would pass, Dickens would articulate a second fundamental ideologeme. The affect accompanying this next literary negation would be not the jubilation of beholding an Incarnation, but the agony of staging an Atonement.

Literary evolution (2): the prostitute meets her clients

We have already glimpsed this second ideologeme at its Dickensian origin – the stationer's daughter in "Shops and Their Tenants" of late 1834, a victim of "the miserable market" for stationers' goods, and soon to become a victim of the same kind of market for women's bodies. The first mention of a sketch featuring this character dates from the dawn of Dickens's success: his response to Macrone's 1835 offer to publish a collection of his sketches, in which he assured Macrone that he had an abundance of materials for the project, including a paper called "The Hospital" (*PL* 1: 81–4). With the advent of *Pickwick*, it was not until a year later that "The Hospital Patient" appeared in the *Carlton Chronicle* of 6 August 1836, part of yet another project called "Leaves from an unpublished Volume by Boz," but buried under the avalanche of work Dickens created for himself in the autumn.

In its original version, "The Hospital Patient" begins with its narrator walking past a public hospital at night. He imagines the scenes of extremity playing out just over his head, in which pain and disease must be endured without the tender ministrations of "mother, wife, or child." Having mused on such institutional incapacity overnight, the narrator happens the next day upon a pickpocket being carried to a nearby police station in a wheelbarrow:

> Somehow I never can resist joining a crowd – nature certainly intended me for a vagabond – so I turned back with the mob, and entered the office, in company with my friend the pickpocket, a couple of policemen, and as many dirty-faced spectators as could squeeze their way in.[41]

In the station he sees "a powerful, ill-looking young fellow at the bar," an ancestor of Bill Sikes, brought up on charges of beating the woman he lives with. The magistrates decide to bring the suspect to her bed, at which decision he blanches: will she identify him?

The mob at the police station has become a party of only a few professional men. These few enter the clinic to figures of escalating misery: a burned child; a severely injured woman, "wildly beating her clenched fists on the coverlet, in an agony of pain"; a girl, "apparently in that heavy stupor so often the immediate precursor of death"; and at the end of the room, the "object of the visit," "a fine young woman of about two or three and twenty":

> Her long black hair had been hastily cut from about the wounds on her head, and streamed over the pillow in jagged and matted locks. Her face bore frightful marks of the ill-usage she had received: her hand was pressed upon her side, as if her chief pain were there; her breathing was short and heavy; and it was plain to see that she was dying fast.

The magistrates order off the perpetrator's hat; she recognizes her tormentor, starts up "with an energy quite preternatural," and bursts into tears. But she will not condemn him ("'for God's sake! I did it myself – it was nobody's fault – it was an accident'"), and reaches out to him as she denies his guilt, at which, "[b]rute as the man was," he too "sob[s] aloud." With this circuit of anguish between victim and aggressor established, the woman goes into her death-throes. In rapid sequence, she begs God's forgiveness, asks "'some kind gentleman'" – the narrator is the only candidate – to take her love to her father, and repeats the judgment that father has long since rendered on her:

> "Five years ago, he said he wished I had died a child. Oh, I wish I had! I wish I had!"
>
> We turned away; it was no sight for strangers to look upon. The nurse bent over the girl for a few seconds, and then drew the sheet over her face. It covered a corpse.

We are not likely to miss the first appearance in this sketch of phrases which will resonate through Dickens's career – his self-description as a "vagabond," later a key term in the 1846 autobiographical fragment, for example, or the provisional title of *Little Dorrit*, "Nobody's Fault," on the lips of the dying prostitute.[42] But we may miss the import of other elements in this scene. The face of the girl whose death is the "immediate precursor" of the prostitute's is "stained with blood, and her breast and arms were bound up in folds of linen," just as the prostitute shows injuries on her face and side. These details – the bloodied face, as under a crown of thorns, the winding sheets already wrapping the wounded side – would indicate to Dickens's audience the sanctified status of these women as gendered symbols of Christ's atoning sacrifice. As Walder has suggested, moreover, Dickens was immersed in Shakespeare throughout the time of the *Sketches'* composition, and was even working on a burlesque entitled *O'Thello* during the period of their revision. Like that play's innocent victim, Dickens's prostitute finally claims to have inflicted her injuries on herself, though Desdemona's exclamation that she dies "a guiltless death" (V. ii. 122–4) appears nowhere in the *Sketches* scene.[43] The prostitute's echo of her father's wish for her death means that Dickens's scene, like Shakespeare's, reaches its climax when it achieves what René Girard would call "violent unanimity": institutional and individual efforts to alleviate suffering have failed, producing a social tension so unbearable as to demand the religious ritual of identification and sacrifice by a mass that finally includes the victim herself.[44]

To the end of his life, Dickens continued to be fascinated by the mass psychology of Atonement. In 1869, as he was insisting on performing the gruesome reading entitled "Sikes and Nancy," he used the same word Girard has employed to describe his huge audiences' reaction to the staging of his sacrificial murder:

> I don't think a hand moved while I was doing [the murder] last night, or an eye looked away. And there was a fixed expression of horror of me, all over the theatre, which could not have been surpassed if I had been going to be hanged to that red velvet table. It is quite a new sensation to be execrated with that unanimity; and I hope it will remain so! (*PL* 12: 329)

The most strenuous ambivalence still pervades Dickens's account of this reading, more than thirty years after he first imagined the murder in *Oliver Twist*. He apparently wants the sensation of unanimous execration to "remain" ever "new," ever shockingly fresh to him, even as he suggests that he would not want to become habituated to the experience through repetition. Escaping this kind of ambivalence by means of the symbolic deployment of violence is the aim of the conclusion of "The Hospital Patient." The prostitute's sacrifice permits the narrator to suppress his own "vagabond" individuality, psychologically and sociologically unstable as it is, in favor of the first person plural, the fantasy voice of a reconstituted community: "[w]e turned away; it was no sight for strangers to look upon." This dramatic shift was, indeed, important enough to constitute the principal revision for the Second Series, when Dickens recast the entire sketch in that voice, deleted his earlier reference to "vagabond" individuality, and effaced this imagined community's violent moment of origin by deleting the sentence I have just quoted.

But our close attention to "The Hospital Patient" may distract us from what should remain obvious: that its scene of Atonement remains in the form of a brief character "sketch," and that the Dickens of late 1836, even after inventing the Cockney Quixote and Sancho Panza, remained a novelist-to-be, still working to assemble both audience and form. The periodical in which the sketch appeared, the *Carlton Chronicle*, itself marks an episode in Dickens's incessant campaign to conquer new readers, whatever their class or politics. Though Dickens's former employer, the *Morning Chronicle*'s John Black, was known for his Whiggism, the *Carlton*'s editorial policy was "to combine politics with literature, and aspire to be at once a vehicle of sound Conservative doctrines in the one, and fair critical opinions in the other"; more to the point, as Dickens noted, its fashionable readers could afford a book costing a guinea or more.[45] In October, the *Carlton* published two Dickens sketches without authorization. But probably because of the access even unauthorized publication in the *Carlton* gave him to such affluent readers, Dickens took care to maintain cordial relations with its publisher, P. W. Bankes.[46]

November brought Dickens new responsibilities and disputes as editor of and leading contributor to *Bentley's Miscellany*. Despite the "no-politics" stance taken in the preface to the first issue, "Oliver Twist" marked a broadening of Dickens's appeal from his Whiggish *Morning Chronicle* base to the Tory and Radical elements now uniting against the New Poor Law: Bentley's close adviser R. H. Barham, for example, deplored the "radicalish" drift of the serial in April.[47] The death of the pauper woman in chapter 5 of "Oliver Twist," appearing in April 1837, was Dickens's most horrible scene since "The Drunkard's Death" of the Second Series. Bankes's appreciative review of both *Pickwick* and "Oliver Twist" cast the two works as parts of a greater whole, just as Bentley, Maginn, and even Dickens himself had all hoped to gather an audience for *Bentley's* across traditional market boundaries:

> We come to "Boz"; but stop, reader! you are going to burst into a guffau! – Stop, we say, for your own credit's sake; you do not understand "Boz." . . . The surface of the stream seems bright, and cheer-

> fully bubbling as it rushes on – but in its windings you come ever and anon upon some place of depth, which is dark at top, and as you look into it, if you pause the while – inscrutable to the vulgar many, and mysterious, because we know it hath within it the voice of an oracle, to the singular few. "Boz" has the sense of the ludicrous, the instinct feeling of the moving panorama, which is human life: he possesses in his sketches the power Rembrandt had, of bringing out to stand forth visibly masses of dark by a few strokes of light. This, with the heart to feel, and the nice art of availing oneself of contact, constitutes the power of pathos which so few, even of the most celebrated authors, have possessed. "Boz" has the power.[48]

To Bankes, Dickens is no longer a Cockney caricaturist, but rather the "oracle" of a creed of "human life" accessible only to the "singular few" – that is, the *Carlton*'s own affluent and cultivated readers. The April installment of "Oliver Twist" shows those readers how to "feel" their way to imaginary "contact" with the humanity of other, less cultivated classes. But though Bankes articulates the political stakes of Conservative humanism for us, his hyperbole analogizes the writer of "Oliver Twist" to the tradition of painterly realism exemplified by Rembrandt, rather than to the English school of drawn and engraved satire exemplified by Cruikshank.[49] Before Dickens could force publishers and readers to recognize him as an artist of this stature, he would have to imagine himself as such, and to turn "Oliver Twist," whatever its miscellaneous origins, into something resembling a novel.

In the few months from the death of Mary Hogarth, on 7 May, to the following November, Dickens's position in the literary field underwent yet another series of consolidations. By the end of June, after nursing Charles and Catherine through the worst of their grief, John Forster had taken on a decisive role in each sphere of Dickens's professional life: as de facto editor of *Pickwick*'s fifteenth number, the first submitted to someone other than Chapman and Hall for review; as critical champion, in the *Examiner*'s "beautiful notice" of that number on 1 July; and as chief negotiator, in the contest between Macrone and Chapman and Hall over the reissue of the *Sketches* (*PL* 1: 274, 280).[50] By the end of September, Dickens and Forster had not only forced Richard Bentley to accept the "Oliver Twist" series as one of the two novels specified in the agreement of August 1836 (the other being the unfinished *Gabriel Vardon*, published years later with Chapman and Hall as *Barnaby Rudge*), but had also wrested back a future interest in half its copyright, a reversion that was to take place three years after the novel's completion. As

Robert Patten was the first to emphasize, these terms were entirely unprecedented in the market for new novels.[51]

The second half of 1837 was also the time, however, when the unprecedented extent of Dickens's success, and the apparent endlessness of its cycles of production, began to disturb even his core audience. Carlyle started reading *Pickwick* after his pupil Charles Buller's comment in the *London and Westminster*'s July issue that Dickensian popularity was extraordinary not only "on account of its sudden growth," but because it included "persons of the most refined taste," as well as "the great mass of the reading public."[52] The haughty *Quarterly Review* agreed in October, admitting at the outset of a generally hostile review that Dickens was "one of the most remarkable literary phenomena of recent times."[53] But accompanying the rising tide of haut bourgeois attention and acclaim was a undercurrent of middle-class hostility. A number of the weeklies were suggesting that "Oliver Twist," and the entire Dickensian enterprise, violated some vague but fundamental distinction between art and commerce. *The Weekly Dispatch* put the matter plainly in September: "we must protest against publishing a long story, bit by bit, in a Magazine, and then reprinting the whole in the shape of a novel." In the same month, *Bell's Weekly* was warning that *Pickwick* was "already exhausted," and *Bell's Life* sniping at the announcement for *Nicholas Nickleby*, "[n]othing like striking while 'the iron is hot'; but even iron may be worn out." Chittick concludes that the outcome of this "skirmish" between upper- and middle-class reviews was, "being conducted on unequal ground," a foregone conclusion.[54] But Dickens's dilemma in the summer of 1837 should not be underestimated. Abandoning serial publication was now unthinkable: the Pickwickian "machinery"[55] had not only pumped July 1837 sales up to a dizzying 40 000 issues, but also taken over the reprints of *Sketches by Boz*. Dickens and his publishers might nonetheless have felt that they would ignore criticism from their core audience at their peril; after all, the now-hostile *Bell's Life* had paid for the last series of sketches to appear consistently, week after week, little more than a year before.[56] The best solution would have it both ways: make "Oliver Twist" into something undeniably and essentially novelistic, a quality which would have to appear in the text itself, independent of its Pickwickian "machinery"; and yet retain that mode of production and the riches it was generating.

As Kathleen Tillotson was the first to suggest, there is no sign of Nancy's later importance for the structure of the complete *Oliver Twist* before the installment of chapters 16 and 17, written as Dickens withheld the October 1837 installment from *Bentley's*. At her first appearance in chapter 9, Nancy and her companion, Bet, were both "not exactly pretty, perhaps; but they had a great deal of colour in their faces, and looked quite stout and hearty," "remarkably free and agreeable in their manners" (*OT* 55).[57] In the original chapter 13, it is Nancy, not Bet, who wore the "red gown, green boots, and yellow curl-papers" of the prostitute; and the sarcasm of chapter 15's title, "Shewing How Very Fond Of Oliver Twist, the Merry Old Jew and Miss Nancy Were," made no distinction between her and Fagin's feelings towards the boy (*OT* 79, 91).

The changes of chapter 16 are immediate and decisive. Its title identifies her as "Nancy," without the mock-fancy "Miss," a change worked back through all subsequent editions. And it soon strikes two notes familiar to us from "The Hospital Patient." The first is that of a Nancy no longer "stout and hearty," but weak and suffering: as Bill Sikes leads the recaptured Oliver through "narrow streets and courts," it is Nancy, not Oliver, who is "quite unable to support, any longer, the rapid rate at which they had hitherto walked" (*OT* 97). The second is a capacity for moral sympathy to match this new physical morbidity. The sound of a Smithfields church-bell brings Nancy to imagine aloud how some of their companions in crime, " 'fine young chaps' " now languishing in nearby Newgate, can hear the same sound. An exasperated Bill reduces her fellow-feeling to its sexual component: " 'Yes; that's all you women think of,' answered Sikes. 'Fine young chaps! Well, they're as good as dead, so it don't much matter.' " Nancy again attempts to rouse his sexual jealousy into moral imagination by insisting that if Bill were held in Newgate, she would " 'walk round and round the place till I dropped' "; but Bill again resists: " 'You might as well be walking fifty mile off, or not walking at all, for all the good it would do me' " (98–9). Instantly, Nancy's body begins to emit messages which only Oliver and the reader are in a position to decode:

> The girl burst into a laugh; drew her shawl more closely round her; and they walked away. But Oliver felt her hand tremble; and, looking up in her face as they passed a gas lamp, saw that it had turned a deadly white. (*OT* 99)

The entire narrative procedure is repeated a few pages later, when Fagin beats Oliver for attempting to escape; and this time, Nancy's "transport of frenzy" prefigures the moment of violent unanimity to come: " 'I wish I had been struck dead in the street, or had changed places with them we passed so near to-night, before I had lent a hand,' " she exclaims, and faints shortly afterward (104). From this sixteenth chapter, then, and not later, Nancy's status as atoning victim seems assured.[58]

Tillotson was the first to argue for this November installment as the moment when "the novel had become more than a serial," corrected by Chittick as the moment when "the serial had become a novel."[59] But what has remained obscure, even to these expert readers, is that its narrator has two central and simultaneous purposes: marking his atoning victim, and announcing his novelistic ambitions. No one can miss Dickens's attention to genre in the metaphor of "streaky bacon" introducing chapter 17: the theatrical "custom" is to alternate "good, murderous melodramas" with broadly comic scenes (*OT* 105). But this theatrical norm is ordered to give way to a new narrative regime in the remainder of the same passage, most of which was omitted and the rest toned down in all later versions of the work:

> [T]here is so much to do, that I have no room for digressions, even if I possessed the inclination; and I merely make this one in order to set myself quite right with the reader, between whom and the historian it is essentially necessary that perfect faith should be kept, and a good understanding preserved. The advantage of this amicable explanation is, that when I say, as I do now, that I am going back directly to the town in which Oliver Twist was born, the reader will at once take it for granted that I have good and substantial reasons for making the journey, or I would not ask him to accompany me on any account. (*OT* 106)

This passage's ambition, the product of the criticisms and victories of the late summer of 1837, is to subject the repetitions of comedy and melodrama to the telos of novelistic "history."[60] It presages a new kind of Dickensian narrator: neither the "vagabond" of the *Carlton Chronicle* sketch of August 1836, nor the archivist of *Pickwick*'s number that same month, nor even the anti-Poor Law polemicist of February 1837; but rather a "historian," who has "no room for digression," "good and substantial reasons" for everything he does, and an unprecedented measure of control over both his commodity-novel and its consumer-reader.

As I have already suggested, Dickens took two giant steps toward becoming a cultural phenomenon when he reoccupied his representations of urban alienation in a literary and commodity form determined by a fundamental opposition from a fading Christian culture. The success of Dickens's first longer literary form sprang from the incarnation of the master Pickwick and the servant Sam in a transcendent relation of brotherly Love and masterful Logos; his second imagines itself a novel just as it conceives the murder of Nancy as an atoning sacrifice presumably designed, like the death of the anonymous *Sketches* prostitute, to enable the imagination of a reconstituted community. The appearance of these ideologemes of Incarnation and Atonement[61] at moments of transformation in the literary field, as in the critical period from the commencement of *Pickwick* in February 1836 to the recasting of *Oliver Twist* in the autumn of 1837, is only the first such episode in the course of Dickens's career. And these related ideologemes have already begun to mingle as *Pickwick Papers* draws to a close.

Winding up *Pickwick*: laughter and despair

Representations of suffering are never entirely absent from *Pickwick Papers*. At first, they are isolated in the shorter individual narratives of disease, obsession, revenge, and death, from the Stroller's Tale (No. 1) to the story of the Bagman's Uncle (No. 17), interpolated into the serial. But with Mr. Pickwick's entry into the Fleet, in the August 1837 number, this idealized representation of humanity, having been found liable in the case of *Bardell v. Pickwick*, begins to apprehend the human suffering made inevitable by a legal apparatus wielding a specialized and perverted discourse. W. H. Auden drew attention long ago to these moments of Pickwickian disenchantment. In his first few days in the Fleet, where he has gone in defiance of the judgment against him, Mr. Pickwick meets what Auden classifies as three kinds of prisoners for debt: thieves, like Smangle; "the childish who believe in magic," a type reaching its epitome years later in Mr. Micawber; and those others, victims of larger forces than mere greed or improvidence, who "have fallen into debt through circumstances which they could neither foresee nor control." Auden's example of these last is a man who is eager to let his prison cell out to Mr. Pickwick for twenty shillings a week, and who (as we later learn) has been unfortunate enough to be named both beneficiary and executor of an estate long since consumed by the costs of a suit in Chancery (*PP* 652, 678–81). What Auden finds significant about these prisoners for debt is their necessarily rich symbolic valence in a world governed by monetary exchange. Such meanings become acutely ironic in the case of the Chancery prisoner, Mr. Pickwick's Fleet landlord: the personification of benevolence secures a private cell with cash payment. Pickwick will soon realize that wealth itself is a form of debt, which he can discharge only through forgiveness and charity.[62]

For his part, however, the Chancery prisoner soon expires, with Sam, Sam's own Fleet landlord (a cobbler), and a guilty Pickwick in attendance. The event is set amidst the same urban roar into which Arthur Clennam and Amy Dorrit will descend at the conclusion of *Little Dorrit* – that is, amidst a form of social life which the Dickens of 1837 already imagines as both immensely powerful and essentially inhuman:

> "Open the window," said the sick man.
>
> [The cobbler] did so. The noise of carriages and carts, the rattle of wheels, the cries of men and boys, all the busy sounds of *a mighty multitude instinct with life and occupation*, blended into one deep murmur, floated into the room. Above the hoarse loud hum, arose, from time to time, a boisterous laugh; or a scrap of some jingling song, shouted forth, by one of the giddy crowd, would strike upon the ear, for an instant, and then be lost amidst the roar of voices and the tramp of foot-steps; the breaking of the billows of the restless sea of life, that rolled heavily on, without. Melancholy sounds to a quiet listener at any time; how melancholy to the watcher by the bed of death! (*PP* 687, emphasis added)

Though Mr. Pickwick is indeed a "watcher by the bed of death," his consciousness, which mingles with the narrator's own in the last sentence's free indirect discourse, is transfixed by what he hears: the sounds of a stage of modernity, gendered as male, in which it is impossible to distinguish those instincts arising from any imaginable preexisting or natural life from those arising from the socially given circumstances of occupation. Dickens is here beginning to render, in his own distinctively figural terms, a sociological judgment like those of Schiller, Marx, and Weber: that the leading determinant of nineteenth-century urban life would be its intensive and ongoing rationalization, including a division of human labor across all categories of work into literally countless parts; and that a fundamental subject for Victorian culture must be the dialectical relation of these developments, figured here as forces of oceanic power and sublimity, to any consciousness struggling to apprehend and survive them.[63]

Once again, Dickens reoccupies this fretful consciousness, generated by the hero's encounter with the misrule of bourgeois law, in a brief narrative cycle of Atonement. A mounting incapacity to react to suffering, a tendency to "muse deeply" on it instead (*PP* 653), has become obvious in Mr. Pickwick by the end of the following chapter. He claims to have "seen enough," and begins to display physical symptoms of his moral disgust, his health "evidently beginning to suffer from the closeness of the confinement" (707). By the September 1837 number, after "three long months" of self-imposed isolation (707), the same period as John Dickens's imprisonment for debt in the Marshalsea,[64] Mr. Perker is pleading with his client to take the "magnanimous revenge" of paying off the judgments against both himself and Mrs. Bardell (726), who has joined him in the Fleet as a result of his refusal to do so. The lawyer's formulation preserves intact the apparently insoluble contradiction between Weber's two kinds of social action: the means-rationality of surviving one's enemies in the world, and the ends-rationality of treating them according to Christianity's golden rule.[65] One last time, Mr. Pickwick is deprived of the opportunity to act, and thus to make what Weber would argue must be an agonizing choice between these alternatives, when Mr. Winkle and Arabella Allen, the latter of whom wears a bridal veil in the illustration, "rush[] tumultuously into the room" (*PP* 728–9).

Of course, the marriage plot, the *deus ex machina* of comedy in general and the Victorian novel in particular, is only an escape from the contradiction between ethical ends and rational means now permeating Mr. Pickwick's consciousness. After his release from the Fleet, this problem comes to define the country through which the hero moves. In the "heart of the turmoil" of the "great working town" of Birmingham, for example, "[t]he hum of labor resounded from every house; lights gleamed from the long casement windows in the attic stories, and the whirl of wheels and noise of machinery shook the trembling walls" (*PP* 776); the stable-yard of Mr. Pickwick's inn is populated by pathetic objects like a rooster, "deprived of every spark of his usual animation, balanc[ing] himself dismally on one leg in a corner," or a donkey, "moping with drooping head under the narrow roof of an outhouse, appear[ing] from his meditative and miserable countenance to be contemplating suicide" (784). The contradiction between the prodigious energy of industrial production and the despair and exhaustion of those creatures condemned to live amidst that production has come to constitute an entire landscape.

At this same time, in the fall of 1837, Dickens seems to have become intermittently aware of the mechanical quality of his creative life. In October, for example, we find him responding to Alexander Heyward's faint praise in the *Quarterly Review*, including the naming of him as "one of the most remarkable literary phenomena of recent times," with a mixture of gratitude and fear regarding the emergent mass market which now bears him along:

> [A]s the Notice contains a great deal that I know to be true, and much more which may be, but of which I am no impartial judge, I find little fault with it. I hope I may truly say that no writer ever had less vanity than I have; and that my only anxiety to stand well with the world in that capacity, originates in authorship being unhappily my trade, as it is happily my pleasure. (*PL* 1: 316)

As always, ambivalent statements like this are more fully developed in the symbolic language of the fiction. Just as this letter was written, Sam Weller enacted the same kind of attraction and repulsion to the source of wealth in his life. In Pickwick's final number, Mr. Pickwick wishes to "free" his servant from the "restraint" of his position as valet by setting Sam up with the cash enabling him not only to marry, but also "to earn an independent livelihood" for himself and his family (*PP* 864–5). But rather than using this offer of capital as the basis for participation in an economic system dedicated to it, Sam insists on joining his master in "repose and quiet" (865) – that imaginary state which, as George Orwell has pointed out, amounts to the Dickensian novel's idea of heaven, a state of "radiant idleness" where getting and spending have at last ceased to be matters of transcendent importance.[66]

Mr. Pickwick's self-immurement in the Fleet, as well as Sam's withdrawal with him at serial's end into repose and quiet, are early examples of Dickens making ever more atonement for his ever-increasing wealth, power and fame – a dialectical series that comes to include *Little Dorrit*'s self-despising hero and record-breaking sales, as well as the Farewell Tour's suicidal reader and massive profits.[67] Near the end of the first volume of *Capital*, Marx would subject the capitalist creed to a withering irony: if that creed is "Accumulate, accumulate! That is Moses and the prophets," then its "beautiful trinity" is "overproduction, overpopulation, overconsumption" – "three very delicate monsters, indeed."[68] These layers of Dickensian production and triumph, transformation and despair, encode a similar verdict that the god of capital will, like its Old and New Testament predecessors, eventually obtain its sacrifice.

2
The Pathos of Distance: Thackeray, Serialization, and *Vanity Fair*

> Without that pathos of distance which grows out of the ingrained difference between strata – when the ruling caste constantly looks afar and looks down upon subjects and instruments and just as constantly practices obedience and command, keeping down and keeping at a distance – that other, more mysterious pathos could not have grown up either – the craving for an ever new widening of distances within the soul itself, the development of ever higher, rarer, more remote, further-stretching, more comprehensive states.
>
> Friedrich Nietzsche, *Beyond Good and Evil* (1886)

Many years ago, the editor and biographer Gordon Ray proposed an explanation for the appearance of *Vanity Fair* from a writer who, despite more than a decade of effort, had not yet produced a serial novel meeting either his or his audience's requirements.[1] After years in which Isabel Thackeray's mental distress, and her husband's unpredictable reactions to its vicissitudes, had allowed only intermittent contact between the father and his children, Thackeray's "scale of values" underwent a profound change as a result of his permanent reunion with his daughters. Ray juxtaposes this rediscovery of his love for his children, and theirs for him, with the conception of *Vanity Fair*'s "dark moral." In the same letter in which he rhapsodized to his mother about the "Divine Benevolence appointed to result from the union between parents and children," Ray argues, Thackeray first states the *vanitas* theme to which readers and reviewers responded so intensely; Charlotte Brontë's characterization of him as "the first social regenerator of the day" is only the best-known of these.[2] The formal result of this moral revolution, Ray concludes, is the emergence of the essentially earnest narrative voice of *Vanity Fair*'s chapter 8, "bound to speak the truth as far as one knows it," even if "a deal of disagreeable matter must come out in the course of such an undertaking" (83): a voice, that is, representing a "loose but temporarily tenable synthesis of ultimately irreconcilable social standards."[3]

A significant refinement of Ray's thesis came in John Sutherland's meticulous 1974 discussion of this same chapter. Having introduced himself as a "moralist" who is not a clergyman but a clown, this narrator playfully distinguishes between his characters' contempt for religion or rank from his own contempt for them, coming as it does "from one which had no reverence except for prosperity and no eye for anything beyond success" (*VF* 83–4). To Sutherland, the number and complexity of the stances taken here, including this final flourish of ironic distance, signify the profound difficulties involved in negotiating the roles of artist and moralist – difficulties elided by moving away from any single character, and in particular the Becky whose letter takes up most of the chapter, and towards a narrative "consciousness" so variegated as to belie the name. The result, he concludes, is an "artistic impasse," a state of contradiction that Thackeray "could only blur with an increasingly virtuosic display."[4]

The middle section of chapter 8's famous coda has received significantly less attention, however. Here, Thackeray juxtaposes two anecdotes in which audiences express enthusiastic outrage at the skillful presentation of villainous characters. A Neopolitan story-teller

> work[ed] himself up into such a rage and passion with some of the villains whose wicked deeds he was describing and inventing, that the audience could not resist it, and they and the poet together would burst out in a roar of oaths and execrations against the fictitious monster of the tale, so that the hat went round and the bajocchi tumbled into it in the midst of a perfect storm of sympathy[,]

while, "on the other hand," one present at a Paris theater

> will not only hear the people yelling out "*Ah gredin, ah monstre!*" and cursing the tyrant of the play from the boxes, but the actors themselves positively refuse to play the wicked parts such as those of *infâmes Anglais*, brutal Cossacks, and what not, and prefer to appear, at a smaller salary, in their real character as loyal Frenchmen. (*VF* 83–4)

The apparent lesson to be gained from these two scenes of performance and moneymaking, set as "one against the other" (84), is that this narrator too forgets that his characters are fictitious, and has "a sincere hatred of them . . . which must find a vent in suitable abuse and bad language."

But a lesson so quickly gained leaves much unsaid. To start with, *Vanity Fair* is not an oral performance, the reproduction of which must involve collective effort in real time, but a commodity in Marx's writerly sense of the word: circulating independently of its creator for the purpose of making money, of course, but also capable of simultaneously recording, prescribing, and mystifying the truth of the social.[5] In this case, though the narrator points out his mercenary motives, and though he reveals himself as neither actor nor audience but producer, we are left undecided whether he is more like the Italian story-teller, who shares his audience's feelings, or like the unnamed capitalist running the Paris theater, who arouses his employees' patriotism for the purpose of securing their services at a lower price.

What is indisputable is that Thackeray has alerted us to the possibility that judgment itself is a feeling pleasant enough to pay for. My purpose here is to consider this result not as ideological or aesthetic compromise, as Ray and Sutherland do respectively, but as an imaginative response to the London literary field of the late 1830s and 1840s – specifically, as a product of Thackeray's ten-year struggle to escape the crushing weight of Charles Dickens in that field. Publishing his first piece of fiction under Dickens's editorship in 1837, and persevering through the long decade to follow, Thackeray veered between imitation of and attacks on his idol and rival. In the intermediate phase of these years of adversity, the author of *Catherine* and *Barry Lyndon* gradually abandoned his earlier pseudonyms in favor of a critical persona he would never abandon, one that allowed him to express both his continued hostility to the social phenomena Dickens represented and his need to achieve a certain salutary distance from these. Thackeray first imagined a link between escaping Dickens's domination of the literary field and articulating a distinctive aesthetic vision of his own as he traveled to the Mediterranean and the Middle East in 1844–5, visiting Bethlehem and Jerusalem, Christianity's sites of Incarnation and Atonement, among other places. A longing for deliverance from the bloody pleasures of revenge, informing his developing and powerful critique of the author of *A Christmas Carol*, would finally issue in *Vanity Fair*'s "pathos of distance." From the exalted ideological position Charlotte Brontë would identify as that of a "prophet," Thackeray would turn a cold and searching light on the struggle between Christianity and capitalism in the age of Dickens.

The weight of Dickens, 1837–1840

In the winter of 1837, just as Dickens was assuming his duties as the editor of and leading contributor to *Bentley's Miscellany*, Thackeray's daily concerns were rapidly hardening into the forms of financial and personal responsibility which would rule the rest of his life. His attempts to earn money by illustrations in 1836–7 included submissions of drawings for *Sketches by Boz* in 1836, all of which Dickens rejected; for Ainsworth's *The Admirable Crichton*, the first edition of which appeared without illustrations in early 1837; and for admission to the Water Colour Society, whose Board apparently turned Thackeray down.[6] With Isabella pregnant with their first child, Thackeray's January letters reach a new pitch of urgency. The letter soliciting Macrone for the Ainsworth job, for example, closes with a plea for a £20 advance on a fantasy project – "a book in 2 Wollums. with 20 drawings. entitled Rambles and Sketches in old and new Paris by W. T." – in short, a Parisian *Sketches by Boz*, a work which duly appeared in 1840 as the *Paris Sketch Book*. From this very beginning of his career as a writer of fiction, Thackeray's relationship with the London literary field would be characterized by a distinctively intense ambivalence over the generative power of the marketplace. Even at this stage, the Paris sketches project must proceed under pressure – "I have not of course written a word of it, that's why I offer it so cheap, but I want to be made to write, and to bind myself by a contract or fine" (*LPP* 1: 328–9) – just as, years later, Thackeray would reminisce about the gambler's mentality of these days, when he would spend his last shillings on a dinner with his wife in order to "nerve and excite myself up to writing."[7]

The same letter proposing what would become the *Paris Sketch Book* also mentions a "large picture," not yet a part of anything more specific than a "hope to procure immortality" (1: 327–8), of one "*Dando.*" This same character would take center stage in "The Professor," Thackeray's first published story, which appeared in the Dickens-edited *Bentley's Miscellany* in July 1837. A historical character of this name appears in *The Times* as early as 1830, when a John Dando was found guilty of the crime of overconsumption, having eaten eleven dozen oysters and run out on the bill; we get a glimpse of the same character in Dickens's 1835 sketch "The River," in which a Thames boatman shares the name with "the defunct oyster swallower."[8] Thackeray's villain is a strapping dancing-master (with a pronounced Cockney accent, despite his exotic name) at a Hackney school for girls. The first half of the tale follows his attempted seduction of Miss Adeliza Grampus, the school's wealthiest student, as well as one of the two sisters who run the establishment; this romantic double-dealing ends with the exposure of the simpering Adeliza as a mere oystermonger's daughter. The tale's other chapter moves to London, where Dando resumes his attentions with a vengeance, extracts money from Adeliza, and finally descends on the luckless Cheapside shop. There, he manages to fondle both daughter and mother, eat two lobsters and eleven dozen oysters, and run up a bill of well over a pound before Mr. Grampus flushes him out: "'What a flat you are,' shouted he in a voice of thunder, 'to think I', a goin' to pay! Pay! I never pay – I'm DANDO!'"[9]

We cannot know the extent of Dickens's involvement in this first published tale, noting only that Dando (and the victimized shopkeeper) remained sufficiently vivid in his mind to appear in a letter written five years later (*PL* 3: 291–2). But it is clear that "The Professor" bears the marks of an ambivalent identification with Dickens that would hardly wane over the next decade. Compare, for example, these two physical descriptions – the first, Thackeray's villain, fallen from the heights of Hackney; the second, his literary sibling Bill Sikes, who had appeared for the first time in the previous month's number of *Bentley's*:

> His costume at present was singularly changed for the worse: a rough brown frock-coat dangled down to the calves of his brawny legs, where likewise ended a pair of greasy shepherd's plaid trousers; a dubious red waistcoat, a blue or bird's eye neckerchief, and bluchers, (or half-boots,) remarkable for thickness and for mud, completed his attire. But he looked superior to his fortune; he wore his grey hat very much on one ear; he incessantly tugged at his smoky shirt-collar, and walked jingling the half-pence (when he had any) in his pocket. (283–4)

> [He] was a stoutly-built fellow of about five-and-forty, in a black velveteen coat, very soiled drab breeches, lace-up half boots, and grey cotton stocking, which inclosed a very bulky pair of legs, with large swelling calves; – the kind of legs, that in such costume, always look in an unfinished and incomplete state without a set of fetters to garnish then. He had a brown hat on his head, and a dirty belcher handkerchief round his neck, with the long frayed ends of which, he smeared the beer from his face as he spoke. . . . (*OT* 118)

Bill Sikes's soiled breeches have become greasy trousers, and a gray hat turns brown; but the spotted "bird's eye" or "belcher" kerchief, powerful (and phallic) calves, dirty linen, and half-boots remain the same.[10] Likewise, two years before *Catherine* (1839–40) would parody Newgate novels in general, and *Oliver Twist*'s "whitewashed saint" "Biss Dadcy" in particular, the hapless Adeliza Grampus suffers the same kind of fainting fit we have seen Dickens's heroine fall into, with more serious short-term effects: "[w]hen Adeliza Grampus rose from that trance she was a MANIAC!" (288).

But even as we note the extent to which the young Thackeray imitates Dickens's Newgate style, distinctive differences are no less clear. The Misses Pidge, Adeliza Grampus, and Dandolo/Dando are all blinded by their appetite for a few more tidbits of status, money, or luxury, without any pole of purity to react against. Dickens never deploys horror for laughs, as Thackeray does in the case of the crazed Adeliza. And even if Dickens would choose to end such a tale with the kind of bombast this narrator does, claiming that if the tale has "deterred one soul from vice, my end is fully answered," he would never have included a postscript disclosing the bombastier behind them: "Please send the proceeds as requested per letter; the bearer being directed not to give up the manuscript without" (288).

Already obvious in the Parisian sketches proposal of 1835, Thackeray's need for money continued to grow as his family expanded in the late 1830s. Even in his own house, he was faced with Dickens's dominant position: as she nursed their second child, friends gave Isabella *Pickwick Papers* to read, just as his daughter Minnie would later demand why her father didn't write more books like *Nicholas Nickelby*, and name her cat after the book's hero.[11] Demanding more pay from James Fraser in March, begging the publisher to distinguish between their commercial and personal relationships, and then quickly apologizing for "bullying you about money matters" (*LPP* 1: 351–2, 364–5), Thackeray wrote in the grip of both admiration and anxiety, as in his first noted magazine serial, *The Yellowplush Correspondence*, the bulk of which ran during 1838.

The narrator of the series, a footman, has been moved to write to *Fraser's Magazine* concerning a book of manners which caught Thackeray's eye, John Skelton's *Anatomy of Conduct* (1837). After skewering Skelton's capacious sense of propriety, which could condemn such phenomena as a knocker on the door of a country house, the Cockney Yellowplush narrates his own early life: his mother, like Becky Sharp, claimed lineage as a Montmorency, while one of his early masters went off to the City every morning not to shuffle paper, as the family thought, but to sweep the corner of Bank and Cornhill for a few pence.[12] In its third number, the *Correspondence* brings Yellowplush into the service of the rascallious Percy Deuceace, whom we first see competing with another gambler for the opportunity to fleece a hapless middle-class aspirant to the bar. This strand proved popular, and followed Percy to Paris as he attempted to escape creditors (just as Thackeray's in-laws had done a few years before), where we meet Lord Deuceace, the ruthless elder of this morally and financially decayed family, who eventually obtains the moneyed woman for whom he is competing with his own son. But as he narrates Percy Deuceace's capture and imprisonment in the Parisian equivalent of the Fleet, Yellowplush admits that "the admiral Boz" had already, "in the history of Mr. Pickwick, made such a dixcripshn of a prizn, that mine wooden read very amyousingly afterwids" (94).

"Mr Yellowplush's Ajew," the last installment of the *Correspondence* for more than a year,[13] marks Thackeray's most extended engagement with the Dickens phenomenon to date, combining an extended satire of Bulwer with a closing parody of *Pickwick*. In the Dickensian original, we recall, Mr. Pickwick makes a well-known offer to Sam Weller: "Supposing I were desirous of establishing them comfortably as man and wife in some little business or situation, where they might hope to obtain a decent living, what should you think of it, Mr. Weller?" (*PP* 864). Thackeray winds up his own serial by inverting this scene. One Lord Crabs, a guest at the literary party dominated by a thinly disguised Bulwer, has been so impressed with the *Correspondence* that he makes Yellowplush an offer:

> "With all my admiration for your talents, Mr. Yellowplush, I still am confident that many of your friends in the servants' hall will clean my boots a great deal better than a gentleman of your genius can ever be expected to do. . . . But . . . I don't wish to throw you upon the whole wide world without means of a livelihood, and have made interest for a little place which you will have under government, and which will give you an income of eighty pounds per annum, which you can double, I presume, by your literary labours." (115)

Yellowplush's reaction is a parody of loving labor: "'Sir,' says I, clasping my hands, and bursting into tears, 'do not – for Heaven's sake, do not! think of any such think, or drive me from suvvice, because I have been fool enough to write in magaseens.'" But though he is foolish enough to accept Lord Crabs's offer, the last lines of the number show that Yellowplush soon regrets his divergence from the Wellerian norm: "it's with a melancholy regret" that he looks back on the decision to become a writer, though he is now "an altered, wiser, and, I trust, better man" (117–18).

Such broad parody and sudden pathos, with its deflations and reversals of Dickensian fellow-feeling, makes it all the more difficult to note the essential innovation in *Yellowplush*: the Dickensian *character* of Cockney labor, set loose to dispense encoded wisdom in the world-city of *Pickwick*, becomes the Thackerayan *narrator*, who has lived through the results of the Pickwickian dispensation, and named its results "melancholy." Thackeray escapes the weight of Dickens, in other words, by means of a narrative voice which – as in the case of Yellowplush himself, who metamorphoses from the worldly Weller of the first three numbers to the gullible and finally chastened scribbler of the last – is essentially various.

However much Thackeray may have felt the need to critique the fantasy of class conciliation embodied in Sam Weller, he continued to represent atoning victims, the dark counterparts of such incarnational formations. As we have seen, his own roster of victimized heroines began with the unfortunate Adeliza Grampus, driven mad by the attentions of the oyster-eater Dando. But the series thus begun is not always as absurd as its first case. The conclusion of the Deuceace tale making up the bulk of the *Yellowplush Correspondence*, for example, comes as the ruined son Percy waves his crippled arm at the carriage containing his triumphant and vindictive father and his ex-servant, the latter of whom is reporting the scene. Once again, as in "The Professor," the tale ends in a blur of frustration and violence; but this time, there is little sign of humor or absurdity, as Percy turns his maimed anger from the father he cannot strike to the wife he can: she "fell, screaming. Poor thing! Poor thing!"[14] As Thackeray would comment in 1840, "amidst much debauch of sentiment, and enervating dissipation of intellect," writers and readers "have from time to time a returning appetite for innocence and freshness."[15]

Thus working through the warring imperatives of benevolence and sacrifice, Thackeray's insights into the literary field gained in both intensity and precision. In a single 1839 *Fraser's* article on the penny press, for example, we are told that three numbers of a twopenny newspaper have more "information," more dependable data on "thieves, ruffians, swindlers of both sexes, more real vulgarity, more tremendous slang, more unconscious, honest, blackguard NATURE, in fact, than Mr.

Dickens will ever give to the public"; and, earlier in the same article, that "we" readers, including Thackeray himself, prefer the imaginary to the real, "are willing to pass off" fictions, whether literary, theatrical or political, "as truth, *and have entered conventionally into an agreement that they shall be received among us in place of the real thing.*"[16] To reveal the social basis of literary production and consumption in this way would have been inconceivable to the Dickens who asserted in 1841 that Nancy speaks "not one word exaggerated or over-wrought," having been extracted, like other forms of Christian vision, from "these melancholy shades of life" (*OT* 6–7).

By 1840, Thackeray's distinctive rhetoric is thus already in place: the skillful deflation of the very illusion he has created, as in the concluding flourish of "The Professor"; and the placement of that urge to deflation in a first-person voice always tending toward disintegration, as in the narrator of *Yellowplush.* His ongoing critique of Dickensian exaggeration, as of the conventional and essentially contractual nature of the relationship between writers and readers, seems to have had an inescapable personal effect, however: an inability to project his own aspirations more or less directly into a literary creation, what D. J. Taylor has recently termed a queasy "suspicion that the muse would turn out to be inconstant."[17] Perhaps he could suspend this disbelief in his own imaginative powers only by freeing himself from old convictions and the disposition they engendered.[18] In order to reach such a state, however, Thackeray would have to invent his own distinctive ideologemes of benevolence and sacrifice even as he intensified his critique of the literary market and the Dickens phenomenon.

Becoming a critic, 1840–1844

One might construct an entire narrative of Thackeray's development around the evolution of his pseudonyms. The young literary adventurer begins with one "Goliah Gahagan," referring to both his Goliath height and his Irish roots; competes with Sam Weller in the person of the Cockney author Charles Yellowplush; becomes George Fitz-Boodle in the Fieldingesque *Barry Lyndon,* retiring that persona along with the story in late 1844; and then appears as Michael Angelo Titmarsh, attendant at galleries, exhibitions, and concerts, in a *Fraser's* review of 1838 entitled "Strictures on Pictures."[19] Given this penchant for disguise, one may reasonably look with some attention at "Going to See a Man Hanged," one of the very few articles published before 1846 under Thackeray's own initials.

D. J. Taylor takes this piece on the public hanging of the murderer Courvoisier, published in August 1840, as the moment where "this immense, teeming world – dominated by the figure of the writer moving within it – first moves into focus."[20] It is true that this piece is narrated from what Jonathan Arac would call a position of overview.[21] But Thackerayan overview is both less ambitious and more generous than its Dickensian equivalent. While Dickens rented a second-storey room especially for the occasion, Thackeray remained on foot. And though Dickens later recalled having a distinct lack of sympathy for the crowd, seeing "nothing but ribaldry, debauchery, levity, drunkenness and flaunting vice in fifty other shapes," and feeling astonished that he "could have ever felt any large assemblage of my fellow creatures to be so odious," Thackeray, though he noted the presence of beggars, thieves, and prostitutes, concluded that he had "never yet" been "in an English mob . . . without wonder at the vigorous, orderly good sense, and intelligence of the people" – proven to him on this occasion by the crowd's imperative that a prostitute cover her exposed shoulders.[22]

Such "republican" sentiments as these were sure to expose Thackeray and his argument against capital punishment to attack from the political right; and thus the piece's rhetorical destination is moral rather than political. Just as he moves at the level of the crowd, observing more than dominating the scene, the novelist finally renders judgment not only on the crowd but on himself, acknowledging his own complicity in the blood-lust which draws them all:

> I may be permitted for my part to declare, that for the last fourteen days, so salutary has the impression of the butchery been upon me, I have had the man's face continually before my eyes; that I can see Mr. Ketch at this moment, with an easy air, taking the rope from his pocket; that I feel myself ashamed and degraded by the brutal curiosity which took me to that brutal sight; and that I pray to Almightly God to cause this disgraceful sin to pass from among us, and to cleanse our land of blood. (158)

Under the sway of this generous benevolence, evidence of the sins of others hastens the contemplation of his own fallen state, rather than the social activism in which Dickens would plunge himself. Chesterton was right, then, when he wrote that Thackeray "stood for the remains of Christian humility, as Dickens stood for the remains of Christian charity," though we should note that the question how extensive these remains are is one Chesterton leaves artfully open.[23]

The literary criticism of the early 1840s adds this new and distinctive note of humility to the ambition and iconoclasm of Thackeray's earlier work. By the time of "A Box of Novels," for example, published in *Fraser's* in February 1844, it is clear that *Yellowplush*-style attacks have been set aside. Instead, we hear an opening confession that even if "Michael Angelo has handled the tomahawk as well as another, and has a scalp or two drying in his lodge," youthful vitriol has given way to the good humor of middle age, which "has yet a mirth of its own," "more lasting than the intoxication of satire."[24] Such good humor is indeed obvious in Thackeray's account of the Irish novelist Charles Lever. Thackeray is most interested, however, in the phenomenon of the hack writer, who moralizes or attacks according to the whims of the periodical market:

> O patriotic critic! what Brutus-like sacrifices will the literary man not commit! . . . Although he knows that the success of one man of letters is the success of all, . . . that to make what has hitherto been a struggling and uncertain calling an assured and respectable one, it is necessary that some should succeed greatly, . . . yet *the virtues of professional literature are so obstinately republican, that it will acknowledge no honours, help no friend, have all on a level*; and so the Irish press is at present martyrising the most successful member of its body. (155–6, emphasis added)

The analogy of the critic as Brutus to the preeminent writer's Caesar emphasizes the overtly political and symbolically violent nature of struggle in the early Victorian literary field: members of the republic of letters would, as Marx would put it, "recognise no other authority than that of competition, the coercion exercised upon them by the pressure of their reciprocal interests."[25]

When ruthless competition can be idealized as moral equality, expressions of domination can masquerade as critical magnanimity. Such are Thackeray's late 1843 comments on Dickens's *Christmas Carol*. It is true that Thackeray identifies Dickens as "the master of all the English humourists now alive," "the young man who came and took his place calmly at the head of the whole tribe, and who has kept it," achieving a "communion" with his readership that is "something continual, confidential, something like personal affection" (167). But under cover of this apparent magnanimity, and in the intensity of his own ambivalence, Thackeray repeats a series of common insults against Dickens that the well-heeled readers of *Fraser's* were likely to remember, if not to believe: that Dickens's books had "lost in art" due to the incessant pace of publication; that they might have been "pruned here and there and improved"; and, while urging his readers to ignore Dickens's lack of classical education, his treatment of low subjects with high rhetoric, and his propensity to write blank verse in prose, that Boz's literary reputation "has been sinking regularly these six years" (167–8). Only the last of these is actually affirmed before praising *A Christmas Carol* as a virtual scripture of sympathy, "a national benefit, and to every man or woman who reads it a personal kindness" (169). But the evidence of Dickens's material overproduction and rhetorical excess have been introduced nonetheless.

What makes this ventriloquistic technique useful, of course, is its capacity to express aggression by indirection: the puppet can say what the puppeteer cannot. And it is only after the release of such aggression, it seems to me, that Thackeray can articulate the origins of Dickensian enjoyment in an iron dialectic of mastery and victimization, brute consumption and atoning sacrifice:

> Had the book appeared a fortnight earlier, all the prize cattle would have been gobbled up in pure love and friendship, Epping denuded of sausages, and not a turkey left in Norfolk. . . . But there is a Christmas for 1844, too; the book will be as early then as now, and so let speculators look out.
>
> As for Tiny Tim, there is a certain passage in the book regarding that young gentleman, about which a man should hardly venture to speak in print or in public, any more than he would of any other affections of his private heart[.] (169)

The certain passage requiring suppression is likely Scrooge's vision, under the hand of the Ghost of Christmas Future, of Tiny Tim's green grave and cold corpse – as powerful a sacrificial image for his Victorian audience in 1844, perhaps, as Nell's deathbed had been; and a painful enough one to require both the well-known correction in proof that Tiny Tim "did NOT die," as well as the excision of Bob Cratchit's visit to the deathbed in the public readings of Dickens's later career.[26]

As we have seen in the case of early Dickens, such images of sacrifice and consumption are the sacred and profane variants of an acquisitiveness going far beyond ordinary greed into a state tantamount to ravenous hunger or obsessed rage. "Such a night as I have passed!" Dickens exclaimed on seeing the poor receipts from *A Christmas Carol*. "I really believed I should never get up again, until I had passed through all the horrors of a fever," Dickens exclaimed to Forster upon finding the profits limited to £230, having "set [his] heart and soul upon a Thousand, clear." "I was never so knocked over in my life," he continued to Thomas Mitton: "though I had got over it by yesterday, . . . I have slept as badly as Macbeth ever since – which is, thank God, a Miracle with me" (*PL* 4: 42–3). This kind of agonized ambivalence (is the "miracle" the getting over of greed, or the persistence of it in a guilty sleep?) is matched only by Thackeray's brilliant fantasy of Dickensian reader-consumers, who rush to purchase "five thousand more copies," who will denude the countryside in their orgies of feasting, and whose whims will make the fortunes of "speculators" – a class in which we must include Dickens himself.[27] By now Dickens's best critic, Thackeray suggests that *A Christmas Carol* fetishizes the same unholy trinity Marx would soon decry: "overproduction, overconsumption, and overpopulation – three very delicate monsters indeed!"[28]

Escape and return, 1844–1846

Having begun eight years before with desultory Paris dispatches on the French political scene, Thackeray's magazine writing was, by the summer of 1844, reaching a volume he would sustain for several years: 85 articles, reviews, serial parts, or illustrations in 1844; 115 in 1845; and 105, not including the forthcoming *Vanity Fair*, in 1846.[29] *The Luck of Barry Lyndon*, appearing under the Fieldingesque pseudonym "George Fitz-Boodle," had begun its run in the January 1844 issue of *Fraser's*, and would continue through December of that year. A fanciful and proleptic "History of the Next French Revolution," set in the Paris of 1884, ran from February through April, while Michael Angelo Titmarsh, whose initials had appeared at the end of the Christmas books review, continued to churn out assorted reviews, political commentary and travelogues all year.[30]

Thackeray seemed to be working no less hard in 1844 to resolve his longstanding domestic difficulties. Having ensconced Isabella in Dr. Puzin's private asylum at Chaillot for the last two years, he was now planning to rent a house in Twickenham where she would have both space and care, and where he would stay two nights a week.[31] Yet all these plans were postponed or abandoned. There may have been little hope, as the summer wore on, that Isabella would improve enough to justify the new arrangement and expense; or, perhaps, there was the sudden offer in early August of a free steamship voyage to the Near East from the Peninsular & Oriental shipping company, arranged by the MP

James Emerson Tennent, the friend of a Reform Club friend and a fellow writer. Despite the practical difficulties involved in a looming departure, including unfinished *Barry Lyndon* parts and unmet *Punch* deadlines, Thackeray found himself bound for Cadiz and points east on 22 August.[32]

Though *Notes of a Journey from Cornhill to Grand Cairo* has received little attention since Saintsbury's time, each of the three strands of Thackerayan development I have been following – Thackeray's position in the literary field, his imagined and real relation to Dickens in particular, and his dispositions on politics and religion – underwent significant change after his departure in August 1844. The first of these is a new awareness of what had become his relatively privileged status: not only a prosperous magazine writer, as a number of his friends noted in this year, but also close enough to the turbines of capital to seize opportunities such as the P&O berth, offered (and accepted) as a publicity stunt for the company.[33]

Thackeray must have suspected that this acceptance might lead to charges of literary prostitution, as when Carlyle compared him to "a blind fiddler going to and fro on a penny ferry-boat," "playing tunes to the passengers for halfpence."[34] Thus the class perspective of the narrative is announced at the start: this is a journey for "young, well-educated men" like a younger Thackeray himself, who, "having their book-learning fresh in their minds, see the living people and their cities, and the actual aspect of Nature, along the famous shores of the Mediterranean" (*CGC* 232). And just in case we miss such people's connection to capital, Thackeray's book title indicates their origins at Cornhill: site of the Bank of England, the new Royal Exchange, and the Stock Exchange in Capel Court. Though the last of these still specialized in the sale of government securities, it would soon engross over half the investment capital of the Victorian world-system, or about £5 billion. This was also the period in which the London financier, rather than the industrialist of the north or Midlands, was giving landowners like the Earl of Portland a run for the big money, with the City home to "a concentration of personal wealth without parallel in the world."[35]

This Cornhill capital was much on Thackeray's mind as he moved through the Middle East, where old belief systems everywhere give way to a disenchanted enlightenment: "Wherever the steamboat touches the shore[,] adventure retreats into the interior, and what is called romance vanishes. . . . the light of common day puts it out, and it is only in the dark that it shines at all" (290–1). This steamboat stands in for a stream of commodities, the same units whose uncanny energy animated the dancing clothes of Dickens's "Meditations on Monmouth-Street"; next comes Thackeray's speculation that "an allegory might be made showing how much stronger commerce is than chivalry, and finishing with a grand image of Mahomet's crescent being extinguished in Fulton's boiler" (291). As Andrew Miller has suggested, *Vanity Fair* would be just this kind of allegory, bearing the "dark moral" that all objects, including human beings and their cultures, are subject to exchange in the modern world-system.[36]

Against this backdrop of "humble incidents of travel" (290), *Cornhill to Grand Cairo* also bears the traces of conflict between the evangelical Christianity Thackeray inherited from his mother and his own emergent humanism. We know that he had been on the lookout for victims including the law student of *The Yellowplush Correspondence* and the lady of *Barry Lyndon*. At Gibraltar, surveying the lives ruined by imperial service, he zeroes in on a new "martyr": the lieutenant in charge of the mail, a man who has served Navy, nation, and empire for three decades, still as proud of the flag flying from his little boat "as if it were flying from the mainmast of a thundering man-of-war" (*CGC* 265, 257). What is remarkable is not that Thackeray noticed this "meek lieutenant" in the first place, or that he commends his "good, kind, wholesome and noble character," but that such impulses suddenly prompt the question what a "good" novel should look like:

> Why should we keep our admiration for those who win in this world, as we do, sycophants as we are? When we write a novel, our great stupid imaginations can go no further than to marry the hero to a fortune at the end, and to find out that he is a lord by right. O blundering lickspittle morality! And yet I would like to fancy some happy retributive Utopia in the peaceful cloudland, where my friend the meek lieutenant should find the yards of his ship manned as he went on board, all the guns firing an enormous salute (only without the least noise or vile smell of powder), and he be saluted on the deck as Admiral Sir James, or Sir Joseph – ay, or Lord Viscount Bundy, knight of all the orders above the sun. (*CGC* 257–8)

Christian morality is immoral when it fails to account for the dark side of its own sympathy: Thackeray's transvalued justice would reject pain and punishment in favor of happiness and reward. In doing so, he approaches the Nietzschean view that nineteenth-century Christianity was more about the suppressed revenge fantasies of its believers than anything else.[37] Thackeray also insists that all moral judgments, and especially his own, are "cheap consolations" invented "to reconcile me to that state of life into which it has pleased Heaven to call me" (*CGC* 303–4). Zarathustra would say the same: that human equality is ideal rather than real, and that deliverance from the longing for equality is the highest hope of all.[38]

One climax of this travel narrative comes at Jerusalem, which Thackeray (like Dante) imagines to be "the centre of the world's past and future history" (*CGC* 357). Judging from letters written the following summer to his mother, Thackeray would seem to have put her ideological inheritance behind him. But as he drafted the Jerusalem section in July 1845, he declared himself stuck, "not wishing to offend the public by a needless exhibition of heterodoxy[,] nor daring to be a hypocrite," and yet sufficiently outraged by the Old Testament's bloodthirsty theology that "I don't dare trust myself to write, and put off my work from day to day" (*LPP* 2: 204). In fact, though he avowed to his mother that evangelical theology had been "solemnly repealed" by the New Testament command of brotherly love (*LPP* 205–6), his writerly consciousness is still entranced by the Old Testament deity:

> There is not a spot at which you look, but some violent deed has been done there: some massacre has been committed, some victim has been murdered, some idol has been worshipped with bloody and dreadful rites. . . . After a man has seen [this gloomy landscape] once, he never forgets it – the recollection seems to me to follow him like a remorse, as it were to implicate him in the awful deed which was done there. Oh! with what unspeakable shame and terror should one think of that crime, and prostrate himself before the image of that Divine Blessed Sufferer! (*CGC* 364–5)

Compared to the intensity of this Jerusalem episode, Thackeray's reactions to Cairo and Bethlehem seem insipid. He admitted that his Egyptian chapter was not really about the place at all, but rather about "England in Egypt"; its highlight, apparently too lighthearted for the book, was the triumphal pasting of a *Punch* advertisement onto the side of a pyramid, thus besting the "Warren's Blacking" graffito Thackeray had espied on Pompey's Pillar in Alexandria (*CGC* 393, 385).[39] Bethlehem's Church of the Nativity is "a vast and noble Christian structure," with tourists and their "robbing Arab" guides milling about in "a scene as Cattermole," Dickens's illustrator, "might paint" – all in all, "a brilliant, romantic, and cheerful picture," and yet one that does not compare to the place his mother imagines, where "the Holy Child was

PUNCH, OR THE LONDON CHARIVARI. 61

PUNCH IN THE EAST.

BY OUR FAT CONTRIBUTOR.

IV.—PUNCH AT THE PYRAMIDS.

The 19th day of October, 1844 (the seventh day of the month Hudjmudj, and the 1229th year of the Mohammedan Hejira, corresponding with the 16,769th anniversary of the 48th incarnation of Veeshnoo), is a day that ought hereafter to be considered eternally famous in the climes of the East and West. I forget what was the day of General Bonaparte's battle of the Pyramids; I think it was in the month Quintidi of the year Nivose of the French Republic, and he told his soldiers that forty centuries looked down upon them from the summit of those buildings—a statement which I very much doubt. But I say the 19th day of October, 1844, is the most important era in the modern world's history. It unites the modern with the ancient civilisation; it couples the brethren of Watt and Cobden with the dusky family of Pharaoh and Sesostris; it joins Herodotus with Thomas Babington Macaulay; it intertwines the piston of the blond Anglo-Saxon steam-engine with the Needle of the Abyssinian Cleopatra; it weds the tunnel of the subaqueous Brunel with the mystic edifice of Cheops. Strange play of wayward fancy! Ascending the Pyramid, I could not but think of Waterloo Bridge in my dear native London—a building as vast and as magnificent, as beautiful, as useless, and as lonely. Forty centuries have not as yet passed over the latter structure, 'tis true; scarcely an equal number of hackney-coaches have crossed it. But I doubt whether the individuals who contributed to raise it are likely to receive a better dividend for their capital than the swarthy shareholders in the Pyramid speculation, whose dust has long since been trampled over by countless generations of their sons.

If I use in the above sentence the longest words I can find, it is because the occasion is great and demands the finest phrases the dictionary can supply; it is because I have not read Tom Macaulay in vain; it is because I wish to show I am a dab in history, as the above dates will testify; it is because I have seen the Reverend Mr. Milman preach in a black gown at Saint Margaret's, whereas at the Coronation he wore a gold cope. The 19th of October was *Punch's Coronation*; I officiated at the august ceremony. To be brief—as illiterate readers may not understand a syllable of the above piece of ornamental eloquence—on the 19th of October, 1844, I pasted the great placard of Punch on the Pyramid of Cheops. I did it. The Fat Contributor did it. If I die, it could not be undone. If I perish, I have not lived in vain.

If the forty centuries *are* on the summit of the Pyramids, as Bonaparte remarks, all I can say is, *I* did not see them. But *Punch* has really been there; this I swear. One placard I pasted on the first landing-place (who knows how long Arab rapacity will respect the sacred hieroglyphic?). One I placed under a great stone on the summit; one I waved in air, as my Arabs raised a mighty cheer round the peaceful victorious banner; and I flung it towards the sky, which the Pyramid almost touches, and left it to its fate, to mount into the azure vault and take its place among the constellations; to light on the eternal Desert, and mingle with its golden sands; or to flutter and drop into the purple waters of the neighbouring Nile, to swell its fructifying inundations, and mingle with the rich vivifying influence which shoots into the tall palm-trees on its banks, and generates the waving corn.

I wonder were there any signs or omens in London when that event occurred? Did an earthquake take place? Did Stocks or the Barometer preternaturally rise or fall? It matters little. Let it suffice that the thing has been done, and forms an event in History by the side of those other facts to which these prodigious monuments bear testimony. Now to narrate briefly the circumstances of the day.

On Thursday, October 17, I caused my dragoman to purchase in the Frank bazaar at Grand Cairo the following articles, which will be placed in the Museum on my return.

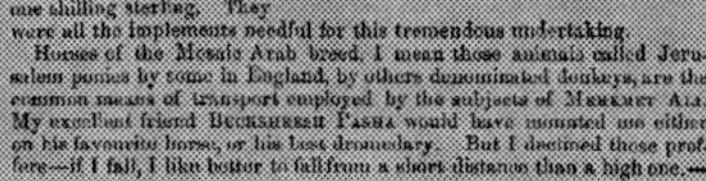

A is a tin pot holding about a pint, and to contain B, a packet of flour (which of course is not visible, as it is tied up in brown paper), and C, a pigskin brush of the sort commonly used in Europe—the whole costing about 5 piastres, or one shilling sterling. They were all the implements needful for this tremendous undertaking.

Horses of the Mosaic Arab breed, I mean those animals called Jerusalem ponies by some in England, by others denominated donkeys, are the common means of transport employed by the subjects of Mehemet Ali. My excellent friend Buckshеesh Pasha would have mounted me either on his favourite horse, or his best dromedary. But I declined those proffers—if I fall, I like better to fall from a short distance than a high one.—I have tried tumbling in both ways, and recommend the latter as by far the pleasantest and safest. I chose the Mosaic Arab then—one for the dragoman, one for the requisites of refreshment, and two for myself—not that I proposed to ride two at once, but a person of a certain dimension had best have a couple of animals in case of accident.

I left Cairo on the afternoon of October 18, never hinting to a single person the mighty purpose of my journey. The waters were out, and we had to cross them thrice—twice in track-boats, once on the shoulders of abominable Arabs,

who take a pleasure in slipping and in making believe to plunge you in the stream. When in the midst of it, the brutes stop and demand money of you—you are alarmed, the savages may drop you if you do not give—you promise that you will do so. The half-naked ruffians who conduct you up the Pyramid, when they have got you panting to the most steep, dangerous, and lonely stone, make the same demand, pointing downwards while they beg, as if they would fling you in that direction on refusal. As soon as you have breath, you promise more money—it is the best way—you are a fool if you give it when you come down.

The journey I find briefly set down in my pocket-book as thus:—Cairo Gardens—Mosquitoes—Women dressed in blue—Children dressed in nothing—Old Cairo—Nile, dirty water, ferry-boat—Town—Palm-trees, ferry-boat, canal, palm-trees, town—Rice-fields—Maize-fields—Fellows on dromedaries—Donkey down—Over his head—Pick up pieces—More palm-trees—More rice-fields—Water-courses—Howling Arabs—Donkey tumble down again—Inundations—Herons or cranes—Broken bridges—Sands—Pyramids.—If a man cannot make a landscape out of *that* he has no imagination. Let him paint the skies very blue—the sands very yellow—the plains very flat and green—the dromedaries and palm-trees very tall—the women very brown, some with veils, some with nose-rings, some tattooed, and none with stays—and the picture is complete. You may shut your eyes and fancy yourself there. It is the pleasantest way, *entre nous*.

The Crusade against the Apple Women.

It will have been seen by the papers that the extermination of the Strand apple-women has been resolved upon, and the result is, that they are being driven "up the country" by the police, something in the same style as the red men were hurried into the far west by the American emigrants. Sergeant Z., accompanied by his staff, marched down from the heights of Southampton-street, and surprised a file of basketiers, who fled with a loss of twenty-four Ribstone pippins, and six nonpareils. Three Seville oranges also fell in the affray, and were picked up by some loiterers, who having got them into quarters, cruelly made away with them. On the side of the police there was a loss of a button from the coat and twenty minutes—being the time occupied in the achievement.

PRESENT OF FRUIT TO THE LORD MAYOR.

The Fruiterers' Company presented a large quantity of fruit to the Lord Mayor, consisting chiefly of apples. One of the deputation neatly observed, that the fruit was intended to furnish an abundance of apple-sauce for the goose of which his Lordship had partaken so plentifully on Lord Mayor's Day. The Lord Mayor smiled, and the deputation bowed and retired.

Figure 3: Punch at the pyramids: Thackeray's illustration to the Cairo number of *Cornhill to Grand Cairo* (1845).

born, and the angels sang, . . . the most sacred and beautiful spot in the earth" (371–2). Such insipid piety suggests that however loudly announced or closely argued in his letters of the following summer, Thackeray's newfound benevolence had still failed to assume a characteristic shape in and for his literary production by 1845.

In the meantime, however, his critique of the Dickens phenomenon would only intensify. In his review for the *Morning Chronicle*, the same newspaper in which many of Dickens's sketches had first appeared, Thackeray argued that the writer of *The Cricket on the Hearth* surpassed even Fortnum and Mason's as "the great monopoliser," producing "extra jovialities in compliment to the season," including a literary form so commodified as to resemble an ideological department store, "illuminated with extra gas, crammed with extra bonbons, French plums and sweetnesses, like a certain Piccadilly palace before mentioned."[40] This is a much more explicit denunciation of Dickensian benevolence than he had made of *A Christmas Carol* the year before, and the complement to *Cornhill to Grand Cairo*'s renunciation of sacrificial Christianity. If Dickensian benevolence was now the "cheap consolation" with which a gorging bourgeoisie could settle its moral queasiness, and if evangelical belief is "almost blasphemous" in its insistence "that any blind prejudiced sinful mortal being . . . should dare to say Lo I am right and my brothers must go to damnation" (*LPP* 1: 206–7), then the only position left seems to have become Chesterton's humility, or some larger impartiality: an aversion from judgment that would be difficult to distinguish from a judgment on those who judge. The problem, of course, would be symbolizing and selling this paradoxical position in the serial market.

The art of aggression: 1846

Perhaps the strongest pointer to Thackeray's ascendancy of 1847 is his triumph in the struggle of the preceding year over the ideological direction of *Punch*. Richard Altick has suggested how much the magazine's early success owed to the timing of its debut in the summer of 1841, just as Peel and his liberal Tories took office.[41] By February 1846, as Thackeray's serial "The Snobs of England" began, Peel finally came out against the Corn Laws, which *Punch* had long considered oligarchic protectionism.[42] Though "The Snobs of England" began as a casually satirical anatomy of London society, it quickly developed into a medium of response to the political developments of 1846, a pulpit for Thackeray's moderate views and against the radical ones of its editor, Douglas Jerrold.

At first, as John Sutherland has noted, the targets in "The Snobs of England" were stock Jerroldian ones: aristocrats, bishops, court flunkies, and other constitutional "relics."[43] But by May, Thackeray's sympathies for a militant Empire and national Church had clearly won out: "The history of the world contains no more brilliant and heroic picture" than that of the army officer eventually responsible for the Sikh slaughter of December 1845, while Chapter 11's clerical subjects get off remarkably lightly, there being "some places," such as cathedrals and churches, "where [*Punch*] acknowledges himself not privileged to make a noise" (44–5).[44] With the serial resulting in the greatest circulation increase in the magazine's brief history, Thackeray could write with justice in 1847 that while in 1845 "I used only to make a passive opposition agst the Anti-church and Bishop sneers," "last year I made an active one (Jerrold and I had a sort of war and I came off conqueror)" (*LPP* 2: 274).[45]

Some of the success of "The Snobs of England" may have been due to the way it filled the vacuum left in Dickens's relative absence from the London scene. Having negotiated both a hefty advance and a badly needed break from his new publishers Bradbury and Evans (also the publishers of *Punch*), and having returned from his first long trip to Italy in July 1845, Dickens was at the beginning of 1846 deeply involved in establishing the *Daily News*, which began publication on 21 January (*DP* 152–6; *PL* 4: 691). But even as circulation increased, other battles raged at the *Punch* table. On one side were the radicals Jerrold and Mark Lemon, with their absent friend Dickens looming in the near background; on the other, noting their colleagues' propensities for eating peas with a knife or salting a gooseberry tart, were Thackeray, John Leech, Gilbert à Beckett, and others of gentlemanly origin.[46]

The differences between *Punch*'s Jerroldian and Thackerayan factions corresponded to their disagreements on the functions of the writer. These differences would intensify the following year, when John Forster took offense at Thackeray's caricaturist series entitled "Punch's Prize Novelists."[47] But even by the early summer of 1846, Thackeray had stated the laissez-faire position in a cutting response to Bulwer-Lytton's sympathetic portrait of the editor and suicide Laman Blanchard. Bulwer-Lytton's account of Blanchard's poverty was "in much too despondent a strain," Thackeray argued, both because Blanchard's life was not as desperate as Bulwer had made out and because "there is not the least call at present to be holding up literary martyrs":

> [M]illions of people in this honest, stupid empire . . . have a right to have books supplied for them as well as the most polished and

> accomplished critics have. The literary man gets his bread by providing goods suited to the consumption of these. This man of letters produces a police report; that, an article contaning some downright information; this one, as an editor, abuses Sir Robert Peel, or lauds Lord John Russell, or *vice versa*; writing to a certain class who coincide in his views, or are interested by the question which he moots.[48]

Forster and Dickens might well have taken as great offense at Thackeray's characterization of the literary field as Bulwer, his ostensible target.

But Thackeray would soon attack both Forster and Dickens more directly. Perhaps a paragon like Dr. Arnold, whom Forster had praised to the skies in an 1844 review,[49] might have deplored the influence of *Pickwick* at Rugby: "Light stories of Jingle and Tupman, and Sam Weller quips and cranks, must have come with but a bad grace before that pure and lofty soul." But perhaps, on the other hand, Arnold's taste is not representative of the society which admires him so much:

> Laughing is not the highest occupation of a man, very certainly; or the power of creating it the height of genius. I am not going to argue for that. No more is the blacking of boots the greatest occupation. But it is done . . . by persons ordained to that calling in life, who arrogate to themselves (if they are straightforward and worthy shoe-blacks) no especial rank or privilege an account of their calling; and not considering boot-brushing the greatest effort of earthly genius, nevertheless select their Day and Martin, or Warren, to the best of their judgment; polish their upper-leathers as well as they can; satisfy their patrons; and earn their fair wage. (333)

Though he seems to include himself in this class of "bootblack" writers, forever barred from reaching the "height of genius," Thackeray suggests too that Dickens is at its head. Who else but Thackeray himself might remain above the fray as a "literary craftsm[a]n, hitting no foul blow, condescending to no servile puffery, filling a not very lofty, but a manly and honorable part"? (334).

The same kind of conflicted aggression roils Numbers 16 and 17 of *The Snobs of England*, published in late June 1846, but omitted, along with Numbers 18–23, from the 1848 and 1855 editions known as *The Book of Snobs*. Thackeray's decision to omit the latter six chapters from these reprints is relatively easy to reconstruct. Written in immediate response to the political crisis begun with the repeal of the Corn Laws on 25 June 1846, and published over the course of the summer, chapters 18–23 may have been either too topical in their references to the details of Peel's administration, or else too controversial in their free-trade rhetoric, to be included two years later.[50]

The suppressed Chapter 17 is a more difficult case. The second of two chapters on literary snobs, John Sutherland calls it "the more savage of the two," likely because Thackeray shifts his aim from relatively easy targets, such as the novelists Catherine Gore and Lady Bulwer and the periodical writers Douglas Jerrold and John Forster, to bigger game, such as Frances Trollope, Thomas Babington Macaulay, and Benjamin Disraeli, among others (220–1). Sutherland suggests that Thackeray did not target Dickens in Chapters 16 or 17 because "he was, perhaps, a little afraid" of him. But Thackeray may have chosen to omit chapter 17 from the 1848 *Book of Snobs*, as he had abandoned plans to include Dickens in "Punch's Prize Novelists" (*LPP* 2: 270), because he had already numbered him amongst his victims. One of Thackeray's chief targets in the suppressed chapter 17 is the novelist "Tom Fustian," whose wife rides in a yellow carriage "lined with pink and a green hammercloth," and whose friend "Libertas" is the literary critic of a periodical called the *Weekly Tomahawk* (68). As I have explained elsewhere, this "Tom Fustian" is likely a caricature of Dickens, while the critic he has spurned resembles Douglas Jerrold, Dickens's foremost ally at the *Punch* table.[51] The animus between the two men would last for many years. Thackeray would be disgusted enough with Dickens's rhetorical and sartorial resplendence at Daniel Macready's 1851 farewell dinner, for example, to call him a "beggar" and a "butterfly" in the same breath (*PL* 6: 303 n.3).

But it would be as unimaginative to attribute Thackeray's attack to mere animus as it would be to attribute Dickens's ostentatious taste to mere vanity. The latter's penchant for self-promotion and display was a sign of the mass audience he assembled, as of its ambivalent relation to its creator. At a Cincinnati dinner of 1843, for example, one attendee noted both the vulgarity of Dickens's dress and the fracas that ensued as fans scrambled for the fallen petals of the rose he had worn in his lapel.[52] What makes Thackeray's caricature both withering and significant is its articulation of the interests which must have informed, even if they did not dominate, the friendship between Dickens and Jerrold, as they informed all relationships in a highly competitive literary world. If no other Victorian writer would assemble an audience on the scale of Dickens's, then, none would have a clearer insight into the irrationalities of that audience, and the correspondingly arbitrary nature of literary friendships, than Thackeray. Never capable of suppressing the contingent nature of any "successful" position, always aware of the dubious status of any claim to vocation, Thackeray's disposition now demanded an aesthetic object capable of subsuming all of these.

The pathos of distance: 1847

As the year of *Vanity Fair* began, Thackeray continued to envy Dickens's capacity to produce powerful scenes of atonement:

> When the fifth number [of *Dombey and Son* for February 1847] appeared, containing the death of little Dombey, Thackeray, with the part in his pocket, went down to the *Punch* office, and startled Mark Lemon by suddenly laying it before him and exclaiming, "There! read that. There is no writing against such power as this – no one has a chance. Read the description of young Paul's death; it is unsurpassed – it is stupendous."[53]

Even at this late date, Thackeray himself apparently felt the inadequacy of blanket statements such as the closing admonition of the "Snobs of England" – "if Fun is good, Truth is still better, and Love best of all" (*BS* 207). The story of *Vanity Fair* is one of turning this loss into gain, as when he refuses to write the history of Amelia's martyrdom to her ageing father as "too dreary and stupid" (*VF* 567), or when he reserves the capacity to characterize Dobbin's love for Amelia to himself: "Any person who appreciated her paid a compliment to the Major's good judgment – that is, if a man may be said to have good judgment who is under the influence of Love's delusion" (601–2).

Though a recognizably incarnational "Love" had gotten the last word in the satirical anatomy *The Book of Snobs* (as we saw death get the same in *Pickwick Papers*), the Thackeray of *Vanity Fair* emphasizes the necessity of moral judgment as much, if not more than, the imperative to love:[54]

> A few years ago I should have sneered at the idea of setting up as a teacher at all, and perhaps at this pompous and pious way of talking about a few papers of jokes in *Punch* – but I have got to believe in the business, and in many other things since them. And our profession seems to me to be as serious as the Parson's own. (*LPP* 2: 282)

These dueling imperatives of benevolence and judgment closely resemble the contradictory definitions of "goodness" that Nietzsche would place at the very origins of European morality. *On the Genealogy of Morals* begins with the juxtapositions of two such definitions: that a typically "English" goodness consists of "unegoistic" acts later deemed "useful" by those to whom the act was done; and, by contrast, that the concept of the good "did *not* originate with those to whom 'goodness' was shown," but rather with the "nobles" as Nietzsche notoriously defined them.[55]

As I have suggested, such competing conceptions of the good are the blurry center of Thackeray's world-view at this critical time, expressed not only in the compressed formulae of *The Book of Snobs'* closing line, but echoed in the sensations of repentance and exaltation *Vanity Fair* would evoke in his audience. John Cordy Jeaffreson reported that "strong men, men not given to emotion, least of all to religious excitement, laid [*Vanity Fair*] down with tearful eyes and full hearts," "prayed earnestly to the Almighty for mercy and help," and finally "rose from their knees with a determination to be men of charity"; Charlotte Brontë imagined Thackeray as a wrathful Micaiah appearing "before the throned Kings of Judah and Israel[,]" speaking "truth as deep, with a power as prophet-like and as vital."[56] These reactions resonate, moreover, with our sense of how Thackeray was simultaneously submitting to and securing his distance from the Dickens phenomenon: Jeaffreson's strong yet tearful men resemble the chastened capitalists Mr. Dombey and Scrooge more than any other Dickens type, while Brontë's prophet resembles the speaker of truth to power whom the Dickens of the 1850s would soon become.

Taken together, the alternately stern and forgiving components of Thackeray's vocation to judgment amount to a pathos of distance, an affect of control that has always attracted praise from literary critics (who take their own pleasure in passing judgment, after all). Brontë was only the first to highlight Thackeray's exceptional "control" and to note how he exudes "the charm and majesty of repose in his greatest efforts."[57] Chesterton emphasized this same quality in 1911, insisting that Thackeray was himself the best representation of "the Englishman in repose." For Gordon Ray in 1955, too, this is what makes Thackeray the unfashionable premodernist worth defending: unlike Flaubert, Joyce, or Woolf, he was "content to work out his literary destiny within the limits imposed by the common life of his age" – content, that is, to strive for what Nietzsche would ridicule as an essentially "*English* happiness" – "comfort and fashion (and at best a seat in Parliament)."[58]

We can return to where we began with a much fuller understanding of the imperatives that brought the ventriloquist of *Vanity Fair*'s chapter 8 into existence. Its narrator begins by articulating the multivalent and stylized differences – economic, ethical, psychological – between the energetic Becky and the enervated Amelia, and ends by affirming the need for emplotted counterpoint: "it is quite as well for our dear Amelia Sedley in Russell Square, that Miss Sharp and she are parted" (*VF* 83).[59] It is a matter of more than formal significance, then, that at the very moment when this decision to innovate a multiplotted novel is made, Thackeray delivers the most distinctive version of the pathos of judgment he had been developing for nearly a decade: "these histories in their gaudy yellow covers," having "Vanity Fair for a title," issue from a "moralist" and "motley" who, though as foolish as his audience, is nonetheless "bound to speak the truth as far as one knows it" (83).

Like Nietzsche's supposedly "positive" morality, Thackeray's incarnational humanism remains open to charges of banality, vagueness, and incoherence. In Nietzsche's case, his new kind of self-mastery, exceptionally difficult to define, seems to require the nearly unimaginable task of simultaneously identifying with and condemning one's own heretofore "evil" passions in the service of an unfamiliar monism. (Unitarianism, the period's most rationalized version of incarnational humanism, was attacked throughout the first half of the century on just these grounds.)[60] Moving "beyond good and evil," if it means anything, must have something to do with "combining all of one's features and qualities, whatever their traditional moral value, into a controlled and coherent whole"[61] – a description by Alexander Nehamas that seems to apply at least as well to *Vanity Fair* as to the philosopher.

Of course, much of the best twentieth-century criticism of *Vanity Fair* is preoccupied with finding just this kind of unity in the work.[62] But the question whether or not *Vanity Fair* attains any such coherence seems less important than its drive to express and contain ideological and rhetorical oscillations so great as to evoke nausea in some of its more fastidious readers.[63]

Only in this nearly total fictional praxis, projecting a potent rhetoric of compromise into the structure of his fiction, does Thackeray finally become an artistic and economic rival of Dickens, capable of succeeding in the elite market for the novel in monthly parts. As we saw at the outset, the Dickensian part had become the prestigious exception to the rule of magazine serialization to which the great part of Thackeray's pre-1847 production complied. The achievement of *Vanity Fair* is the carving out of a unique but transitory position between the hegemony of Dickens, in which literary and economic forms of consecration confirm each other, and the recognizably modernist field of Baudelaire, Flaubert, and James, in which commercial success and artistic achievement have become opposed.[64] Only after becoming Dickens's best critic did Thackeray join him at the pinnacle of the period's distinctive hierarchy of commodity forms.

3
Dickens Breaks Out: the Public Readings and *Little Dorrit*

> Try this uncertainty and this *not putting of them* together, as a new means of interest.
>
> Dickens's working note to the first number of *Little Dorrit*

> The right to nostalgia, to transcendental knowledge, to a dangerous life cannot be validated.
>
> Max Horkheimer, as quoted by Theodor Adorno

In the 1857 essay entitled "On the Modern Element in Literature," Matthew Arnold identified two essential qualities of his own mid-century: the abundance, both material and theoretical, of its "copious and complex present"; and the state of "bafflement" in which the beneficiaries of this abundance lived. Speaking this longstanding contradiction – between modernity's power to liberate people from the positions and dispositions to which they were born and the radical contingency and uncertainty this liberation brings – makes news to this day, as when the political scientist Robert E. Lane informs us that the affluent citizens of today's "market democracies" are substantially less happy than most of their predecessors and contemporaries.[1]

Such is the uncannily familiar story of Dickens in the 1850s. Serial publication's averaging of profits and costs over an extended period, and its creation of an audience for the completed work in volume form, kept both Dickens and his publishers at the top of the literary marketplace throughout the decade. Demand for *Bleak House*'s first number caught everyone by surprise, with thousands of additional copies and advertisements required before the first day of publication was over; serial sales would eventually earn Dickens almost £11000 – more than the exceptional £10000 paid for the copyrights of George Eliot's *Romola*

(1861) and Disraeli's *Endymion* (1880) – with the American profits, though exaggerated at the time, also substantial. In addition, and though Dickens's annual profits from Chapman and Hall's Cheap Edition hovered at a few hundred pounds a year (a pittance at a time when his annual household expenses were between £8000 and £9000), *Household Words* produced nearly £1000 a year, augmented by £1500 from the volume sale of *Hard Times*.[2] Accompanying all this, however, is a steady drumbeat of hostile reviews, financial setbacks, and personal turmoil. Though it sold well, *Little Dorrit*'s overt radicalism would continue to enrage critics through the summer of 1857.[3] In that September, Dickens's longtime adviser John Forster and his publishers Bradbury and Evans talked him into the deluxe Library Edition, priced at 6*s*. per volume, the early losses from which would lead his serial enterprise back to Chapman and Hall, the publishers of *Pickwick*. By the same December, even the author of *A Christmas Carol* had forsworn celebrations of the season, surely because he was contemplating the separation from his wife completed in May 1858 – now begun in earnest with his sealing of the passage between their old bedroom and his new one.[4]

Of course, amidst these signs of strain in Dickens's systems of writing and living, getting and spending, there are also those of transformation. Just as his marriage foundered at last, he began the round of theatrical activities which would eventually bring him into contact with the Ternan sisters – first Maria, who cradled him (as *The Frozen Deep*'s dying Richard Wardour) in front of audiences ranging from Bradford workers to the Queen herself; and then her sister Ellen, who would become the most important female companion of the rest of his life. Likewise, having begun as private entertainments, Dickens's public readings were also assuming forms they would keep until his death. By the end of 1858, for example, earnings from the first of many reading tours would be far greater than those made from the "reading edition" of the *Carol* reprinted at this time; by 1870, the readings would have generated nearly half of the £93000 Dickens would leave his wife and children at his death.[5]

Gaining perspective on *Little Dorrit*, the serial novel which emerged from this nexus of continuation, suffering, and transformation, is not simply a matter of narrating the events and forms which throng its conception, composition, and appearance. There is also a massive critical history to this work. Through the 1970s, the American revisions of Trilling's inaugural 1953 reading consistently located the force of this novel in its metaphors of the labyrinth, the shadow, the taint, and the prison, while treating the marriage of Amy Dorrit and Arthur Clennam as a sign that relief from the inhuman forces at work in that society might come, if at all, only in the personal or private sphere.[6] Marxian and poststructuralist criticism has, by contrast, most often insisted on the centrality of the novel's inheritance plots. If, as Trilling had suggested, the work's "great images," and by implication any utopian prescriptions embedded there, are "very hard to grasp and judge," the force of its critique must reside principally in those plots, "too frequently dismissed or undervalued," as William Myers and others have argued.[7] Both lines of criticism have fallen into disrepair, however – the metaphorical line of inquiry into strictures about Amy Dorrit's "ultimate" status as "a contradictory and disruptive figure who sustains nothing more than a sadly dysfunctional family," and the metonymic one into baroque deconstructions of plot, as when the Clennam will is construed as an elaborately indirect representation of Arthur's father's sexual cruelty.[8]

Here, I explore how *Little Dorrit* hollows out the core functions that serial novels had assumed for Victorian culture: literary forms working to imagine alternatives to human lives utterly determined and yet radically estranged from society; and commodity forms invoking a Christian cultural inheritance as a veil for those conditions. Even as he amplified his attacks on public incompetence and corruption, experimented with new theatrical and journalistic forms, and prepared to dissolve his failed marriage, Dickens was refiguring the transcendent effects of his own literary past, the tropes of overviewing mastery and atoning sacrifice with which he had first assembled his audience.

As David Simpson has suggested, however, *Little Dorrit*, as much or more than any other of Dickens's works, will always remain "nothing but figure": a virtual menagerie of literary forms, many of which we must recognize as "modernist," both in the semantic autonomy they claim and in the discriminating readers they demand.[9] It is true that only a few of these forms have previously been identified as such. My purpose in touring this literary menagerie, however, is not simply to place the Dickens of *Little Dorrit* as Victorian vanguard in a conventional literary history moving from Romantic transcendent to Victorian compromise to modernist shock, from vision to doubt to disavowal. As it breaks out of the figurations of the past, now become imprisoning, *Little Dorrit* interrogates the very largest categories of modern, as opposed to merely "modernist," meaning: commodity and art, society and individual, development and trauma, psyche and text. As he transformed himself from adored entertainer to ruthless social critic, from oppressed part producer to acclaimed public reader, and from tormented husband to unrepentant bachelor, Dickens produced a novel that is finally about examining the relations between these massive categories. Like the greatest works of the century with which it belongs, and like the seminal modern tragedy it continually evokes, *Little Dorrit* contains more than literary history has yet dreamed of.

Figuring a disordered totality, 1855

Though many of its readers would express distaste for its radical conclusions, the period of *Little Dorrit*'s conception was a time when politics sold both newspapers and serials. By January 1855, William Howard Russell's *Times* dispatches from the Crimea were making the case for army mismanagement "clearer from day to day" to Dickens, and surely to many others as well; Russell's publisher Routledge would soon suggest an expanded history of the Crimean War, "to appear in shilling monthly parts, with illustrations either from photographs or from artists who have been there . . . like Dickens's works."[10] To this politically acute literary market, aristocrats and bureaucrats were cogs in a system fostering poverty, disease, and death. Lord Seymour had joked about the expiring powers of the Board of Health in Parliament, earning Dickens's outraged sarcasm in an article published in September 1854; Palmerston's neglect of sanitary reform contributed to the cholera from which Dickens's daughter Mary suffered at Boulogne that month; and thus the first two chapters of the work tentatively entitled *Nobody's Fault*, drafted in late May 1855, place the Meagleses in an atmosphere of French taint and quarantine, presided over by an "officer of health, and a variety of humbugs in cocked hats" (I. 1: 16). When spring testimony before Parliament blamed the winter's thousands of Crimean troop deaths on red tape, including the refusal of requests for rations submitted on the wrong form, Assistant Secretary of the Treasury Trevelyan "succeed[ed] in shifting the blame from his own department," and from his aristocratic superiors; Dickens attacked him in print; and thus "the statesman at the head of the Circumlocution Office . . . sat a little uneasily in his saddle, by reason of some *vagabond* making a tilt at him in a newspaper" (I. 10: 103 [emphasis added]).[11] Here, as in "The Hospital Patient" and the 1846 autobiographical fragment, the epithet "vagabond" is Dickens's code name for himself.

Other, less public events must also have impressed on Dickens how people talk themselves out of human connection. Of course, the sudden reappearance of his early love Maria Beadnell spurred a weeks-long sequence of memory, desire, and disenchantment:

> As I was reading by my fire last night, a handfull of notes was laid down on my table. I looked them over, and, recognizing the writing of no private friend, let them lie there, and went back to my book. But I found my mind curiously disturbed, and wandering away through so many years to such early times in my life, that I was quite perplexed to account for it. . . . [A]t last it came into my head that it must have been suggested by something in the look of one of those letters. So I turned them over again, – and suddenly the remembrance of your hand, came upon me with an influence that I cannot express to you. Three or four and twenty years vanished like a dream, and I opened it with the touch of my young friend David Copperfield when he was in love. (*PL* 7: 532, emphasis added.)

Ever since his stenographic days, when he was one of bureaucratic London's fastest "automatic" writers, Dickens had associated the act and result of handwriting with the unconscious sources of his prodigious creativity. To Maria's synecdochic "hand" on an envelope, Dickens responded with a "touch" which is both eroticized and fictionalized.[12] Clennam's meeting with Flora Finching, of course, is this moment disenchanted, the moment when "his gaze no sooner fell upon the object of his old passion, than it shivered and broke into pieces" (I. 13: 142).

The lesson of the Beadnell encounter was that love, imagination, and fetishization might only be distinguishable after the fact. And yet Dickens, having had painful proof of this in his own life, had no choice but to continue to produce serial novels: specifically, to work in a literary form consisting of lengthy metonymic sequences, brought into some kind of transcendent or mythic sense by metaphoric analogy or synecdochic displacement. We know early on in *Little Dorrit* that when such metonymic sequences are brought under the rule of a mechanical metaphor, the movement created is either futile or harmful, as in Mrs. Clennam's routine, "always the same reluctant return of the same pieces of machinery, like a dragging piece of clockwork" (I. 29: 387–8), or in the Circumlocution Office, which "went on mechanically, every day, keeping this wonderful, all-sufficient wheel of statesmanship, How not to do it, in motion" (I. 10: 146). This novel's great difficulty is twofold: how to bind this old metonymic energy into comprehensible units; or, failing this, how to liberate it to new purposes.

Though it makes some early attempts at the latter, *Little Dorrit*'s norm is diffusion and infection, a norm to which even its most energetic characters succumb. When Mr. Meagles suggests following Doyce to the site of the latter's factory, Clennam shows a quite uncharacteristic enthusiasm ("'Bleeding Heart Yard?' said Clennam. 'I want to go there'" [I. 10. 165]); in the next chapter of the same invigorated number, Cavalletto flees Rigaud as a tiny organic body liberated from oppressive constraint, "a black speck" moving against "the flat line of the horizon" (I. 11: 175), speeding north from Marseille to Chalon, where he rejoins Rigaud by chance, and finally to London, stopping at last only when a careening mail-coach runs him down in the City (I. 13: 203). By the end of the fourth number, however, Arthur's first "audacious doubts" about Mr. Casby, like the "swift thought" that his mother's paralysis is in fact a form of self-punishment (I. 8: 129), are subsumed in organic terms derived from developing infectious theory, "afloat in the air," mere "motes and specks of suspicion in the atmosphere of that time" (I. 13. 190).[13] The symbolic center of this rhetoric of disease is, sensibly enough, the place where Cavalletto is finally brought to a halt: the ancient and depopulated City, that lifeless core of the nineteenth-century world-system, associated with an undead Christian culture at least since Paul Dombey's christening, still sounding here as the "deadly-lively" church bell of Clennam's dismal homecoming (I. 3: 68).

As always in Dickens, synecdoche continues to be the means by which plot makes apparent progress. After Clennam kisses Amy's hand in gratitude for her care, the same hand, "with a very gentle lingering where it was," seems "to court being retained," creeps "up a little nearer his face" and away again, until finally, "[l]ocked in his arms," "she drew the slight hand round his neck, and clasped it in its fellow-hand" (II. 34: 884–6). As we shall see, however, this denouement of the romantic plot is highly equivocal, just as *Little Dorrit*'s other major means of metonymic connection, its inheritance plots, continually signify their own meaninglessness. The very notion of the "rightful" heir, already under strain in *Martin Chuzzlewit*, is negated before our eyes, on two counts. The Clennam plot is a matter of the obstruction of the wishes of the Clennam testator, Arthur's great-uncle. But its specifics remain unknown to Arthur with the destruction of the codicil to that great-uncle's will, just as the story of that obstruction is difficult to reconstruct and virtually impossible to recall. The problem of recalling and construing the past, for which this inheritance plot has itself become a metaphor, is as intractable as remembering and knowing the many meanings of the paternal command "Do Not Forget" – a list that includes the existence of the codicil; Mrs. Clennam's judgment of her own guilt; the relation between Arthur's father and biological mother; and Arthur's relation to his great ancestor in unheroic subjectivity, Hamlet.[14] The Dorrit inheritance plot is simply the next stage in the depletion of synedochically generated significance: because no testator exists, the story of the frustration and resolution of this testator's intention cannot be told, just as the plot's incessant movement of capital, culminating in William Dorrit's release from the Marshalsea, demonstrates only a deep and traumatic fixity.[15]

As Trilling was the first to note, *Little Dorrit*'s metaphors are as diffuse as they are omnipresent, sometimes extending over hundreds of pages before exploding into violence. Dickens's treatment of the traditional emblem of the shipwrecked soul reminds us of this quality. This symbol was already in use on the covers of *Dombey and Son*'s monthly parts (1846–8), which had Florence reaching out from shore to the drowning Mr. Dombey.[16] *Little Dorrit*'s early numbers take up this symbol in a series of distinctions between victimized characters, likened to small craft, and their victimizers, compared to larger vessels (I. 27: 368, I. 13: 193; I. 5: 92, I. 13: 191, II. 12: 614). This metaphoric series reaches a higher level of abstraction when Dickens imagines social collectivities as single ships. One is, as we would expect, the Circumlocution Office, with Lord Decimus Tite Barnacle as its "Pilot," who "prosper[s] in the private loaf and fish trade ashore, the crew being able, by dint of hard pumping, to keep the ship above water without him" (I. 34: 455); another is the Convent of St. Bernard, which floats like an "Ark" on the darkness coming "up the mountain like a rising water" (II. 1: 483). The Convent is a *Gemeinschaft*, a true community of shared beliefs and complementary acts; the Circumlocution Office is a perversion of this, headed by an absentee Messiah "in the private loaf and fish trade ashore"; and British society is its negation, a highly rationalized *Gesellschaft* brought to ruin by Merdle the financier:

> The admired piratical ship had blown up, in the midst of a vast fleet of ships of all rates, and boats of all sizes; and on the deep was nothing but ruin; nothing but burning hulls, bursting magazines, great guns self-exploded tearing friends and neighbors to pieces, drowning men clinging to unseaworthy spars and going down every minute, spent swimmers floating dead, and sharks. (II. 26: 777)

While *Dombey* refused any transcendent solution to the problem of Mr. Dombey's selfishness, it nonetheless sustained a faith in "genial society as an end in itself."[17] By this point in *Little Dorrit*, by contrast, Merdle's exposure is a matter of fire, detonation, dismemberment, and death, producing the oceanic shapelessness of the world before Creation or after the Flood.

Little Dorrit's patterns of figuration, both metonymic and metaphoric, thus cast virtually all motion as diseased or destructive, from Mrs. Clennam's mechanical repetition to Cavalletto's specklike travel to Merdle's polluting flow. Individual psychology functions according to the same disordered rules. Here is Arthur Clennam's first conversation on his return from China, as he sits in a City coffee-house on a stifling Sunday evening:

> "Beg pardon, sir," said a brisk waiter, rubbing the table. "Wish see bed-room?"
>
> *"Yes I have just made up my mind to do it."*
>
> "Chaymaid!" cried the waiter. "Gelen box num seven wish see room!"
>
> "Stay," said Clennam, rousing himself. *"I was not thinking of what I said; I answered mechanically.* I am not going to sleep here. I am going home."
>
> "Deed, sir? Chaymaid! Gelen box num seven, not go sleep here, gome." (I. 3: 69–70; emphasis added)

In a virtual demonstration of urban psychology as it would be described by the sociologist Georg Simmel in 1903, Dickens represents Clennam's act of restoring conscious control over his own mechanized thought by restoring punctuated breaks to his responses. Under the conditions of urban modernity, the individual may develop what Simmel calls the "protective organ" of an intensified rationality. Even if he does, however, he will experience a loss of consciousness as a result, will feel like a mere "cog" in a huge social machine.[18] Clennam uses metonym to escape connection in just this way, as when, induced by the flow of the same river Little Dorrit so often looks into, he fends off his desire for Pet Meagles: "suppose such a man were to come to this house, and were to yield to the captivation of this charming girl, and were to persuade himself that he could hope to win her; what a weakness it would be!" A narrative of "somebody," developing in temporally linear fashion, produces a condemnation of desire as "weakness"; and from this masochistic negation of desire comes a negation of the self itself: "Why should he be vexed or sore at heart? It was not his weakness that he had imagined. It was nobody's, nobody's within his knowledge" (I. 16: 244).[19]

Nearly all of these examples have come from the first five numbers of *Little Dorrit*, written before the death of John Sadleir, the ex-Treasury lord whose suicide from poison on Hampstead Heath would provide the basis for the increasingly important Merdle plot.[20] These early numbers thus suggest how the serial novelist had begun to negate the symbolic practice of his earlier work: elaborating metaphors of social disorder to points of apocalyptic violence; translating emplotted connections between characters into underlying psychological states; and suggesting how the social purpose of such states is to evade human connection. These categories of society, psychology, and language have already fused into a social body, in other words, as European modernists from Baudelaire to Adorno would imagine it: a massive, inhuman, and disordered totality.

Failed escape, 1855–1856

Amidst this atmosphere of political, personal, and symbolic bafflement, new forms were soon jostling for breathing room. Dickens's audience, that old totality of Pickwickian readers ranging from Lord Denman on the bench to servants under stairs, was segmenting into two fundamental parts, each of which seemed to require a theatrical supplement to the increasingly disenchanted symbolics of the Dickensian serial novel. The private melodrama would serve the first of these segments and the public reading the second before the two merged once again in the Farewell Tours of the late 1860s.

This part of the cycle begins in May 1855, when Dickens leapt at the opportunity to play a guilt-ridden murderer in Wilkie Collins's *The Lighthouse*, based on a *Household Words* piece published two years before.[21] Still unpublished, the melodrama is most often noted for the culprit Aaron Gurnock, who faces death by starvation along with his son and old friend, stranded in a lighthouse, but whose greatest agony is his guilt over the robbery and murder years ago of one beneficent Lady Grace.[22] Letters of the period make clear how much Dickens relished Collins's set-pieces of confession, paranoia, and confrontation, whatever he may have thought of the blanket pardon a restored Lady Grace issues as the curtain falls: "The privilege of forgiving, Aaron Gurnock, is a right that we may all insist upon. Great attribute of Him in whom we live, And who forgives us as we do forgive!"[23] But the more interesting character for the reader of *Little Dorrit* may be Aaron's son Martin, played by Collins that same June. Incapable of claiming the lover to whom he is engaged because of his shame over his father's guilt, but equally incapable of leaving her behind, Martin repeatedly begs for a familiarly Shakespearean kind of delay: "Whichever way I turn, whatever I do, the chance that I may commit some dreadful error, or be guilty of some unmanly deception, terrifies me into silence – Give me a little time longer to think what I ought to do; and trust in me mercifully till that time arises!"[24] Just as *Hamlet*'s ghost admonishes, and as the motto on Arthur Clennam's watch repeats, Martin of *The Lighthouse* cannot forget the sins of his parents, and is a psychic cripple as a result.

The second theatrical form to emerge from this tumultuous period was the public reading, dating from a command performance of *A Christmas Carol* at the house of the British consul at Genoa ten years before. In 1845, Dickens had taken the stage only after balking at a guest list he had not approved, protesting too much as to his own "invincible repugnance to that kind of exhibition." Despite such misgivings, though, he had realized that same year that such performances, even if "odd," would likely be highly profitable (*PL* 4: 317, 631). For the next decade, Dickens labored to maintain this distinction between profitable and public literary production, with its familiar journalistic forms and routines on one hand, and private and non-profit theatrical activities, including Tavistock House productions and charity readings, on the other. But it was in 1855, according to Philip Collins's estimate, that the reading version of the *Carol,* his most often performed piece over the next fifteen years, took its definitive form.

Even as his serial novels became more overtly political than ever before – in tune, as we have seen, with his readers and fellow writers – Dickens began to expunge politically charged elements, and especially the waifs Ignorance and Want and accompanying commentary, from his prompt-text of *A Christmas Carol.*[25] But though his public readings were becoming less rather than more Radical, his enemies were both feeling the lash of his pen in *Household Words* and lashing back by pointing out the theatrical quality of his political activities. In June 1855, Dickens's friend Austen Layard assailed Palmerston at a rally in Hyde Park for having failed to effect any change in the Crimea. Palmerston responded with a sneer in Parliament on 18 June, directed at the *Lighthouse* success, concerning "the private theatricals at Drury Lane," until finally, in a speech to the Administrative Reform Association on 27 June that was the most pointed political statement of his life, Dickens blasted back with a parable of politicians as incompetent servants, who consult "exploded cookery books in the South" when commanded to serve "dinner in the North." If the ruling class kept up their "obstinate adherence to rubbish," Dickens warned, the whole structure of society would go up in smoke as speedily as the rotten beams in the recently burned Palace of Westminster.[26]

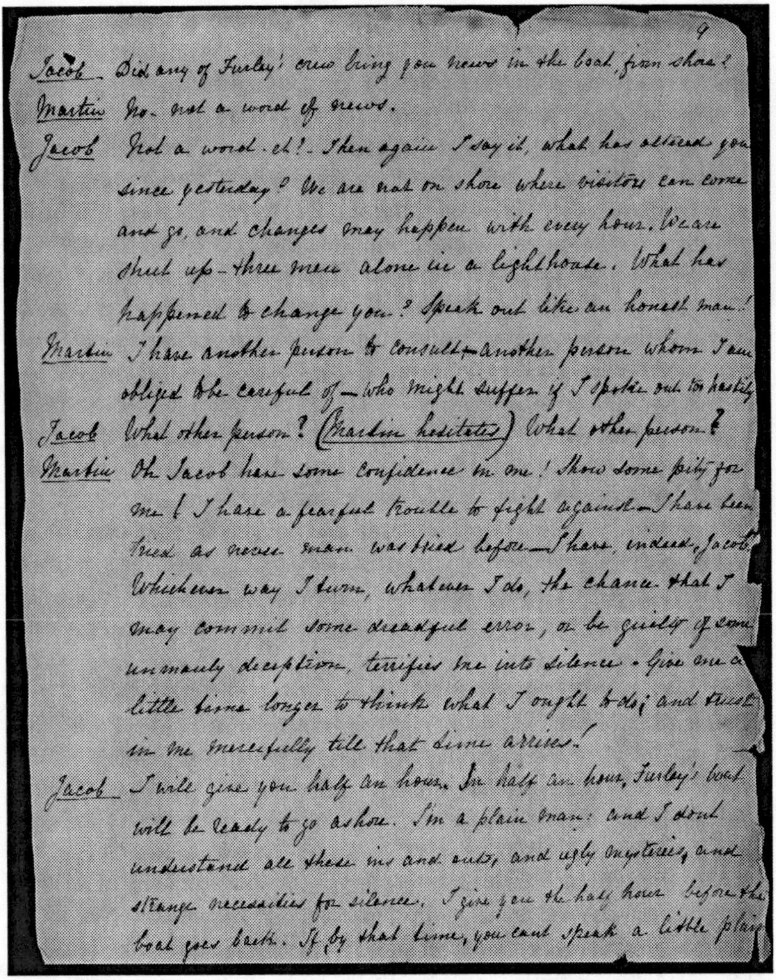

9

Jacob — Did any of Furley's crew bring you news in the boat, from shore?

Martin — No — not a word of news.

Jacob — Not a word — eh! — Then again I say it, what has altered you since yesterday? We are not on shore where visitors can come and go, and changes may happen with every hour. We are shut up — three men alone in a lighthouse. What has happened to change you? Speak out like an honest man!

Martin — I have another person to consult — another person whom I am obliged to be careful of — who might suffer if I spoke out too hastily.

Jacob — What other person? (Martin hesitates) What other person?

Martin — Oh Jacob have some confidence in me! Show some pity for me! I have a fearful trouble to fight against — I have been tried as never man was tried before — I have, indeed, Jacob! Whichever way I turn, whatever I do, the chance that I may commit some dreadful error, or be guilty of some unmanly deception, terrifies me into silence. Give me a little time longer to think what I ought to do; and trust in me mercifully till that time arrives!

Jacob — I will give you half an hour. In half an hour, Furley's boat will be ready to go ashore. I'm a plain man: and I don't understand all these ins and outs, and ugly mysteries, and strange necessities for silence. I give you the half hour before the boat goes back. If, by that time, you can't speak a little plain

Figure 4: Hamlet at sea: fair-copy of Wilkie Collins's *The Lighthouse* (1855), Act II.

But whatever his darker fears or harsher judgments, Dickens would always hope that he could keep the masses in the Victorian social fold by appealing to their intelligence, morality, and taste.[27] The last of the Birmingham readings of December 1853 was just such an occasion, advertised for "working people," and featuring ticket prices cut to sixpence. W. H. Wills wrote that day that "[i]f Dickens does turn Reader he will make another fortune. He will never offer to do so, of course. But if they *will* have him he will do it, he told me today."[28] That night, the first part of the fantasy came true. Dickens thought his listeners "the most remarkable thing that England could produce, I think, in the way of a vast intelligent assemblage," an audience that "lost nothing, misinterpreted nothing, followed everything closely, laughed and cried with most delightful earnestness, and animated me to that extent that I felt as if we were all bodily going up into the clouds together" (*PL* 7: 244). Nor did it take long for such feelings to turn into more durable materials. In this original version of 1853–4, the *Carol* reading ran almost three hours, with the Birmingham hosts thankful enough, and the charitable take large enough, to send silver plate to Mr. and Mrs. Dickens afterwards (*PL* 7: 250). A few years later, audiences at Coventry and Chatham had an equally rapturous response to a newer, shorter version; in its gratitude, the Coventry Institute later sent Dickens a watch worth 75 guineas – an amount not much less than the average annual salary of one of their members (*PL* 8: 498, 718). The reception of these early readings suggests once again how ironclad the linkage had become between Dickens's vocation to write benevolence and his drive to profit thereby.

With the benefits temporarily behind him, and with the new year wearing on, Dickens found that only theatrical activity of the kind begun in *The Lighthouse*, supplemented with continued public reading, could relieve his inner turmoil. Once again, Wilkie Collins provided it, this time in the form of the character of Richard Wardour in *The Frozen Deep*. The play had its origins in Dickens's interest in the fate of the Franklin expedition, lost somewhere in the Arctic since 1845. Nine years later, the well-known explorer and Hudson's Bay Company official Dr. John Rae published a report in *The Times* suggesting that Franklin's company had resorted to cannibalism before their deaths: Rae's conclusion, drawn from Eskimo witnesses, was that "the mutilated state of many of the corpses and the contents of the kettles" suggested that the company "had been driven to that last resource – cannibalism – as a means of prolonging existence."[29] In the course of 1854, Dickens wrote two lengthy *Household Words* articles attempting to refute Rae's claim, insisting repeatedly that Eskimo treachery, rather than English depravity, was responsible for the explanation of cannibalism; Rae's rejoinder was printed, with final rebuttal, soon afterwards.[30] But the lengthy exchange with Rae did not exhaust Dickens's fascination with the case's matrix of elemental extremity, interracial violence and ambiguous death. Still aglow with the guilty pleasures of *The Lighthouse*, Dickens and Collins conceived *The Frozen Deep* in the spring of 1855; the second melodrama was revised in the late summer and early fall.

On the very day in August 1856 that Collins arrived at Boulogne to begin working on revisions of the script, Dickens had protested that the conventional hero of an "English book," including any by Scott, "is always uninteresting – too good – too natural, &c," particularly to English emigrés, who "pass their lives with Balzac and Sand" (*PL* 8: 178). However conventional its ending, the final version of the play was a concerted break with this moralism and prudishness. After an exposition in which we learn that the heroine's ex-lover Wardour and her fiancé Aldersley are both on the expedition, Act I ends with an "admirable idea" Collins may have adapted from Scott's *Redgauntlet*: the prophecy of the household's Scottish nurse that Aldersley will die at the jealous Wardour's hand. In a September letter, Dickens suggested not only the definitive wording of the nurse's vision, which announces the imminent sacrifice of an atoning victim, but also, in an extraordinary final parenthesis, projected his own intense guilt temporarily into the scene: "'I see the lamb in the grasp of the lion – your bonnie bird alone with the hawk. . . . Blood! The stain of his blood is upon you, *(C.D.)*!'"[31] Act II heightens the threat to Aldersley by two principal means: the representation of Wardour's "ice-bound soul," frozen into hate by jealousy, and his discovery of Aldersley's identity. Taken with a weakening of Esther's prophetic powers, Wardour's heroic rescue of his old rival would appear more plausible, and his death in the arms of his childhood love more affecting.[32] Dickens's revisions thus made the play more realistic and its hero more complex than the supernatural plot and maniacal villain of Collins's draft, even as he kept the work's essentially stark and melodramatic character intact.[33]

What is immediately striking about the reception of *The Frozen Deep* is the success with which Dickens converted his fashionable audience to a hero riven by jealous passion and guilty self-loathing: as Queen Victoria wrote to Dickens after the command performance of 4 July 1857, the point of the play was that Wardour's "better and nobler feelings" triumphed over "the evil passions," including lust, jealousy, hate, and rage. John Oxenford's comments in *The Times* were no less enthusiastic and considerably more interesting. First came praise for the character Richard Wardour: by "daring" to deliver Wardour's life story in a "*monotonous*" style, demonstrating thereby the "oppressive and almost humiliating burden" under which Wardour suffers, Dickens produced what Oxenford called a "most perfect representation" of obsession.[34]

It is hardly controversial to identify this spell of monotony as the same under which Arthur Clennam sits in his London coffee-house on a Sunday evening, with "[n]othing for the spent toiler to do, but to compare the *monotony* of his six days, [and] think what a weary life he led, and make the best of it – or the worst, depending on the probabilities" (I. 3: 67–8). In a more fashionable London coffee-room, Nicholas Nickleby had awakened from a doze to hear his sister's name, and waited for Sir Mulberry Hawk to take up his challenge with "the monotonous ticking of a French clock" in his ears; the tormented author of the autobiographical fragment of 1846 mulls over the words "MOOR EEFFOC" on the plate-glass window before him.[35] But European literary and visual art would remain riveted by this kind of visionary dreariness long after Dickens's death. The energetic ancestors of these coffee-room customers were the dealers in probability who founded an insurance syndicate in Edward Lloyd's London coffee-house; their listless descendants would come to include the absinthe drinkers of Manet and Degas, painted between 1875 and 1882.[36] And nearly three decades after the creation of Arthur Clennam, the decadent anti-hero of J. K. Huysmans' *A Rebours* (1884) would also sit in a London lounge over a cup of coffee, though this one is laced with gin. As he listens to the Englishmen around him talking about the rain, notes how his Bond Street suit matches theirs, and feels "highly pleased to find himself not out of tone with his surroundings, glad to be, in a kind of superficial way, a naturalized citizen of London," he imagines that Little Dorrit is serving him.[37]

No less important to *The Times* reviewer than this ideologeme of negated transcendence is the exceptional nature of those who can discern it. A psychologically sophisticated creation like Wardour, Oxenford also insisted, "can only be appreciated by the most careful study on the part of the spectator." This kind of audience will feel "admiration" rather than "delight," and show themselves capable of "careful study" even if they also weep (as many did) at the death of Wardour: "There was literally a gasp of applause when the curtain descended, and the conversation that ensued during the interval . . . was composed of a laudatory criticism of details." In short, the audience of *The Frozen Deep* knows its own collective power as a group of elite cultural consumers: "not only talking men, but men whose talk is sure to find listeners," who are " 'up to everything,' especially in matters of public amusement, and whose organ of veneration is by no means largely developed."[38] As we have seen, Thackeray presented a very early and attenuated version of this cultivated audience reader at the end of *Vanity*

Fair's chapter 8: Italian sailors and French actors make the pleasurable mistake of hating villains too closely, an identification Thackeray both encourages and warns against in language borrowed from Drury Lane. In time, as we shall also see, this audience would become sufficiently important, and its most representative novelist sufficiently attuned to its needs, that George Eliot would not only cast the intellectuals Lydgate and Ladislaw as the heroes of *Middlemarch*, but also publish the novel on a bimonthly schedule that allowed her readers time, as one clergyman put it in 1872, "to master the teacher's lessons." In 1857, however, this *haut bourgeois* audience was just coming into focus.

If *The Frozen Deep* and *Little Dorrit* project themselves towards the negated subjects and discriminating consumers of high European modernism, then, we should not be surprised that the great serial novel also negates the two ideologemes on which, as we have seen, the Dickensian audience was first assembled: the male spirit of overview, which had long craved mastery of the urban environment; and the atoning heroine, whose body had provided that environment with its occult moral center. Dickens's novels from *Dombey and Son* forward, including *Bleak House*, *Little Dorrit*, and *Our Mutual Friend*, each make different claims for the powers of the Carlylean spirit of overview imagined in *Dombey and Son*, the "good spirit who would take the house-tops off, with a more potent and benignant hand than the lame demon in the tale[.]"[39] By the opening of *Bleak House*, the "dark shapes" of *Dombey and Son*'s "Vice and Fever" have become an entire noxious atmosphere.[40]

In *Little Dorrit*, this ideology of overview is still at work; the human objects it tracks, however, are vanishing from sight. Possessed by the guilty obsession that "there is [a] wrong entrusted to us to make right" (88) – that is, possessed by the novel's already psychologized inheritance plot – Arthur Clennam's first significant act is diverting his gaze from himself to Amy (I. 5: 96). What is never quite clear is how, like Nancy before her, Little Dorrit has managed to resist the moral toxicity of her environment: "What her pitiful look saw" in her childhood, "how little of the wretched truth it pleased God to make visible to her[,] lies hidden with many mysteries" (I. 7: 111). After her father has been told of his impending liberation after years of imprisonment, Amy objects that he should have to pay "in life and money both" – an entirely reasonable argument that human suffering should have some worth in a society which fetishizes credit and debt in the transcendent categories of Atonement theology. The narrator, however, takes her attack on the link between financial and moral restitution as "the first speck Clennam had ever seen," "the last speck Clennam ever saw, of the prison atmosphere upon her" (I. 35: 472): Dickens imposes the taint at precisely the moment when Amy has the courage to question the ancient Protestant linkage between debt and redemption.[41]

The marriage plot too shows how Amy's transcendental goodness is a matter of capital, the sign of an invisible surplus-value. For Clennam, accepting Amy's love has as its prerequisite taking his fetishistic, worthless love from "its old sacred place" and "danc[ing] upon it" (I. 13: 191). Thus begun, the action of divestment ends when Arthur's guilt for this old fetishism takes on the potentially infinite status of unlimited economic liability: "What wretched amends I can make must be made. I must clear my unfortunate partner's reputation. I must retain nothing for myself. . . . I must work out as much of my fault – or crime – as is susceptible of being worked out in the rest of my days" (II. 26: 779).[42] Even in the Marshalsea, Clennam persists in thinking that the surrender of wealth can only be a "sacrifice" rather than a gift (II. 29: 828), a state of mind which Maggy does not hesitate to identify as a form of sickness (830). And though Amy's offer of love will liberate him from his prison cell, her voice and body speak the inhuman language of capital. The only "fortune" remaining to Little Dorrit, the thing not yet "shared" with Arthur, is her sexuality, for which her questing hand is the synecdoche: "I am yours anywhere, everywhere!" But this offer, made at the moment of escape from capital, is imagined simultaneously as an offer of labor, the source of capital: "I would rather pass my life here with you, and go out daily, working for our bread, than I would have the greatest fortune that ever was told" (886). Just as Little Dorrit's hand signifies the offer of her body, that body signifies the offer of her labor, the nineteenth-century coin of her love.[43]

The metaphorical counterpart of this metonymic procedure, which suggests how incarnational love can slip into sexual commodification, is the designation of Amy as a "vanishing point," the ground zero of abstract benevolence: "Every thing in its perspective led to her innocent figure . . . it was the center of interest of his life; it was the termination of everything that was good and pleasant in it; beyond, there was nothing but mere waste and darkened sky" (II. 27: 801–2). We have seen how Dickens's early characters personify sympathy, becoming exhibits for what Benjamin calls the "resplendent but ultimately noncommittal knowledge of an absolute."[44] The "ultimately noncommittal" nature of such knowledge comes through clearly in this figuration of *Little Dorrit*'s good angel. Though she is purported to be "the center of interest" in Clennam's life, she is no less its organizing abstraction. The atoning heroine, whom Dickens has previously represented as mediating the gap between phenomena and noumena, here emerges as an unmistakable symptom of that gap, shuttling between extremes of meaningful- and meaninglessness.[45] Discourse has become virtually detached from representation, with the result that thought is brought back, as in modernist writing from Mallarmé and Nietzsche to Foucault and Derrida, "towards language itself, towards its unique and difficult being."[46]

Little Dorrit does include a professional overviewer: Physician, who combines the faculties of his *Bleak House* predecessors Allan Woodcourt and Mr Bucket in diagnosing the ills of London life. But while Mr. Bucket's power to supervise deviancy had operated in the narrative present – from his position atop the "tower in his mind," "[m]any solitary figures he perceives" – the connections Physician makes are literally things of the past: "Few ways of life *were* hidden from [him].... Many wonderful things *did* he see and hear" (II. 25: 768). It is consistent with this belatedness that Physician's hermeneutics is consistently literary, preoccupied as he is by the question of Merdle's "deep-seated recondite complaint," a phrase which links his physical state to a complex of meanings which cannot emerge without an effort of interpretation.[47] Thus, "[b]eing a great reader of all kinds of literature (and never at all apologetic for that weakness)," Physician is reading at the very moment he is called away to attend Merdle's corpse (II. 25: 771).

By the end of this same chapter, moreover, we have learned the *Little Dorrit* narrator is as beset as Physician, his surrogate. A modern city, now perceived in *narrative* as much as *geographical* terms, produces interpretations of the disasters which inevitably occur within itself. As rumors about Merdle's death circulate through the city, it is not long before "appalling whispers," coming from "east, west, north and south," assert the connections between Merdle the character and Merdle the social phenomenon:

> [T]he talk, lashed louder and higher by confirmation on confirmation, and by edition after edition of the evening papers, swelled into such a roar when night came, as might have brought one to believe that a solitary watcher on the gallery above the Dome of St. Paul's would have perceived the night air to be laden with a heavy muttering of the name of Merdle, coupled with every form of execration. (II. 25: 776)

We have previously understood the sound Mr. Pickwick heard at the prison bedside of the Chancery prisoner as the phantasmatic "murmur" and "roar" rising from the London streets of 1836–8 (*PP*, 44: 718); the same oceanic sound recurs here. But this "roar" is the sound of an emergent mass media, "lashed louder and higher" by "edition after edition of the evening papers." If the cinematic analogue of the opening of *Bleak House* is the camera zoom, then the equivalent here is a montage, with a shot of the "solitary watcher" followed by close-ups of furious, distorted and cursing faces, with a soundtrack in which whispers swell into "a heavy muttering of the name of Merdle, coupled with every form of execration." We might even imagine that Dickens is throwing off a prophecy of the leading formal characteristics of modernist cinema here – that totality of *mise en scène*, camerawork, editing, and sound Eisenstein would call "vertical montage."[48] As it makes thus visible the rupture between "Merdle" as emplotted character and recurring name, as between the narrator as masterly overviewer and benighted watcher, *Little Dorrit* approaches "the abyss into which language plunges when it tries to become name and image."[49] The counterpoised structure of *Bleak House* has become a single but multivalent voice, attempting to represent its own submersion in tides of meaning.

Breaking out, 1857

What is left standing after the detonations and tidal waves of 1856, either in or outside of this great serial novel? Bakhtin has suggested that the narrator's descriptions of Merdle manipulate a variety of discourses within the same sentence for comic and satiric effect, "mak[ing] use of language without wholly giving himself up to it" in the liberatory play he calls "heteroglossia." Substantial parts of the sixteenth and seventeenth numbers use a different strategy, however, alternating between the same two univocal modes which Bakhtin *opposes* to heteroglossia – "scattered direct speech" (the transcriptions of William Dorrit's dinner speech, Physician's diagnosis) as well as "purely authorial speech" (the comments on Dorrit's "poor maimed spirit" [II. 19: 710], the account of the "solitary watcher" on St. Paul's dome). While Bakhtinian heteroglossia may be pleasurable and liberatory to a point, then, it can also become overwhelming, a sign of misunderstanding and anarchy rather than dialogue and consensus.[50] Even in Bakhtin's own terms, the denouement of *Little Dorrit* seems to have featured a multivalent *narrative voice*, univocal, dialogic, and heteroglossic by turns. In this, it seems more akin to a modernist literary form, which attempts to represent its autonomy from modern life by means of defamiliarization and shock; and *Little Dorrit* itself does not escape the verdict that its pleasures demanded the discriminating and self-disciplinary consumer of modernist art as much if not more than they satisfied the popular taste for Pickwickian play.[51] It is worth explaining, then, how *Little Dorrit*'s denouement includes a number of distinct formal episodes, each possessing what Bakhtin calls "its own verbal and semantic forms for assimilating various aspects of reality."[52]

The first of these forms closely resembles those of psychoanalysis. As Trilling first noted, Arthur's inspired guess about the origin of his mother's paralysis anticipates the theory of neurosis which Freud would come to in the course of *Studies on Hysteria*: "In that long confinement to her room, did his mother find a balance to be struck?" (I. 8: 129).[53] For the Calvinist Mrs. Clennam, virtue and guilt are still a matter of "balancing her bargains with the Majesty of heaven, posting up the entries to her credit, strictly keeping her set-off, and claiming her due" (I. 5: 89); her paralysis is what Freud would call "a symbolic expression of her painful thoughts," taking the form of "the intensification of her sufferings."[54] But the extent of the congruence goes well beyond Trilling's suggestion. Forced to marry Flintwinch without warning and against her will, Affery suffers from the same sensations of giddiness, choking and suffocation, the same terror of being surprised from behind by a man who admonishes her to silence with unspeakable threats, as her Freudian counterpart Katharina (*SE* 2: 126). So, too, Amy's wage relation to the Clennam family, as well as the thwarted womanhood symbolized in her status as nearly invisible object (I. 8: 125; I. 9: 130, 134) or captive bird (I. 9: 144) has its Freudian counterpart in Lucy R.'s relation to her rich cousins. In both cases, economic differences have blocked familial love in the past, and sexual love in the future, with this blockage manifesting itself in depression, fatigue, and impaired appetite.[55] Nor can we omit Mr. F's Aunt, existing in a "cataleptic" state (I. 23: 319, *SE* 2: 14), and producing speech on "some system of her own," the "key" to which is missing (I. 13: 198–9), just as Freud would call the symptoms of Cäcilie M. "a regular collection of symbolizations" (*SE* 2: 180).[56]

Freud's women deliver moral judgments in astonishingly complex and idiosyncratic forms (*SE* 2: 131). In all these cases, and especially in the no less astonishing Flora Finching, Dickens reached heights of insight he would never again equal. Like that of her Freudian counterparts, Flora Finching's speech functions paradigmatically rather than syntagmatically. We have seen how the novel's romantic plot winds up by means of synecdoche, with Little Dorrit's hand announcing her desire for Clennam by "[creeping] up a little nearer his face" (II. 34:

884–5). Flora offers her sexuality, the subject of a hilariously grim analogy to a kidney pie, to Clennam in the similarly synecdochic form of a "hand of true regard." But accompanying this similarity is a critical difference. Whereas the figuration of Little Dorrit's sexual offer is enacted at the level of plot, Flora's speech repeats and then dismantles that synecdoche at the level of discourse:

> "[1] but being aware that tender relations are in contemplation beg to state that *I heartily wish well to both* and find no fault with either not the least,
>
> [2] it may be withering to know that ere *the hand of Time* had made me much less slim than formerly and dreadfully red on the slightest exertion particularly after eating I well know when it takes the form of a rash, it might have been and was not through the interruption of parents and mental torpor succeeded until the mysterious clue was held by Mr. F.
>
> [3] still I would not be ungenerous to either and *I heartily wish well to both*." (II. 34: 887, emphases added)

We must first understand Flora's coded self-references, here as elsewhere: the life with Arthur effaced by "the hand of time"; her hopes destroyed by Mr. Casby's matchmaking; and finally, after seven proposals and twelve months of chastity at Flora's request (I. 13: 196, 194), the taking of her sexuality, which remains a "mysterious clue" to Flora herself, by her new husband.

But Flora also has the capacity to name her fantasies as such. When she does so, she temporarily shatters her own spell, allowing not only a repetition of her congratulations, but also a return to her own first-person selfhood: "I heartily wish well to both" [1, 3]. Though Clennam has earlier found Flora "wholly destitute of the power of separating herself and him from their bygone characters" (I. 13: 201), her last appearance shows her working at just this separation, rising out of metonymic self-cancellation into self-awareness [1], and back again [2], and out again [3], like the "mermaid" Dickens twice calls her (196, 201). To call her speech mere "paratactic babble,"[57] then, is thus to underestimate its relation to not only the traumatic encryptions of the Freudian hysteric, but also the pleasurable exclamations of Molly Bloom.

One final example both restates the correlations between *Little Dorrit*'s women and modernist prose poetics and returns us to matters of overview and genre. Both Mrs. Clennam and the subject of Freud's final case-history in the *Studies on Hysteria*, Elisabeth von R., are paralyzed by guilt as a result of their thwarted ambition. Mrs. Clennam, resisting marriage as Elisabeth would, and like her "jealously guard[ing] everything that was bound up with" her class position (*SE* 2: 140), eventually accomplishes what Elisabeth von R. only imagines – the elimination of her sexual rival and the adoption of that rival's child as her own (II. 30: 843–4; *SE* 2: 142, 156). But we can associate Mrs. Clennam with the literary future in another, more concrete way. Unlike Lady Dedlock, who returns to her lover's grave through variegated *geographical* terrain, the urban space through which Mrs. Clennam travels is various only in a *psychological* sense. It differs from the space she remembers many years before, and makes her seem different in turn:

> More remarkable by being so removed from the crowd it was among than if it had been lifted on a pedestal to be seen, *the figure attracted all eyes*. Saunterers pricked up their attention to observe it; busy people, crossing it, slackened their pace and turned their heads; companions pausing and standing aside, whispered one another to look at this spectral woman who was coming by; and the sweep of the figure as it passed seemed to create a vortex; drawing the most idle and the most curious after it. (II. 31: 855–6, emphasis added)

The first two categories of those "observing" and "crossing" this "figure" are just those Benjamin points out in Poe: the "saunterers" or *flâneurs*, and the busy "men of the crowd," with the couples mediating the relatively intense and faint interest of these other categories of walkers.[58] Though Mrs. Clennam is in a position even "more remarkable" than *Bleak House*'s position of overview, "as if lifted on a pedestal," like Mr. Bucket on his tower, she ascends into that position not to see from above, but "to be seen" *from below*, to become "the object of all eyes" rather than the overviewing subject.

At this second demise of overview, however, a new and signal possibility is put into play: in her exceptional and interior position as a "sleep-walker," Mrs. Clennam looks "as if she were environed by distracting thoughts, rather than by external humanity and observation" (856). When this capacity for distraction, here already a working defense against the attention of the urban crowd, is reconceptualized as a *successful adaptation* rather than an *adverse reaction* to the conditions of urban life, Leopold Bloom will be able to endure a boring conversation with McCoy by thinking about the foot of a woman who is standing nearby.[59] In their own time, Benjamin and Adorno would have one of their bitterest arguments over the same question: whether modern distraction should be considered "progressive reaction" or "infantile regression."[60]

Simply put, the difference between *Dombey and Son*'s drive towards overview and its negation in Mrs. Clennam is the very important one between wishing for something and analyzing that wish. In the same way, we saw the speech of Flora Finching turn from projection to insight and back, and back again, and can add Miss Wade's "History of a Self-Tormentor" to the list as well.[61] The novel must use transcription to maintain its claim as a truthtelling mode; the monologue or autobiography chooses to efface such marks in order to foreground subjectivity's inescapable presence in all telling, truthful or not. Like the Baudelairean narrator, Miss Wade's history formalizes this problematic by making her obsessions determined by the absent urban crowd, as she announces at the outset: "I have the misfortune of not being a fool. From a very early age I detected what those about me thought they hid from me" (II. 21: 725). Dickens's early wish that her history might be "impossible of separation from the main story" gave way, after a struggle, to a fictional method having the *negation* of synthesis as its implicit principle. Once again, Dickens seems to be working towards Adorno's modernist definition of "great narrative": the form of Miss Wade's history, like Flora's speech and Mrs. Clennam's distraction, questions its own ways of meaning by representing its difference from those forms which have preceded it.[62]

How to do it

By now, my list of analogies between *Little Dorrit* and modernist forms is bewilderingly large, including not only Huysmans and Joyce, but also Freud, Simmel, Benjamin, and Adorno. But it seems to me that this novel encompasses much more literary history than we have been able to understand before. Each of these theorists were, like Dickens, wondering in his own distinctive way about Schiller's epochal claim that modern literary representation has lost the magical power to stand for the society which has produced it, and thus, paradoxically, its autonomous status as an aesthetic object.[63] Arthur Clennam and Amy Dorrit, Physician and Flora Finching and Miss Wade seem to be part of the same massive historical situation as the modernism of a century later, a situation in which, as Fredric Jameson has written, "the relationship between the individual and the system seems ill-defined, if not fluid, or even dissolved."[64]

If we demand some escape from Dickens's own "negative dialectics," we might begin by looking to the single character who, we are told, knows "how to do it" by the end. The indefatigable Pancks learns that the landlord Casby, for example, has been the "Works" to Pancks's "Winder" (II. 32: 869): greed is the human urge which gives capitalism its inhuman energy. And it is to Pancks also that Dickens grants the privilege of articulating his final, and arguably most significant, trope for modernity:

> How he had felt his way inch by inch, and "Moled it out, sir" (that was Mr. Pancks's expression), grain by grain. How in the beginning of the labour described by *this new verb*, and to render which the more expressive Mr. Pancks shut his eyes in pronouncing it and shook his hair over them, he had alternated from sudden lights and hopes to sudden darkness and no hopes, and back again, and back again. (I. 35: 460, emphasis added)

Pancks, the human mole, also known as a "journeyman Hamlet" (II. 13. 642), is the comic sibling of the two other Hamlets from the period of *Little Dorrit*'s composition: the hapless Martin Gurnock of *The Lighthouse*, caught between his father's guilt and his lover's appeal, and the vacillating Arthur Clennam, whose watch echoes the old ghost's admonition not to forget. The truth of *Hamlet*'s old mole, of course, is that there are "more things in heaven and earth than have been dreamt of" in any philosophical system (I. 5), including the unconscious sequences and mythic comparisons on which Dickens and his fellow novelists had long relied. What Hamlet's father's ghost commands is what the Dickens of *Little Dorrit* knows: that the work of the individual in modernity, its "new verb," is the exploration of the furthest reaches of human experience for the sake of a future life located not in heaven, but on earth.[65] Such a massive effort applies also to Dickens's compositional procedures in this novel, his meticulous planning and abstention from synthesis.[66]

If I am correct, then glimmers of worldly hope and good humor should shine even in the darkest corner of this text: the prison, that metaphorical center of *Little Dorrit* from its original frontispiece to Trilling's inaugural modern reading, and especially its eighteenth number, which is spent entirely within the walls of the Marshalsea. The first and last of this number's three chapters are interviews with John

Chivery and Little Dorrit, ironized versions of the aspiring hero and long-suffering heroine at the eternal and unstable center of Dickens's romantic plots.[67] But there is strangeness in Book II's chapter 28: a discrepancy between its title, "An Appearance in the Marshalsea," and the three characters who in fact appear there. Two of these are the newfangled and oldfangled villains Ferdinand Barnacle and Rigaud/Blandois. Between them, and at the very center of the number as a whole, comes an encounter with Mr. Rugg, the lawyer Pancks recommends to him: a "ruddy-headed gentleman," who "shone in at the door, like a elderly Phoebus" (II. 28: 807) – a fancified version of the elderly Mr. Pickwick, who had "burst like another sun from his slumbers" two decades before (*PP* 2: 72). We are already acquainted with Rugg from the end of the previous number, when he attempts to talk his client out of incarceration at the Marshalsea, as Mr. Perker had on his client's behalf (II. 26: 780–1, 784; *PP* 40: 655–6). The uncanny quality of this series is only heightened when we consider Rugg's conversational tic: his repeated references to his daughter, once the successful plaintiff in an action for breach of promise of marriage – the same cause of action, of course, which brought Pickwick into the Fleet (II. 26: 780, 28: 808). In short, the only way to find the single "appearance" of the chapter title is to interpret the term as referring not to a new character but to an old book: what appears, or reappears, I am suggesting, is *Pickwick Papers*.[68]

Like Pickwick before him, Clennam has a complex relation to capital. While each hero takes a moral stand against self-interest, a position that lands both in debtor's prison, the quality of these stands, their conception of the means of reaching justice as an ultimate end, is worlds apart. Pickwick first burst into Dickens's fiction as the incarnation of capital "in all its might and glory," the soul of a soulless world; resisting the greed personified in Dodson and Fogg meant refusing to submit to the judgment rendered by a corrupt economic and legal system. Clennam wants to redeem himself, but does not know either the quality or the extent of his wrongs; instead, he can pledge only to "work out as much of my fault – or crime – as is susceptible of being worked out in the rest of my days" (II. 26: 779). For him, as for Dickens/Wardour in *The Frozen Deep*, conquering infection by greed requires that he declare himself both guilty agent and atoning victim, and thereby to make "[t]he only real atonement in his power":

> The disclosure was made, and the storm raged fearfully. Thousands of people were wildly staring about for somebody alive to heap

reproaches on; and this notable case, courting publicity, set the living *somebody* so much wanted, on a scaffold. (II. 26: 782, 783)

This moment of violent unanimity – declaring his guilt "publicly and unreservedly," even "courting publicity," as the society hungry to identify its scapegoat sees it – is the climactic one in Dickens's fiction, dramatizing as it does the irrationality and violence bound to accompany efforts to reclaim meaning from modernity.

It is true that unlike Nancy or Richard Wardour, Clennam's life is not sacrificed, although he does become sufficiently enervated in the Marshalsea to turn his face repeatedly to the wall (*LD* 786, 818). But the problem of imagining meaningful action remains. Perhaps it would help to recall that *Pickwick*'s plot gets underway when Mr. Pickwick speaks to his landlady, Mrs. Bardell, about having Sam Weller come to live with him as his manservant. Mrs. Bardell fancies that "she observed a species of matrimonial twinkle in the eyes of her lodger"; and Mr. Pickwick speaks of "the person I have in my eye (here he looked very hard at Mrs. Bardell)" (*Pickwick* 12: 230–1). We know, as Mr. Pickwick does not, that his innocent look will be misunderstood; and we also know, as Mrs. Bardell does not, that he has Sam Weller, not her, in his mind's "eye." Dickens's very first plot, in other words, was engendered in a dialectical play between the contiguity of objects, including metonymic human beings in modernity, and the continuity of interpretations, including the myths of love and sacrifice inherited from a Christian past.

Arthur Clennam's encounter with Rugg shows Dickens attempting to survive this dialectical play in an allegory of his own development through 1857, a development to and beyond the limits of a serial form attempting to integrate both modes of signification into a single disordered totality. For Dickens to recall *Pickwick* at this moment is thus to remember its kind of missed, absent, or meaningless connections, and to evoke the possibility, and only this, of a joyful and hilarious rather than agonized and grieving knowledge in that remembrance. Having begun with the ambition to sanctify bourgeois society, and having worked through its inhuman nature, *Little Dorrit*'s forms of comedy – the language of Flora, the jubilation of Pancks, the reappearance of *Pickwick Papers* in the prison cell – amount to a way of representing the history of society: like the awesome tragicomedies of Hegel and Marx, this novel is "the form which reflection takes after it has assimilated the truths of Tragedy to itself."[69] It not only asks the central questions of European modernism – can humanity in society survive the discovery of an unconscious? the disenchantment of the world? – but also suggests that literary culture has become what it has remained ever since: a mindful deviation from a reified and forgetful norm, compelled to make interiority and remembrance its central subjects, and enlightenment its endless horizon.

4
A Dance of Indecision: George Eliot's Shorter Fiction

> The religious ethic of brotherliness stands in dynamic tension with any purposive-rational conduct that follows its own laws. In no less degree, this tension occurs between the religious ethic and "this-worldly" life-forces, whose character is essentially non-rational or basically anti-rational. Above all, there is tension between the ethic of religious brotherliness and the spheres of esthetic and erotic life.
>
> Max Weber, "Religious Rejections of the World and their Directions" (1915)

To begin reading George Eliot is speedily to encounter the conviction that modernity is best approached from an oblique angle. While Dickens's earliest fictions are emphatically timely, his persona amounting to what Bagehot called "a special correspondent for posterity" from modernity's urban front, George Eliot's fictions usually displace us from that front in two ways: they return us to the provincial settings of Austen and Scott; and they set their action in historical pasts which, as we read along, soon appear quite specific. The earlier of these settings is around the turn of the nineteenth century, as in "Mr. Gilfil's Love Story" (1857), *Adam Bede* (1859), and most of *Silas Marner* (1861); the later is the Reform period of the late 1820s and early 1830s, as in "The Sad Fortunes of the Reverend Amos Barton" (1857), "Janet's Repentance" (1857), *The Mill on the Floss* (1860), *Felix Holt* (1866), and *Middlemarch* (1871–2).

The same twenty-five or thirty-year period separates these two apparently distinctive historical settings from each other, as from the 1857 present in which Marian Evans became George Eliot. This periodicity of a single human generation, playing out at moments of perceived crisis in Victorian Britain's recent prehistory, already suggests that the ways in which families and societies perpetuate themselves will preoccupy George Eliot's fiction, as we have seen the Dickens of the same year preoccupied with the disintegration of the high Victorian social body.[1] A glance at the plots of her works confirms this hunch. The common subject of the works George Eliot sets in the 1790s is how the social structure of the British *ancien régime* cannot contain the destructive forces of sexual passion, from the *Scenes'* Caterina and Captain Wybrow to *Adam Bede*'s Hetty Sorrel and Arthur Donnithorne to *Silas Marner*'s Molly Farren and Godfrey Cass. In those works set around 1830, plot usually concerns the trials of marriage for what would have been her parents' generation, from the *Scenes'* Bartons and Dempsters to the Casaubons, Lydgates, and Bulstrodes of *Middlemarch*. Resolving such plots of erotic destruction and marital reconstruction, we soon learn, can be a symbolic task of apparently extreme difficulty – so much as to require the final flood of *The Mill on the Floss*, to take the most striking example, though the unsuitable marriages of *Felix Holt* seems to cause not only old Mr. Transom's dementia but also Annette's decline and death.[2]

Another register in this developing counterpoint is George Eliot's negotiation of what she called "the Nightmare of the Serial" (*L* 3: 236) – that is, her ambiguous relation to the literary and commodity form innovated by Dickens.[3] Her first principle was vaulting aspiration: as G. H. Lewes would remind John Blackwood in November 1856, "that which I suspect most writers would be apt to consider as success," George Eliot would consider failure, "so high is his ambition" (*L* 2: 276). The goal, then, would be to satisfy this aspiration while achieving the financial independence the couple had lived so long without, including the burdens of raising Lewes's three sons and supporting his wife's four additional children by T. L. Hunt.[4] The publication history of *Scenes of Clerical Life*, with its well-known sequence of submission, conditional acceptance, partial withdrawal, reassurance, and resumption, suggests how difficult this task would always be. In the years to follow, indeed, precisely half of George Eliot's works would be published serially; of these, in turn, half would appear in periodicals, with the remainder published in separate parts.[5] Eventually, her success would lead her into negotiations with Dickens himself. In November 1859, just after having dinner with them for the first time, he made the Leweses an offer to serialize Marian Evans's work in *All the Year Round*, "on any terms perfectly satisfactory," including the Leweses' reservation of copyright and choice of publisher for any completed novel. The answer would be a characteristically equivocal no. After an apparent misunderstanding over the offer and its refusal, and referring to his "delicate kindness in a recent matter," Marian Evans would write to Blackwood the following spring that her single complimentary copy of *The Mill on the Floss* should go to Dickens, with all others marked "From the Publisher," "that they may not be imagined to come from me."[6]

Given the consistency with which George Eliot maintained these fiercely negotiated and supervised distances from the historical, geographical, and literary modernities of the 1850s, moments of particular strain or outright disruption deserve our close attention. Such are both of the works I consider in detail here. The third and last "scene of clerical life," "Janet's Repentance," bears the familiar features of George Eliot's later English fictions: a provincial and Reform-era setting, a troubled marriage, a scandal featuring an evangelical with sins in his past. Some of her most powerful readers found this story distinctly unpleasurable, even objectionable: John Blackwood feared the story might cause Mudie's to reject the planned volume at the end of the series (*L* 2: 344–5). This time, George Eliot's response was unequivocal. She refused substantially to allay the painful quality of her tale, and threatened to end the series at once (*L* 2: 348). In exchange for the excision of a few passages, Blackwood wrote that "[i]n continuing to write for the Magazine I beg of all things that you will not consider himself hampered in any way" – a reply that eventually evoked the plan for *Adam Bede*, originally conceived as a fourth scene, as a novel to be serialized at Blackwood's option (*L* 2: 352, 381, 387). *Silas Marner* also claims exceptional status in George Eliot's corpus. Drafting *Adam Bede* and *The Mill on the Floss* for serialization had been a difficult experience, though both eventually appeared in traditional three-volume format; by 1860, she was already anticipating the "great deal of study and labour" that the serial *Romola* would require. By contrast, the one-volume, non-serialized tale of the weaver of Raveloe appeared with none of the symptoms of mental and physical torment characteristic of a novelist who would compare the process of completing *Middlemarch*, a bimonthly serial, to "a sort of nightmare in which I have been scrambling on the slippery bank of a pool, just keeping my head above water" (*L* 3: 41, 3: 307, 5: 301).[7]

A more traditional approach to these patterns of mindfulness would be to ask whether George Eliot's texts "exemplify the basic dilemma which is their main concern didactically," as William Myers has put it: the "discernment of the laws of necessity," and the "resolution in spite of them to conduct one's life in their light." If her fictions succeed in embodying this dilemma, then, as Myers concludes, her fictions are essentially "honest"; if not, as other readers have suggested, her greatest effort is spent fending off her own moments of profoundest insight.[8] But perhaps the question is more compelling than any single answer could be. One reason why the ethics of her work remain in question is that though her brand of incarnationalism had been utopian and "Radical" in the 1840s, it had become hegemonic across the fields of theology, economics, and social thought by 1870, as Boyd Hilton has suggested.[9] More generally, evaluating George Eliot's "complicity" with the dominant ideologies of her time seems less useful than approaching the question of how we continue to produce conceptions of the literary author from the same matrix of subjectivity her works map so well. "Janet's Repentance," for example, is so elaborate an attempt to mediate between Comtean and Feuerbachian "positive truths" and George Eliot's own critical insights into the Victorian family that its movements between incarnational philosophy and psychosexual pathology have been either denigrated as "melodrama" or ignored altogether.[10] Assisted a few years later by the Germanic *Novelle* tradition, *Silas Marner* mobilizes the same ideologeme of pathology, so apparently destructive in "Janet's Repentance," for the improvement of the Victorian social body, riven by class and gender divisions as it had always seemed in George Eliot's moments of dreariest Wordsworthian vision.[11]

If the essayist of the early 1850s worked to develop her own disposition between the enchantments of religious faith and the truths of historical consciousness, these two works exemplify both George Eliot's persistently ambivalent position in the Victorian literary market, poised between the Dickensian serial audience and the fashionable segment of it that she would later dominate. The Janus-faces of her early career are the longing to incarnate Victorian life in a still theological sense, to induce belief in its transcendent quality, and the vocation to incorporate that life into some larger and more rationalized system of knowledge. Like Dickens before her, she wrote a "cult of man in the abstract," in both its benevolent and its suffering modes, as the private, readerly, and commodified antidote to modern disenchantment. But though she steps artfully across the gaps between theology and science, economics and culture, it is also worth noting how her dance, like Silas Marner's cloth, sometimes seems to issue "from pure impulse, without reflection."[12] In this and other ways, she resembles her successor sociologist Max Weber. Though sometimes succumbing to the old cadences of violent sacrifice, both of these writers would illuminate the mundane conflicts of bourgeois life as scenes from a titanic cultural struggle between Christianity and modernity.

The early career of the incarnational intellect

Marian Evans's future status as an eminent incarnational intellectual became imaginable, at least to her partner and collaborator George Henry Lewes, at the moment she made her most concerted attack on the Atonement theology of her youth.[13] The subject of the essay "Evangelical Teaching: Dr. Cumming" (1855), a man whose preaching was popular enough to exact pew rents of £1500 at his rebuilt church at Covent Garden,[14] served as straw man for Marian's real target, the theologian and political economist Thomas Chalmers. Marian derided Cumming's popular *Apocalyptic Sketches* for such absurdities as its scene of "Dr. Chalmers and Mr. Wilberforce being caught up to meet Christ in the air, while Romanists, Puseyites, and infidels are given over to gnashing of teeth," or its imagination of Chalmers issuing a doomsday summons to Linnaeus and Newton, who promptly confess that their respective sciences of botany and astronomy have "only served to show more clearly that Jesus of Nazareth is enthroned on the riches of the universe" (*E* 41, 42).

Such witticisms impressed Lewes enough to identify this essay, during a walk in Richmond Park, as that which convinced him of his companion's "true genius" (*L* 2: 218).[15] But as vehemently as it rejects evangelical piety for its vindictiveness and complacency, the essay on Cumming itself relies on a species of transcendent and alienated suffering. To a Chalmersian, as Marian Evans objected, "[t]he man who endures tortures rather than betray a trust, the man who spends years in toil in order to discharge an obligation from which the law declares him free," must do so not from humanist sympathy, but for "the glory of God." But only the concrete apprehension of suffering in another can evoke the right kind of social action:

> Benevolence and justice are strong only in proportion as they are directly and inevitably called into activity by their proper objects: pity is strong only because we are strongly impressed by suffering; and only in proportion as it is compassion that speaks through the eyes when we soothe, and moves the arm when we succour, is a deed strictly benevolent. (*E* 66)

This humanist reviewer places suffering and compassion in the balance, using the same trope of proportionality featured in the King James prayer to "forgive us our debts, as we forgive our debtors." But more remarkable than this echo of Calvinism is the isolation to which the social actor is herself condemned – an isolation as transcendent, in fact, as the old encounter with depravity, that essential first step towards grace: "If the soothing or the succour be given because another being wishes or approves it, the deed ceases to be one of benevolence, and becomes one of defence, of obedience, or self-interest, or vanity" (*E* 66). As Myers has also noted, this species of judgment is the point where Protestant piety meets Feuerbachian conviction. For Feuerbach's man, as for Calvin's God, the movement of judgment, "the discrimination of the praiseworthy, of the perfect from the imperfect," is the originary act of faith.[16]

Even in her declaration of independence from the popular evangelicalism of Wilberforce and Chalmers, then, Marian Evans remained committed to its isolated subjectivity, just as newfangled Comtean positivism would evoke a native skepticism. As early as her first review to be published in London, a discussion of her friend Richard Mackay's *The Progress of the Intellect* (1850), she found Mackay's work animated by the "faith that divine revelation is not contained exclusively or pre-eminently in the facts and inspirations of any one age or nation, but is coextensive with the history of human development," and agreed that the "master key" to this "revelation" is "the recognition of the presence of undeviating law in the material and moral world" (*E* 270–1). Comte was the author of this world-view; Marian Evans made her first recorded reference to him in this article.[17] But though her language is Comtean in both its emphasis on the "undeviating" nature of the laws governing phenomena, and in the comprehensive action of those laws, she also distances herself from positivism's totalizing urges:

> though the teaching of positive truth is the grand means of expelling error, *the process will be very much quickened if the negative argument serve as its pioneer*; if, by a survey of the past, it can be shown how each age and each race has had a faith and a symbolism suited to its need and its stage of development, and that for succeeding ages to dream of retaining the spirit along with the forms of the past, is as futile as the embalming of the dead body in the hope that it may one day be resumed by the living soul. (*E* 269, emphasis added)

Philosophical overambition might result in an undead social theory; better, then, to describe difference than to prescribe unity.

If the searching light of "negative argument" sometimes found out objects dear to consciousness, it could also create a sensation tantamount to physical pain. Though the Mackay review echoes David Friedrich Strauss's praise of another friend's work (Charles Hennell's *An*

Inquiry Concerning the Origin of Christianity [1838]), Strauss's own *Life of Jesus* was sufficiently excruciating to make its translator "Strauss-sick – it made her ill dissecting the beautiful story of the crucifixion"; only a Thorwaldsen cast of the risen Christ, standing 20 inches high in her study, allowed her to go on with her work (*L* 1: 206).[18] Not for the last time in George Eliot's career, the aura of transcendence illumines the transcription of disenchantment.

Perhaps the most effervescent byproduct of this ferment of native evangelicalism and imported idealism is "The Natural History of German Life," an appreciation of and response to the German sociologist Wilhelm Riehl, whose *Bourgeois Society* (1851) and *Country and People* (1853) she first looked into in June 1856. In a passage she was careful to footnote as her own "interpretation" and "illustration" of Riehl, Evans praised his conclusions as "evolved entirely from his own gradually amassed observations":

> The views at which [Riehl] has arrived by this inductive process, he sums up in the term – *social-political- conservatism*; but his conservatism is, we conceive, of a thoroughly philosophical kind. He sees in European society *incarnate history*, and any attempt to disengage it from its historical elements must, he believes, be simply destructive of social vitality. (*E* 127)

This kind of "incarnate history" would accomplish a connection between "the external conditions which society has inherited from the past" and "inherited internal conditions in the human beings which compose it" in a language at once scientific and humane. But this conception is still "the fundamental *idea* in Riehl's books," rather than the form in which those books are written. Organic connections between past and present, are not only "necessary" but also "delicate" (*E* 128); and they will be more difficult to establish, maintain or extend in England than elsewhere, since "Protestantism and commerce have modernized the face of the land and the aspects of society in a far greater degree than in any continental country" (*E* 129).

Only Weber, writing half a century later, would match this level of insight into the simultaneously archaic and precocious nature of Victorian modernity. In the meantime, however, Marian Evans continued to look to marriage as the institution with the best chance of sustaining or extending lively social connections. Comte's *Cours de philosophie positive* (1830–42) had argued for marriage as the best form of mediation between individuals and their society; his *Système de politique*

Figure 5: Coping with Strauss-sickness: cast of Thorvaldsen *Risen Christ* used by Marian Evans during translation of Strauss's *Life of Jesus*, 1845–6.

positive (1851–4) went further, calling marriage "the highest type of all sympathetic instincts," and "the most elementary and yet the most perfect mode of social life."[19] Feuerbach also cast marriage as a model for the mediation of private desires and public needs:

> [Marriage] is sacred in itself, by the very nature of the union which is therein effected. That alone is a religious marriage, which is a true marriage, which corresponds to the essence of marriage – of love. And so it is with all moral relations. Then only are they moral, – then only are they enjoyed in a moral spirit, when they are regarded as sacred in themselves.[20]

The problem was that *The Essence of Christianity*'s "concluding application," the place where philosophy was supposed to become reality, contains no application at all: Feuerbach told his readers neither how to construct such marriages nor how to identify the love at their basis.[21]

It was a failing shared by every member of this intellectual generation. In the course of his influential essay on the Incarnation, for example, published as part of *Theological Essays* in 1853, F. D. Maurice had argued that the very persistence of ideals like brotherhood pointed to the existence of God. In her review of the work for the *Westminster*, Marian had praised Maurice's conception of the Jewish nation and the man Jesus "not as exceptional cases in the world's history, but as types of the normal relations to God"; the implication of this conception was that Christian comfort must extend to all humanity, whatever their faith. But in the course of his argument, Maurice unwittingly suggested that the Victorian family is organized by forces whose power comes not from above, but from below:

> Friendships, sadly and continually interrupted, suggest the belief of an unalterable friendship. Every brother awakens the hope of a love stronger than any affinity in nature; and disappoints it. Every father demands a love, and reverence, and obedience, which we know is his due, and which something in him as well prevents us from paying. . . . Men have asked, "Are all these delusions? Is this goodness we have dreamed of all a dream? this Truth a fiction of ours? Is there no Brother, no Father *beneath* those, who have taught us to believe there must be such?"[22]

In passing, Maurice locates the truth not above the relation of brother to brother or father to son, in some divine sphere, but beneath such family relations, suggested by them but hidden from view. Among mid-century philosophers of the family, only Marx would see that determining the "analytic fact" of Christianity's anthropological significance, as Feuerbach had, was only a first step towards a critique of a nominally Christian society whose religious practice was now centered on the bourgeois family: "[A]fter the earthly family is discovered to be the secret of the holy family, the former must then itself be criticized in theory and revolutionized in practice."[23] Engels's *The Origin of Family, Private Property, and State* would be one form of the critique Marx had in mind; psychoanalysis, another.

Throughout the summer of 1856, as she confided to her journal that she did "not ever remember ever feeling so strong in mind and body as I feel at this moment" (*J* 62), Marian Evans continued to be denied public work. But this condition seems only to have stimulated her productivity, with her work for the *Westminster* including not only her usual expert summary of art and literature, but also the brilliant essay on Riehl. As evidence for the interpenetration of leisure and vocation, the journals kept at this time are especially noteworthy.[24] Alternating between zealous work and mindful recreation, lugging a hamper full of specimen jars from London only to have "the satisfaction of discovering [them] to be quite unfit for our purpose," Marian Evans seems both caught in and amused by her taste for self-chastening recreation. Having previously mused on "the wide difference there is between having eyes and seeing" (*J* 219), and "climbing about for two hours without seeing one anemone," for example, the couple eventually found the creatures they were searching for, their "crescendo of delight" reaching a comically horrific "*fortissimo* when [Marian] for the first time saw the pale fawn tentacles of an Anthea Cereus viciously waving like little serpents" (*J* 265). Begun with Philip Gosse's *A Naturalist's Rambles on the Devon Coast* (1853), and extended in Lewes's own *Seaside Studies*, begun in *Maga* that August, the craze for Ilfracombe's tidal pools soon stripped them bare. By 1865, Gosse himself was bewailing that "such has been the invasion of the shore by crinoline and collecting jars, that you may search all the likely and promising rocks within reach of Torquay, . . . and come home with an empty jar and an aching heart, all being now swept as clean as the palm of your hand."[25]

As we shall see, an amalgam of morally instructive comedy and Medusa-haunted horror would resurface in "Janet's Repentance," written the following summer. For now, however, "between work and zoology and bodily ailments," as she wrote to Charles Bray in early June, "my time has been full to overflowing" (*L* 2: 252). Indeed, Marian

Evans's career as a critic ended, and George Eliot's as a novelist began, in a long-postponed essay on the poet Edward Young, finally completed in December 1856. The first half of this final *Westminster* article surveys Young's long search for preferment, culminating around 1730–1 (at the age of fifty) in a Hertfordshire living and a prosperous marriage; the long poem *Night Thoughts*, an early favorite of hers, made him a literary success. Now, however, Young seemed stranded within "the same narrow circle of thoughts, the same love of abstractions, the same telescopic view of human thoughts, the same appetency towards antithetic apothegm and rhapsodic climax" – faults which add up to his "*radical insincerity as a poetic artist,*" just as his biography suggests his ignorance of "virtue or religion as it really exists" in "ordinary life" (*E* 186, 194, 199). Where Young failed, perhaps George Eliot would succeed: moving between the intellectual and popular sectors of the literary field, between *Westminster* other-worldliness and Dickensian this-worldliness, working out her vocation in the culture of modernity.

The horror of incarnate history

Like the essay on Riehl in which she had first imagined the category of "incarnate history," "Janet's Repentance" casts industrial capitalism and Protestantism as the two principal markers of modernity.[26] At the narrative present, the town of Milby boasts not only a "handsome" commuter station lit by "brilliant gas-light," but also an affluent rector "who keeps his own carriage," a church grown "by at least five hundred sittings," and a local school "conducted on reformed principles."[27] "Janet's Repentance" seems fundamentally involved in penetrating this surface of technological, moral, and ideological improvement, narrating as it does the old lawyer Dempster's wifebeating, alcoholism, and final delirium on one hand, and the young curate Tryan's past sins, new passion, and consumptive death on the other. But there are also suggestions that reading this tale will not be easy: the "drowsy London traveller" who can see only "sober papas and husbands" as he glides out of Milby station is obviously meant to warn Marian Evans's urban readers not to get drowsy themselves (196).

In contrast to the brilliant but opaque surfaces of 1857, one can read scandal on the face of 1832 Milby. From the story's opening exclamation ("'No!'"), Dempster is in the grip of an indiscriminate and negative fury, unleashed not only on Tryan, who is agitating for Sunday evening lectures open to the entire town, but on anyone who comes into his path, and especially on his wife Janet. Dempster is the leader of the male, anti-Tryanite camp, set out in the tavern scene of the first chapter; the third shows Mr. Tryan's female supporters gathered at the house of an older woman bearing the Wordsworthian name of Linnet, whose daughter is among the converted. Both groups are meeting to discuss the tactics they should adopt on the matter of Mr. Tryan's proposed lectures, with the men nearly unanimously opposed to him and his plan, the women unanimously in favor. In the fourth chapter, these gendered spheres are brought together, with violent results: Dempster moves from the Red Lion, where he has just delivered an anti-Tryanite speech, to his house, where we first see him beat Janet. And there is much evidence, in addition to the structure of this first number of "Janet's Repentance," to suggest that Tryan and Dempster are doubled representatives of feminized good and masculinized evil.[28] Dempster's devilish nature is clearest to those at a distance, whether of age or of class, from the ideological struggles Evangelicalism has brought to Milby, such as Mrs. Linnet and Boots the tapboy (213, 223). Tryan's mundane Passion begins when he "shed[s] hot tears" alone in his study on returning from the garden house of his supporter, Mr. Jerome, as Christ shed tears alone on the Mount of Olives; reaches its public climax with his entrance into Milby on a Sunday to face a hostile mob; and ends with his death at thirty-three, the age at which Jesus died (248, 251, 217).

It seems obvious at first that Dempster has no reasonable grounds for objecting to Tryan's Sunday evening lectures. He attacks the Sunday evening lectures on the absurd ground of protecting "our young people" from being "demoralized and corrupted by the temptations of vice notoriously connected" with them, and casts Tryan as a kind of incubus "who sneaks into our homes perverting the faith of our wives and daughters" (222).[29] But if Dempster is wrong about Tryan's present comportment, he is not so far off about this evangelical's shameful past. The son of a politician, Tryan seduced "a lovely girl of seventeen" named Lucy while at college, abandoned her, and months later just happened to see her expire on Gower Street, "with paint on her cheeks," a suicide by poison. After this "hideous" episode, "only one thing could make life tolerable" to Tryan: "to spend all the rest of it in trying to save others from the ruin [he] had brought on one" (289–90).

Readers have always criticized this Lucy story as hackneyed; Lewes himself described it as such (*L* 2: 378).[30] But its very starkness, the way in which its conventionality circumscribes speculation or interpretation, suggests an important contrast. While the tale's obvious function is to explain Tryan's extraordinary selflessness, there is no similarly simple explanation for Dempster's equally extraordinary rage. We know that Dempster had "known caresses" as "the first born darling son of a fair little mother" (233–4), but is now "callous in worldliness, fevered by sensuality, enslaved by chance impulses" (237). But it is entirely uncertain how maternal affection has been transformed into filial depravity; there is no indication, for example, that Dempster has been manifesting this "sensuality" in the kind of illicit sexual activity attributed to the lawyer Wakem in *The Mill on the Floss*.[31] Why has Dempster made a habit of beating his wife, who reports later that "I loved my husband very dearly when we were married, and I meant to make him happy – I wanted nothing else" (286)? Only a few readers have noted this absence of explanation for Dempster's "case"; none has accounted for it.[32]

The history of the Dempster marriage survives in the town's gossip, the linguistic form memory takes in those "small communities in which everyone is acquainted with everyone else," and a persistent source of revelation in George Eliot's fiction.[33] Mrs. Pettifer remembers Dempster as the "cleverest man in Milby," one of the few young men "fit to talk to Janet," who was "the handsomest bride that ever came out of Milby church" (214–15); Mr. Jerome, the honorable representative of "Old Dissent" who pledges his assistance to Tryan in chapter 8, can still picture the two: "'I think I see 'em fifteen year ago – as happy a young couple as iver was'" (303). But the most interesting speculation comes from the member of the older generation closest to the pair: Mrs. Dempster, who lives with her son and daughter-in-law. As she muses about Janet's "want of housekeeping skill and exactness," she wonders: "'[W]hat use is it for a woman to be loving, and making a fuss with her husband, if she doesn't take care and keep his home just as he likes it . . .? That was what I did when I was a wife, though I didn't make half so much fuss about loving my husband'" (267). Having earlier suggested that her son needed the "right woman – a meek woman like herself, who would have borne him children, and been a deft, orderly housekeeper" (234), Mrs. Dempster now returns to the idea, making it the *coup de grâce* of Janet's failures: "'Then, Janet had no children.'" The narrator's response comes in a rush, after the first ellipsis in Marian Evans's fiction:

> . . . Ah! there Mammy Dempster had touched a true spring, *not perhaps of her son's cruelty*, but of half Janet's misery. If she had had babes to rock to sleep – little ones to kneel in their night dress and say their prayers at her knees – sweet boys and girls to put their young

> arms round her neck and kiss away her tears, *her poor hungry heart would have been fed with strong love,* and might never have needed that fiery poison to still its cravings. Mighty is the force of motherhood! says the great tragic poet to us across the ages, finding, as usual, the simplest words for the sublimest fact[.] (267–8, ellipsis in original, emphasis added)

After this effusion, however, the equivocation as to whether Janet's childlessness is the cause of Dempster's violence is immediately eliminated: "[D]o not believe that it was anything either present or wanting in poor Janet that formed the motive of her husband's cruelty. Cruelty, like every other vice, requires no motive outside itself – it only requires opportunity" (268).

In the face of the narrator's imperatives "not to believe" Mrs. Dempster's suspicions, "not to suppose" that Dempster is drinking to escape something, we are only left with both the question, and the denial of any answer to that question, stated more forcefully than ever: Dempster's rage is caused by something which remains unnarratable.

The only other substantial source of information about Dempster's psyche is his deathbed case of the D.T.'s, during which his unconscious mind first imagines Janet as a murderous Medusa, her black hair and white arms dragging him down into watery depths, and then casts Tryan as both predator and prey:

> . . . "I'll hunt you down like a hare . . . prove it . . . *prove that I was tampered with* . . . prove that I took the money . . . prove it . . . you can prove nothing . . . you damned psalm-singing maggots! I'll make a fire under you, and smoke off the whole pack of you . . . I'll sweep you up . . . I'll grind you to powder . . . small powder . . . (here his voice dropt to a low tone of shuddering disgust) . . . powder on the bed-clothes . . . running about . . . black lice . . . they are coming in swarms . . . Janet! come and take them away . . . curse you! why don't you come? Janet!" (308, emphasis added)

Though Dempster's attention has shifted to Tryan, the driving anxieties remain the same. In a swift inversion of harm threatened against others into harm accomplished against himself, and in the midst of his defiance over the misdemeanors which Mrs. Linnet suggested to us, Dempster imagines that he has become the victim of a "tampering," and then returns to his earlier fear of proliferating serpents, both white and black (maggots and lice, like Janet's arms and hair).[34] The delirium continues:

> "Not there, isn't she?" he went on in a defiant tone. "Why do you ask me where she is? I'll have every drop of yellow blood out of your veins if you come questioning me. Your blood is yellow . . . in your purse . . . running out of your purse . . . What! you're changing it into toads, are you? They're crawling . . . they're flying . . . they're flying about my head . . . the toads are flying about. Ostler! ostler! bring out my gig . . . bring it out, you lazy beast . . . ha! you'll follow me, will you? . . . you'll fly about my head . . . you've got fiery tongues . . . Ostler! curse you! why don't you come? Janet! come and take the toads away! . . . Janet!" (308)

The money which Dempster has drained from the purses of his clients never appears as a solid. Instead, it remains a yellow liquid, preserving its association with blood and yellow bile; "runs out" of a "purse" as urine may seem to run out of the vagina; and then spawns a brood of toads, a monstrous offspring. The fourth section of the delirium returns to the image of Janet as Medusa, while the fifth replays Dempster's final, fatal ride.[35]

We cannot say that Janet has had some kind of reproductive mishap, such as the miscarriage suffered by the virtuous Milly of "The Sad Fortunes of the Reverend Amos Barton."[36] But we can say, on the basis of his delirium's imagery, that Dempster *imagines* the physiology of female sexuality and reproduction in horrific terms – an act of imagination, moreover, for which there is no emplotted explanation, and on which George Eliot, despite Blackwood's objections, would not compromise.[37] Like older members of the community, Janet continues to remember a time when Dempster could participate in the active sexuality of their courtship and early marriage, "the days when they sat on the grass together, and he laid scarlet poppies on her black hair, and called her his gypsy queen" (311). But Janet herself suspects that her own "strong love" has called out Dempster's violence: "What had she ever done to him but love him too well – and believe in him too foolishly? He had no pity on her tender flesh; he could strike the soft neck he had once asked to kiss" (268). Such is the grim obverse of the Feuerbachian scenario: if fetishization and obsession, love and idealization, are two sets of names for the same process, then a violent and immoral marriage may operate according to the same rules of association and cathexis as a "religious" and "true" one.

If Dempster raves about Janet in terms which betray intense, densely encoded anxieties over matters of love and reproduction, and projects these anxieties into the struggle over Milby's religious practices, the male narrator likewise links the heroine of "incarnate history" to an entire range of psychosexual, theological, and political disenchantments. Immediately before Janet's first appearance, for example, the narrator recalls a "heretical" wish, made at his long-ago confirmation, that the "ceremony" marking the passage into adulthood be "confined to the girls" (*SCL* 227), just as Freud's later description of male panic analogized adult anxieties over questions of religious and political domination to some earlier experience of sexual difference. The boy feels anxious on discovering the difference between his body and a woman's, just as "[i]n later life grown men may experience similar panic, perhaps when the cry goes up that throne and altar are in danger."[38]

John Blackwood apparently felt enough of this male panic to suggest that "[s]ome allusion to the solemn and affecting sight that a confirmation ought to be" would surely "destroy the chance of any accusation of irreverence or wish to make the ceremony ridiculous" (*L* 2: 360). It is consistent with this reaction that Janet's leading characteristic is her capacity to produce an amalgam of desire and anxiety on the part of the story's own male narrator:

> [N]o other woman in Milby has those searching black eyes, that tall graceful unconstrained figure, set off by her simple muslin dress and black lace shawl . . . And, ah! – now she comes nearer – there are those sad lines about the mouth and eyes on which that sweet smile plays like sunbeams on the storm-beaten beauty of the full and ripened corn. (*SCL* 227–8)

Janet's beauty is represented in two related ways: her submission to the rules of appearance for a lawyer's wife, and her contact with male sexuality and violence. Her face as the synecdoche for her body, a sexualized "field" across which her "sweet speaking smile plays like sunbeams."

In the *Critique of Judgment*, Kant proposed that in sculpture, "the mere *expression* of ideas is the main intention," while architecture's purpose is "a certain *use* of the artistic object to which, as the condition, the aesthetic ideas are limited."[39] The representation of Janet follows these two Kantian steps: the naturalized "storm" of male violence brings her "beauty" to light, so that her body can be compared to a structure of the highest possible cultural value – "a glorious Greek temple, which, for all the loss it has suffered from time and barbarous hands, has gained a solemn history, and fills our imagination the more because it is incomplete to the sense" (272). Janet has become a sublime object here, a representation of historical process which discloses its own inadequacy as a totalizing symbol of that process.[40] But the narrator's reaction to her is not that transcendent ecstasy such as Mr. Pickwick's "might and glory" produced, but rather a vision of disenchantment, a waking nightmare: "In this artificial life of ours, it is not often we see a human face with all a heart's agony in it, uncontrolled by self-consciousness; when we do see it, it startles us as if we had suddenly waked into the real world of which this everyday one is but a puppet-show copy" (287). Even after Janet and Tryan have made contact, the two take on the stiffness of the religious icons for which they are meant to be substitutes: "She might have been taken for an image of passionate strength beaten and worn with conflict; and he for an image of the self-renouncing faith which has soothed that conflict into rest" (293).

To compensate for this failure of transcendence, a classic statement of incarnational humanism has already been made: "Blessed influence of one true loving human soul on another! Not calculable by algebra, not deducible by logic, but mysterious, effectual, mighty as the hidden process by which the tiny seed is quickened, and bursts forth into tall stem and broad leaf, and glowing tasseled flower" (293). Kant called this kind of sympathy "blind but indispensable," seeking to convert the affect of loss arising from a deployment of rationality on the problem of God into a new kind of gain associated with unconscious states.[41] And like Hegel's *Geist*, Marian Evans's "influence" aspires to be simultaneously synchronic and diachronic, apprehending the movement of history as it maintains a belief in its transcendent subject, the "blessed influence of one true loving human soul on another." The difficulty, however, is that putting Janet's story into prose is as sexualized a process as incarnating her body:

> Ideas are often poor ghosts; our sun-filled eyes cannot discern them; they pass athwart us in thin vapour, and cannot make themselves felt. But sometimes they are made flesh: they breathe upon us with warm breath, they touch us with soft responsive hands, they look at us with sad sincere eyes, and speak to us in appealing tones; they are clothed in a living human soul, with all its conflicts, its faith, and its love. Then their presence is a power, then they shake us like a passion, and we are drawn after them with gentle compulsion, as flame is drawn to flame. (293)

The writer's and reader's desire for the idea of repentance can be awakened only when it is represented in the "flesh" of language, with all the dangers of "passion," "compulsion," and "flame" suggested here.

What we have located, then, is a contradiction, visible both in the relation of Dempster and Tryan and in the narrator telling the tale of their conflict, between this story's overt and covert representations of bourgeois love. "Janet's Repentance" describes the Dempster marriage as replete with turmoil, irrationality, and violence, having their origins in male panic, and yet goes to extraordinary lengths to bury those origins in elaborate textual defenses. Likewise, it states the incarnational ideology of "blessed influence" even while associating that force with guilt, madness, and death. The aesthetic of incarnation constructed around Janet Dempster strains towards the raptures of the saint before collapsing into the shameful movements of the hysteric.

Disenchantment and its cure: *Silas Marner*

One is tempted to identify "Janet's Repentance" as a novella merely on the basis of its anomalous and intermediate length: significantly longer than either of the other two "scenes of clerical life"; but significantly shorter than *Adam Bede*, the novel which began as a fourth scene before John Blackwood's ambivalent response to "Janet's Repentance" brought the series to a close. As James Diedrick has explained, however, there is a more substantial basis for applying this generic term to intermediate-length works in English by a novelist who began her professional life translating Strauss and Feuerbach. Each of the shorter works of fiction she produced between 1858 and 1861 – "The Lifted Veil" (1859), "Brother Jacob" (1860, published 1874), and *Silas Marner* (1861) – is an experiment in the *Novelle* genre of German Romanticism, which from its origins in Goethe and Novalis had investigated extreme psychological states of the kind explored in the delirium scenes of "Janet's Repentance."[42]

This prose form was well suited for the exploration of George Eliot's ambivalent disposition and mediated position in the Victorian literary field. The stories collected as *Scenes of Clerical Life* had been written for a literary market organized in gender and class terms: as an early review of "Amos Barton" put it, their author "writes with an ease and aptitude, and a delightful mixture of humour and pathos, that it is refreshing to meet with in these days of filtered, ladylike sentiment and forced buffonery."[43] Lewes, Blackwood, Dickens, and others also spoke in terms of the *Scenes'* successfully transgendered quality, its combination of masculine "humour" and feminine "pathos" (*L2*: 269, 272, 423). The overdetermined representations of reproductive capacity of "Janet's Repentance," as well as the psychosexual panic of the work's male narrator, were written while Marian Evans continued to live as a woman and write as a man before finally abandoning her anonymity in 1859.

In the same way, the epigraph to "The Lifted Veil," written many years after that story's completion, made a plea for "completer manhood" long after George Eliot had ceased to be a man in all but name (*L* 5: 380). Latimer, its protagonist and narrator, sees and feels the future, and in particular his marriage to the serpentine Bertha Grant, a blonde ancestor of Rosamond Vincy, with horrifying specificity. Gillian Beer categorizes Latimer's pathology as "hyperaesthesia," "the particular disease of the Victorian consciousness," and an obvious precursor of Freudian conversion hysteria.[44] Permeated by the same symptoms as the narrator of "Janet's Repentance," and taken up in great part with the narration of his own pathology from its origins in a childhood episode of blindness, a common symptom of castration anxiety, Latimer's narrative also relates the emergence of Bertha's dark double in the form of one Mrs. Archer, the subject of the gruesome (and unsuccessful) experiment in revivification with which the story ends. The tale, which Marian called a "*jeu de melancholie*," unsettled John Blackwood enough to require suppression of its author's pseudonym in *Maga* for July 1859; not until 1874, in the Cabinet edition, did Eliot make her authorship public.

In 1968, U. C. Knoepflmacher showed this tale to be a summa of the Gothic literary and philosophical tradition George Eliot inherited from Mary Shelley. The feminist readings that followed emphasized the transgressive power of this tradition, even if the creator of Latimer failed to gain access to that power.[45] But it seems no less plausible, and significantly less speculative, to read both the timid narrator of "Janet's Repentance" and the raving one of "The Lifted Veil" as mediations of an accelerating and acute gender polarization after 1850, contributions to a complex mid-century debate on "manly nerves" only recently recovered for us.[46] Mark Micale has shown, for example, that although the long Hippocratic tradition of a feminine and feminizing hysteria persisted throughout the medical establishment, an entirely different strand of British scholarship, dating as far back as 1837, theorized hysterical disorders on a psychogenic and sex-neutral rather than somatic and female model.[47] The former was the majority view, of course, and the one to which the narrator of "Janet's Repentance" seems to subscribe when he diagnoses Janet Dempster as a woman in desperate need of the "strong love" of children. But George Eliot would have just such a diagnosis leveled against her: in memoirs published in 1930, the famous alienist James Crichton-Browne (1840–1938) delivered his opinion that "motherhood and the laughter of children of her own" might have kept "the demon" of Marian Evans's own depression at bay.[48] When a great part of the representational effort of "Janet's Repentance" is spent asking, rather than answering, where hysteria comes from and what it means, we can conclude that the work exists in the no-man's-land of a war over the meaning of gender for culture.

Apprehending this historical and ideological complexity is the complement to the interpretation of hysteria as a polysemic cultural phenomenon. As Christopher Lane has argued, even if some analogy must still be maintained between Freudian and materialist models of psychological and political repression, psychoanalysis, more than any other critical apparatus, allows both modern hysteric and modern novelist a large role in the formation and definition of sexual identity. As "the transitive element overriding men's and women's sexual asymmetry," fiction-making can thus play both repressive and liberatory roles in the socially adaptive work of culture[49] – just as we have read "Janet's Repentance" as an effort not only to sanctify Victorian modernity as (humanist) organic development and (evangelical) transcendent sacrifice, but also to gain insight into these processes of sanctification.

Another way of relating Lane's "Victorian asymmetry" to literary history is to recall the young Mary Ann Evans's favorite books. By 1857, more than fifty years had passed since the incarnational poet William Wordsworth and the evangelical politician William Wilberforce were themselves young.[50] Both of the works she loved best of all – Wordsworth's *Excursion* and Wilberforce's *Life* – cast male depression as a symbolic site where vocation is forged through suffering. The Prospectus to *The Excursion*, Wordsworth's best-known longer work before the posthumous publication of *The Prelude* in 1850, and a perennial favorite of the Leweses, casts this fragment of Wordsworth's "philosophical poem" in incarnational terms, a "spousal verse," whose subject is a "great consummation" between "individual Mind" and "external World." Its most memorable character, however, is the Solitary, a middle-aged man whose spiritual despondency has its origins in the French Revolution's failed premises of progress and enlightenment. Shortly before her death, Marian Lewes would add the Solitary's description of his wife's beautiful but reproachful face as a sight more horrifying than any antique Fury to the manuscript of Lewes's *Life of Goethe*; as we have seen, her early villain Dempster likewise reimagines his wife's face as a Medusa's head.[51] Psychological distress plays a similarly large role in Wilberforce's *Life*, written by his sons, published in 1838, and immediately devoured by the young Mary Ann. The central event of this first great Victorian biography is the terminus of Wilberforce's relatively fashionable and frivolous youth in the depression which struck him while traveling in 1785. To his family, the Wilberforce of the following year was a man morally improved and socially activated by the experience of suffering: though "[t]here were indeed no external symptoms to announce the change which had passed over him[,] . . . many silent intimations now bespoke the presence of higher motives than a mere desire of personal distinction."[52]

This cluster of associations has important implications for the gender categories "Janet's Repentance" is so concerned with reproducing and repressing, as it does for *Silas Marner*, the last *Novelle* George Eliot would write. As James Eli Adams has explained, high and late Victorian culture would repudiate the kind of turmoil Wordsworth portrayed and Wilberforce experienced by branding it as deviance from a nominally neutral but effectively gendered norm of self-discipline.[53] Only ten years after the publication of the last "scene of clerical life," for example, another late Victorian alienist, Henry Maudsley (1835–1918), could criticize his own father-in-law John Conolly (1794–1866), the pioneer of the humane asylum movement, as "of a feminine type," "no gift of fortune to a man having to meet the adverse circumstances and pressing occasions of a tumultuous life."[54] And *Silas Marner*, George Eliot's last *Novelle*, begins at the same intersections of rationalization and its opposite: sociological critique and Protestant fervor, psychological case-history and domestic ideology.

Silas Marner continues to grapple with the objective realities and subjective effects of modernization, and to mediate those disenchanted effects by symbolic means. Just as Schiller's modern worker is tormented by "the monotonous sound of the wheel that he turns," "never develop[ing] the harmony of his being," George Eliot's account of Silas working at his loom likewise broadens into sociological explanation: "He seemed to weave, like the spider, from pure impulse, without reflection. Every man's work, pursued steadily, tends in this way to become an end in itself, and so to bridge over the loveless chasms of his life" (*SM* 64). The translation of this broadly sociological significance into personal pathology begins with the symbolization of Silas's alienation in the form of his cataleptic fits, or "chasms of consciousness," as the same passage calls them – the emplotted form of Silas's impoverished working and emotional life, its distance from the satisfactions of traditional community.[55] But like those of Dempster's rage and violence, the origins of Silas's isolation have been neglected, a condition reinforced by longstanding critical hostility to the centrality of his "cataleptic" fits in the work's plot.[56]

As we have learned in the opening chapter, Silas was originally banished from his Calvinist religious community, Lantern Yard, as the result of treachery by his childhood friend, William Dane. The adolescent Silas is feminized in similar terms to those Henry Maudsley would use to describe his oversensitive father-in-law: just as John Conolly was not tough enough to meet the "adverse circumstances of a pressing and tumultuous life," Silas possesses "one of those impressible self-doubting natures which, at an inexperienced age, admire imperativeness and lean on contradiction." This nature, expressed physiologically in Silas's "defenceless, deer-like gaze," apparently found its master in William Dane; indeed, the two became intimate to the extent that the Lantern Yard community referred to them as David and Jonathan (*SM* 57). But Silas was responsible for the event which brought a decisive change in this relationship:

> It had seemed to the unsuspecting Silas that the friendship had suffered no chill even from his formation of another attachment of a closer kind. For some months he had been engaged to a young servant-woman, waiting only for a little increase to their mutual savings in order to their marriage; and it was a great delight to him that Sarah did not object to William's occasional presence in their Sunday interviews. *It was at this point in their history that Silas' cataleptic fit occurred.* (*SM* 58, emphasis added)

Even after Silas has become engaged to the young woman Sarah, the "history" under narrative consideration is "their history" – that is, the history told in this and the previous paragraph of "the friendship" between Silas and William; and Silas's trances begin at the very moment a woman is introduced into this relation. Silas's "tendency to dissociation," and his resulting banishment from Lantern Yard, thus seem to be the result of his unconscious apprehension of the homosocial quality of his relation with his boyhood friend, with whom, as Silas twice says, he has been going "in and out" for "years" (60, 203) – the same kind of sexual etiology we have found behind Dempster's ferocious rage and Tryan's suicidal guilt in "Janet's Repentance."[57]

But the sexualization of Silas's alienation, its transformation from Schillerian disenchantment to Freudian hysteria, is only half of the story. Sally Shuttleworth has shown that the "catalepsy" affecting Silas was a medical ailment as vague to Victorian writers and readers as the related or conflated terms of hypochondriasis, hysteria, and neurasthenia.[58] There are, however, more exalted resonances to the term, sounded at the outset. According to the *Oxford English Dictionary*, the words "catalepsy" and "cataleptic" appeared in two different contexts from the seventeenth through the nineteenth centuries: medical usage, for which *Silas Marner* itself is the example; and philosophical usage, in which the adjective is defined as "pertaining to apprehension." One of the quotations which the *OED* provides as proof of this second, epistemological meaning is taken from G. H. Lewes's first great success, *A Biographical History of Philosophy* (1847–8), a work Marian Evans would obviously have known well. Lewes's treatment of Zeno and the Stoics features this second, philosophical usage of the term "cataleptic." The Stoics "held that there was one criterium of truth for man, and it was what they called the Cataleptic Phantasm." After glossing this term as "the Sensuous Apprehension," Lewes continues:

> Of true Phantasms, some are cataleptic (apprehensive), and others non-cataleptic. The latter are such as arise from disease or perturbation of the mind: as, for instance, the innumerable Phantasms produced in frenzy or hypochondria. *The cataleptic Phantasm is that which is impressed by any object which exists, which is a copy of that object, and can be produced by no other object.*[59]

Of these "true phantasms," the "cataleptic" is the species of representation which comes closest to the real. In it, existing objects are apprehended with such intensity as to transform the activity of apprehension into a sensation of moral certitude – whether in the unconscious, "delusional" case of the nineteenth-century cataleptic, whose body tells the symbolized "truth" of repressed experience, or in the hyperconscious, "philosophical" case of the Stoics, who "fought for morality, which they thought endangered" (1: 289).

The second term of Lewes's paradigm of moral apprehension is "phantasm," a term which, like "catalepsy," also appears at an early and critical point in the work – that is, the narrator's self-introduction:

> To them pain and mishap present a far wider range of possibilities than gladness and enjoyment: their imagination is almost barren of the images that feed desire and hope, but is all overgrown by recollections that are a perpetual pasture to fear. "Is there anything you

> can fancy that you would like to eat?" I once said to an old labouring man, who was in his last illness, and who had refused all the food his wife had offered him. "No," he answered, "I've never been used to nothing but common victual, and I can't eat that." *Experience had bred no fancies in him that could raise the phantasm of appetite.* (*SM* 53, emphasis added)

Such psychic phenomena call out a familiar ethic of sympathy: the narrator is in the position of trying to arouse a "phantasm" without which the starving man will die.

Silas's "catalepsy," then, is the symbol of an alienation which, having an apparent socioeconomic cause in the advent of textile technology, and bearing the heavy philosophical and moral freight I have just sketched out, has its emplotted origins in sexual anxiety – just as Janet Dempster's story began with her husband's hysterical denials, and just as the "blessed influence" between her and Tryan turns out to resemble nothing so much as sexual attraction. The emplotted significance of Silas's trances are one principal means by which the term "catalepsy" is overdetermined; the philosophical and sociological interest of the narrator in "cataleptic phantasms" is another, no less important one. As a pair exhibiting the familiar ambivalence between philosophical aspiration and modernist case-history, these overdeterminations prepare us for the symbolic work of the novella's denouement. When Silas finds a means of expressing his unconscious love, the results will have the kind of significance to which the theorist of "incarnate history" has long aspired.

Eppie's transformation of Silas's life involves transforming the diffuse incarnational rhetoric of "Janet's Repentance" into instructions on producing a loyal working class – the same sublime object Dickens had voiced a generation before when he devoted Sam Weller to "Pickwick and principle." The linkage between the economic survival of one generation and the biological survival of the next is clear from the start: how can Silas raise Eppie even when he is "forced to sit in the loom," as the wise Dolly puts it? She approves of Silas's idea to tie Eppie to it with a piece of cloth on the ground that girls are "easier persuaded to sit i' one place nor the lads" (181). But Eppie defeats Dolly's feminizing distinction when she cuts the cloth and strays away. When Silas finds her playing in the mud, the moment of the cure is at hand: "overcome with convulsive joy at finding his treasure again," he can "do nothing but snatch her up, and cover her with half-sobbing kisses" (187). What is vindicated here is child-rearing as a matter of "convulsive joy," a relation characterized by the physical expression of love denied Silas in earlier life.[60]

It is true that Silas is following a Wordsworthian example of trans-gendered affection here: the novel's epigraph from Wordsworth's "Michael" reminds us how the latter gave his son Luke "female service," "as with a woman's gentle hand" (ll. 152, 158), just as Silas makes his hut a "soft nest" for Eppie, "lined with downy patience" (189). But George Eliot's departure from Wordsworth is as significant as this similarity. The old Michael loses his son Luke forever by sending him away to work in the city – a loss available to us only through the mediation of the poet, who knows the meaning of the unfinished sheepfold with which the narration of Michael's tale begins. By contrast, Silas's child decides to remain with her father, repudiating her biological father Godfrey Cass's offer of social and economic betterment: "I wasn't brought up to be a lady, and I can't turn my mind to it. I like the working folks, and their victuals, and their ways. And," she ended passionately, "I'm promised to marry a working man, as 'll live with father, and help me to take care of him" (*SM* 234).

With this symbolic result in mind, we are in a better position to understand the sensations of pleasure and ease which accompanied the conception and composition of *Silas Marner*. The peasant introduced at the narrator's first appearance was used only to "common victual," and thus had "no fancies in him that could raise the phantasm of appetite"; likewise, Eppie's final word on the matter of her adoption is that she can eat only the "victuals" of "working folks." Silas has succeeded in cathecting his "convulsive" affection, which took longstanding pathological form in his cataleptic trances and money fetishism, to Eppie; the result is the latter's own psychology, impervious not only to persuasion or bribery, but even to ambition. In this broadly sociological and fundamentally conservative result, *Silas Marner* is a triumphant coda to both the literary and philosophical tradition of "The Lifted Veil" and the humanist religion of "Janet's Repentance."

One way to conclude is to admit that George Eliot's capacity for observation, specification, and generalization defies paraphrase. Take this metaphor from Lyell's *Principles of Geology* (1830–3), for example, with which she organizes the contents of her own mind at the age of twenty:

> I have lately led so unsettled a life and have been so desultory in my employments, that my mind, never of the most highly organized genus, is more than usually chaotic, or rather it is like a stratum of

> conglomerated fragments that shews here a jaw and rib of some ponderous quadruped, there a delicate alto-relievo of some fernlike plant, tiny shells, and mysterious nondescripts, encrusted and united with some unvaried and uninteresting but useful stone. My mind presents just such an assemblage of disjointed specimens of history, ancient and modern, scraps of poetry picked up from Shakspeare, Cowper, Wordsworth, and Milton, newspaper topics, morsels of Addison and Bacon, Latin verbs, geometry entomology and chemistry, reviews and metaphysics, all arrested and petrified and smothered by the fast thickening every day accession of actual events, relative anxieties, and household cares and vexations. (*L* 1: 29)[61]

But with this astonishing and precocious mindfulness comes the need to escape from it, as in a letter written to the same Maria Lewis a few months later:

> [W]hen I had been [at the dance] some time the conviction that I was not in a situation to maintain the *Protestant* character of the true Christian, together with the oppressive noise that formed the accompaniment to the dancing, the sole amusement, produced first headache and then that most unwretched and unpitied of afflictions, hysteria, so that I regularly disgraced myself. (*L* 1: 41)

To forever "maintain" the forces of repression, to continue to "protest" against enjoyment, is not yet possible, particularly in a situation where dancing is "the sole amusement"; and the result is a mixed denial of and submission to desire, a form of enjoyment which, while "disgraced," has its own secret order as well.

In the next European generation, after an equally long apprenticeship as well as a nervous breakdown from which he never fully recovered, Max Weber would also devote his maturity to the study of culture as a repository of oppositions between moral, economic, and asthetic purposes.[62] Perhaps George Eliot never became so disenchanted as to believe, with Weber, that "only within the smallest and most intimate circles, in personal situations, in *pianissimo*," could sympathy, that which "corresponds to the prophetic *pneuma*, which in former times swept through the great communities like a firebrand, welding them together," be possible;[63] or perhaps, on the other hand, *Middlemarch* is one long testimony to such a belief. In any case, the sociological novelist, recognizing the intractable conflict between means and ends in a disenchanted modernity, and continuing to write from, not beyond, the personal and ideological conflicts she had lived, made a choice: to "set to work and meet the "demands of the day,' in human relations as well as in our vocation," acts "plain and simple, if each finds and obeys the demon who holds the fibers of his very life."[64] From such a choice there could be no liberating progress. Intimations of disease and derangement would haunt both professional accomplishments and personal comforts, reaching a puzzling coda in her second marriage, decline, and death.[65] Vocation and guilt, responsibility and horror, animate her work with modernity's apparently inhuman energy. For us, perhaps, the challenge should be to move beyond a mere appreciation of its complex movements, beyond even an explanation of its origins and features, to find terms as charged and as motivating for ourselves as George Eliot's seem to have been for her.[66]

5
The Production of Belief: the Serial, *Middlemarch*

Why should one expect the truth to be consoling?

George Eliot to Edith Simcox[1]

Though the novelist Edward Bulwer-Lytton and the publisher John Blackwood had discussed the idea more than two decades before, *Middlemarch* was the first Victorian serial novel to be published in eight half-volumes, or "books," priced at 5*s*., issued bimonthly from November 1871 to December 1872.[2] It is possible that George Henry Lewes got the idea from Victor Hugo's 1862 half-volume sale of *Les Misérables*; what is certain is that *Middlemarch* marked one in a series of attempts by the Leweses and Blackwood to escape the power of Mudie's and other lending libraries, which were by 1871 exacting large discounts on large orders. The potential benefits of half-volume bimonthly publication were numerous: freedom from the pressures of the monthly norm dating from the onset of *Pickwick Papers* in 1836; the opportunity for end-page advertising; a greater chance of obtaining reviews of each part; and thus an accelerating sale to the appearance of the work in its final, four-volume form (*L* 5: 146, 179–80).[3] The success of the experiment was not immediately obvious, however. At the outset of his year-long series of reviews in the *Spectator*, for example, R. H. Hutton expressed surprise that George Eliot could prosper writing novels in which painful enlightenment so apparently outweighed any pleasurable kind: "The ground-note of dissatisfaction, of pain, runs through all its melody. On your wedding day, toothache is the governing thought. . . . No doubt life is like that, but how one sighs sometimes that the great novelists and dramatic poets of our day would give us a little more of the ideal."[4]

As a number of readers have noted, a large part of this novel's symbolic effort is spent describing the "disaggregation" of Victorian culture from other persistent or emergent nineteenth-century discourses, including theology, law, economics, and social theory: those who fail to accept the consequences of an ongoing division of cultural labor will produce only their own keys to all mythologies.[5] But even as readers absorb the history of Lydgate's intellectual development in chapters 15 and 16, for example, the suggestion is made that insight itself, rather than the objects glimpsed by means of it, should now be the object of their desire – "the imagination that reveals subtle actions inaccessible by any sort of lens, but tracked in that outer darkness through long pathways of necessary sequence by the inward light which is the last refinement of Energy, capable of bathing even the ethereal atoms in its ideally illuminated space" (*M* 16: 161–2). So great a definitional effort already suggests that, by 1870, George Eliot's vocation as a messenger of disaggregation, one who emphasizes negative arguments over positive prescriptions, also required some compensatory sacralization of a highly rationalized but still imaginative intellect, some consecration of this "instrument by which the moral mission of culture is propagated" as "ideally illuminated space."[6]

The great historical paradox, to which *Middlemarch* does better justice than any other Victorian novel, is that one principal means of obtaining assent to the very modernity responsible for desacralization was to infuse literary culture with a moral authority it had never before been asked to assume. This mode of modernization predates the nineteenth century, of course. Fredric Jameson has characterized the seventeenth-century Puritanism so fascinating to Max Weber as a "vanishing mediator" between traditional and modern cultures, an ideology which temporarily intensified the sacral qualities of everyday life so as to infuse it with a significance traditionally reserved to religion. Hans Blumenberg makes the same kind of argument when he characterizes Marxian utopianism as a leading example of the "reoccupation" of religious culture's now-vacant "position," long "consecrated for consciousness," by rationalized forms of thought: the project of enlightenment proceeds in a rhetoric inherited from Christian theology.

In both of these cases, a modernizing ideology accomplishes "not the secularization of eschatology but rather secularization *by* eschatology": by means of each, modernization is accomplished "not by making life less religious, but by making it *more* so," after which time the particular ideology "disappears from the historical scene."[7] Dickens's public readings, continuing through the 1860s, were another high Victorian cultural practice attempting this kind of work. As we have seen in chapter 1, the young Dickens had constructed his emergent serial novel around characters like Mr. Pickwick and Nancy, who embodied the perennial Christian values of incarnate benevolence and atoning sacrifice; fashionable audiences of 1869 were still being brought down from the horrors of Nancy's murder via the Pickwickian party at Bob Sawyer's or the conversion of Scrooge to benevolence – as profitable a mix of sentiment and gore in these latter days as it had been in 1837. Appearing in part in the *Cornhill* of July and October, 1871, and in book form in 1873, finally, Matthew Arnold's *Literature and Dogma* would argue that culture's capacity to link emotion and morality made it religion's best hope in a rationalized society.[8]

George Eliot concerned herself with similar tasks in the years just after Dickens's death in 1870. Even within the conventions of the Victorian multiplot novel, the plot of *Middlemarch* abstains from adjusting the economic positions of its characters: the pages of what N. N. Feltes would call its commodity-text remain substantially innocent of the movements of capital.[9] The Leweses' correspondence with John Blackwood, on the other hand, features two capitalist enterprises dealing at a friendly arm's length, weighing risk frankly and prudently, and finally acting to produce an innovative commodity-book – the bimonthly serial novel – in pursuit of profit.[10] But both the literary work *Middlemarch* and the public figure identified with that work's narrator offer certain compensations for this set of abstentions and engagements. Like the humanist social theory of the period, the capital plot of *Middlemarch* struggles to divest itself of an inherited evangelical economics but maintains many of the latter's fundamental assumptions. As important to our understanding of this novel's mediation of religious belief and literary commodification is the response of its evangelical and humanist readers. Whatever their other differences, these readers were unanimous in their praise of those moments where the text worked hardest at Jameson's "mediation" and Blumenberg's "reoccupation." Modern discussions of *Middlemarch* often reproduce this response, suggesting that its readers still struggle to separate moral message from symbolic work.[11]

As George Eliot constructed the most thoroughly mediated novel of the age of Dickens, the author herself began to assume a new and increasingly idealized cultural position. Her refusal to imagine certain kinds of social action correlates to a series of changes in her relations with both friends and readers in the years just after the Second Reform Act.[12] In the early 1870s, George Eliot assumed the role of novelist as "Great Teacher," as a West End clergyman named her in late 1872.[13] The text of *Middlemarch*, of course, intensifies an ideologeme of mindful effort, as in the comment on Lydgate's imagination, such that the novelist may be said to have accomplished some "immediate good" in the consciousnesses of her readers even as the male intellectuals she has created – the historian Casaubon, the scientist Lydgate, and even the politician Will Ladislaw – all fail.[14] But if George Eliot had a more satisfying financial success with *Middlemarch* than any of her characters did in their own vocations, she seemed also to require a more immediate form of compensation than ever before in her relationships with her fans, and in particular the feminist, labor activist, and writer Edith Simcox. This chapter explores the tension between Eliot's literary and financial success and her apparent need for more than these provided. Perhaps because Eliot felt the contradiction between her serial novel's static treatment of capital and its innovative commodity form so acutely, she remains our preeminent novelist of sympathy, arisen from the tomb of Christian belief.

The politics of atonement and incarnation

If seventeenth-century Puritanism was grounded in the certainty of original sin, early nineteenth-century theology and economics was forced to settle for its probability, as in Bishop Butler's *The Analogy of Religion, Natural and Revealed, to the Constitution and the Course of Nature* (1736). Having gone through only ten editions between 1736 and 1800, Butler's treatise would warrant another twenty-nine before 1850, becoming a seminal theological and philosophical text for a generation of Victorian male intellectuals. At Oxford's Oriel College of the teens and twenties, Whately, Hampden, and Keble set the *Analogy* alongside Heraclitus and Aristotle in the Greats curriculum; its students eventually included Newman, Gladstone, and Matthew Arnold.[15] Newman found the Butlerian principle that "probability is the guide of life" at the core of his own lifelong conviction of the existence of God, as well as throughout his "master" Keble's *The Christian Year,* which sold an average of 10000 copies a year for fifty years after its publication in 1827.[16] The reading materials we find in Dorothea's boudoir at the moment of Casaubon's death are a jumble of these and other cultural inheritances, books "of various sorts," as the manuscript of the novel categorized them: Herodotus, whom she is reading under the eye of her university-trained husband; Pascal, the unorthodox "old favorite" introduced to us in the first paragraph of the novel; and, lest we think Dorothea's intellectual independence already accomplished, *The Christian Year* as well (48: 465).

Just as evangelical theologians attempted to prove original sin by analogy from the perceived moral disorder of early nineteenth-century social life, evangelical political economists argued that the convulsions of postwar capitalism were divergences from what should be a virtually static economic equilibrium. In his influential *On Political Economy* (1832), Thomas Chalmers cited the "clear and convincing expositions of Malthus on the subject of population" on his way to concluding that a progressive division of labor constituted "no security" against either "continuous pressure" on wages or some "severe ultimate pressure, augmenting, perhaps, and becoming more intense and intolerable, with every approach that is made to the extreme limit of the country's resources."[17] Chalmers's economic model made out an implicit argument for the social relations Michael Mann has called "old regime liberalism," featuring a central government generally refusing to involve itself in intranational arrangements of wages, apprenticeships, and guilds, but vigorously defending its industries from foreign competition through the 1840s. This laissez-faire rule might give way only in exceptional cases such as child labor, which attracted legislative attention from Peel's Health and Morals of Apprentices Act of 1820 to the Whig creation of factory commissioners in 1833 and 1836 to the Tory limitations on working hours in the Factory Act of 1844.[18]

As late as the depression of 1836–7, however, Chalmersian political economists succeeded in convincing the old regime, whether Whig or Tory, that the dissemination of capital across class lines should remain a matter of personal conscience, to be enforced by Malthusian moral restraint – an idea both Mill and Marx would later ridicule. In sermons collected under the title *The Application of Christianity to the Commercial and Ordinary Affairs of Life* (1820), Chalmers held his audiences in sway by veering between two contradictory tenets of postwar evangelicalism: that "selfishness" could indeed be "a means of promoting honesty," as the subtitle of one sermon claimed; but that such honesty could be inculcated only under threat of retribution:

> [T]he preacher is not bringing down Christianity – he is only sending it abroad over the field of its legitimate operation, when he goes with it into your counting-houses, and there rebukes every selfish inclination that would carry you ever so little within the limits of fraudulency; when he enters into your chambers of agency, and there detects the character of falsehood, which lurks under all the plausibility of your multiplied and excessive charges. . . . He is not, by all this, vulgarizing religion, or giving it the hue and the character of

> earthliness. He is only asserting the might and the universality of its sole preeminence over man.[19]

The deal was that as long as Chalmers's bourgeois imagined himself under the eye of a wrathful God, his coins would avoid the fingers of a covetous State; the broader social bargain, that the misery of the bankrupt or pauper made a salutary propitiation for all national sin, and especially British greed. In the name of the poor's suffering at the hands of speculators, analogized to the atoning and redemptive suffering of Christ, Chalmers campaigned throughout his life against all nationalized forms of economic assistance, whether by old Poor Laws or new, traditional apprentice assistance or newfangled factory reform; instead, the traditional unit of local government, the parish, was to be restored to its ancient and communal glory, even in the new industrial cities.[20]

George Eliot's generation of intellectuals, coming of age after 1832, worked to articulate that kinder, gentler variant of Chalmersian theology and economics Boyd Hilton has named "incarnational" social thought: opposed to Atonement ideology, but also sharing some fundamental assumptions with it.[21] High Victorian theologians like F. D. Maurice would redeploy Butlerian probability on behalf of not damnation but salvation: "God reveals His law to men in their consciences," thereby saving them from the necessity of punishment or humiliation. Whereas conscience had spoken to the older generation only of sin, Maurice heard in it a message of fatherly love epitomized not by the Atonement, but by the Incarnation, without which "it is impossible to know the Absolute and Invisible God as man needs to know Him."[22] J. Llewelyn Davies, rector of the fashionable Christ Church, Marylebone, likewise argued in 1871 that theology now owed a "debt" to the clarifying light of "secular influences": developments in religious freedom, democracy, political economy, and physical science all pointed towards the radically brotherly content of Jesus's teachings, with God's justice now conceived as "a living active harmony of intelligences and wills throughout his world."[23] The author of *Middlemarch* shared intellectual and social contexts with both men. Though George Eliot privately termed Maurice's *Theological Essays* "dim and foggy" in 1853, Maurice's sister Esther was calling on her long before the 1870s; the novelist called Maurice's letter in praise of *Romola* "the greatest, most generous tribute ever given to me in my life" (*L* 2: 125, 4: 101–2). Llewelyn Davies and his wife were close friends of the Leweses, often accompanying them over many years to Sunday afternoon concerts at St. James's Hall; their son's copy of Samuel Lawrence's 1860 portrait of George Eliot, now at Girton College, Cambridge, is reproduced on the cover of the 1985 Penguin edition of Gordon Haight's biography.[24]

The sentiments of this incarnational school also informed the life and work of John Stuart Mill, whose *Principles of Political Economy*, first published in 1848, was read with care by both Maurice and George Eliot.[25] According to the early draft of the *Autobiography*, Maurice played an important part in Mill's recovery from his breakdown of 1826–7. The former's German idealism, which Mill rightly called a species of "European reaction against the [British empiricist] philosophy of the eighteenth century," had helped "to build up [his] new fabric of thought." By the publication of *On Liberty* in 1859, the philosophical incarnationalism of Goethe and his disciple Maurice had taken its place as Mill's third stage of modern cultural development, after his nation's Reformation and his father's Enlightenment.[26]

As a whole, the *Principles* attempted to reconcile the two traditions of political economy with which Mill's famous education had begun: Ricardo's macroeconomic theory of surplus, in which a quantity of labor, objectively measured, produces a commodity which saves a subsequent user or purchaser from expending that labor, with resulting efficiencies amounting to economic growth; and Smith's microeconomic theory of competitive equilibrium, in which both wages and profits tend naturally, by the operation of the market's "invisible hand," to reach some optimal point. After the 1870s, these two schools of thought would split into the open antagonism of Marxist and neoclassical economics.[27] In the third quarter of the nineteenth century, however, Mill's compound of "hard-headed rules and utopian aspirations was just exactly the doctrine that Victorians of goodwill yearned for," effectively postponing any substantial developments in British economic theory until the 1880s.[28]

Chalmers had relied on morality, enforced by the fear of a Malthusian apocalypse, to chasten private greed and, in doing so, to limit the need for public redistribution. Mill argued that both Malthus's hypothesis and Chalmers's remedy were incorrect – the first an "unlucky attempt to give numerical precision to things which do not admit of it," and the second better accomplished by the publicity which would prevent fraud than by any "moral restraint in reference to the pursuit of gain" (*Works* 2: 353, 3: 571). Moreover, Mill believed, working-class sexual and economic prudence would increase in proportion to working-class wealth, on condition that the state provide a minimum in both education and subsistence sufficient to "extinguish extreme poverty for one whole generation": the affluence created by industrial modernity, in combination with the simple ethical premise that "human beings should help one another," together made "the amplest reason" for poor relief "as by *any* arrangement of society it can be made" (2: 374, 3: 960 [emphasis added]). But despite these dynamic conceptions of capital formation and governmental action, Mill's economic theory, like Chalmers's, had a nearly static equilibrium, or "stationary state," as its ideal destination, in which "there would be as much scope as ever for all kinds of mental culture, and moral and social progress." Finally, to the third (1852) and all subsequent editions, Mill added that "[p]rivate charity can give more to the more deserving" – an echo of the position Chalmers had long held (3: 756, 3: 962).[29]

The situation of Dorothea Brooke at the outset of *Middlemarch* is precisely that of being "shut out" from both evangelical and incarnational forms of social action (*M* 3: 28). In the first place, her own "ardent, theoretic and intellectually consequent" nature condemns the politics of Mary Ann Evans's provincial youth, and in particular its constricted life of "village charities, patronage of the humbler clergy, the perusal of [Mrs. Frances Elizabeth King's] 'Female Scripture Characters,' unfolding the private experience of Sara under the Old Dispensation, and Dorcas under the New, and the care of [a woman's] soul over her embroidery in her own boudoir" (*M* 3: 28). With her activities limited to ineffectual charity, bankrupt religion and empty domesticity, only divine intervention could save a woman of the gentry from a life of isolation and futility. Even by 1870, this sacrificial conception of female vocation was still worth spending sarcasm on, so that the best of her readers might have wondered, with Gillian Beer, whether times had really changed in forty years.[30]

When she chose the historical and geographical setting she did for her "study of provincial life," George Eliot also blocks Dorothea's access to the incarnational liberalism her creator shared with Maurice, Davies, and Mill. Her most important associations with schemes like Dorothea's would have been formed many years before, particularly by her contacts with Robert Owen and Harriet Martineau. In her early twenties, Marian Evans had met the manufacturer and utopian socialist Owen through Charles and Cara Bray; of course, the novel's series of allusions to utopian reformers, beginning with Dorothea's daydream of the spirit of the eighteenth-century pastor Oberlin passing over the neighborhood "to make the life of poverty beautiful," culminates in Will Ladislaw's flirtation with joining Owen's experimental community in New Harmony, Indiana (*M* 3: 31, 82: 790).[31]

George Eliot's relationship with Harriet Martineau was more intellectually and emotionally substantial, though often difficult. After their first meeting in January 1852, Marian Evans wrote that Martineau had been "very kind and cordial, but unhappily not able to stay long enough to dispel the repulsion excited by the *vulgarity* (I use the word in a moral sense) of her looks and gestures"; granting her "powers and industry," Marian "should be glad to think highly of her" (*L* 2: 4–5). Despite such doubts, Marian accepted invitations to visit her and the phrenologist George Combe and his wife that October – perhaps out of an obligation to humor one of the *Westminster*'s new contributors, but also needing to escape a brutul routine of anonymous reviewing, thankless editing, and the Strand flat, with "the light one might expect midway up a chimney" (*L* 8: 66).[32] In such circumstances, the Combes' comfortable house and soothing drives around Edinburgh were the sheerest relief; next "came the tonic in the shape of Harriet Martineau with her simple energetic life, her winter Lectures and her cordial interest in all human things" (*L* 2: 64–5). In the swirl of scandal that broke out around the Leweses' elopement to Germany in 1854, however, the same George Combe would lead the moral charge against the couple, even accusing Marian Evans of "morbid mental aberration" (*L* 8: 129); for her part, Martineau circulated a rumor, denied in writing by both the Leweses, that Marian had written her an offensive message before leaving for Germany (*L* 2: 177, 180; 8: 124).[33]

Nearly twenty years later, George Eliot first conceived of Dorothea's plan to build cottages on her uncle's estate – the kind of relief Mill argued must be accomplished by "any arrangement of society," whether private or public – and then ruled out its realization: as Sir James Chettam points out, such a plan is just "sinking money; that is why people object to it," since laborers "can never pay rent to make it answer" (*M* 3: 30). But Martineau had implemented just such a project by the time she met George Eliot. Not long after visiting the radical manufacturer W. R. Greg, whose *The Creed of Christendom* her brother James reviewed for the *Westminster* in the summer of 1851, preempting Marian's own review in the process, Martineau purchased a Lake District property in 1845, with new neighbors including the Wordsworths, Isabella Fenwick, and the Matthew Arnolds.[34] She soon began work on a housing scheme in which poor families would contribute to a common fund of subscribed capital. Fifteen cottages were eventually built, over the objections of virtually every vested interest in the neighborhood, from neighbors fearful of a rise in servant wages resulting from improved housing stock as well as her own agent in the purchase, who refused to allow a remeasurement of land because it might have antagonized the local parson.[35]

The capital plot of *Middlemarch* finally affirms this adverse verdict on all forms of poor relief, including the collaborative model of Martineau's Ambleside. An older and wiser Dorothea does offer her fortune to Lydgate's New Hospital, abandoned by Bulstrode in the course of his disgrace. But she is free to do so, and to be refused, because Chettam and Brooke have talked her out of it once and for all: "'I wished to raise money and pay it off gradually out of my income which I don't want, to buy land with and found a village which should be a school of industry; but Sir James and my uncle have convinced me that the risk would be too great'" (76: 754). Better, perhaps, to redirect Dorothea's vocation beyond specification: still aspiring as late as halfway through the novel to "work which would be directly beneficent[,] like the sunshine and the rain," her "full nature" will finally, in a last whisper of capital loss, "spen[d] itself in channels which [have] no great name upon the earth" (48: 466; 825).

If *Middlemarch* finds Dorothea's benevolent impulses impossible to implement, honest profitmaking cannot be imagined at all. Bulstrode's capital is, of course, the ill-gotten gain of his father-in-law's East London trade in stolen goods (61: 602–3), becoming the basis of his "sleeping" or silent partnership with Ned Plymdale, who in turn extracts fraudulent profits from both ends of his textile trade. "'[O]ne of those who suck the life out of the wretched handloom weavers in Tipton and Freshitt,'" as Mrs. Cadwallader calls him, Plymdale uses defective dyes both he and Bulstrode know to rot silk, and sells the adulterated fabric to feckless customers including Mr. Vincy, who manufactures furnishings including silk braids (*M* 36: 333). The only character who manages to create wealth without engaging in morally reprehensible activity is Caleb Garth. But as Alan Mintz has argued, Caleb is simultaneously the "least interesting" character in this disenchanted work, a "fading canvas in a gallery of arresting portraits," and the one producing its most vivid iconography of labor. With its "echoes of the great hammer where roof or keel were a-making, the signal-shouts of the workmen, the roar of the furnace, the thunder and plash of the engine," the "myriad-headed, myriad-handed" creature we would call unalienated labor – never involved in the transfer of money, always relying on the land and its products – is a patently "sublime" object, as this same passage twice claims (24: 246). Thus insulated from modernity, and like Janet Dempster's abused body, which "fills our imagination the more because it is incomplete to sense" (*JR* 282), Caleb's conception of exchange is a fetish marking a limit to his creator's imagination as well as his own: "it would be difficult to convey to those who had never heard him utter the word 'business,' the particular tone of fervid veneration, of religious regard, in which he wrapped it, as a consecrated symbol is wrapped in its gold-fringed linen."[36]

The generalization just made, however – that the symbolic systems of *Middlemarch* somehow forbid any substantial movement of capital, whether profitable or charitable – applies only to its text, and not at all to its circumstances of production. As Carol Martin has suggested, the Leweses' correspondence and negotiations with the publisher John Blackwood could serve as a model for the risk-taking Mill imagined to be the dynamo of economic growth, as well as the mutual benefits supposed to result from such risk-taking. Even as *Middlemarch* rejected the evangelical economics of Atonement, and failed, like other forms of incarnational social theory, to imagine any substantial alternative to this economics, it succeeded dramatically as an innovative commodity-form. What remains to be explained is the symbolic compensation made for this gap, both within and beyond the text of the work: that is, the reoccupation of the serial novelist's ethic of sympathy in cultural positions long associated with English Protestantism.

The poetics of reoccupation

Peter Mandler has characterized the late 1820s as a moment of uneven transition (exemplified in Grey's 1830 grab-bag government of Old Whig grandees, incipient Liberals, and Tory free-traders) between an aristocratic politics of incremental reform and a bourgeois one of nationally organized parties, candidates, and handlers.[37] George Eliot represents this transition with uncanny precision in the form of Mr. Brooke, the representative of the old regime and its reformist veneer. A combination of hidebound Tory squire and absent Whig grandee, he collects his rents personally, but ignores advances in agricultural practice and makes no improvements to his properties (*M* 38: 370). Like the historical group Mandler calls "moderate gentlemen," Brooke cannot survive the professionalization of post-aristocratic politics: spending his own money and promising to serve in only one Parliament, he loses badly in the end (51: 489, 495). And he is as lost in the fields of culture as on those of agriculture and politics. No one, least of all Will Ladislaw, could be "a sort of Burke with a leaven of Shelley" (51: 490), just as "severe classical nudities and smirking Renaissance-Correggiosities" make for absurd results at the Grange (9: 72).

Casaubon is the ecclesiastical counterpart to Brooke, but with even greater assets at his disposal: a sinecure including a "considerable mansion, with much land attached to it"; the responsibility only to preach the Sunday morning sermon, leaving less glamorous work to the curate; and a private income large "enough to give lustre to his piety" (*M* 5: 51, 1: 11). From this position of privilege, Casaubon faces modernity with a Chalmersian disposition consisting of two core beliefs: that humanity consists of the elect and the fallen, perhaps obscured in this world, but certainly revealed in the next (42: 411); and that concern for the material well-being of others must take second place to "zeal for the glory" of God (7: 63). More specifically, Casaubon conceives of sexual love as a fundamentally "immoderate passion." In an elaboration later deleted, George Eliot ascribed this conception of sexuality as part of "a general conspiracy of men," presumably including both Malthus and Chalmers (*M* 7: 62).[38] For Casaubon, even sexuality and repression are analogous to capital expenditure and preservation – as when he fantasizes that his long bachelorhood "had stored up for him a compound interest of enjoyment, and that large drafts on his affections would not fail to be honored" (*M* 10: 84).

Nicholas Bulstrode suffers from neither the dullness of Brooke nor the risk-aversion of Casaubon. But though he is capable of adaptation to changed external conditions, and "organic" to that extent, his repressed past, pathologized and reified in the villain Raffles, inexorably dominates and subverts present scruple.[39] Evangelical and incarnational readers alike consumed the Bulstrode/Raffles narrative as a moral parable easily separated from the rest of the work. The Methodist *London Quarterly Review*'s retrospective article of April 1873 concentrated almost exclusively on Bulstrode:

> We have dwelt more particularly on this man's character and career, not because he is one of the principal characters in the drama of Middlemarch life, regarded from an artistic point of view, but because all that relates to him is of vital interest to every serious-minded person, and is not so difficult to separate from the book as some portions of greater beauty and more artistic importance.[40]

At the opposite end of the spectrum of belief, Henry James would also emphasize the separability of the Bulstrode plot, its "artificial cast" and "melodramatic tinge," as "unfriendly to the richly natural coloring of the whole," and thus as evidence for his summary verdict of "indifferent" formal unity.[41]

There was unanimous praise, however, for the scene of reconciliation between Bulstrode and his wife Harriet, with the London correspondent for the *Nation* calling it "as pathetic as anything George Eliot has ever written," and James likewise taking the view that Harriet Bulstrode "emerges at the needful moment, under a few light strokes, into the happiest reality."[42] We get a clue as to the quality of this need towards the end of James's review, when he makes the generalization that Eliot, having "commissioned herself to be real, her native tendency being that of an idealist," has produced "a very fertilizing mixture" (359). This organic metaphor is more discreet than the one George Eliot deploys:

> The man whose prosperity she had shared through nearly half a life, and who had unvaryingly cherished her – now that punishment had befallen him it was not possible to her in any sense to forsake him. There is a forsaking which still sits at the same board and lies on the same couch with the forsaken soul, withering it the more by unloving proximity. She knew, when she locked her door, that she should unlock it ready to go down to her unhappy husband and *espouse his sorrow*, and say of his guilt, I will mourn and not reproach. (*M* 74: 740, emphasis added)

The text figures Harriet's compassion as both self-sacrifice and erotic consummation, in accordance with a humanism which held marriage, with its subordination of individual desire to social need, the archetype for an anthropocentric religious practice.[43] If the compassionate spouse is Feuerbach's gentle deity, Harriet's "espousal" of her husband's sorrow reaches for the status of humanist sacrament, a claim reinforced by other hints of ordination, confession, and absolution: "Her hands and eyes rest[ed] gently on him. . . . His confession was silent, and her promise of faithfulness was silent" (74: 741). The scene as a whole thus attempts to reoccupy two familiar cultural functions – the demand for a victim whose suffering symbolizes the regenerative effects of the Atonement, and the celebration of that sacrifice as consummation and renovation – with a gendered Feuerbachian humanism.[44] James's claim for the "happiest reality" of the Bulstrodes' reconciliation, then, shows just how successful George Eliot was at suffusing disenchanting analysis with Christian aura.

As the *Spectator* reviewer would have pointed out, however, such pleasurable moments are the exception to *Middlemarch*'s painful rule, laid out most extensively in the career of Tertius Lydgate. Unlike his benefactor Bulstrode or his uncle Sir Godwin, Lydgate occupies the dominated bourgeois fraction of the still-dominant aristocratic class, having the latest (French) medical training, but few (British) connections or cash. The defeat of his scientific ambitions follows from his failure to understand his ambiguous social position, as Mr. Farebrother explains it: either to "wear the harness and draw a good deal where your yoke-fellows pull you," or to "keep yourself independent" – and "[v]ery few men can do that" (*M* 17: 170). Though capable of growth, Lydgate cannot preserve his cosmopolitan independence because his consciousness is, like Bulstrode's, pathologically divided: "[T]hat distinction of mind which belonged to his intellectual ardor, did not penetrate his feeling and judgment about furniture, or women, or the desirability of its being known (without his telling) that he was better born than other country surgeons" (15: 147–8).[45] Lydgate fails to perceive similarities and differences *across* conventional categories – between his taste in furniture, as here, or the fashionable clothes he wears with "a certain natural affinity, without ever having to think about them" (27: 262), and his comparatively low status position as a provincial doctor of 1830; or between a mate who would assist in the realization of both vocation and ambition (such as Farebrother points out in Mary Garth), and one who, like Rosamond Vincy, serves principally as "adornment," Lydgate's leading criterion among "wifely functions" (17: 171, 11: 93).

Such characteristics amount to Lydgate's not-so-distinctive self, his habitus, doomed finally to be "packed by the gross" (15: 142).[46] Caught as he is in the contradiction between inherited disposition and current position, Lydgate underestimates the intractability of his wife's own *arriviste* habitus, with its premises of class ambition, consumption, and display.[47] Eliot symbolizes this incapacity in terms which negate Harriet Bulstrode's lively sympathy. When Lydgate fails to recognize Rosamond's tears as artifice, he joins her in a mindless chain of events – each lover acting "mechanically" or "instantaneously," like inorganic substances – until that "crystallizing" moment which "shook flirtation into love," and transformed private attraction into public engagement (*M* 31: 294). When she characterized Lydgate's moment of sexual choice as mere inorganic abreaction, George Eliot was joining a rising chorus of incarnational writers engaged in the refiguration of Hell as the consciousness of "opportunities neglected," or simply as "arrested growth," as the theologian Henry Jones put the matter in an 1891 volume entitled *Browning as a Philosophical and Religious Teacher.*[48] To this incarnational school, Lydgate's fall into love would be tantamount to "some terrific explosion," as James put it (357), because the willed personal development sacred to them is there figured as impossible.

Like both Bulstrode and Lydgate, Dorothea occupies a structurally ambiguous position in Middlemarch society, the resultant of the "mixed conditions" of class advantage and gender disadvantage: a solid annual income of £700, as we have seen, and a future interest by entail in another £3000; but also a "toy-box" education, distinctly inadequate by the standards of 1870s London (*M* 10: 84–5). This ambiguity bears a close resemblance to what Henry James called this character's "indefinable moral elevation," a "spiritual sweetness" powerful enough to suggest some comforting recuperation from unbelief, if not an outright conversion: "we believe in her as in a woman we might providentially meet some fine day when we should find ourselves doubting of the immortality of the soul" (357).[49]

D. A. Miller takes a large first step towards the historicization of this effect by pointing out how the climax of Dorothea's narrative collapses the verticalities of class: she rises from her climactic night on the floor at Lowick to see a peasant family through her picture-window, and thus to imagine a new life of "labour and endurance" (*M* 80: 777).[50] But this aura also seems to be an appropriately vague symbolization of an incarnational humanism sharing more than has been acknowledged with the evangelical theology and economics it replaced. As early as the 1830s, Edward Irving had decried Atonement "stock-jobbing" theology for its insistence "that God wanted punishment, and an infinite amount of it[,] which Christ gave for so many."[51] The statistician William Atkinson had argued in 1838, against Malthus and Chalmers, that capital would grow geometrically, while population would do so only arithmetically, with the corollary that aid to the poor must be considered "the great social law of the Christian faith" – the same position taken in print by Charles Bray as early as 1841.[52] The Christian Socialists of the 1870s would likewise eschew both liberal and Marxist descriptions of labor-power – the first assuming that legal freedom guaranteed the independence of labor, the second that this factitious freedom guaranteed its servitude – in favor of fantasies of urban melioration. Like Harriet Martineau at Ambleside, they hoped that a judicious application of capital would alleviate working-class suffering, thus discharging any responsibility for its causes.[53]

As I have been suggesting, the common cause of George Eliot's circle in the 1870s was to inscribe such fashionable ideas into the covenants of Victorian culture. Given that "[p]ower is descending into the hands of the many," as the Marylebone theologian and the Leweses' concert companion Llewelyn Davies argued in 1872, "the side of Our Master is the side of the weak."[54] Such sentiments, enabled by what Gladstone called the "intoxicating augmentation of wealth and power" of the propertied classes, were far more soothing to readers of the 1870s than the virulent evangelicalism of their parents and grandparents. Just as Dorothea's life will have an "incalculably diffusive effect" (825), Gladstone expressed the hope on the floor of Parliament in 1863 that such wealth and power, even when "entirely confined" to the propertied classes, surely "*must* be of *indirect* benefit to the labouring population."[55] Finding the proper symbolic expression for Dorothea's "moral elevation," then, seems to involve the translation of her charitable impulses into *intraclass* economic assistance: first shunted away from cottage-building into the hospital plan, itself left adrift by Bulstrode's disgrace; thwarted there not only by Lydgate's newfound convictions of his own inadequacy, but also by his vague sense that "the whole thing is too problematic"; and finally issuing in the form of a £1000 check payable to the needy doctor himself (*M* 76: 754, 756–9).

As in this case of inherited capital, which begins with praise for Dorothea's idealism and ends with the emplotment of class solidarity, the text's imagination of labor also resists a newer sympathy. As agricultural laborers threaten to attack railway surveyors, Caleb Garth intervenes:

> There was a striking mixture in him – which came from his having always been a hard-working man himself – of rigorous notions about workmen and practical indulgence towards them. To do a good day's work and do it well, he held to be part of their welfare, as it was the chief part of his own happiness; but he had a strong sense of fellowship with them. (*M* 56: 545)

What "strikes" the narrator here is precisely the discrepancy between Caleb's conception of work as an individual rather than communal enterprise, with its inevitable corollaries of working-class laziness and bourgeois "unproductive consumption," on the one hand, and his fantasy of "fellowship" with that working class on the other. John Stuart Mill provides us with a final example of these kinds of wishes and their inexorable limit. Though he had argued as early as 1851 that "nothing valid can be said against socialism in principle," and though Harriet Taylor had moved the seventh edition of the *Principles* significantly to the left of its predecessors, the 1871 edition nonetheless asserted

– as had every edition since 1848 – that laissez-faire "should be the general practice," with "the burthen of making out a strong case, not on those who resist, but on those who recommend, government interference."[56]

In short, the character whose moral beauty Henry James found irresistible was also the one whom George Eliot finally could not imagine spending money for the benefit of the laborers on her uncle's estate. The mysteries remaining include why the novelist's own moral beauty became marginally more public at just this time. In an emergent and still substantially private theater of sympathy, George Eliot exuded a new kind of attraction to a small group of reader-acolytes; at the same time, as the *Middlemarch* narrator delivered disenchantment in the century's first bimonthly serial, its readers gave thanks that they had been given time thus to learn the Great Teacher's lessons.

The theater of sympathy

In a *Century Magazine* commemorative profile of 1881, Frederic Myers began the circulation of one of the most familiar anecdotes about George Eliot: how, years before, in the Fellows' Garden of Trinity College, Cambridge, she had delivered the verdict that if "God" was "inconceivable" and "Immortality" likewise "unbelievable," the category "Duty" nonetheless remained "peremptory and absolute":

> I listened, and night fell; her grave, majestic countenance turned towards me like a sibyl's in the gloom; it was as though she withdrew from my grasp, one by one, the two scrolls of promise, and left me the third scroll only, awful with inevitable fates. . . . I seemed to be gazing, like Titus at Jerusalem, on vacant seats and empty halls, – on a sanctuary with no Presence to hallow it, and heaven left lonely of a God.[57]

The conquering rationalist can only gape at a plundered Holy of Holies; an aura of transcendence uncannily persists at the very pronouncement of its absence. In the same article, Myers also describes the scene at the Sunday afternoon salons gathering momentum from the late 1860s: the "thin hands that entwined themselves in their eagerness, the earnest figure that bowed forward to speak and hear, the deep gaze moving from one face to another with a grave appeal." Such physical signs seemed to Myers the "transparent symbols of a wise benignant soul," the manifestations of a will not only "to utter words which should remain as an active influence for good," but also to mark the limit beyond which even literary language must not go, to convey "the mystery of a world of feeling that *must remain untold*" (61, emphasis added).

In such public appearances, then, George Eliot seems to have compensated for her text's messages of disaggregation and disenchantment by projecting an extraordinary and charismatic sympathy. Such moments could occur at any gathering of the cultural elite – at a St. James's Hall concert of 1874, for example, when the Leweses, in the company of Llewelyn Davies and his wife Emily, allowed an elderly woman to kiss George Eliot's hand, only to be faced with a younger and more ardent woman who, after kissing the same apostolical hand, declared herself only "one of the many thousands" of such devotees (*L* 6: 27 n.3). We might call such scenes examples of Max Weber's "charisma of illumination," by which George Eliot sought not only to transmit a typically Christian "ethic of brotherliness," but also to forestall inquiries into the fashioned status of her own authority – inquiries which the leader is certain to condemn as "the misleading and deceptive surrogates which are given out as knowledge by the confused impressions of the senses and the empty abstractions of the intellect."[58] By late 1871, indeed, the Leweses had already begun a series of relationships which emphasize this charismatic side of George Eliot's emergent cultural authority.

One of the first of these was a correspondence with an admirer from the Scottish coast named Alexander Main, who lived with his mother, and spent entire days reading his favorite author aloud at the seashore. Having responded to her first thanks for his interest with a long outpouring on *Romola*, and continuing to show what Marian called "perfect insight" in a letter on the *Spanish Gypsy*, Main was duly rewarded with permission to publish a selection of her narratorial interventions eventually entitled *Wise, Witty and Tender Sayings in Prose and Verse*. Lewes' response to Main's proposal shows the former in a perpetual search for new markets:

> Some years ago a lady suggested that "texts" should be selected from the works to hang up in schoolrooms and railway waiting rooms in view of the banal and often preposterous bible texts, thus hung up and neglected. Your idea is a far more practical one . . . it would I think be both a treasure for readers, and a good speculation for the publisher. (*L* 5: 192–3)

The position in the field of literary production to which the Leweses' enterprise of sympathy aspired, it seems, is that previously occupied by the evangelical tract – "undeniable Sunday reading," as Blackwood's

PROPOSED ST. JAMES'S HALL, LONDON.—MR. OWEN JONES, ARCHITECT.

Figure 6: Proposed interior, St. James's Hall, designed by Owen Jones, site of concerts attended by the Leweses, late 1860s.

wife characterized the *Sayings* to a theological friend over lunch (*L* 5: 230).[59] The profitmaking motive in this enterprise was apparently too much for Marian, who handed over the plans and negotiations to her partner; Main's and Lewes's scheme was so transparent that even John Blackwood demurred at first. But when Marian again acknowledged Main's talent at maxim selection, Blackwood gave in to the fan he called "the Gusher" – the commodity in question being not oil but morality. *Wise, Witty and Tender Sayings,* which sold well enough to justify later editions including material from *Middlemarch* and *Daniel Deronda,* thus unveils the doctrine of sympathy in its most thoroughly commodified form since *A Christmas Carol.*[60]

Main was kept at arm's length after the publication of *Wise, Witty, and Tender Sayings;* more discreet admirers would gain more intimate access. In January 1873, Marian Lewes began a correspondence with and soon sent Main's volume along to another Scottish fan named Elma Stuart, whose first gift of a carved book-slide earned her the assurance that "there is no wealth now so precious to me (always excepting my husband's love) as the possession of a place in other minds through the writings which are the chief result of my life." The gift itself was taken as a fetish of the cult: "My eyes see much more of it, just as they see much more than marble where pious feet and lips have worn a mark of their pressure." It is again Lewes, always looking to shore up his partner's fragile ego, who confirmed in a letter of the same day that what gave the author "a thrill of exquisite pleasure" was not mere critical praise, but the more sublime expressions of "*sympathy*" – which he, like his partner, immediately distinguished from sexual love as an "acknowledgement of influence such as your letter so sweetly expresses" (*L* 5: 244–5, emphasis in original). The relationship would last until George Eliot's death in 1880. Elma contributed ever more personal gifts – a letter case, a purse, a shawl, slippers, belts, shirt patterns – and was rewarded with responses including a lock of hair, "anxious" admonitions from both "spiritual parents" to abandon her experiments with valerian and opium, and a blessing as "an angel of mercy" for taking in an orphaned dog. Only to Elma could Marian Lewes write a letter about underwear; and only Elma, of all the novelist's "spiritual daughters," would finally lie next to her idol in Highgate Cemetery (*L* 6: 84–66, 327–8).[61]

Weber suggests that any ethic of brotherliness, a category in which we must include George Eliot's sympathy, will always remain in a state of profound tension not only with economic, aesthetic, and intellectual activity, but with erotic activity as well.[62] Thus George Eliot's most talented and accomplished fan was the one whose relation to her would, as Weber leads us to expect, anatomize the psychosexual terms of charismatic influence. Edith J. Simcox was a shirt manufacturer, labor activist and periodical writer by the time she finally met George Eliot in late 1872. Her first book, *Natural Law, An Essay on Ethics*, was written as an act of devotion. Published with the Leweses' assistance in late 1877, the work's final sentence opposes Simcox's own erotic longings, which seemed to her "a hell of sensuality and hardened cruelty," with the "heaven of love and wisdom" occupied by the adored author, "a tender smile upon her gracious lips, and yearning prophecy in the melting depths of her unfathomable eyes."[63] From the vantage point of an idealized sympathy, it seems, Simcox's erotic obsession was from the first associated in her own mind with brutality, as Weber observes is often the case.[64]

George Eliot's lack of response to Simcox's passionate inscription of her "idolatrous love" at the end of her gift copy of *Natural Law* apparently forced the younger woman to begin the narrative, entitled *Autobiography of a Shirtmaker*, published in full only in 1998.[65] In it, we repeatedly glimpse Simcox in the coils of passion: making jokes about poisoning the shirts of Johnny Cross, George Eliot's husband-to-be; fondling and kissing the novelist's cheek, hands, and feet; acknowledging a recurrent and "conscious unsatisfied craving," both psychological and physical; and making "reckless love," seconded by Lewes, in avowals that "5 centuries hence there would be no one as adorable as" Marian, and that Simcox's only ambition was "to be allowed to lie silently at her feet as she pursued her occupations."[66] Only later, years after her idol's death, would Simcox understand why her "alternations from the tone of rapturous delighted adoration and devotion to still unsatisfied questioning" must have exasperated George Eliot: because Simcox's adoration was understood by both parties as an attack on heterosexual norms, to which the younger woman was repeatedly urged to conform; and because her questions broke the rule of naiveté by which she would have obtained the maximum of maternal love.[67]

As we have seen, one task for *Middlemarch* was the reoccupation of incarnational humanism in the cultural position of a religious practice. The apparent corollary to this work of reoccupation was the consecration of the novelist as a figure who, in the course of representing the failure of traditional transcendence most forcefully, herself becomes an object of worship. Emerging in this mostly private atmosphere of religious enthusiasm and sexual obsession, the conception of the Great Teacher mediated not only the nineteenth-century novelist's past and future roles – Dickensian entertainer and Jamesian connoisseur – but also the immense and irregular abandonment of Christianity that would include Nietzsche's completion, in 1873, of an essay concerning "truth and lies in an extramoral sense."[68]

The authority of the teacher depended, of course, on the size and influence of the audience reading her. Perhaps a more material innovation than the theatrical supplements just described was *Middlemarch*'s unprecedented, if transitory, commodity form: the bimonthly serial, which she judged afterwards to have been "of immense advantage to the book in deepening the impression it produces" (*L* 5: 297).[69] Reviewers had warned that a half-volume installment "must have great intrinsic merit" to maintain interest through the two months before the next.[70] But with the aid of strategic repackaging along the way – a first installment long enough to justify the separate reviews of each part following it; Book 2's last-minute inclusion of Dorothea's honeymoon troubles to satisfy that character's already vocal fans; Book 3's suspenseful appeal, in the form of the expiring Featherstone, to an inheritance dispute in the news; and accelerated publication of the later parts to allow the appearance of the four-volume whole in time for the Christmas gift season – *Middlemarch* succeeded in creating the taste by which it would be relished.[71]

Having begun by noting Book 1's many "happy turns of thought still more happily expressed," and then imagining page after page of such expressions, Blackwood's reading practice has become even more worshipful by the time Book 6 is complete: he is now "turning over the sheets of the Book, looking at the different points and wondering what is most perfect," and agreeing with his wife that it "requires the most undivided attention[;] I know that if a line or a word escapes me I find out as I read on that I have missed something and I turn back" (*L* 5: 148, 230, 293–4). A review from the *Examiner* shows this style of reading working through the market as early as the appearance of Book 3, in March 1872:

> We heard the other day of a husband and wife who find in each two-monthly instalment as much as they can read in the two months, two or three pages affording the text for a whole evening's thought and discussion, and we both understand and admire their state of mind. There is hardly a page of *Middlemarch* in which there is not enough condensed wisdom to furnish an hour's profitable reflection, and they who have time thus thoroughly to master the teacher's lessons are much to be envied.[72]

By December, Hutton's *Spectator* series was expressing the same views – "that no story gets so well apprehended, so completely mastered in all its aspects, as one which, written as a whole, is published in parts"; and that bimonthly publication, moreover, allowed its readers "those frequent discussions of the various Middlemarch personages by which *their exact social function and position have been fixed in our minds*."[73] Narrative and marketing form, in other words, correlates to sociological and ideological function. Dorothea's money circulates within its class of origin, buying Lydgate's future as a servant of the cosmopolitan elite; and final four-volume publication goes forward at the new and low price of 21*s*., made possible by "thinner paper and narrower margin," with the enterprising George Eliot, having rejected Blackwood's early offer of £6000 for the copyright, collecting a 40 percent royalty (*L* 5: 348).[74]

Such circumstances as these allow us to extend D. A. Miller's suggestion that "while the narrator's discourse is merely *in* the novel, the novelist's discourse quite simply *is* the novel"[75]: written text, marketed book, and performed author entwine the contradictions of disenchantment and sympathy, perspective and charisma, into a cultural form of unprecedented authority and durability. A traditional means of marking the emergence of this form is to indicate *Middlemarch*'s status as a cusp of literary history, as Henry James did. But we might also think of this "limit" to the "old-fashioned English novel" as its own "cosmos of more and more consciously grasped independent values which exist in their own right," providing an imaginary "*salvation* from the routines of everyday life, and especially from the increasing pressures of theoretical and practical rationalism."[76] Even if it was George Eliot's only bimonthly serial, even if its quadruple-decker format would soon die out, the sum of texts and circumstances we call *Middlemarch* has not yet exhausted its mediating power because neither the educated class it soothes, nor the modernity to which that class must perpetually reconcile itself, shows any sign of passing from the scene.[77]

Epilogue

The Sacred Monster: the Serial Novelists' Reenchantment

"Terror To The End"

Last stage direction in Dickens's prompt-copy of "Sikes and Nancy" (1869), with double underlines

On the evening of 29 April 1858, Charles Dickens stepped out on the stage of St. Martin's Hall, London, to cheers from his audience. Two weeks before, he had given readings in the same venue for the benefit of the Hospital for Sick Children. Now, he was making the first public appearance of his life undertaken for his own profit; on the program was *The Cricket on the Hearth*, the tale written for Christmas 1845.[1] Before starting, Dickens felt it necessary to say a few words about what he was doing, and why. Having given a number of charity readings in the past, undertaken "at some charge to [himself], both in time and money," and with "accumulating demands" for more of the same, he faced a decision "between now and then reading on my own account" and "not reading at all."

From the beginning, then, his decision to read for profit took place in a world where clocks and accounts were always running, with his talent and his life the things charged against. In public, that night, he made three justifications for his decision. The first was that a reading career could "involve no possible compromise of the credit and independence of literature" – a topic on which he and Thackeray had been jousting for more than a decade.[2] The second was that "in these times," which he considered so bleak that no functional democracy could hope to emerge from them, "whatever brings a public man and his public face to face, on terms of mutual confidence and respect, is a good thing"; and the third, really a restatement of the last, that it was his "great privilege and pride," as it was his "great responsibility," to continue this

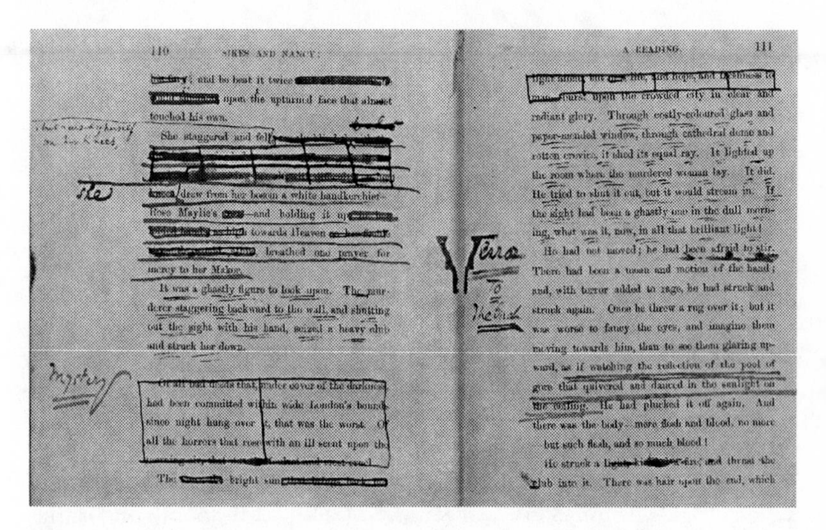

110 SIKES AND NANCY:

; and he beat it twice upon the upturned face that almost touched his own.

She staggered and fell; drew from her bosom a white handkerchief—Rose Maylie's—and holding it up towards Heaven, breathed one prayer for mercy to her Maker.

It was a ghastly figure to look upon. The murderer staggering backward to the wall, and shutting out the sight with his hand, seized a heavy club and struck her down.

Of all bad deeds that, under cover of the darkness, had been committed within wide London's bounds since night hung over it, that was the worst. Of all the horrors that rose with an ill scent upon the

The bright sun

A READING. 111

upon the crowded city in clear and radiant glory. Through costly-coloured glass and paper-mended window, through cathedral dome and rotten crevice, it shed its equal ray. It lighted up the room where the murdered woman lay. It did. He tried to shut it out, but it would stream in. If the sight had been a ghastly one in the dull morning, what was it, now, in all that brilliant light!

He had not moved; he had been afraid to stir. There had been a moan and motion of the hand; and, with terror added to rage, he had struck and struck again. Once he threw a rug over it; but it was worse to fancy the eyes, and imagine them moving towards him, than to see them glaring upward, as if watching the reflection of the pool of gore that quivered and danced in the sunlight on the ceiling. He had plucked it off again. And there was the body—mere flesh and blood, no more—but such flesh, and so much blood!

He struck a light, kindled a fire, and thrust the club into it. There was hair upon the end, which

Figure 7: "Terror to the end": the murder of Nancy in Dickens's personal prompt-copy of "Sikes and Nancy" (1869).

"tried means" of reinforcing his relations "with a multitude of persons who will never hear my voice nor see my face."[3] The audience sitting before him had come to stand for the community of readers he could now only imagine.

Certainly Dickens felt these latter motives of political renovation and public communion. Paul Schlicke, for example, finds the reading career the "culmination of his lifetime's dedication to the cause of popular entertainment," in which Dickens made a choice – "conscious, concerned, heroic, even tragic" – to provide "carefree, innocent amusement" to the Pickwickian totality his novels could no longer assemble.[4] But this is also to oversimplify a complex phenomenon: the spectacle of the exemplary cultural producer of the age deciding to exhibit not only his own voice, but now his own body, for pleasure, profit, and more. John Forster was against the readings from the first, repeating his objections even from the biographer's podium:

> It was a substitution of lower for higher aims: a change to commonplace from more elevated pursuits; and it had so much of the character of a public exhibition for money as to raise, in the question of respect for his calling as a writer, a question also in respect of himself as a gentleman.[5]

Dickens himself would admit to no such debasement, even though his 1858 conversations with Forster, his 1862 consideration of an offer to tour Australia, and his decision to undertake the American tour of 1867–8 all featured his financial responsibilities.[6]

However exalted, mundane, or mixed Dickens's motives may have been, Forster was right to sense that Dickens's will to perform had, in some fundamental sense, superseded his need to write. From the completion of *Great Expectations* in 1861 to the enforced truncation of the British Farewell Tour in April 1869, Dickens would interrupt his reading career only once. Though he had thought of the title two years before, he made no progress on *Our Mutual Friend* until October 1863, shortly after conceiving the reading of Nancy's murder from *Oliver Twist*, "something so horrible," as he then said, that he was "afraid to try it in public" (*PL* 10: 75, 250, 300). The truth of the reading Dickens, then, is surely some complex and fractured whole of artistic aspiration and pecuniary motive, with the titanic personality subsuming both. Dickens's biographers have had justifiable difficulty rendering this whole in any single, chronologically ordered narrative. Fred Kaplan, for example, uses the November 1868 trial performance of "Sikes and Nancy" as a cue for his final psychological sketch, featuring the symbolic murder of the two women Dickens hated most. Peter Ackroyd intersperses his narrative with imaginary meetings between himself and his subject; in this last section of his biography, he even resorts to reporting on his own fearful dreams of Dickens in the room next to his, or traveling with him in a railcar.[7]

My aim has been to describe the status of Dickens's serial novels, as well as those of his two greatest rivals in the form, as emblems of Victorian modernity – delivering their news of alienation and disenchantment in and for a historical consciousness, but simultaneously invoking myths of benevolence and sacrifice from a lost Christian culture. From Mr. Pickwick to Thackeray's meek lieutenant to George Eliot's Caleb Garth, each novelist worked to symbolize the cult of abstract humanity and benevolence Marx would call "the most appropriate form of religion for a society of commodity producers." As George Eliot leaned towards her Sunday afternoon visitors, she was working to supplement what had previously been left to the principally linguistic means of serial fiction.[8] In his late rush into the theatrics of Atonement, Dickens was showing himself, as well as his actual and imaginary audiences, that benevolence and violence were two sides of the same social coin.

The three most significant reading texts for these purposes are the "Trial from Pickwick," a thirty-minute closer, and the most frequently performed of all the readings; the "Carol," the first and perhaps the "quintessential" of them, as Philip Collins says; and "Sikes and Nancy," the last reading to appear, but speedily taking pride of place in the repertoire. The programs for his last two public appearances (on 8 and 15 March 1870) were "Sikes and Nancy" and "A Christmas Carol" respectively, each followed by "The Trial from Pickwick."[9] The latter was a staple of the Victorian lectern long before Dickens himself performed his virtual transcription of the famous confrontation between the lawyer Buzfuz and the valet Sam Weller. As such, the reading was quite short – too short, according to Kate Field, who argued that Dickens should have included the scene in which Mrs. Bardell collapses into Mr. Pickwick's arms, with their discovery leading to her nefarious lawsuit for breach of promise to marry (*PR* 197–8).

Nor was this criticism the only one of "The Trial from Pickwick." Dickens's portrayal of Sam Weller was often second-guessed, particularly at first, when he seemed, as W. P. Frith put it to him, to have "lowered his voice to the tones of one who was ashamed of what he was saying, and afraid of being reproved for the freedom of his utterances." Much later, in Boston, an audience member from Maine likewise declared that Dickens "knows no more about Sam Weller 'n a cow does of pleatin' a shirt[;] at all events that ain't *my* idea of Sam Weller, anyhow."[10] Perhaps many more agreed with the reviewer for the *Manchester Guardian* of August 1874, who did not fail to repeat the famous joke about Mrs. Bardell's husband having "stamped his likeness on a little boy" before seeking in death "that repose and peace which a custom-house can never afford":

> Talk to us of Garrick and his Protean powers! Mr. Justice Stareleigh, and Mr. Sarjeant Buzfuz, and Mr. Nathaniel Winkle himself, all appeared in succession in Mr. Dickens's face and voice, and, like the image of Mrs. Bardell's departed exciseman, will remain "stamped on" us forever. If Mr. Samuel Weller failed to attain to a similar incarnation, it is only because, like his own personal illustrations, he has already become to us a mythical personage incapable of realization in this imperfect world.[11]

Much of my own essential Dickens is on the very surface of these responses: the sense that the Dickens phenomenon had always exceeded the understanding of the man himself; the hilarious yet disturbing displacement of a natural relationship between father and child into a mechanical one of stamping out coin; the hint of transcendence in Sam's very failure to achieve a satisfactory "incarnation"; and finally, Dickens's and his works' status as essential Victorian myth, vehicles of longing for what Steven Marcus has called "the ideal possibilities of human relations in community."[12]

Though it surely contains Dickens's most powerful expression of his doctrine of benevolence, dramatized in Scrooge's eleventh-hour conversion, the printed version of *A Christmas Carol* is already one large step away from myth and into ideology, just as its thirst for atonement scarifies the Christmas tableau. Take, for example, the Cratchit dinner, the longest passage to survive the print version:

> [T]he two young Cratchits set chairs for everybody, not forgetting themselves, and mounting guard around their posts, crammed spoons into their mouths, lest they should shriek for goose before their turn came to be helped. At last the dishes were set on, and grace was said. It was succeeded by a breathless pause, as Mrs. Cratchit, *looking slowly all along the carving-knife, prepared to plunge it in the breast*; but when she did, and when the long expected gush of stuffing issued forth, one murmur of delight arose all round the board, and even Tiny Tim, excited by the two young Cratchits, beat on the table with the handle of his knife, and feebly cried Hurrah![13]

Though in a comic mode, this too is a scene of violent unanimity, like the death of the prostitute in "The Hospital Patient." It is true that Dickens's murderous intentions concerning Tiny Tim are first diverted by the substitution and consumption of a goose, and then tied off in the famous last-minute revision of the print version to the effect that he "did NOT die."[14] But such tropes of hunger, consumption, and sacrifice vary only in these matters of substitution and degree.

As in the case of George Eliot around 1870, then, any account of Dickens's cultural significance at this time must include not only the new trend towards novelist worship – George Eliot's fans rushed up to kiss her hand in the same St. James's Hall where Dickens delivered nearly all his London readings – but also the note of sacrifice sounding beneath the class liturgy. Late nineteenth-century sociology would remain fundamentally concerned with these categories. For Durkheim, the moment of sacrifice is the archetype of the positive religious ritual, the symbolic act which confirms, in its own ostracizing and bloody way, that "regardless of the blow that has fallen upon it, the collectivity is not breached," and that "even at this moment, society is more alive and active than ever." For his part, Weber would condemn his fellow intellectuals' urge "to furnish their souls" with the "guaranteed genuine antiques" of religious practice as a sacrifice of their vocation to irrational ends.[15] Neither sociologist, however, could restrain himself from enacting the irrationality both worked so hard to comprehend – Durkheim in the "inversive circularity" of his conviction that religion must have a place in an age of sociology, and Weber in the enthusiasm with which he embraced the blood rites of the First World War.[16]

George Eliot was too mindful ever to let her private torments and relationships become a matter for sustained public display. For Dickens, however, who had surrendered a theatrical vocation only with difficulty, "Sikes and Nancy" proved an irresistible opportunity to link three parts of his personality in a single aesthetic act. The first of these was his inclination to attract the attention of those around him by means of self-display – a trait which had long attracted disapproval, as in Thackeray's 1851 mutterings to his dinner companion about the "beggar" looking like a "butterfly" in a blue silk dress-coat, satin vest and collar, and embroidered shirt (*PL* 6: 303 n. 3). The second was his longstanding drive to make money, and even, like the literary capitalist he had become, to make new ways of making it. What makes "Sikes and Nancy" the capstone to the reading career, however, is its linkage of Dickens's longstanding drive to sacrifice his own talent, his own energy, his very body, to these other goals.

The origins and history of the "Sikes and Nancy" reading are well known. Sidelined after the American tour of 1867–8, which he had finished as a virtual cripple, Dickens soon returned to the scenes he had abandoned in 1863.[17] His reasons for reading had always featured a need for money; the economic incapacity of his wife, his children and their spouses was a constant source of irritation to him. The reaction to the November 1868 trial reading, however – sure to be the greatest "sensation" in fifty years, or certain, if even one woman screamed, to produce "a contagion of hysteria all over the place" – convinced Dickens and others that this one would have an effect like none before it.[18]

As it came inevitably to dominate the 1868–9 winter season, the stage manager George Dolby added his own note of warning to Forster's longstanding objections to all the readings. Since the tours were a complete financial success, and since Dickens was again approaching collapse (as in a London cancellation on 16 February), Dolby finally argued that he should read it less often, perhaps in the larger venues only. In a fury, Dickens refused, shattering a dinner plate as he slammed his arms down on the table.[19] His obsession to repeat the piece would never leave him

– from the hours after each performance, when he always felt either a manic hilarity or a need to climb the platform again, to a day or two before his death, when he was seen on the grounds of Gads Hill re-enacting the murder once more.[20]

Chapter 48 of *Oliver Twist* struggles to keep its distance from the consciousness of Sikes, veering between narration of his frantic flight and reportage of his vision of the dead Nancy's "widely staring eyes, so lustreless and so glassy." The trial reading version of 14 November 1868 transcribed sections of this and the previous three chapters, ending with Sikes's flight from Nancy's body; later excisions to this version slightly reduced its length. But on suggestions from Charles Kent and Wilkie Collins, and overcoming his own anxiety that no audience would tolerate anything after the murder, Dickens added passages assuming the criminal's point of view:

> Hark!!!! A great sound coming on like a rushing fire! What? *Tracked so soon*? the hunt was up already? Lights gleaming below, voices in loud and earnest talk, hurried tramp of footsteps on the wooden bridges over Folly Ditch, a beating on the heavy door and window-shutters of the house, a waving crowd in the outer darkness like a field of corn moved by an angry storm! (*PR* 485)[21]

Whether walking the streets after a trial reading with a "vague sense of being 'wanted,'" or later, noting how his audiences seemed to view him as a man marked for death, with a "fixed expression of horror . . . which could not have been surpassed if I had been going to be hanged to that red velvet table," Dickens was murdering both Nancy and the murderer he himself had become.[22] In a prophetic representation of the distance between the utopian dream of market society as lively entity and the ideological work of pretending that it is so, he completed his transformation into that *monstre sacré*, the worshipped and victimized celebrity.[23]

As he approached the platform for the last performance of "Sikes and Nancy," Dickens whispered to George Dolby: "I shall tear myself to pieces." If we are to interpret this as something more than a deranged suicide note, it may help to imagine the forces at work on him: not only the ever-dueling imperatives to sanctify and to profit, but also the union of literary production and theatrical reproduction he was struggling to maintain. No future novelist would achieve the success of Dickens's late combinations. For a young Thomas Hardy, for example, this same spring of 1870 was a season of submission. Having had his first novel rejected by George Meredith, the powerful reader at Chapman and Hall, and having written a second to Meredith's specifications of oblique sensation and elaborate plot, Hardy had to face the verdict of John Morley at Macmillan's, who called the rape at the center of *Desperate Remedies* a "disgusting and absurd outrage," and asked his employer to "beg the writer to discipline himself to keep away from such incidents."[24] By the 1890s, novelists were either attacking the publishing establishment head on, as Gissing did in *New Grub Street* (1891), or, like Hardy, abandoning the form altogether.[25] And for those few novelists who did aspire to make both serious art and serious money, the news was not good, as Henry James found out in 1895. On the disastrous opening night of *Guy Domville*, with the cheers from Wilde's *An Ideal Husband* still ringing in his ears, he was driven off his own stage; only playwrights like Wilde and Shaw would henceforth succeed at Dickens's dangerous game.[26]

Finally, then, the public reader of "Sikes and Nancy" is the last of what I have come to realize are a series of figures not unlike those at Madame Tussaud's, which establishment opened a Baker Street branch in 1835. The first figures in my own theater of sympathy include the young Dickens, swiftminded as Faust, who "thought of Mr. Pickwick and wrote the first number"; the twenty-year-old Mary Ann Evans grimacing with headache at a provincial dance; and the creator of Tiny Tim, gnashing his teeth over his Christmas book accounts. Towards the center might come Dickens the resplendent keynoter, with a frowning Thackeray keeping his distance; or the impresario of *The Frozen Deep* as the dying Frank Wardour, attended by Ternans in costume; or the Leweses lugging their specimen jars to the tidal pools of Ilfracombe.

Last would come the two St. James's Hall tableaux over which I have puzzled longest: the author of *Middlemarch*, sitting next to Lewes with her hand outstretched, accepting the obeisance of an elderly woman as another, younger woman looks eagerly on; and the murderer of Nancy, a wild expression on his face, bringing down the club. If the former is clearly what Audrey Jaffe would call a "scene of sympathy," we must finally wonder that the same description must also apply to the latter, in which Dickens, like Goethe's rat, mistakes the pain of the poison he has eaten for the love he feels.[27] We may prefer to turn away from the starkness of the contrast between these two scenes. If we do, however, we avert our gaze from the very gap between enchantment and disenchantment the smiles and tears worked so hard to close.

Notes

Introduction

1. Though the Gardens were well into their second century, they had begun to decline long before they were first opened to daytime visitors in 1836, and were closed for good in 1859. Charles Dickens, *Sketches by Boz*, ed. Dennis Walder (Harmondsworth: Penguin, 1995), 601; see also Paul Schlicke, *Dickens and Popular Entertainment* (London: Allen & Unwin, 1985), 41–2. Michael Slater's *Sketches by Boz and Other Early Papers* (Columbus: Ohio State University Press, 1994) reprints the 1867–8 "Charles Dickens Edition" of the *Sketches* without explanation (*id.*, viii). All further citations are thus to Walder's reprint of the 1837–9 Chapman and Hall serial. On the *Sketches* and their generic predecessors, see Walder, "Introduction" to *Sketches*, xviii; Andrew Sanders, *Dickens and the Spirit of the Age* (Oxford: Clarendon Press, 1999), 1–16; and F. S. Schwarzbach, *Dickens and the City* (London: Athlone Press, 1979), 35–9.
2. For the phrase "creative destruction," see Joseph Schumpeter, *History of Economic Analysis* (New York: Oxford University Press, 1994), 389, 441, 630–1.
3. I rely here on Regenia Gagnier, *The Insatiability of Human Wants: Economics and Aesthetics in Market Society* (Chicago: University of Chicago Press, 2000), 21–53.
4. Karl Marx, *Capital, Volume One*, trans. Ben Fowkes (Harmondsworth: Penguin – New Left Books, 1976), 180, 302, 740–1.
5. Max Weber, *Ancient Judaism*, trans. and ed. H. H. Gerth and Don Martindale (New York: Free Press, 1952); *The Rational and Social Foundations of Music*, trans. and ed. Don Martindale, Johannes Riedel and Gertrude Neuwirth (Carbondale: Southern Illinois University Press, 1958); "Science as a Vocation," in *From Max Weber: Essays in Sociology*, trans. and ed. H. H. Gerth and C. Wright Mills (New York: Oxford University Press, 1946), 148–9, 155, 333–4. For successors to Weber, see, for example, Fredric Jameson, "Marxism and Historicism" (1979), rpr. in *The Ideologies of Theory: Essays 1971–1986*, 2 vols (Minneapolis: University of Minnesota Press, 1988), 149; Franco Moretti, "The Moment of Truth," in *Signs Taken for Wonders*, rev. edn (London: Verso, 1988), 261; Marcel Gauchet, *The Disenchantment of the World: a Political History of Religion*, trans. Oscar Burge (Princeton: Princeton University Press, 1997); Clark, *Farewell to an Idea*, 7–8.
6. See, for example, Max Weber, *The Protestant Ethic and the Spirit of Capitalism*, trans. Talcott Parsons (New York: Scribners, 1958), 183; compare Ellen Meiksins Wood, *Democracy Against Capitalism* (Cambridge: Cambridge University Press, 1995), 146–78, and Lawrence A. Scaff, *Fleeing the Iron Cage: Culture, Politics and Modernity in the Thought of Max Weber* (Berkeley: University of California Press, 1989), 34–49. For the problems created by Weber's tendency to substitute the terms "disenchantment" and "intellectualization" for the broader processes he generalized as "rationalization," see

Anthony Giddens, "Politics and Sociology in the Thought of Max Weber" (1972), in *Politics, Sociology and Social Theory: Encounters with Classical and Contemporary Social Thought* (Stanford: Stanford University Press, 1995), 44.

7. Weber, "The Social Psychology of the World Religions" (1922), in *From Max Weber*, 267–301, 280.
8. See Gerth and Mills, "Introduction" to *From Max Weber*, 63–4; Scaff, *Fleeing the Iron Cage*, 92; Wolfgang Mommsen, *The Political and Social Theory of Max Weber* (Chicago: University of Chicago Press, 1989), 54–5. On Bourdieu's relation to classical sociology, see David Swartz, *Culture and Power: the Sociology of Pierre Bourdieu* (Chicago: University of Chicago Press, 1997), 38–48.
9. Arnold, "Stanzas from the Grande Chartreuse" (1855), ll. 85–6; see also Walter E. Houghton, *The Victorian Frame of Mind, 1830–1870* (New Haven: Yale University Press, 1957), 9–10.
10. Karl Marx, *The Eighteenth Brumaire of Louis Bonaparte* (New York: International, 1963), 15; J. G. A. Pocock, *The Ancient Constitution and the Feudal Law* (New York: Norton, 1967), 30–69; and see Linda Colley, *Britons: Forging the Nation, 1707–1837* (New Haven: Yale University Press, 1992), 336–7.
11. Weber, "Science as a Vocation," *From Max Weber*, 149; on Weber as an "important supplement and corrective" to Marx, see Eric Hobsbawm, *On History* (New York: New Press, 1997), 167–8.
12. See William Warner, *Licensing Entertainment: the Elevation of Novel Reading in Britain, 1684–1750* (Berkeley: University of California Press, 1998), 150–1, 192–9, 270–1; on this longstanding "secular-religious antithesis," see also John Richetti, *Popular Fiction Before Richardson: Narrative Patterns, 1700–1739*, 2nd edn (Oxford: Clarendon Press, 1992), xxiv–xxv, 264–5; Franco Moretti, *The Way of the World: the Bildungsroman in European Culture* (London: Verso, 1987), 185–9; Moretti, *Atlas of the European Novel, 1800–1900* (London: Verso, 1998), 131–2; Nancy Armstrong, *Desire and Domestic Fiction* (Oxford: Oxford University Press, 1987), 193–4.
13. Victorian serial novels do not successfully secularize an inherited Protestant culture, in other words, but haphazardly "reoccupy" it in a modern literary and commodity form. See Hans Blumenberg, *The Legitimacy of the Modern Age*, rev. edn, trans. Robert M. Wallace (Cambridge: MIT Press, 1983), 46–9. On the diffuse nature of early nineteenth-century British discourse, amounting to "a revolution in ideological power relations," see Michael Mann, *The Sources of Social Power, Volume 2: the Rise of Classes and Nation-States, 1760–1914* (Cambridge: Cambridge University Press, 1993), 105; for one terminus for the idea of modernity as a totality characterized by disorder, see Theodor W. Adorno, "Sociology and Psychology," *New Left Review* 46–7 (1967–8): 69.
14. See Boyd Hilton, *The Age of Atonement: the Influence of Evangelicalism on Social and Economic Thought, 1795–1865* (Oxford: Clarendon Press, 1988), *passim*.
15. Legh Richmond, "The Dairyman's Daughter" (1810), in *Annals of the Poor, or Narratives of the Dairyman's Daughter, The Negro Servant, and The Young Cottager* (New York, [1856]) (emphasis in original), n.p. The anecdote of Victoria's reading appears in Ian Bradley, *The Call to Seriousness: the Evan-*

gelical Impact on the Victorians (London: Jonathan Cape, 1976), 36, without attribution, and is repeated in Stanley Weintraub, *Victoria: an Intimate Biography* (New York: E. P. Dutton, 1987), 77; for a thorough account, see Lynne Vallone, *Becoming Victoria* (New Haven: Yale University Press, 2001), 40–7.

16. Quoted in Christine L. Kreuger, *The Reader's Repentance: Woman Preachers, Woman Writers, and Nineteenth-Century Social Discourse* (Chicago: University of Chicago Press, 1992), 131 (emphasis added).
17. See Bradley, *The Call to Seriousness,* 19–26; Elisabeth Jay, *The Religion of the Heart: Anglican Evangelicalism and the Nineteenth-Century Novel* (Oxford: Clarendon Press, 1979), 54–82.
18. See Stewart J. Brown, *Thomas Chalmers and the Godly Commonwealth in Scotland* (Oxford: Oxford University Press, 1982), 129–51.
19. Chalmers to James Brown, 30 January 1819, quoted in Hilton, *Age of Atonement*, 88.
20. Hilton, *Age of Atonement*, 131.
21. Quoted in Hilton, *Age of Atonement*, 96.
22. Hilton, *Age of Atonement*, 21, 131–2.
23. Maurice, "On the Atonement," in *Theological Essays* (1853; New York: Harper, 1953), 102; on "incarnationalism," see Hilton, *The Age of Atonement*, 298–339; on Maurice's intellectual disposition, see David Newsome, *Two Classes of Men: Platonism and English Romantic Thought* (London: John Murray, 1972), 73–90. On the incarnational rhetoric of 1830s reform, see Colley, *Britons*, 328, 340.
24. Marx, *Capital, Volume One*, 93.
25. James Phillips Kay, *The Moral and Physical Condition of the Working Classes Employed in the Cotton Manufacture in Manchester*, 2nd edn (London: James Ridgeway, 1832), 63–4, quoted in Mary Poovey, *Making a Social Body: British Cultural Formation, 1830–1864* (Chicago: University of Chicago Press, 1995), 85.
26. For the eighteenth-century origins of sympathy, see Christopher Lawrence, "The Nervous System and Society in the Scottish Enlightenment," in *Natural Order: Historical Studies of Scientific Culture*, ed. Barry Barnes and Steven Shapin (London: Sage, 1979), 19–40.
27. Poovey, *Making a Social Body*, 116–17; see also Joseph Childers, *Novel Possibilities: Fiction and the Formation of Early Victorian Culture* (Philadelphia: University of Pennsylvania Press, 1995), 72–109, and Elaine Freedgood, *Victorian Writing About Risk: Imagining a Safe England in a Dangerous World* (Cambridge: Cambridge University Press, 2000), 48–60.
28. N. N. Feltes, *Modes of Production of Victorian Novels* (Chicago: University of Chicago Press, 1986), 13–14.
29. Linda K. Hughes and Michael Lund, *The Victorian Serial* (Charlottesville: University Press of Virginia, 1991), ch. 3; James Chandler, *England in 1819* (Chicago: University of Chicago Press, 1998), 24, 203–7, 216–25, 307, 358.
30. Charles Dickens, "Passage in the Life of Mr. Watkins Tottle," *Morning Chronicle* (Jan. and Feb. 1835), rpr. in Dennis Walder, ed., *Sketches by Boz*, 494–535, 514–16; W. M. Thackeray, "The Professor," *Bentley's Miscellany* 2 (Sept. 1837): 277–88; George Eliot, "The Sad Fortunes of the Reverend Amos Barton," in

Scenes of Clerical Life, ed. Thomas A. Noble (Oxford: Clarendon Press, 1985), 10. On George Eliot's historicism, see especially Steven Marcus, "Literature and Social Theory: Starting in with George Eliot," in *Representations: Essays on Literature and Society*, 2nd edn (New York: Columbia University Press, 1990), 183–213.

31. After John Sutherland, *Victorian Novelists and Publishers* (Chicago: University of Chicago Press, 1976) and Robert L. Patten, *Dickens and his Publishers* (Oxford: Clarendon Press, 1978), see Kathryn Chittick, *Dickens and the 1830s* (Cambridge: Cambridge University Press, 1990); Peter Shillingsburg, *Pegasus in Harness: W. M. Thackeray and Victorian Publishing* (Charlottesville: University Press of Virginia, 1992) and Edgar Harden, *A Checklist of Contributions by William Makepeace Thackeray to Newspapers, Periodicals, Books, and Serial Part Issues* (Victoria: University of Victoria Press, 1996); and Carol Martin, *George Eliot's Serial Fiction* (Columbus: Ohio University Press, 1994). On the categories of series, capital, and commodity, see Laurie Langbauer, *Novels of Everyday Life: the Series in English Fiction, 1850–1930* (Ithaca: Cornell University Press, 1999), Jeff Nunokawa, *The Afterlife of Property: Domestic Security in the Victorian Novel* (Princeton: Princeton University Press, 1994), and Andrew Miller, *Novels Behind Glass: Commodity Culture and Victorian Narrative* (Cambridge: Cambridge University Press, 1995). After John Sutherland, "Dickens's Serializing Imitators," in *Victorian Fiction: Writers, Publishers, Readers* (New York: St. Martin's Press, 1995), 87–106, see Graham Law, *Serializing Fiction in the Victorian Press* (Basingstoke: Palgrave Macmillan, 2000); Laurel Brake, *Print in Transition, 1850–1910: Studies in Media and Book History* (Basingstoke: Palgrave Macmillan, 2001); Deborah Wynne, *The Sensation Novel and the Victorian Family Magazine* (Basingstoke: Palgrave Macmillan, 2001).
32. Sutherland, *Victorian Fiction*, 89–95, 103–4; *PL* 10: 287.
33. Sutherland, *Victorian Fiction*, 94; Brake, *Print in Transition*, 12; Altick, *The English Common Reader*, 295.
34. David Simpson, *Fetishism and Imagination: Dickens, Melville, Conrad* (Baltimore: Johns Hopkins University Press, 1982), 40–2, 62–8.
35. [Marian Evans], "The Natural History of German Life," *Westminster Review* (July 1856), rpr. in *Selected Essays, Poems and Other Writings*, ed. A. S. Byatt and Nicholas Warren (Harmondsworth: Penguin, 1990), 128–9 (emphasis added). For the intellectual context of "incarnate history," see A. S. Byatt, "Introduction" to *Essays*, xx–xxxi; Peter Allan Dale, *In Pursuit of a Scientific Culture: Science, Art, and Society in the Victorian Age* (Madison: University of Wisconsin Press, 1989), chs 3–4.
36. See, for example, Thomas Chalmers, *On Political Economy, in Connexion with the Moral State, and Moral Prospects of Society* (1832) (New York: Kelley, 1968), 425–49; John Stuart Mill, "Inaugural Address delivered to the University of St. Andrews" (1867), in *The Collected Works of John Stuart Mill*, ed. J. M. Robson (Toronto: University of Toronto Press, 1963–91), 31: 215–57, 253; Elie Halévy, *England in 1815*, trans. E. I. Watkin and D. A. Barker (New York: Peter Smith, 1949), 509, 525; G. M. Young, *Portrait of an Age: Victorian England*, annotated edn (London: Oxford University Press, 1977), 21–31; Altick, *The English Common Reader*, 99 (citing Halévy); Hilton, *Age of Atonement, passim.*

37. On the categories of modernity and spectatorship in Victorian literary culture, see also Audrey Jaffe, *Scenes of Sympathy: Identity and Representation in Victorian Fiction* (Ithaca: Cornell University Press, 2000).
38. See Charlotte Elizabeth [Tonna], *Helen Fleetwood* (1840–1), in *The Works of Charlotte Elizabeth,* 2 vols (New York: M. W. Dodd, 1849), 1: 533–4, 678.
39. Sutherland, *Victorian Novelists and Publishers,* 135.
40. Sutherland, *Victorian Novelists and Publishers,* 145.
41. Anthony Trollope, *Framley Parsonage* (1861), ch. 2.
42. Trollope, *An Illustrated Autobiography* (Wolfeboro: Alan Sutton, 1989), 104, 106–7, 109.
43. See Mary Hamer, *Writing by Numbers: Trollope's Serial Fiction* (Cambridge: Cambridge University Press, 1987), 69–74; Sutherland, *Victorian Novelists and Publishers,* 133, 148–9, 151.
44. Altick, *The English Common Reader,* 309–12; Law, *Serializing Fiction,* chs 3–4.
45. Law, *Serializing Fiction,* 24–7; Wynne, *The Sensation Novel, passim.*
46. Laurel Brake, *Subjugated Knowledge: Journalism, Gender, and Literature in the Nineteenth Century* (New York: New York University Press, 1994), 106; Haight, 437, *L* 5: 183, 199–200, 9: 22–4; Sutherland, *Victorian Novelists and Publishers,* 71.
47. Henry James, *The Portrait of a Lady,* ed. Geoffrey Moore (Harmondsworth: Penguin, 1986), 39; for real and imagined links between the two novelists, see Leon Edel, *Henry James: the Conquest of London, 1870–1881* (New York: Avon, 1978), 368–71.
48. Marx, *Capital, Volume One,* 274; Trollope, *Autobiography,* quoted in Sutherland, *Victorian Novelists and Publishers,* 148.
49. See, for example, Marx, *Capital, Volume One,* 172–7; and note Eric Hobsbawm, *On History,* 159: "The first volume of *Capital* contains three or four fairly marginal references to Protestantism, yet the entire debate on the relationship between religion in general, and Protestantism in particular, and the capitalist mode of production derives from them." See also David Simpson, "Introduction" to *The Origins of Modern Critical Thought* (Cambridge: Cambridge University Press, 1988), 1–22.
50. Hilary Schor, "Fiction," in Herbert Tucker, ed., *A Companion to Victorian Literature and Culture* (London: Blackwell, 1999), 326; see also Kathryn Chittick, *Dickens and the 1830s* (Cambridge: Cambridge University Press, 1990), ch. 2.
51. See George Orwell, *Dickens, Dali and Others* (New York: Reynal and Hitchcock, 1946), 59–65; John Bowen, *Other Dickens* (Oxford: Oxford University Press, 2000), 51–7.
52. See E. J. Hobsbawm and George Rudé, *Captain Swing* (New York: Pantheon, 1968), 223–30, and Appendix III ("Table of Incidents"), *passim.*
53. On Dickens's modernism, see especially Steven Marcus, "Language into Structure: *Pickwick* Revisited," in *Representations: Essays on Literature and Society,* 2nd edn (New York: Columbia University Press, 1990), 49–53; Bowen, *Other Dickens,* 34–5 and n. 89; Ned Lukacher, *Primal Scenes: Literature, Philosophy, Psychoanalysis* (Ithaca: Cornell University Press, 1986), 275–336; Kevin McLaughlin, *Writing in Parts: Imitation and Exchange in Nineteenth-Century Literature* (Stanford: Stanford University Press, 1995), 120. On modernism as a "rearguard action against the truths it has stumbled on,"

see T. J. Clark, *Farewell to an Idea: Episodes in a History of Modernism* (New Haven: Yale University Press, 1999), 35, 88–90.

54. Perhaps Dickens's best-known articulation of his sacrificial aesthetic is the 1841 preface to *Oliver Twist*, a piece Hilary Schor calls "a catalogue of realism's alibis." See Schor, *Dickens and the Daughter of the House* (Cambridge: Cambridge University Press, 1999), 19–21, as well as Jonathan Arac, *Commissioned Spirits: the Shaping of Social Motion in Dickens, Carlyle, Melville, and Hawthorne*, 2nd edn (New York: Columbia University Press, 1989), 65.
55. See also Barry Qualls, *The Secular Pilgrims of Victorian Fiction: the Novel as Book of Life* (Cambridge: Cambridge University Press, 1984), 23–4, 104–9; Bowen, *Other Dickens*, 98–104.
56. On the conflict between the gods of Christianity and capitalism, see Max Weber, "Science as a Vocation," *From Max Weber*, 149; for the massive literature on early Dickens, see for example Adorno, "On Dickens's *Old Curiosity Shop*: A Lecture," in *Notes to Literature* (New York: Columbia University Press, 1992), 2: 170–7; Steven Marcus, *Dickens from Pickwick to Dombey* (New York: Norton, 1965), 16–17, 73–7; David Simpson, *Fetishism and Imagination* (Baltimore: Johns Hopkins University Press, 1982), 14, 56; Robert F. Patten, "Serialized Retrospection in *The Pickwick Papers*," in *Literature and the Marketplace*, 131–4; McLaughlin, *Writing in Parts*, ch. 2; Bowen, *Other Dickens*, 138–51.
57. Emile Durkheim, *The Elementary Forms of Religious Life*, trans. Karen E. Fields (New York: Free Press, 1995), 330, 208.
58. Durkheim, *The Elementary Forms of Religious Life*, 208–9; Aron, *Main Currents in Sociological Thought II: Durkheim, Pareto, Weber* (New York: Anchor-Doubleday, 1970), 55–66.
59. Susan Mizruchi, *The Science of Sacrifice: American Literature and Modern Social Theory* (Princeton: Princeton University Press, 1998), 33. On the relation between Weber's sacrificial sociology and his German nationalism, see Perry Anderson, *A Zone of Engagement* (London: Verso, 1992), 190–7.
60. Gauchet, *The Disenchantment of the World*, 9; compare Arjun Appadurai, *Modernity at Large: Cultural Dimensions of Globalization* (Minneapolis: University of Minnesota Press, 1996), 6–7.

1. The Cockney and the Prostitute

1. Quoted in Asa Briggs, *Victorian Cities*, rev. edn (1970; Berkeley: University of California Press, 1993), 93. *The People's Journal*, appearing from 1847 to 1851, was also known as *Howitt's Journal of Literature and Popular Progress*. See J. F. C. Harrison and Dorothy Thompson, *Bibliography of the Chartist Movement, 1837–1976* (Sussex: Harvester Press, 1978), 116.
2. For accounts of the Athenaeum soirée, see *PL* 3: 581–2 n.4; *Speeches of Charles Dickens*, ed. K. J. Fielding (Oxford: Clarendon Press), 44 n.4; Briggs, *Victorian Cities*, 93–95; *Benjamin Disraeli Letters*, ed. J. A. W. Gunn et al. (Toronto: University of Toronto Press, 1982–), 4: 108–9 nn.1–3. For accounts of the public lecture in early Victorian Manchester, see Martin Hewitt, "Ralph Waldo Emerson, George Dawson, and the Control of the Lecture

Platform in Mid-Nineteenth Century Manchester," *Nineteenth-Century Prose* 25.2 (Fall 1998): 1–23, as well as Howard M. Wach, "Culture and the Middle Classes: Popular Knowledge in Industrial Manchester," *Journal of British Studies* 27 (1988): 375–404.

3. Quoted in Wach, "Culture and the Middle Classes," 381.
4. Adam Smith, *The Nature and Cause of the Wealth of Nations*, ed. R. H. Campbell and A. S. Skinner (Oxford: Clarendon Press, 1976), 781–2. For a historical summary of the concepts of division of labor and alienation, see Dietrich Rueschemeyer, *Power and the Division of Labor* (Stanford: Stanford University Press, 1986), 1–14.
5. See David Simpson, *Romanticism, Nationalism and the Revolt against Theory* (Chicago: University of Chicago Press, 1993), 52, 57–9.
6. Byron, *Selected Letters and Journals*, ed. Leslie A. Marchand (Cambridge: Belknap-Harvard University Press, 1982), 167.
7. There is no clear evidence for Dickens's knowledge of *Sartor Resartus* until chapter 37 of *The Uncommercial Traveller*, the series of essays which first appeared in *All the Year Round* in 1860. See Michael Goldberg, *Carlyle and Dickens* (Athens: University of Georgia Press, 1972), 20–3.
8. For the literary origins of British critique, see Raymond Williams, *Culture and Society* (New York: Columbia University Press, 1983), 271 and *passim*; Perry Anderson, *Arguments within English Marxism* (London: New Left Books, 1980), 158–60. For the distinction between British and German discourses, the latter's debt to Protestantism, and the rehabilitation of German thought in Britain between 1815 and 1830, see Simpson, *Romanticism, Nationalism and the Revolt against Theory*, 100–2 and *passim*, as well as his introduction to Simpson, ed., *The Origins of Modern Critical Thought: German Aesthetic and Literary Criticism from Lessing to Hegel* (Cambridge: Cambridge University Press, 1988), 4–9.
9. Friedrich Schiller, *Letters on the Aesthetic Education of Man* (1795), trans. E. M. Wilkinson and L. A. Willoughby (Oxford: Oxford University Press, 1967), 33–5.
10. G. W. F. Hegel, *The Phenomenology of Mind*, trans. J. B. Baillie (New York: Harper & Row, 1967), 238.
11. Karl Marx and Friedrich Engels, *The German Ideology*, ed. C. J. Arthur (New York: International, 1970), 68–9, 77–8.
12. E.g., "Men are the producers of their conceptions, ideas, etc., – real, active men, as they are conditioned by a definite development of their productive forces and of the intercourse corresponding to these, up to its furthest forms" (*German Ideology* 47). For a description of Marx's ambiguity on the category of "real activity," and an argument for the division of labor as "the connecting link" between early "anthropological" and later "abstract" Marxisms, see Paul Ricoeur, *Lectures on Ideology and Utopia* (New York: Columbia University Press, 1986), 83 and ch. 5 *passim*.
13. Søren Kierkegaard, *Fear and Trembling* (1843), ed. and trans. Walter Lowrie (Princeton: Princeton University Press, 1983), 49–51; *Either/Or* (1843), 2 vols, ed. and trans. Howard V. Hong and Edna H. Hong (Princeton: Princeton University Press, 1987), 1: 290.
14. J. Hillis Miller, "The Fiction of Realism: *Sketches by Boz, Oliver Twist* and Cruikshank's Illustrations," in *Charles Dickens and George Cruikshank*, ed.

Ada A. Nisbet (Los Angeles: William Andrews Clark Memorial Library, 1971), 31.

15. George Eliot, "The Natural History of German Life" (1856), *Essays*, 129.
16. Philip Collins, *Dickens and Crime* (London: Macmillan, 1962), 33.
17. "A Visit to Newgate" (February 1836), "Our Next-Door Neighbors" (March 1836), "Meditations in Monmouth-Street" (Sept. 1836), "Scotland-yard" (October 1836), "Doctors' Commons" (October 1836), rpr. in *Sketches by Boz* (London: Chapman and Hall, 1837–9), rpr. in *S* at 248, 66, 101, 90, 115. Robert L. Patten argues that the *Sketches'* preoccupation with death, exemplified by "Meditations in Monmouth-Street," is more a matter of the *flâneur*'s own bachelor detachment from "life or wife" than the downward spiral of any social phenomenon. Patten, *George Cruikshank: His Life, Times, and Art*, 2 vols (New Brunswick: Rutgers University Press, 1992, 1996), 2: 39.
18. "The Great Winglebury Duel," the only sketch written especially for the second volume of February 1836, became the operetta *The Strange Gentleman*, premiering in September; "Mrs. Joseph Porter" depicts a family "infected with the mania for Private Theatricals" (*S* 482); "The Steam Excursion" subjects a river party to *Paul et Virginie* excerpts and seasickness; and "Sentiment" concerns a schoolmistresses' ball involving "[p]reparations, to make use of theatrical phraseology, 'on a scale of magnitude never before attempted'" (*S* 379).
19. See Patten, *George Cruikshank*, 2: 42–5.
20. Kathryn Chittick, *Dickens and the 1830s* (Cambridge: Cambridge University Press, 1990), 49.
21. The three versions, the third a combination and revision of the previous two, are: (1) "Some Account of an Omnibus Cad," *Bell's Life in London and Sporting Chronicle* (1 November 1835) (superseded beginning and ending rpr. in Virgil Grillo, *Charles Dickens' Sketches by Boz: Ends in the Beginning* [Boulder: Colorado Associated University Press, 1974], 104, and John Butt and Kathleen Tillotson, *Dickens at Work* [London: Methuen, 1957], 54, respectively); (2) "Hackney-Cabs, and their Drivers," *Carlton Chronicle* (17 September 1836): 170, rpr. in Duane DeVries, *Dickens' Apprentice Years: the Making of a Novelist* (New York: Harvester/Barnes and Noble, 1976), Appendix B, 164–6; and (3) "The Last Cab-Driver, and the First Omnibus Cad," *Sketches by Boz* (London: Macrone, 1836), rpr. with minor changes in Chapman and Hall's Part 7 (May 1838), and in *S* 170–81.
22. Compare, for example, David Hume, *A Treatise on Human Nature*, ed. L. A. Selby-Bigge (Oxford: Clarendon Press, 1978), 618; Adam Smith, *The Theory of Moral Sentiments*, ed. D. D. Raphael and A. L. Macfie (Oxford: Clarendon Press, 1976), 9–16; G. W. F. Hegel, "The Spirit of Christianity," trans. T. M. Knox, in *Early Theological Writings*, ed. Richard Kroner (Philadelphia: University of Pennsylvania Press, 1971), 246–7; and George Eliot, "The Natural History of German Life," *Essays* 128.
23. Quoted in Butt and Tillotson, *Dickens at Work*, 54.
24. D. A. Miller, *The Novel and the Police* (Berkeley: University of California Press, 1988), 59.
25. Jonathan Arac, *Commissioned Spirits: the Shaping of Social Motion in Dickens, Carlyle, Melville, and Hawthorne*, rev. edn (New York: Columbia University Press, 1989), 22–3, 87, 121 and *passim*.

26. See Roman Jakobson, "Two Aspects of Language and Two Types of Linguistic Disturbances" (1956), in *Language and Literature*, ed. Krystyna Pomorska and Stephen Rudy (Cambridge: Belknap-Harvard University Press, 1987), 95–114.
27. Perker is referring to *Reports of Cases in the Court of King's Bench, 1817–1834*, ed. R. V. Barnewell (London, 1836), and Sam to *The History of George Barnwell, or the London Merchant*, a melodrama first produced in 1731. See *The Pickwick Papers*, ed. Robert L. Patten (Harmondsworth: Penguin, 1972), 937 n.14, 938 n.15.
28. See J. Hillis Miller, "Sam Weller's Valentine," in *Literature and the Marketplace: Nineteenth-Century British Publishing and Reading Practices*, ed. John O. Jordan and Robert L. Patten (Cambridge: Cambridge University Press, 1995), 114–16.
29. On the modern state's monopoly on force, see Max Weber, "Politics as a Vocation" (1919), in *From Max Weber: Essays in Sociology*, trans. and ed. H. H. Gerth and C. Wright Mills (New York: Oxford University Press, 1946), 78, and Michel Foucault, *Discipline and Punish: the Birth of the Prison*, trans. Alan Sheridan (New York: Vintage, 1979). On Dickens's and Thackeray's objections to public execution arising from the Courvoisier case of 1840, see Collins, *Dickens and Crime*, 224–6.
30. Karl Marx, *Economic and Philosophic Manuscripts of 1844*, trans. Martin Mulligan, ed. Dirk J. Strunk (New York: International, 1964), 136; see also Jeff Nunokawa, *The Afterlife of Property: Domestic Security and the Victorian Novel* (Princeton: Princeton University Press, 1994), 32–3.
31. Karl Marx, *Capital, Volume One*, trans. Ben Fowkes (Harmondsworth: Penguin/New Left Books, 1976), 172.
32. For literary form as "veiled revelation" of the kinds of conclusions to which sociology aspires, see Pierre Bourdieu, "The Structure of *Sentimental Education*," trans. Claude DuVerlie, in *The Field of Cultural Production*, ed. and intro. Randal Johnson (New York: Columbia University Press, 1993), 158–9. For *Pickwick*'s status as sucn, see N. N. Feltes, *Modes of Production of Victorian Novels* (Chicago: University of Chicago Press, 1986), 15–16.
33. Chittick, *Dickens and the 1830s*, 64; see also Alexander Welsh, "Waverley, Pickwick and Don Quixote," *Nineteenth Century Fiction* 22 (1967–8): 19–30. On the novel's larger patterns of disruption and reversal, see Patten's introduction to the 1972 Penguin edition, 28–9.
34. *Athenaeum* 2 January 1828, quoted in John Sutherland, *Victorian Novelists and Publishers* (Chicago: University of Chicago Press, 1976), 12; see also *DP* 50.
35. E.g., "The Boarding House, No. 2," *Monthly Magazine* 18 (August 1834): 177–92; "The Steam Excursion," *Monthly Magazine* 18 (October 1834): 360–76; "Passage in the Life of Mr. Watkins Tottle," *Monthly Magazine* 19 (January and February 1835): 15–24, 121–37.
36. Chittick, *Dickens and the 1830s*, 45–6, 58.
37. On *Bell's Life*, see Butt and Tillotson, *Dickens at Work*, 41 n.3. Ackroyd states that Dickens's payment for the "Scenes and Characters" series was more than his *Chronicle* salary, but does not give the amount; nor does Johnson. See Peter Ackroyd, *Dickens: a Life* (London: Sinclair-Stevenson, 1990), 169;

Edgar Johnson, *Charles Dickens: His Tragedy and Triumph*, 2 vols (New York: Simon and Schuster, 1952), I, 103.

38. *DP* 51; Richard D. Altick, *The English Common Reader* (Chicago: University of Chicago Press, 1957), 335, 333.
39. *DP* 46; Sutherland, *Victorian Novelists and Publishers*, 21.
40. Chittick, *Dickens and the 1830s*, 67.
41. Charles Dickens, "The Hospital Patient," *Carlton Chronicle* (6 August 1836): 139. All further quotations are taken from this original 1836 version.
42. John Forster, *The Life of Charles Dickens*, ed. A. J. Hoppé, 2 vols (London: J. M. Dent, 1966), 1: 25, 2: 179.
43. Walder, "Introduction" to *S*, xxx. I am indebted to James Hirsh for the *Othello* reference.
44. René Girard, *Violence and the Sacred*, trans. Patrick Gregory (Baltimore: Johns Hopkins University Press, 1977), 81; see also Michiel Heyns, *Expulsion and the Nineteenth-Century Novel: the Scapegoat in English Realist Fiction* (Oxford: Clarendon Press, 1994), ch. 2.
45. *Carlton Chronicle* (11 June 1836): 1; *PL* 1: 160.
46. See, e.g., *PL* 1: 204.
47. Chittick, *Dickens and the 1830s*, 74; "Preface," *Bentley's Miscellany* 1 (Jan. 1837): 1; *PL* 1: 279 n.2.
48. *Carlton Chronicle* (8 April 1837): 635.
49. Other reviews also called him "the Cruikshank of writers," "our modern Hogarth." See David Paroissien, *Oliver Twist: an Annotated Bibliography* (New York: Garland, 1986), 100–1, 104. On the details of the collaboration and friendship between Dickens and Cruikshank during the composition of *Oliver Twist*, as well as the emerging artistic and personal differences between the two, see Patten, *George Cruikshank*, 2: 36–7, 50–94.
50. Though not present at the climax of the Macrone negotiations on 17 June (when Hall admitted that Macrone's valuation of the copyright at £2000 was not excessive in light of expected profits, bought up Macrone's extra stock for an additional £250, and made Dickens an equal partner), Dickens had sought Forster's advice throughout (*DP* 41).
51. *DP* 79.
52. Chittick, *Dickens and the 1830s*, 80; see also Philip Collins, ed., *Dickens: The Critical Heritage* (London: Routledge & Kegan Paul, 1971), 52.
53. Collins, *Critical Heritage*, 56.
54. See Chittick, *Dickens and the 1830s*, 83.
55. The term is of course Dickens's own (*PL* 1: 273).
56. Grillo, *Sketches by Boz*, 96.
57. On the sudden transformation of Nancy and its negative implications for Tillotson's own thesis concerning any "long incubation" of the work, see Dickens's letter of 3 November expressing his "hope to do great things with Nancy[,] [i]f I can only work out the idea I have formed of her, and of the female [Rose Maylie] who is to contrast with her," *PL* 1: 328, as discussed in Burton M. Wheeler, "The Text and Plan of *Oliver Twist*," *Dickens Studies Annual* 12 (1983): 41–61, 44.
58. For Nancy's primordial status for Dickens, see Hilary Schor, *Dickens and the Daughter of the House* (Cambridge: Cambridge University Press, 1999), 21–31; for the broader cultural significance of the atoning female body, see also

Elisabeth Bronfen, *Over Her Dead Body: Death, Femininity and the Aesthetic* (New York: Routledge, 1992).
59. Tillotson, "Introduction" to *Oliver Twist*, xxxv–xxxvi; Chittick, *Dickens and the 1830s*, 87; Wheeler, "The Text and Plan of *Oliver Twist*," 48.
60. Tillotson herself dismisses the passage as "a particularly garrulous paragraph, which reads as if it had been written to fill space in the original installment" (*OT* xxxvi); Wheeler ("The Text and Plan of *Oliver Twist*") takes it as suggesting "Dickens's awareness of the complexities before him now that he has extracted the new agreement from Bentley" (51).
61. See generally Boyd Hilton, *The Age of Atonement: the Influence of Evangelicalism on Social and Economic Thought, 1795–1865* (Oxford: Clarendon Press, 1988).
62. W. H. Auden, "Dingley Dell and the Fleet," in *The Dyer's Hand and Other Essays* (New York: Random House, 1962), 424–6.
63. On this passage, see also Dennis Walder, *Dickens and Religion* (London: Allen & Unwin, 1981), 26.
64. Johnson, *Charles Dickens: His Tragedy and Triumph*, 1: 42.
65. See, e.g., Weber, "Politics as a Vocation," 118–19, 127.
66. George Orwell, *Dickens, Dali and Others* (New York: Reynal and Hitchcock, 1946), 53.
67. *DP* 251; Johnson, *Charles Dickens: His Tragedy and Triumph*, 2: 1144–5.
68. Marx, *Capital, Volume One*, 742, 787 n.15.

2. The Pathos of Distance

1. On the equivocal reception of *Catherine* (1839–40) and *The Luck of Barry Lyndon* (1844), as well as Thackeray's own judgments on these serial novels, see, for example, *Catherine*, ed. Sheldon Goldfarb (Ann Arbor: University of Michigan Press, 1999), 144–6; *The Luck of Barry Lyndon*, ed. Edgar F. Harden (Ann Arbor: University of Michigan Press, 1999), 232–6; and *LPP* 2: 193 (Thackeray's conclusion in June 1845, six months after completing *Barry Lyndon*, that "I can suit the magazines, but I can't hit the public, be hanged to them").
2. *LPP* 2: 309; Gordon N. Ray, "*Vanity Fair*: One Version of the Novelist's Responsibility," *Essays by Divers Hands* 25 (1950): 87–101, 95–6, 101.
3. Ray, "Novelist's Responsibility," 96.
4. John Sutherland, *Thackeray at Work* (London: Athlone Press, 1974), 30–1; for a similar conclusion, see Peter Garrett, *The Victorian Multiplot Novel: Studies in Dialogical Form* (New Haven: Yale University Press, 1980), 110–12.
5. See Kevin McLaughlin, *Writing in Parts: Imitation and Exchange in Nineteenth-Century Literature* (Stanford: Stanford University Press, 1995), 10–12.
6. *LPP* 1: 327–9; Gordon N. Ray, *Thackeray: the Uses of Adversity* (New York: McGraw-Hill, 1958) (hereafter "Ray"), 169, 189.
7. Quoted in Ray, 201. For the most complete analysis of Thackeray's career to 1840, including especially his stints as owner of and principal writer for *The National Standard* (1833–4) and as foreign correspondent for *The Constitutional* (1836–7), see Richard Pearson, *W. M. Thackeray and the Mediated Text:*

Writing for Periodicals in the Mid-Nineteenth Century (Aldershot: Ashgate, 2000), especially chapters 1, 3, and 5.

8. John S. Farmer, *Slang and its Analogues Past and Present* (1890; rpr. New York: Kraus, 1965), 2: 251–2; Dickens, *SB*, 123.
9. [W. M. Thackeray,] "The Professor," *Bentley's Miscellany* 2 (September 1837): 277–88, 287. For the indispensable listing of Thackeray's periodical output, see Edgar F. Harden, *A Checklist of Contributions by William Makepeace Thackeray to Newspapers, Periodicals, Books, and Serial Part Issues, 1828–1868* (Victoria: University of Victoria Press, 1996). Citations to unreprinted works are hereafter identified by both title and their number in this list (i.e., "Harden no. 117").
10. According to the *OED*, the adjective "belcher" signifies the blue and white spots on the kerchiefs preferred by a famous Regency fighter, Jim Belcher.
11. See Ray, 203; Hester Thackeray Ritchie, ed., *Thackeray and His Daughter* (New York: Harper, 1924), 61–2, quoting Thackeray's lecture "Charity and Humour" (1853), and including Thackeray's own illustration of Minnie reading *Nicholas Nickleby*.
12. W. M. Thackeray, *The Yellowplush Correspondence* (1837–8, 1840), ed. Peter L. Shillingsburg (New York: Garland, 1991), 12, 26. For a thorough study of Thackeray's contributions to *Fraser's* in this period, as well as a list of incorrectly attributed articles, cited by Harden with approval, see Edward M. White, "Thackeray's Contributions to *Fraser's Magazine*," *Studies in Bibliography* 19 (1966): 67–84. In particular, there seems no basis for the misattribution to Thackeray of the article entitled "Charles Dickens and his Works," *Fraser's Magazine* 21 (April 1840): 381–400, as in Robert L. Patten, *George Cruikshank: His Life, Times, and Art*, 2 vols (New Brunswick: Rutgers University Press, 1992, 1996), 2: 56–7 n. 28.
13. Compare "Mr. Yellowplush's Ajew," *Fraser's Magazine* 18 (August 1838): 195–200 (Harden no. 117), and "Epistles to the Literati – No. XIII," *Fraser's Magazine* 21 (January 1840): 71–80 (Harden no. 158), a parody of Bulwer-Lytton's *The Sea Captain* narrated by Yellowplush and another footman friend, and included in later editions of the *Yellowplush Correspondence*, including Peter Shillingsburg's, on that basis.
14. *Yellowplush Correspondence*, 109.
15. See "A Shabby Genteel Story," *Fraser's Magazine* 21–22 (1840) (Harden nos. 169, 173, 177, 181), 21: 681, 22: 91, 101, 233.
16. [W. M. Thackeray,] "Horae Catnachianae," *Fraser's Magazine* 19 (April 1839): 407–24 (Harden no. 136), 408–9 (emphasis added).
17. D. J. Taylor, *Thackeray: a Life* (London: Chatto & Windus, 1999), 286.
18. See, for example, Walter Kaufmann, *Nietzsche: Philosopher, Psychologist, Antichrist*, 4th edn (Princeton: Princeton University Press, 1974), 355.
19. [W. M. Thackeray,] "Strictures on Pictures. A Letter from Michael Angelo Titmarsh, Esq." *Fraser's Magazine* 17 (June 1838): 758–64 (Harden no. 115).
20. Taylor, *Thackeray*, 283.
21. Jonathan Arac, *Commissioned Spirits: the Shaping of Social Motion in Dickens, Carlyle, Melville and Hawthorne*, 2nd edn (New York: Columbia University Press, 1989), 89–93.
22. *PL* 2: 86–7n. and 4: 509n.; Dickens's letter of 28 February 1846 to the *Daily News*, quoted in Philip Collins, *Dickens and Crime* (London: Macmillan,

1962), 225–6; Thackeray, "Going to See a Man Hanged," *Fraser's Magazine* 22 (August 1840): 150–8 (Harden no. 176), 153–4.

23. G. K. Chesterton, "Introduction" to *The Book of Snobs* (London, 1911), ix, quoted in Ray, 377.
24. [W. M. Thackeray,] "A Box of Novels," *Fraser's Magazine* 29 (February 1844): 153–69 (Harden no. 268), 153.
25. Karl Marx, *Capital, Volume One,* trans. Ben Fowkes (Harmondsworth: Penguin, 1976), 1: 12: 4.
26. Charles Dickens, *A Christmas Carol* (New York: Modern Library, 1995), 94; see also *PR*, 29n.
27. Thackeray, "A Box of Novels," 168–9; *DP*, 148–50; on "A Christmas Carol" as a "spectacle of sympathy," see Audrey Jaffe, *Scenes of Sympathy: Identity and Representation in Victorian Fiction* (Ithaca: Cornell University Press, 2000), 35.
28. See *Capital, Volume One,* 787 n. 15.
29. Harden nos. 262–568.
30. E.g., Harden nos. 272, 293, 304, 306, 342.
31. *LPP* 2: 173; see also Taylor, *Thackeray*, 211.
32. Taylor, *Thackeray*, 212–13.
33. Taylor, *Thackeray*, 212.
34. Quoted in Ray, 301.
35. See Stephen Inwood, *A History of London* (New York: Carroll & Graf, 1998), 352, 479–80, 493; see also W. D. Rubinstein, *Men of Property: the Very Wealthy in Britain since the Industrial Revolution* (New Brunswick: Rutgers University Press, 1981), 61.
36. See Andrew H. Miller, *Novels Behind Glass* (Cambridge: Cambridge University Press, 1995), 34.
37. Nietzsche, *Thus Spake Zarathustra*, ed. and trans. Walter Kaufmann, in *The Portable Nietzsche* (New York: Viking/Penguin, 1982), 211–14; see also John R. Reed, *Dickens and Thackeray: Punishment and Forgiveness* (Athens: Ohio University Press, 1995), 202.
38. E.g., Nietzsche, *Thus Spake Zarathustra,* 212: "You preachers of equality, the tyrannomania of impotence clamors thus out of you for equality: your most secret ambitions to be tyrants thus shroud themselves in words of virtue."
39. For a comparison of the serial and book versions of this passage, see Catherine Peters, *The Thackeray Universe: Shifting Worlds of Imagination and Reality* (London: Faber and Faber, 1987), 123.
40. [W. M. Thackeray,] "Christmas Books – No. 1," *Morning Chronicle* (24 December 1845): 5–6 (Harden no. 460), rpr. in *W. M. Thackeray's Contributions to the Morning Chronicle*, ed. Gordon N. Ray (Urbana: University of Illinois Press, 1955), 86–8.
41. Richard D. Altick, *Punch: the Lively Youth of a British Institution, 1841–1851* (Columbus: Ohio State University Press, 1997), 246.
42. Altick, *Punch*, 278; see also Boyd Hilton, *The Age of Atonement: the Influence of Evangelicalism on Nineteenth-Century Social Thought, 1785–1865*, 2nd edn (Oxford: Clarendon Press, 1991), 250.
43. W. M. Thackeray, *The Book of Snobs*, ed. and intro. John Sutherland (New York: St. Martin's Press, 1978), 16.

44. Sutherland attributes the charitable tone of chapter 11 ("On Clerical Snobs") to its status as a counterattack against Jerrold's fiercely anticlerical *The Chronicles of Clovernook*, reprinted in April 1846 ("Introduction" to *Book of Snobs*, 16).
45. See also Ray, 370–1; Sutherland, "Introduction" to *Book of Snobs*, 11, 16.
46. Ray, 362, 370.
47. For details, see Judith McMaster, "Novels by Eminent Hands: Flattery from the Author of *Vanity Fair*," *Dickens Studies Annual* 18 (1989): 309–36.
48. [W. M. Thackeray,] "A Brother of the Press on the History of a Literary Man, Laman Blanchard, and the Chances of the Literary Profession," *Fraser's Magazine* 33 (March 1846): 332–42 (Harden no. 474), 333–4.
49. Dickens called Arthur Stanley's *Life of Dr. Arnold* (1844) "the text-book of my faith," while Forster regretted Arnold's dislike for Dickens's works (*PL* 4: 201 and nn.).
50. Sutherland, "Introduction" to *Book of Snobs*, 20.
51. For the details of these identifications, see David Payne, "Thackeray v. Dickens in *The Book of Snobs*," *Thackeray Newsletter* 51 (May 2000): 1–6, 52 (Nov. 2000): 1–2; on the omission of Dickens from *Punch's Prize Novelists*, see Altick, *Punch*, 106–7; McMaster, "Novels by Eminent Hands."
52. Edgar Johnson, *Charles Dickens: His Tragedy and Triumph*, 2 vols (New York: Simon and Schuster), 1: 410, citing William Glyde Wilkins, *Charles Dickens in America* (New York: Scribner, 1911), 207–9.
53. Hatton, *Critic* (17 January 1885): 34–5, quoted in Ray, 427.
54. See Kathleen Tillotson, *Novels of the Eighteen-Forties* (Oxford: Clarendon Press, 1954), 245.
55. Nietzsche, *On the Genealogy of Morals*, trans. Walter Kaufmann and R. J. Hollingdale (New York: Vintage, 1989), 25–6.
56. Brontë called Thackeray the "son of Imlah" (*VF* 763); for Micaiah's denunciation of Ahab, against the word of 400 other prophets, see 1 Kings 22: 1–40.
57. Quoted in *VF* 751 (emphasis added).
58. G. K. Chesterton, *Masters of Literature: Thackeray* (London, 1909), xxxii, quoted in Ray, *Adversity*, 16; Nietzsche, *Beyond Good and Evil*, sect. 228, trans. Walter Kaufmann (New York: Vintage, 1966), 157.
59. Edgar F. Harden, "The Discipline and Significance of Form in *Vanity Fair*," *PMLA* 82 (1967): 530–41, in *VF*, 710–30, 719; see also Garrett, *Victorian Multiplot Novel*, 116.
60. Alexander Nehamas, *Nietzsche: Life as Literature* (Cambridge: Harvard University Press, 1985), 221–3. On the institutional and ideological failure of Victorian Unitarians, who had long held incarnational and monist views, after 1850, see Hilton, *The Age of Atonement*, 300–4.
61. Nehamas, *Nietzsche: Life as Literature*, 227; on the essential place of art in Nietzsche's "transvaluation of values," see Richard Schacht, *Nietzsche* (Routledge & Kegan Paul, 1983), 367–79.
62. E.g., Tillotson, *Novels of the Eighteen-Forties*, 240.
63. Harden, "Discipline and Significance of Form," 719; Tillotson, *Novels of the Eighteen-Forties*, 253.

64. See, for example, Pierre Bourdieu, "Principles for a Sociology of Cultural Works," in *The Field of Cultural Production*, ed. Randal Johnson (New York: Columbia University Press, 1993), 183–91.

3. Dickens Breaks Out

1. Matthew Arnold, "On the Modern Element in Literature" (1857), *Macmillan's Magazine* 19 (February 1869): 304–14, rpr. in R. H. Super, ed., *The Complete Prose Works of Matthew Arnold* (Ann Arbor: University of Michigan Press, 1968), 1: 18–37, 20; Robert E. Lane, *The Loss of Happiness in Market Democracies* (New Haven: Yale University Press, 2000).
2. *DP* 224, 227–33, 239–46.
3. For Dickens's riposte to James Fitzjames Stephen's ongoing attacks in both the *Saturday Review* and the *Edinburgh Review*, for example, see "Curious Misprint in the Edinburgh Review," *Household Words* 16 (1 Aug. 1857): 97–100; *PL* 3: 389 n. 2.
4. *DP* 254–5; *PL* 8: 465, 566 n. 5.
5. *DP* 258; *PR* xxix.
6. After Lionel Trilling, "*Little Dorrit*" (1953), rpr. in *The Opposing Self: Nine Essays in Criticism* (New York: Viking, 1955), see, e.g., J. Hillis Miller, *Charles Dickens: the World of His Novels* (Bloomington: Indiana University Press, 1958), 246; Edwin Eigner, *The Metaphysical Novel in England and America: Dickens, Bulwer, Melville, and Hawthorne* (Berkeley: University of California Press, 1978), 116; Avrom Fleishman, "Master and Servant in *Little Dorrit*," in *Fiction and the Ways of Knowing: Essays on British Novels* (Austin: University of Texas Press, 1978), 73; Peter Garrett, *The Victorian Multiplot Novel: Studies in Dialogical Form* (New Haven: Yale University Press, 1980), 45, 84–5.
7. William Myers, "The Radicalism of *Little Dorrit*," in John Lucas, ed., *Literature and Politics in the Nineteenth Century: Essays* (London: 1971), 89, 77; see also Sylvia Manning, "Social Criticism and Textual Subversion in *Little Dorrit*," *Dickens Studies Annual* 20 (1991): 127–47.
8. See, for example, Patricia Ingham, "'Nobody's Fault': the Scope of the Negative in *Little Dorrit*," in John Schad, ed., *Dickens Refigured: Bodies, Desires and Other Histories* (Manchester: Manchester University Press, 1996), 98–116, 114; David Suchoff, *Critical Theory and the Novel: Mass Society and Cultural Criticism in Dickens, Melville and Kafka* (Madison: University of Wisconsin Press, 1994), 65, 84–5.
9. David Simpson, *Fetishism and Imagination: Dickens, Melville, Conrad* (Baltimore: Johns Hopkins University Press, 1982), 62; Astradur Eysteinsson, *The Concept of Modernism* (Ithaca: Cornell University Press, 1990), ch. 1.
10. Quoted in *DP* 249; see also *PL* 7: 509.
11. For the details of the Treasury and Commissariat affairs, see Trey Philpotts, "Trevelyan, Treasury, and Circumlocution," *Dickens Studies Annual* 22 (1993): 283–301.
12. *PL* 7: 533; see also Georgina Hogarth, Memorandum of 2 February 1906, MS Dickens House, quoted in Peter Ackroyd, *Dickens: a Life* (London: Sinclair Stevenson, 1990), 728.

13. For a description of developments in miasma and germ theory in this period, see Margaret Pelling, *Cholera, Fever and English Medicine, 1825–1865* (Oxford: Oxford University Press, 1978), 297–305 and *passim*.
14. See Jonathan Arac, "Hamlet, *Little Dorrit*, and the History of Character," in *Critical Conditions: Regarding the Historical Moment*, ed. Michael Hays (Minneapolis: University of Minnesota Press, 1992), 82–96, 86–8.
15. See also Peter Garrett, *The Victorian Multiplot Novel*, 75; Peter Brooks, *Reading for the Plot: Design and Intention in Narrative* (New York: Vintage, 1985), 141.
16. Barry Qualls, *The Secular Pilgrims of Victorian Fiction: the Novel as Book of Life* (Cambridge: Cambridge University Press, 1982), 93–6.
17. Qualls, *The Secular Pilgrims of Victorian Fiction*, 97.
18. Georg Simmel, "The Metropolis and Mental Life" (1903), in *Individuality and Social Forms*, ed. Donald N. Levine (Chicago: University of Chicago Press, 1971), 337.
19. See also Simpson, *Fetishism and Imagination*, 66.
20. See Sucksmith, "Introduction" to *Little Dorrit*, xxvi–xxvii.
21. Wilkie Collins, "Gabriel's Marriage," *Household Words* 7 (16, 23 April 1853): 149, 181.
22. Wilkie Collins, *The Lighthouse*, MS No. 545563B, Berg Collection, New York Public Library.
23. Collins, *The Lighthouse*, Act 2, page 23, MS No. 545563B, Berg Collection.
24. Collins, *The Lighthouse*, Act 2, page 9, MS No. 545563B, Berg Collection.
25. For the details of Dickens's revisions of *A Christmas Carol* at this time, see Philip Collins, *Charles Dickens: the Public Readings* (Oxford: Clarendon Press, 1975), xxxvi, lxv, 2–3, and *A Christmas Carol: the Public Reading Version*, ed. and intro. Philip Collins (New York: New York Public Library, 1971).
26. *PL* 7: 656 n. 3; *Speeches* 198, 200, 203, 205; and see generally Philpotts, "Trevelyan, Treasury, and Circumlocution," 292–9.
27. For a monochromatic view of Dickens's public readings as "wholly consonant with his responsibilities as an artist," "the culmination of his lifetime's dedication to the cause of popular entertainment," see Paul Schlicke, *Dickens and Popular Entertainment* (London: Allen & Unwin, 1985), 228, 226.
28. Quoted in *PR*, xx.
29. See "The Lost Arctic Voyagers," *Household Words* (2 Dec. 1854), *"Gone Astray" and Other Papers from Household Words, 1851–59*, ed. Michael Slater (Columbus: Ohio State University Press, 1999), 255; "The Lost Arctic Voyagers," *Household Words* (9 Dec. 1854), rpr. in *Miscellaneous Papers*, ed. B. W. Matz, 2 vols (London: Chapman and Hall, 1911), 1: 509–26.
30. *Household Words* (23 Dec. 1854), rpr. in Harry Stone, ed., *CD's Uncollected Writings from Household Words, 1850–59*, 2 vols (Bloomington: Indiana University Press, 1968), 2: 513–22.
31. *PL* 8: 184, 186 (emphasis added).
32. *PL* 8: 366 n.; see also Lillian Nayder, *Unequal Partners: Charles Dickens, Wilkie Collins, and Victorian Authorship* (Ithaca: Cornell University Press, 2002), 60–99. For an account of *The Frozen Deep* featuring the developing relationship with the Ternan family, see Claire Tomalin, *The Invisible Woman: the Story of Nelly Ternan and Charles Dickens* (New York: Knopf, 1991), 96–100.

33. For an analysis of the revisions, including the Scott mechanism and the changes in Wardour's character, see Robert Brannan, *Under the Management of Charles Dickens: His Production of* The Frozen Deep (Ithaca: Cornell University Press, 1966), 37–45.
34. John Oxenford, "The Late Mr. Douglas Jerrold," *The Times* (13 July 1857): 12.
35. *Nicholas Nickleby*, ed. Michael Slater (Harmondsworth: Penguin, 1986), 497; on the coffee-room in the 1846 fragment, see John Forster, *The Life of Charles Dickens*, ed. A. J. Hoppé (London: Dent, 1966), 1: 25; G. K. Chesterton, *Charles Dickens* (1906; New York: Schocken, 1965), 47; John Bowen, *Other Dickens* (Oxford: Oxford University Press, 2000), 14.
36. See Jürgen Habermas, *The Structural Transformation of the Public Sphere: an Inquiry into a Category of Bourgeois Society* (Cambridge: MIT Press, 1989), 57–67; T. J. Clark, "A Bar at the Folies Bergère," in *The Painting of Modern Life: Paris in the Art of Manet and his Followers*, rev. edn (Princeton: Princeton University Press, 1999), 203–58.
37. J. K. Huysmans, *Against the Grain (A Rebours)* (New York: Dover, 1969), 127–8.
38. Oxenford, "The Late Mr. Douglas Jerrold," *The Times* (13 July 1857): 12.
39. See generally Raymond Williams, *The Country and the City* (New York: Oxford University Press, 1964), 153–64, and "Introduction," *Dombey and Son* (Harmondsworth: Penguin, 1970), 11–34; Jonathan Arac, *Commissioned Spirits: the Shaping of Social Motion in Dickens, Carlyle, Melville, and Hawthorne*, 2nd edn (New York: Columbia University Press, 1989); and Priscilla Ferguson, *Paris as Revolution: Writing the Nineteenth-Century City* (Berkeley: University of California Press, 1994).
40. Compare D. A. Miller, *The Novel and the Police* (Berkeley: University of California Press, 1988), 61.
41. See also Alexander Welsh, *The City of Dickens* (Oxford: Clarendon Press, 1971), 116; Myers, "The Radicalism of *Little Dorrit*," 82.
42. See N. N. Feltes, "Community and the Limits of Liability in Two Mid-Victorian Novels," *Victorian Studies* 17 (1973–4): 360–5.
43. Though he does not discuss the synecdoche of the hand, Jeff Nunokawa has likewise argued on the basis of this scene that "domestic estate in the novel resembles the formation of, rather than a flight from, capital." See *The Afterlife of Property: Domestic Security and the Victorian Novel* (Princeton: Princeton University Press, 1994), 33.
44. See Walter Benjamin, "Allegory and Trauerspiel," in *The Origins of German Tragic Drama*, trans. John Osborne (London: New Left Books, 1977), 159–60.
45. See also Audrey Jaffe, *Vanishing Points: Dickens, Narrative, and the Subject of Omniscience* (Berkeley: University of California Press, 1991), 1, 150; Hilary Schor, *Dickens and the Daughter of the House* (Cambridge: Cambridge University Press, 1999), 142–9.
46. Foucault, *The Order of Things*, 306, quoted in Eysteinsson, *The Concept of Modernism*, 49.
47. See also Janet Larson, *Dickens and the Broken Scripture* (Athens, Ga.: University of Georgia Press, 1985), 252; Myers, "The Radicalism of *Little Dorrit*,"

93. While George Levine convincingly makes out the novel's entropic ontology, he overstates Physician's ability to resist it, calling him unambiguously "negentropic" and "almost divine." See *Darwin and the Novelists* (Cambridge: Harvard University Press, 1988), 157–8.

48. See Sergei Eisenstein, "Vertical Montage," in *Towards a Theory of Montage*, Michael Glenny and Richard Taylor, eds, *Selected Works*, vol. 2 (London: BFI Publishing, 1991), 327–99, esp. 329–30.
49. See Theodor W. Adorno, "On Epic Naiveté," trans. Shierry Weber Nicholson, in *Notes to Literature*, ed. Rolf Tiedemann, 2 vols (New York: Columbia University Press, 1991), 2: 24–9, 28.
50. See Franco Moretti, *The Way of the World: the Bildungsroman in European Culture* (London: Verso, 1987), 194.
51. See, for example, E. B. Hamley, "Remonstrance with Dickens," *Blackwood's* 81 (1857): 497 ("[W]e sit down and weep when we remember thee, O Pickwick!")
52. M. M. Bakhtin, "Discourse in the Novel," in *The Dialogic Imagination*, trans. Caryl Emerson and Michael Holquist (Austin: University of Texas Press, 1981), 299, 316, 321.
53. See Trilling, *The Opposing Self*, 54–5.
54. Josef Breuer and Sigmund Freud, *Studies on Hysteria* (1893–5), in *Standard Edition* 2: 152. All further citations appear in the text as "*SE*."
55. The wish to avoid eating in the company of anyone else is "the great anxiety of Little Dorrit's day" (I. 5: 93), just as Freud's Lucy R. suffers from both diminished appetite and smell disturbances (*SE* 2: 121).
56. On the origins of Mr. F's aunt's rage, see also Elaine Showalter, "Guilt, Authority and the Shadows of *Little Dorrit*," *Nineteenth-Century Fiction* 34 (1979): 20–40; for the Freudian analogue, see *SE* 2: 60, 62 n. 1, 63.
57. Garrett Stewart, *Dickens and the Trials of Imagination* (Cambridge: Harvard University Press, 1976), 183, 253 (index entry).
58. Benjamin, "On Some Motifs in Baudelaire," trans. Harry Zohn, in *Illuminations*, ed. Hannah Arendt (New York: Schocken, 1968), 170–3.
59. See James Joyce, *Ulysses* (New York: Random House, 1961), 73–4; Erving Goffmann, "Alienation From Interaction," in *Interaction Ritual: Essays on Face-to-Face Behavior* (Garden City: Anchor Books, 1967), 132–4; Franco Moretti, *Modern Epic: the World System from Goethe to Garcia-Marquez* (New York: Verso, 1996), 156.
60. Benjamin, "The Work of Art in the Era of Mechanical Reproduction," in *Illuminations*, 236; Adorno, "On the Fetish Character in Music and the Regression of Listening" (1938), trans. unattributed, in Arato and Gebhardt, eds, *The Essential Frankfurt School Reader* (Oxford: Basil Blackwell, 1978), 270–99, 286; see also Martin Jay, *The Dialectical Imagination: a History of the Frankfurt School of Social Research, 1923–50* (1973; Berkeley: University of California Press, 1996), 189, 210–11.
61. On the sociological significance of the dramatic monologue, see, for example, Isobel Armstrong, *Victorian Poetry: Poetry, Poetics and Politics* (London: Routledge, 1993), 136–46; Loy D. Martin, *Browning's Dramatic Monologues and the Post-Romantic Subject* (Baltimore: Johns Hopkins University Press, 1985), 106–8, 127–30; Robert Langbaum, *The Poetry of Experience* (New York: Random House, 1957), 159, 216, 232. For Miss Wade's paper in

relation to that poetic form, see Carol Bock, "Miss Wade and George Silverman: the Forms of Fictional Monologue," *Dickens Studies Annual* 16 (1987): 113–26.

62. Adorno, "On Epic Naiveté," 28.
63. Jay, *The Dialectical Imagination*, 179, citing Adorno and Marcuse on Schiller's *Letters on Aesthetic Education*.
64. Fredric Jameson, *Late Marxism: Adorno, Or, The Persistence of the Dialectic* (London: Verson, 1990), 252.
65. G. W. F. Hegel, *Lectures on the History of Philosophy*, trans. E. S. Haldane and Frances H. Simpson, 3 vols (New York: Humanities Press, 1974), 3: 552–3; Marx, "The Eighteenth Brumaire of Louis Bonaparte," in *The Marx–Engels Reader*, 2nd edn, ed. Robert C. Tucker (New York: Norton, 1978), 606; Freud, *Interpretation of Dreams*, *SE* 4: 262 ff., and "Psychopathic Characters on the Stage," *SE* 7: 309–10. For much more on the connections between *Hamlet* and *Little Dorrit*, see also Ned Lukacher, *Primal Scenes: Literature, Philosophy, Psychoanalysis* (Ithaca: Cornell University Press, 1986), chs 6–8.
66. See *Little Dorrit*, ed. Harvey Peter Sucksmith (Oxford: Clarendon Press, 1979), Appendix B, 806 (emphasis in original); *Dickens's Working Notes for His Novels*, ed. and intro Harry Stone (Chicago: University of Chicago Press, 1987), 258.
67. The developmental studies of the early 1970s consider John Chivery and Amy Dorrit as elements in this series. See James R. Kincaid, *Dickens and the Rhetoric of Laughter* (Oxford: Clarendon Press, 1971), 217; Alexander Welsh, *The City of Dickens* (Oxford: Clarendon Press, 1971), 150–4.
68. On the relation between *Little Dorrit* and *Pickwick*, see also Steven Marcus, *Dickens from Pickwick to Dombey* (New York: Norton, 1965), 47–8; Kincaid, *Dickens and the Rhetoric of Laughter*, 192.
69. Hayden White, *Metahistory: The Historical Imagination in Nineteenth-Century Europe* (Baltimore: Johns Hopkins University Press, 1973), 93–4.

4. A Dance of Indecision

1. On George Eliot's historicity, see also Steven Marcus, "Literature and Social Theory: Starting in with George Eliot," in *Representations: Essays on Literature and Society* (New York: Random House, 1975), 183–201.
2. Though she was already ill, Annette is married and dies on the same page. See *Felix Holt, the Radical*, ed. Peter Coveney (Harmondsworth: Penguin, 1972), 173.
3. Compare Ian Duncan's metaphor of the nineteenth-century British novel as ideological symphony rather than liberatory polyphony, moving from "the minor mode of historical conflict to the major mode of idyllic repose" (*Modern Romance and Transformations of the Novel: the Gothic, Scott, Dickens* [Cambridge: Cambridge University Press, 1992], 150).
4. Gordon S. Haight, *George Eliot: a Biography* (Harmondsworth: Penguin, 1985) (hereafter "Haight"), 131–2, 370.

5. *Letters of George Eliot*, 2: 269–70, 272, 273, 275 (hereafter cited as "*L*"); and see Carol A. Martin, *George Eliot's Serial Fiction* (Columbus: Ohio State University Press, 1994), 3–4.
6. On Dickens's offer and its aftermath, see Martin, *George Eliot's Serial Fiction*, 116 and nn.30–1, citing *L* 3: 203, 205, 261, 279; see also Margaret Harris and Judith Johnston, eds, *The Journals of George Eliot* (Cambridge: Cambridge University Press, 1998) (cited in the text as "*J*"), 81–2.
7. See Martin, *George Eliot's Serial Fiction*, 63–8, 2.
8. William Myers, *The Teaching of George Eliot* (Totowa: Barnes & Noble, 1984), 241; compare, for example, Deirdre David, *Intellectual Women and Victorian Patriarchy* (Ithaca: Cornell University Press, 1987), 167–72; Daniel Cottom, *Social Figures: George Eliot, Social History, and Literary Representation* (Minneapolis: University of Minnesota Press, 1987), 121–3, 169–72. For a recent defense, see Henry Staten, "Is *Middlemarch* Ahistorical?", *PMLA* 115 (2000): 991–1005, esp. 1000, 1003.
9. See, for example, Boyd Hilton's account of the triumph of an "optimistic and expansionist" conception of free trade, culminating in the adoption of limited liability in 1856, over its "evangelical or retributive" predecessors (*The Age of Atonement: the Influence of Evangelicanism on Nineteenth-Century Social Thought, 1785–1865*, 2nd edn [Oxford: Clarendon Press, 1991], 255).
10. For an uncharacteristically simple reading, see U. C. Knoepflmacher, *George Eliot's Early Novels* (Berkeley: University of California Press, 1968), 73–88.
11. See Wordsworth, *The Prelude* (1805), XI. 310.
12. George Eliot, *Silas Marner, The Weaver of Raveloe*, ed. Q. D. Leavis (1861; Harmondsworth: Penguin, 1967), 64.
13. The definitive account of her intellectual development is still Basil Willey's, in *Nineteenth-Century Studies* (New York: Columbia University Press, 1949; rpr. Harper and Row, 1966), 204–36; but see also U. C. Knoepflmacher, *Religious Humanism and the Victorian Novel: George Eliot, Walter Pater, and Samuel Butler* (Princeton: Princeton University Press, 1965), 24–71; Bernard J. Paris, *Experiments in Life: George Eliot's Quest for Values* (Detroit: Wayne State University Press, 1965), 89–113; Myers, *The Teaching of George Eliot*, Part I.
14. Haight, 186.
15. See also Haight, 186, citing John Cross, *George Eliot's Life as Related in her Letters and Journals*, 3 vols (Edinburgh: Blackwood, 1885), 1: 384, and "How I Came to Write Fiction," *J* 289.
16. Myers, *The Teaching of George Eliot*, 184–6.
17. Compare Auguste Comte, *Cours de Philosophie Positive*, trans. Harriet Martineau, in *Auguste Comte and Positivism: the Essential Writings*, ed. and intro. Gertrud Lenzer (New York: Harper & Row, 1975), 72, 76. Thomas Pinney identified Marian Evans's first reference to Comte in his *Essays of George Eliot* (New York: Columbia University Press, 1963), 28 n.
18. See also Haight, 58.
19. Comte, *The Essential Writings*, ed. Lenzer, 267, 268 (First System); 338–40, 377 (Second System).
20. Ludwig Feuerbach, *The Essence of Christianity*, trans. Marian Evans (New York: Harper, 1957), 271.
21. On this omission, see also Barry Qualls, "George Eliot and Religion," in *The Cambridge Companion to George Eliot*, ed. George Levine (Cambridge: Cambridge University Press, 2001), 119–37, 123.

22. [George Eliot,] [Review of *Theological Essays*,] *Westminster Review* (April 1853), quoted in Knoepflmacher, *Religious Humanism*, 50; F. D. Maurice, "On the Incarnation," in *Theological Essays* (1853; New York: Harper and Bros., 1957), 85–6 (emphasis added).
23. Karl Marx, *Theses on Feuerbach*, Thesis IV, rpr. in *The Marx–Engels Reader*, ed. Robert C. Tucker (New York: Norton, 1978), 144.
24. The poignancy of that interpenetration seems lost on the journals' recent editors. Though their headnotes record both the couple's zoological "zeal" and their relentless work, for example, they find these accounts simply "delightful," and praise the Leweses for being both "thoroughly professional in meeting deadlines, and well practised in the craft of prose composition" – the latter quality evident even in "the splendidly controlled report" of their brush with a pig (*J* 259–60).
25. See John F. Travis, *The Rise of the Devon Seaside Resorts, 1750–1900* (Exeter: University of Exeter Press, 1993), 168–9, quoting Gosse, *Land and Sea*, new edn (1879).
26. The most detailed treatment of "Janet's Repentance" as "incarnate history" appears in David Carroll, *George Eliot and the Conflict of Interpretations* (Cambridge: Cambridge University Press, 1992), 63, 70–2; see also Carroll, "'Janet's Repentance' and the Myth of the Organic," *Nineteenth-Century Fiction* 35 (1980): 331–48.
27. "Janet's Repentance" (1857), rpr. in *Scenes of Clerical Life*, ed. Thomas A. Noble (Oxford: Clarendon Press, 1985), 196.
28. See Knoepflmacher, *George Eliot's Early Novels*, 78; Carroll, *George Eliot and the Conflict of Interpretations*, 64.
29. Sanctimoniousness, hypocrisy, and ambition were "qualities commonly attributed to Evangelical preachers," but the tracts of High Church organs like the Society for Promoting Christian Knowledge stopped short of accusing evangelical preachers of sexual irregularities. See, e.g., *A Dialogue between a Minister of the Church and His Parishioner concerning Those Who are Called Gospel Preachers or Evangelical Ministers* (London, 1804), quoted in Thomas A. Noble, *George Eliot's* Scenes of Clerical Life (New Haven: Yale University Press, 1965), 173–5, 174 n.5.
30. Blackwood apparently used the term first in a letter which has not survived.
31. Wakem has an unspecified number of sons towards whom "he held only a chiaroscuro parentage," including the feckless Jetsome, who takes occupancy of Dorlcote Mill after the downfall of the Tullivers. See *The Mill on the Floss*, ed. A. S. Byatt (Harmondsworth: Penguin, 1979), 341.
32. See Derek and Sybil Oldfield, "*Scenes of Clerical Life:* the Diagram and the Picture," in Barbara Hardy, ed., *Critical Essays on George Eliot* (New York: Barnes and Noble, 1970), 11; compare J. Clinton McCann, Jr., "Disease and Cure in 'Janet's Repentance': George Eliot's Change of Mind," *Literature and Medicine* 9 (1990): 69–78.
33. See, for example, Alexander Welsh, *George Eliot and Blackmail* (Cambridge: Harvard University Press, 1985), 136–7, 249–55.
34. On the Medusa, see, for example, Freud, "Medusa's Head" (1940 [1922]), *Standard Edition* 18: 273–4; Jean LaPlanche, *The Language of Psycho-Analysis*, trans. D. Nicholson-Smith (New York: Norton, 1973), 59; Peter Brooks, *Reading for the Plot: Design and Intention in Narrative* (New York: Vintage, 1985), 56–7, nn.21, 22; Mary Jacobus, "Judith, Holofernes, and the Phallic

Woman," in *Reading Woman: Essays in Feminist Criticism* (New York: Columbia University Press, 1986), 110–36; Jacques Lacan, *Feminine Sexuality: Jacques Lacan and the école freudienne*, ed. and intro. Juliet Mitchell and Jacqueline Rose (New York: Norton, 1982), 36–43; Kaja Silverman, *Male Subjectivity at the Margins* (London: Routledge, 1992), 42–8; Jean-Joseph Goux, *Oedipus Philosopher* (Stanford: Stanford University Press, 1993), 25–39.

35. To Gilbert and Gubar, this imagery "suggests that Dempster is simply mad with guilt over his mistreatment" of Janet. *The Madwoman in the Attic: the Woman Writer and the Nineteenth-Century Literary Imagination* (New Haven: Yale University Press, 1979), 489. But there is nothing simple about Dempster's guilt: his memories of Janet are represented as an unconscious agency in his mind.
36. See Marcus, "Literature and Social Theory: Starting In with George Eliot," 206–13.
37. "Should there be so much of Dempster's delirium? I daresay the effect would be lessened if it were shortened" (*L* 2: 387).
38. Sigmund Freud, "Fetishism," *Standard Edition* 21: 152–57.
39. Kant, *The Critique of Judgment*, trans. James Meredith (Oxford: Oxford University Press, 1952), 186.
40. For a description of the processes generally at work in such objects, see Slavoj Zizek, *The Sublime Object of Ideology* (London: Verso, 1989), 203; for another critique of its function here, see Myers, *The Teaching of George Eliot*, 107–9.
41. Kant, *Critique of Pure Reason* (2nd edn, 1787), trans. N. Kemp Smith (London, 1929), 103. For a classification of Kant as the first modern hysteric, see Zizek, *The Sublime Object of Ideology*, 190–2.
42. See James Diedrick, "Eliot's Debt to Keller: *Silas Marner* and *Die drei gerechten Kammacher*," *Comparative Literature Studies* 20 (1983): 376–87; and "George Eliot's Experiments in Fiction: 'Brother Jacob' and the German *Novelle*," *Studies in Short Fiction* 22 (1985): 461–8.
43. *Illustrated Times* (7 Feb. 1857): 91, quoted in Martin, *George Eliot's Serial Fiction*, 44–5.
44. Gillian Beer, "Myth and the Single Consciousness: *Middlemarch* and 'The Lifted Veil,'" in Ian Adam, ed., *This Particular Web: Essays on Middlemarch* (Toronto: University of Toronto Press, 1975), 96–7, 100.
45. See Knoepflmacher, *George Eliot's Early Novels*, 128–61; Gilbert and Gubar, *The Madwoman in the Attic*, 447–77; Mary Jacobus, *Reading Woman*, 249–74.
46. See Janet Oppenheim, *"Shattered Nerves": Doctors, Patients, and Depression in Victorian England* (New York: Oxford University Press, 1991), ch. 5.
47. Mark S. Micale, "Hysteria Male/Hysteria Female: Reflections on Comparative Gender Construction in Nineteenth-Century France and Britain," in Marina Benjamin, ed., *Science and Sensibility: Gender and Scientific Inquiry, 1780–1945* (Oxford: Basil Blackwell, 1991), 200–39, 223–5; see also Micale, *Approaching Hysteria: Disease and its Interpretations* (Princeton: Princeton University Press, 1995), 125–9, 161–8, 239–48.
48. Sir James Crichton-Browne, *What the Doctor Thought* (London: Ernest Benn, 1930), 279, quoted in Oppenheim, *"Shattered Nerves"*, 207.
49. See Christopher Lane, *The Burdens of Intimacy: Psychoanalysis and Victorian Masculinity* (Chicago: University of Chicago Press, 1999), 39.

50. For Mary Ann's early enthusiasm for both writers, see *L* 1: 34 (Wordsworth), 1: 12 (Wilberforce).
51. See *The Excursion*, Prospectus 57–65, as well as III. 850–5, cited in Haight, 527: "Feebly must they have felt / Who, in old time, attired with snakes and whips / The vengeful Furies. *Beautiful* regards / Were turned on me – the face of her I loved; / The Wife and Mother pitifully fixing / Tender reproaches, insupportable!"
52. R. and S. Wilberforce, *The Life of William Wilberforce*, 5 vols (London: 1838), 1: 82–138, 89, 113.
53. See James Eli Adams, *Dandies and Desert Saints: Styles of Victorian Masculinity* (Ithaca: Cornell University Press, 1995), esp. 4–10.
54. Quoted in Elaine Showalter, *The Female Malady: Women, Madness, and English Culture, 1830–1980* (New York: Pantheon, 1985), 116.
55. For an extensive description of the relationship between nineteenth-century social theory, including Tonnies's distinction between *Gemeinschaft* community and *Gesellschaft* society, and George Eliot's fictional forms, see Suzanne Graver, *George Eliot and Community* (Berkeley: University of California Press, 1984).
56. E. S. Dallas objected in *The Times*: "As in one fit of unconsciousness he lost his all, so in another fit of unconsciousness he obtained a recompense. In either case he was helpless, had nothing to do with his own fate. . . . From this point forward in the tale, however, there is no more chance – all is work and reward, cause and effect, the intelligent mind shaping its own destiny." Quoted in David Carroll, ed., *George Eliot: The Critical Heritage* (London: Routledge & Kegan Paul, 1971), 183–4. More than a century later, Q. D. Leavis was still calling Silas's trances "unsatisfactory," "since it is not a product of his misfortunes but the cause of them, posited for the plotting – after which Silas ceases to have any fits on stage." Leavis, "Introduction" to *Silas Marner*, 26.
57. On the category of the homosocial, see Eve Kosofsky Sedgwick, *Between Men: English Literature and Male Homosocial Desire* (New York: Columbia University Press, 1985), 21–7.
58. Sally Shuttleworth, "Fairy Tale or Science? Physiological Psychology in *Silas Marner*," in L. J. Jordanova, ed., *Critical Essays on Science and Literature* (New Brunswick: Rutgers University Press, 1986), pp. 244–88.
59. G. H. Lewes, *A Biographical History of Philosophy*, 2nd edn, 2 vols (New York: Appleton, 1857), 1: 286–7 (emphasis added).
60. Compare Jeff Nunokawa, *The Afterlife of Property: Domestic Security and the Victorian Novel* (Princeton: Princeton University Press, 1994), 120.
61. On her familiarity with Lyell's *Principles of Geology* (1830–3), though not proven as early as 1838, when this letter was written, see Sally Shuttleworth, *George Eliot and Nineteenth-Century Science* (Cambridge: Cambridge University Press, 1984), 13–14.
62. On the link to Weber, see generally Alan Mintz, *George Eliot and the Novel of Vocation* (Cambridge: Harvard University Press, 1975); on Weber's breakdown of 1897–1903, from which he never fully recovered, and the resulting turn from political economy and law to religion and the sociology of culture, see Marianne Weber, *Max Weber: a Biography*, trans. and ed. Harry Zohn (New Brunswick: Transaction Books, 1988), 226–64, 303–42.

63. Weber, "Science as a Vocation," *FMW* 155.
64. "Science as a Vocation," *FMW* 156.
65. See Rosemarie Bodenheimer, *The Real Life of Mary Ann Evans* (Ithaca: Cornell University Press, 1994), 114.
66. See, for example, Franco Moretti, "The Spell of Indecision," in *Signs Taken for Wonders*, rev. edn (London: Verso, 1988), 240–8.

5. The Production of Belief

1. Simcox recalled the question in July 1880 from a conversation of March 1873. See *The Letters of George Eliot*, ed. Gordon S. Haight (New Haven: Yale University Press, 1954–78), 9: 315 (hereafter "*L*"); Edith Simcox, *A Monument to the Memory of George Eliot: Edith A. Simcox's the Autobiography of a Shirtmaker*, ed. Constance M. Fulmer and Margaret E. Barfield (New York: Garland, 1998), 129.
2. The only exception to the bimonthly rule was the final Book 8, written sufficiently early to appear in December 1872, in time for the Christmas gift season, and only one month after November's Book 7 (*L* 5: 290, 293, 297).
3. See also Carol A. Martin, *George Eliot's Serial Fiction* (Columbus: Ohio State University Press), 182–6; John Sutherland, *Victorian Novelists and Publishers* (Chicago: University of Chicago Press, 1976), 193–7.
4. [R. H. Hutton,] [Review of *Middlemarch*], *Spectator* (3 August 1872): 975.
5. See Mary Poovey, *Making a Social Body: British Cultural Formation, 1832–1865* (Baltimore: Johns Hopkins University Press, 1995), 6–14; see also David Carroll, *George Eliot and the Conflict of Interpretations* (Cambridge: Cambridge University Press, 1992), 236.
6. Gauri Viswanathan, *Outside the Fold: Conversion, Modernity, and Belief* (Princeton: Princeton University Press, 1998), 46; see also Forrest Pyle, *The Ideology of Imagination: Subject and Society in the Discourse of Romanticism* (Stanford: Stanford University Press, 1995), 158–71; Alan Mintz, *George Eliot and the Novel of Vocation* (Cambridge: Harvard University Press, 1978), 167–81.
7. Hans Blumenberg, *The Legitimacy of the Modern Age*, trans. Robert M. Wallace (Cambridge: MIT Press, 1985), 85–7, 45; Fredric Jameson, "The Vanishing Mediator, or, Max Weber as Storyteller," in *Ideologies of Theory: Essays 1971–1986* (Minneapolis: University of Minnesota Press, 1988), 2: 23–5.
8. For the exemplary discussion of the relation between George Eliot and Arnold in the early 1870s, see U. C. Knoepflmacher, *Religious Humanism and the Victorian Novel: George Eliot, Walter Pater, and Samuel Butler* (Princeton: Princeton University Press, 1965), 60–71; on *Literature and Dogma* and its reception, see Lionel Trilling, *Matthew Arnold* (New York: Columbia University Press, 1949), 331–43.
9. See, for example, Patrick Brantlinger, *The Spirit of Reform: British Literature and Politics, 1832–67* (Cambridge: Harvard University Press, 1977), 5–9; John Kucich, *Repression in Victorian Fiction: Charlotte Brontë, George Eliot and Charles Dickens* (Berkeley: University of California Press, 1987), 166–71; Jeff Nunokawa, *The Afterlife of Property: Domestic Security and the Victorian Novel* (Princeton: Princeton University Press, 1994), 120–5. On the distinction between commodity-text and commodity-book, see N. N. Feltes, *Modes of*

Production of Victorian Novels (Chicago: University of Chicago Press, 1986), 48–9, 55.

10. See Martin, *George Eliot's Serial Fiction*, 182–210 *passim*.
11. Compare J. Hillis Miller, "Narrative and History," *ELH* 41 (1974): 455–73, as discussed in Daniel Cottom, *Social Figures: George Eliot, Social History and Literary Representation* (Minneapolis: University of Minnesota Press, 1987), 112; David Lodge, "*Middlemarch* and the Idea of the Classic Realist Text," in *New Casebooks: Middlemarch*, ed. John Peck (New York: St. Martin's Press, 1992), 45–64, 60–2.
12. For an explanation of the Weberian concept of "social action," emphasizing both subjective intention and inherited disposition, see Raymond Aron, *Main Currents of Sociological Thought II: Durkheim, Pareto, Weber*, trans. Richard Howard and Helen Weaver (New York: Anchor-Doubleday, 1970), 220–4.
13. The phrase first occurs in *L* 5: 333; see also William Myers, *The Teaching of George Eliot* (Totowa: Barnes & Noble, 1984), 1–4 and *passim*.
14. There is no end to this novel's drive to qualify, as the inscription of Ladislaw's fate suggests. Though he does become "an ardent public man, working well" (this last adverb much worried over in manuscript), his success is no less about earning his own way in life by "getting at last returned to Parliament by a constituency which paid his expenses" (*M* 822). Compare Henry Staten, "Is *Middlemarch* Ahistorical?", *PMLA* 115 (2000): 991–1005, 1002–3.
15. See David Newsome, *Two Classes of Men: Platonism and English Romantic Thought* (New York: St. Martin's Press, 1974), 73–4.
16. John Henry Newman, *Apologia pro vita sua* (Boston: Houghton Mifflin-Riverside, 1956), 39; Stephen Prickett, *Romanticism and Religion: the Tradition of Coleridge and Wordsworth in the Victorian Church* (Cambridge: Cambridge University Press, 1976), 104.
17. Thomas Chalmers, *On Political Economy, in Connection with the Moral State, and Moral Prospects of Society* (1832; New York: Kelley, 1968), 445–6.
18. Michael Mann, *The Rise and Fall of Nation-States, 1765–1915* (Cambridge: Cambridge University Press, 1990), 101, 534.
19. Thomas Chalmers, *The Application of Christianity to the Commercial and Ordinary Affairs of Life*, 3rd edn (Glasgow, 1820; New York, 1821), 63–5.
20. Stuart J. Brown, *Thomas Chalmers and the Godly Commonwealth in Scotland* (Oxford: Oxford University Press, 1982), 108–44; Poovey, *Making a Social Body*, 98–106.
21. See Boyd Hilton, *The Age of Atonement: the Influence of Evangelicalism on Nineteenth-Century Social Thought, 1795–1865*, 2nd edn (Oxford: Clarendon Press, 1991), *passim*.
22. Quoted in Hamish F. G. Swanston, *Ideas of Order: Anglicans and the Renewal of Theological Method in the Middle Years of the Nineteenth Century* (Assen: Van Gorcum, 1974), 85.
23. J. Llewelyn Davies, *Theology and Morality* (New York, [1873]), 27.
24. Girton College itself was founded through the efforts of Emily Davies and Barbara Bodichon, including the £50 subscription the two obtained in 1860 from George Eliot. See Gordon S. Haight, *George Eliot: a Biography* (1968; Harmondsworth: Penguin, 1985), 339 n.5 (hereafter "Haight"); Sheila R.

Herstein, *A Mid-Victorian Feminist: Barbara Leigh Smith Bodichon* (New Haven: Yale University Press, 1985), 177–9.

25. See Frederick Maurice, *The Life of Frederick Denison Maurice*, 2 vols (London: Macmillan, 1884), 2: 52–3; Edward R. Norman, *The Victorian Christian Socialists* (Cambridge: Cambridge University Press, 1987), 15–6; George Eliot, *Felix Holt, The Radical*, ed. Fred C. Thompson (Oxford: Clarendon Press, 1980), 403.
26. John Stuart Mill, *The Collected Works of John Stuart Mill*, ed. J. M. Robson (Toronto: University of Toronto Press, 1963), 1: 160, 18: 243; see also *Life of Maurice*, 1: 62, 468, and Bernard Semmel, *John Stuart Mill and the Pursuit of Virtue* (New Haven: Yale University Press, 1984), 23.
27. Ernesto Screpanti and Stefano Zamagni, *An Outline of the History of Economic Thought*, trans. David Field (Oxford: Clarendon Press, 1993), 62–3, 96.
28. Jacob Viner, "Bentham and J. S. Mill: the Utilitarian Background" (1949), in *Essays on the Intellectual History of Economics*, ed. Douglas A. Irwin (Princeton: Princeton University Press, 1991), 175; Pedro Schwartz, *The New Political Economy of J. S. Mill* (London: Weidenfeld and Nicolson, 1972), 17.
29. See also Samuel Hollander, *The Economics of J. S. Mill* (Toronto: University of Toronto Press, 1985), 58–60.
30. See Gillian Beer, *George Eliot* (Bloomington: Indiana University Press, 1986), 179; for the stories of Sara and Dorcas, see Genesis 16, 17, 18 and Acts 9: 36–43.
31. On George Eliot's meeting Owen at the Brays, see Haight, 45–6.
32. See Haight, 123–4, 125.
33. See Rosemarie Bodenheimer, *The Real Life of Mary Ann Evans: George Eliot, Her Letters and Fiction* (Ithaca: Cornell University Press, 1994), 90–1; on Martineau's "pathological" attitude towards female sexuality, including her complaints against Elizabeth Barrett Browning and Charlotte Brontë, see Kathryn Hughes, *George Eliot: the Last Victorian* (New York: Farrar Straus & Giroux, 1999), 154.
34. Haight, 89, 93.
35. On Ambleside and the housing project, see R. K. Webb, *Harriet Martineau: a Radical Victorian* (New York: Columbia University Press, 1960), 254–62.
36. See Mintz, *George Eliot and the Novel of Vocation*, 136–7; compare Staten's claim that Garth's "mystified but accurate" notion of business expresses the work's "unblinkingly materialist substratum" ("Is *Middlemarch* Ahistorical?", 1000).
37. See Peter Mandler, *Aristocratic Government in the Age of Reform: Whigs and Liberals 1830–1852* (Oxford: Clarendon Press, 1990), 69–72, 100; for a reminder of the persistence of aristocratic rule, see Staten, "Is *Middlemarch* Ahistorical?", 992.
38. See Hilton, *Age of Atonement*, 78.
39. See Lawrence Rothfield, *Vital Signs: Medical Realism in Nineteenth-Century Fiction* (Princeton: Princeton University Press, 1992), 106–7, 110.
40. H. Buxton Forman, [Rev. of *Middlemarch*], *London Quarterly Review* 40 (April 1873): 99–110, 109.
41. David Carroll, ed., *George Eliot: the Critical Heritage* (London: Routledge & Kegan Paul, 1971), 358, 353.
42. *The Critical Heritage*, 352, 358.

43. Ludwig Feuerbach, *The Essence of Christianity*, trans. Marian Evans (1852; New York: Harper, 1957), 271.
44. Compare Blumenberg, *The Legitimacy of the Modern Age*, 78.
45. On Lydgate's consciousness, see also Rothfield, *Vital Signs*, 107, 113; David Carroll, *George Eliot and the Conflict of Interpretations* (Cambridge: Cambridge University Press, 1992), 256; Staten, "Is *Middlemarch* Ahistorical?", 1001.
46. See Pierre Bourdieu, "Field of Power, Literary Field and Habitus," trans. Claud DuVerlie, in *The Field of Cultural Production*, ed. Randal Johnson (New York: Columbia University Press, 1993), 169–75.
47. See Andrew Miller, *Novels Behind Glass: Commodity Culture and Victorian Narrative* (Cambridge: Cambridge University Press, 1995), 197–204.
48. Henry Jones, *Browning as a Philosophical and Religious Teacher* (London, 1891), 123.
49. See also Kucich, *Repression in Victorian Fiction*, 171; Neil Hertz, *The End of the Line: Essays in Literature and Psychoanalysis* (Ithaca: Cornell University Press, 1985), 95–6; Jill Matus, *Unstable Bodies: Victorian Representations of Sexuality and Maternity* (Manchester: University of Manchester Press, 1995), 217.
50. See D. A. Miller, *Narrative and its Discontents: Problems of Closure in the Traditional Novel* (Princeton: Princeton University Press, 1984), 178.
51. Quoted in Hilton, *The Age of Atonement*, 285.
52. See Hilton, *Age of Atonement*, 322–5.
53. James Mill, *Elements of Political Economy*, 3rd edn (1826), rpr. in *James Mill: Selected Economic Writings*, ed. Donald Winch (Edinburgh: Oliver & Boyd, 1966), 323; Marx, *Capital, Volume One*, trans. Ben Fowkes (Harwordsworth: Penguin – New Left Books, 1976), 718; Edward R. Norman, *The Victorian Christian Socialists* (Cambridge: Cambridge University Press, 1987), 16–17.
54. J. Llewelyn Davies, *Theology and Morality* (New York, [1873]), 275, 277.
55. Quoted in Marx, *Capital, Volume One*, 806 (emphasis added).
56. John Stuart Mill, *Works* 5: 444, 3: 944–5; see also Schwartz, *The New Political Economy of J. S. Mill*, 118–24.
57. Frederic W. H. Myers, "George Eliot," *Century Illustrated Monthly Magazine* 23 (November 1881): 57–64, 62.
58. Max Weber, "Zwischenbetrachtung" ["Intermediate Reflections"] (1915), trans. H. H. Gerth and C. Wright Mills as "Religious Rejections of the World and Their Directions," in *From Max Weber: Essays in Sociology*, ed. Gerth and Mills (New York: Oxford University Press, 1946), 341, 352.
59. See also *L* 5: 164, where Haight identifies Barbara Blackwood's lunch companion as John Tulloch, Principal and Professor of Theology at St. Mary's College, St. Andrews, and notes that Tulloch had called on the Leweses twice in 1870.
60. See Haight, 439–40; *L* 5: 185, 192–3, 194, 208, 212, 230; Bodenheimer, *The Real Life of Mary Ann Evans*, 244–8; and Leah Price, *The Anthology and the Rise of the Novel* (Cambridge: Cambridge University Press, 2000), 105–37.
61. See also Bodenheimer, *The Real Life of Mary Ann Evans*, 249–52; Haight, 452.
62. Weber, "Religious Rejections of the World and Their Directions," 340–1.
63. Simcox, *Autobiography of a Shirtmaker*, 5 n.14.
64. Weber, "Religious Rejections of the World and Their Directions," 348.

65. Simcox, *Shirtmaker*; Bodenheimer, *The Real Life of Mary Ann Evans*, 252–5; *L* 9: 203; K. A. McKenzie, *Edith Simcox and George Eliot* (London: Oxford University Press, 1961).
66. See Simcox, *Shirtmaker*, 4, 6, 13, 49, 10, 25, 26, 119.
67. Simcox, *Shirtmaker*, 5, 13, 117–18, 126.
68. Friedrich Nietzsche, "Über Wahrheit und Lüge im aussermoralischen Sinne" (1873), trans. Daniel Breazeale as "On Truth and Lies in a Nonmoral Sense," in *Philosophy and Truth: Selections from Nietzsche's Notebooks of the early 1870's*, ed. Breazeale (Atlantic Highlands, NJ: Humanities Press, 1979), 79–97.
69. Although *Daniel Deronda* also appeared in eight serial parts, Blackwood suggested monthly publication, over his staff's objections, on the ground that two months would give "the Librarians a better opportunity of starving their supplies"; George Eliot's head start allowed her to agree to the monthly schedule (*L* 6: 186; Martin, *George Eliot's Serial Fiction*, 213–16).
70. Quoted in Martin, *George Eliot's Serial Fiction*, 187.
71. Martin, *George Eliot's Serial Fiction*, 196–7; on the self-consecration of the artist, see also William Wordsworth, *The Letters of William and Dorothy Wordsworth*, ed. Ernest de Selincourt and Mary Moorman, 2nd edn (Oxford: Clarendon Press, 1969), 2: 150; Pierre Bourdieu, "Outline of a Sociological Theory of Art Perception" (1968), in *The Field of Cultural Production*, ed. Randal Johnson (New York: Columbia University Press, 1993), 234.
72. Quoted in Martin, *George Eliot's Serial Fiction*, 245–6.
73. *The Critical Heritage*, 305–6 (emphasis added).
74. See also Feltes, *Modes of Production of Victorian Novels*, 49.
75. Miller, *Narrative and its Discontents*, 152–3 n.20.
76. *Critical Heritage*, 359; Weber, "Religious Rejections of the World and Their Directions," 342.
77. On the persistence of modernity, see T. J. Clark, *Farewell to an Idea: Episodes from a History of Modernism* (New Haven: Yale University Press, 1999), 7–8; Raymond Williams, *The Politics of Modernism* (London: Verso, 1989), 44–7.

Epilogue: The Sacred Monster

1. Though it had been even more popular in print than its predecessor *A Christmas Carol*, the *Cricket* reading proved less successful, and was soon dropped from Dickens's repertoire (*PR* 35). For the essential tabulation and explanation of these texts and performances, see Philip Collins, "Introduction" to *The Public Readings*, xxvii–xxx, as well as the appendices of public readings in *PL* 8: 752–3, 10: 479, and 11: 533–5.
2. See Craig Howes, "*Pendennis* and the Controversy on the 'Dignity of Literature,'" *Nineteenth-Century Literature* 41 (1986): 269–98; Peter Shillingsburg, *Pegasus in Harness: Victorian Publishing and W. M. Thackeray* (Charlottesville: University Press of Virginia, 1992), 17–19.
3. *The Speeches of Charles Dickens*, ed. K. J. Fielding (Oxford: Clarendon Press, 1960), 264.
4. See Paul Schlicke, *Dickens and Popular Entertainment* (London: Allen & Unwin, 1985), 227, 245.

5. John Forster, *The Life of Charles Dickens*, ed. A. J. Hoppé, 2 vols (London: J. M. Dent, 1966), 2: 200.
6. See, for example, Fred Kaplan, *Dickens: a Biography* (New York: William Morrow, 1988), 381–5, 444–50, 503–13.
7. Kaplan, *Dickens*, 532–8; Peter Ackroyd, *Dickens: a Life* (London: Sinclair Stevenson, 1990), 1059–60.
8. On the persistent need for pictorial and theatrical supplements for serial fiction, see especially Martin Meisel, *Realizations: Narrative, Pictorial, and Theatrical Arts in 19th-Century England* (Princeton: Princeton University Press, 1983).
9. On the details of the final London readings, see *PR* 2 ("Carol"), 471 ("Sikes and Nancy"), 199 ("Trial from Pickwick").
10. W. P. Frith, *Autobiography and Reminiscences*, 2 vols (London, 1887), 1: 311–12, quoted in Collins, *PR*, 198; George Dolby, *Charles Dickens as I Knew Him: the Story of the Reading Tours in Great Britain and America, 1866–70* (London, 1885), 175–6.
11. *Manchester Guardian* (4 Feb. 1867), quoted in *PR* 197.
12. Steven Marcus, *Dickens from Pickwick to Dombey* (New York: Norton, 1965), 17.
13. *A Christmas Carol: the Public Reading Version: a Facsimile of the Author's Prompt-Copy*, intro. and ed. Philip Collins (New York: The New York Public Library, 1971), 88–96, 92–3.
14. On the last-minute revision to save Tiny Tim, as well as twentieth-century responses to the discovery, see Paul Davis, *The Lives and Times of Ebeneezer Scrooge* (New Haven: Yale University Press, 1990), 133–5, reproducing the manuscript in the collection of the Pierpont Morgan Library, New York, MA 97, 65–6.
15. Emile Durkheim, *The Elementary Forms of Religious Life* (New York: Free Press, 1995), 405; Weber, "Science as a Vocation," in *From Max Weber* (New York: Oxford University Press, 1946), 154; and see Susan Mizruchi, *The Science of Sacrifice: American Literature and Modern Social Theory* (Princeton: Princeton University Press, 1998), 49–55.
16. Mizruchi, *The Science of Sacrifice*, 53. Weber called his brother's battlefield death of 1915 "beautiful," having occurred in "the only place where it is worthy of a human being to be at the moment." Marianne Weber, *Max Weber: a Biography* (New Brunswick: Transaction Books, 1988), 531.
17. For a description of the final New York dinner, and the ministrations necessary to allow Dickens to attend, see Dolby, *Charles Dickens as I Knew Him*, 310–21.
18. Dolby, *Charles Dickens as I Knew Him*, 351.
19. Dolby, *Charles Dickens as I Knew Him*, 380–1, 387–8.
20. Dolby, *Charles Dickens as I Knew Him*, 386; *PR* 471, quoting John Hollingsworth, *According to my Lights* (London, 1900), 19.
21. Emphasis in original. Philip Collins calls this revision "more interesting than in any of the other Readings" (*PR* 467).
22. *PL* 12: 221, 329.
23. The phrase, as in Cocteau's *Les Monstres Sacrés* (1940), is now translated as "superstar"; see also Paul Ricoeur, *Lectures on Ideology and Utopia*, ed. George H. Taylor (New York: Columbia University Press, 1986), 9–10.

24. See John Sutherland, *Victorian Novelists and Publishers* (Chicago: University of Chicago Press, 1976), 215–17.
25. On the serial fate of Hardy's last novel, *Jude the Obscure* (1895), see Linda K. Hughes and Michael Lund, *The Victorian Serial* (Charlottesville: University Press of Virginia, 1991), 230–43.
26. For the classic account of the *Guy Domville* débâcle, see Leon Edel, *Henry James: the Treacherous Years, 1895–1901* (New York: Avon, 1969), 64–80.
27. See *Faust, Part One*, Auerbach's Cellar in Leipzig, l. 2141; Marx, *Capital, Volume One* (Harmondsworth: Penguin – New Left Books, 1976), 302.

Bibliography

Ackroyd, Peter. *Dickens: a Life*. London: Sinclair Stevenson, 1990.

Adams, James Eli. *Dandies and Desert Saints: Styles of Victorian Masculinity*. Ithaca: Cornell University Press, 1995.

Adorno, Theodor. *Notes to Literature*. 2 vols. Ed. Rolf Tiedemann. New York: Columbia University Press, 1991.

—"On the Fetish Character in Music and the Regression of Listening." 1938. Trans. unattributed. *The Essential Frankfurt School Reader*. Ed. Andrew Arato and Eike Gerhardt. Oxford: Basil Blackwell, 1978. 270–99.

—"Sociology and Psychology." *New Left Review* 46 (1967): 67–80 and 47 (1968): 79–97.

Allen, James Smith. *In the Public Eye: a History of Reading in Modern France, 1800–1940*. Princeton: Princeton University Press, 1991.

Altholz, Josef. *The Religious Press in Britain, 1760–1900*. New York: Greenwood Press, 1989.

Altick, Richard D. *The English Common Reader*. Chicago: University of Chicago Press, 1957.

—*Punch: the Lively Youth of a British Institution, 1841–1851*. Columbus: Ohio State University Press, 1997.

Anderson, Perry. *Arguments Within English Marxism*. London: New Left Books, 1980.

—*A Zone of Engagement*. London: Verso, 1992.

Anonymous. "Charles Dickens and his Works." *Fraser's Magazine* 21 (April 1840): 381–400.

Appadurai, Arjun. *Modernity at Large: Cultural Dimensions of Globalization*. Minneapolis: University of Minnesota Press, 1996.

Arac, Jonathan. *Commissioned Spirits: the Shaping of Social Motion in Dickens, Carlyle, Melville, and Hawthorne*. 2nd edn. New York: Columbia University Press, 1989.

—"Hamlet, *Little Dorrit* and the History of Character." *Critical Conditions: Regarding the Historical Moment*. Ed. Michael Hays. Minneapolis: University of Minnesota Press, 1992. 82–96.

Armstrong, Isobel. *Victorian Poetry: Poetry, Poetics and Politics*. London: Routledge, 1993.

Armstrong, Nancy. *Desire and Domestic Fiction: a Political History of the Novel*. New York: Oxford University Press, 1987.

Arnold, Matthew. *Literature and Dogma*. 1871, 1873. Vol. 6 of *The Complete Prose Works of Matthew Arnold*. Ed. R. H. Super. Ann Arbor: University of Michigan Press, 1968.

—"On the Modern Element in Literature." 1857; *Macmillan's Magazine* 19 (February 1869): 304–14. Vol. 1 of *The Complete Prose Works of Matthew Arnold*. 18–37.

Aron, Raymond. *Main Currents in Sociological Thought II: Durkeim, Pareto, Weber*. Trans. Richard Howard and Helen Weaver. New York: Anchor-Doubleday, 1970.

Auden, W. H. "Dingley Dell and the Fleet." *The Dyer's Hand and Other Essays.* New York: Random House, 1962. 407–28.

Bakhtin, Mikhail. *The Dialogic Imagination.* Ed. and trans. Caryl Emerson and Michael Holquist. Austin: University of Texas Press, 1981.

Basch, Françoise. *Relative Creatures: Victorian Women in Society and the Novel.* Trans. A. Rudolph. New York: Schocken, 1971.

Beer, Gillian. *Darwin's Plots: Evolutionary Narrative in Darwin, George Eliot and Nineteenth-Century Fiction.* London: Routledge & Kegan Paul, 1983.

—*George Eliot.* Bloomington: Indiana University Press, 1986.

—"Myth and the Single Consciousness: *Middlemarch* and 'The Lifted Veil.'" *This Particular Web: Essays on Middlemarch.* Ed. Ian Adam. Toronto: University of Toronto Press, 1975. 91–115.

Benjamin, Walter. "On Some Motifs in Baudelaire." Trans. Harry Zohn. *Illuminations.* Ed. Hannah Arendt. New York: Schocken, 1968. 155–200.

—*The Origins of German Tragic Drama.* Trans. John Osborne. London: New Left Books, 1977.

—"The Work of Art in the Era of Mechanical Reproduction." *Illuminations.* Ed. Hannah Arendt. New York: Schocken, 1968.

Bennett, Scott. "Revolutions in Thought: Serial Publication and the Mass Market for Reading." *The Victorian Periodical Press: Samplings and Soundings.* Ed. Joanne Shattock and Michael Wolff. Toronto: University of Toronto Press, 1982. 225–57.

Blumenberg, Hans. *The Legitimacy of the Modern Age.* Trans. Robert Wallace. Rev. edn. Cambridge: MIT Press, 1985.

Bock, Carol. "Miss Wade and George Silverman: the Forms of Fictional Monologue." *Dickens Studies Annual* 16 (1987): 113–26.

Bodenheimer, Rosemarie. *The Real Life of Mary Ann Evans: George Eliot, Her Letters and Fiction.* Ithaca: Cornell University Press, 1994.

Bourdieu, Pierre. *The Field of Cultural Production.* Ed. and intro. Randal Johnson. New York: Columbia University Press, 1993.

Bowen, John. *Other Dickens.* Oxford: Oxford University Press, 2000.

Bradley, Ian. *The Call to Seriousness: the Evangelical Impact on the Victorians.* London: Jonathan Cape, 1976.

Brake, Laurel. *Print in Transition, 1850–1910: Studies in Media and Book History.* Basingstoke: Palgrave Macmillan, 2001.

—*Subjugated Knowledge: Journalism, Gender, and Literature in the Nineteenth Century.* New York: New York University Press, 1994.

Brantlinger, Patrick. *The Spirit of Reform: British Literature and Politics, 1832–1867.* Cambridge: Harvard University Press, 1977.

Breuer, Josef and Sigmund Freud. *Studies on Hysteria.* 1893–5. New York: Basic Books, n.d. Vol. 2 of *The Standard Edition of the Complete Psychological Works of Sigmund Freud.* Trans. and ed. James Strachey. 24 vols. London: Hogarth Press, 1953–74.

Briggs, Asa. *Victorian Cities.* Rev. edn. Berkeley: University of California Press, 1993.

Bronfen, Elisabeth. *Over Her Dead Body: Death, Femininity and the Aesthetic.* New York: Routledge, 1992.

Brooks, Peter. *Reading for the Plot: Design and Intention in Narrative.* New York: Vintage, 1985.

Brown, Stewart J. *Thomas Chalmers and the Godly Commonwealth in Scotland.* Oxford: Oxford University Press, 1982.
Butt, John, and Kathleen Tillotson. *Dickens at Work.* London: Methuen, 1957.
Byron, George Gordon. *Selected Letters and Journals.* Ed. Leslie A. Marchand. Cambridge: Belknap-Harvard University Press, 1982.
Carlisle, Janice M. "*Little Dorrit*: Necessary Fictions." *Studies in the Novel* 7 (1975): 175–214.
The Carlton Chronicle. London. 11 June 1836–13 May 1837.
Carlyle, Thomas. *The French Revolution: a History.* 1837. New York: Modern Library, 1934.
—*On Heroes and Hero-Worship, and the Heroic in History.* 1840. *Works of Thomas Carlyle.* Vol. 5. London: Chapman and Hall, 1897; New York: AMS, 1969.
Carroll, David. *George Eliot and the Conflict of Interpretations.* Cambridge: Cambridge University Press, 1992.
—" 'Janet's Repentance' and the Myth of the Organic." *Nineteenth-Century Fiction* 35(3) (Dec. 1980): 331–48.
—ed. *George Eliot: the Critical Heritage.* London: Routledge & Kegan Paul, 1971.
Chadwick, Owen. *The Secularization of the European Mind in the 19th Century.* 1975. Cambridge: Cambridge University Press, 1993.
Chalmers, Thomas. *The Application of Christianity to the Commercial and Ordinary Affairs of Life.* 3rd edn. Glasgow, 1820; New York, 1821.
—*On Political Economy, in Connection with the Moral State, and Moral Prospects of Society.* 1832. New York: Kelley, 1968.
Chandler, James. *England in 1819: the Politics of Literary Culture and the Case of Romantic Historicism.* Chicago: University of Chicago Press, 1998.
Chesterton, G. K. *Charles Dickens.* 1906. Intro. Steven Marcus. New York: Schocken, 1965.
— "Introduction." *The Book of Snobs.* By W. M. Thackeray. London, 1911.
—*Masters of Literature: Thackeray.* London, 1909.
Childers, Joseph. *Novel Possibilities: Fiction and the Formation of Early Victorian Culture.* Philadelphia: University of Pennsylvania Press, 1995.
Chittick, Kathryn. *Dickens and the 1830s.* Cambridge: Cambridge University Press, 1990.
Church, R. W. *The Oxford Movement: Twelve Years, 1833–1845.* 1891. Ed. and intro. Geoffrey Best. Chicago: University of Chicago Press, 1970.
Clark, T. J. *Farewell to an Idea: Episodes from a History of Modernism.* New Haven: Yale University Press, 1999.
—*The Painting of Modern Life: Paris in the Art of Manet and his Followers.* Rev. edn. Princeton: Princeton University Press, 1999.
Cohen, Jane R. *Charles Dickens and his Original Illustrators.* Columbus: Ohio State University Press, 1980.
Coleman, John. *Fifty Years of an Actor's Life.* 2 vols. London, 1904.
Colley, Linda. *Britons: Forging the Nation, 1707–1837.* New Haven: Yale University Press, 1992.
Collins, Philip. *Dickens and Crime.* London: Macmillan, 1962.
—ed. *Charles Dickens: the Critical Heritage.* London: Routledge & Kegan Paul, 1971.
—ed. *Charles Dickens: the Public Readings.* Oxford: Clarendon Press, 1975.

Collins, Wilkie. "Gabriel's Marriage." *Household Words* 7 (April 1853): 149–57, 181–90.
—*The Lighthouse*. MS No. 545563B. Berg Collection, New York Public Library.
—*Under the Management of Mr. Charles Dickens: His Production of* The Frozen Deep. Ed. R. C. Brannan. Ithaca: Cornell University Press, 1966.
Comte, Auguste. *Auguste Comte and Positivism: the Essential Writings*. Ed. and intro. Gertrud Lenzer. New York: Harper & Row, 1975.
Cottom, Daniel. *Social Figures: George Eliot, Social History and Literary Representation*. Minneapolis: University of Minnesota Press, 1987.
Cross, John. *George Eliot's Life as Related in her Letters and Journals*. 3 vols. Edinburgh: Blackwood, 1885.
Curran, Stuart. *Poetic Form and British Romanticism*. New York: Oxford University Press, 1986.
Dale, Peter Allan. *In Pursuit of a Scientific Culture: Science, Art, and Society in the Victorian Age*. Madison: University of Wisconsin Press, 1989.
David, Deirdre. *Intellectual Women and Victorian Patriarchy*. Ithaca: Cornell University Press, 1987.
Davies, J. Llewelyn. *Theology and Morality*. New York, [1873].
Davis, David Brion. *Slavery and Human Progress*. London: Oxford University Press, 1984.
Davis, Lennard. *Factual Fictions: Origins of the English Novel*. New York: Columbia University Press, 1983.
Davis, Paul. *The Lives and Times of Ebeneezer Scrooge*. New Haven: Yale University Press, 1990.
Derrida, Jacques. *Specters of Marx*. London: Routledge, 1994.
DeVries, Duane. *Dickens's Apprentice Years: the Making of a Novelist*. New York: Harvester–Barnes and Noble, 1976.
Dickens, Charles. *Bleak House*. 1852–3. Ed. George Ford, Sylvere Monod. Norton Critical Edition. New York: Norton, 1977.
—"City of London Churches." *All the Year Round*. 5 May 1860. *Selected Short Fiction*. Ed. Deborah A. Thomas. Harmondsworth: Penguin, 1976.
—*A Christmas Carol: the Public Reading Version: a Facsimile of the Author's Prompt-Copy*. Intro. and ed. Philip Collins. New York: New York Public Library, 1971.
—*A Christmas Carol*. New York: Modern Library, 1995.
—*Dickens's Working Notes for his Novels*. Ed. and intro. Harry Stone. Chicago: University of Chicago Press, 1987.
—"The Hospital Patient." *Carlton Chronicle*. 6 August 1836: 139.
—*The Letters of Charles Dickens [Pilgrim Edition]*. Gen. eds. Madeline House, Graham Storey, and Kathleen Tillotson. 12 vols. Oxford: Clarendon Press, 1965–2002.
—*Little Dorrit*. 1855–7. Ed. Harvey Peter Sucksmith. Oxford: Clarendon Press, 1979.
—*Little Dorrit*. 1855–7. Ed. John Holloway. Harmondsworth: Penguin, 1967.
—"The Lost Arctic Voyagers." *Household Words*, 2 and 9 December 1854. *Miscellaneous Papers*. Ed. B. W. Matz. 2 vols. London: Chapman & Hall, 1911. 1: 499–526.
—"The Lost Arctic Voyagers." *Household Words*, 23 December 1854. *Charles Dickens's Uncollected Writings from* Household Words, *1850–59*. Ed. Harry Stone. 2 vols. Bloomington: Indiana University Press, 1968. 2: 513–22.

—*Nicholas Nickleby.* 1838–9. Ed. Michael Slater. Harmondsworth: Penguin, 1986.
—*Oliver Twist.* 1837–9. Ed. Kathleen Tillotson. Oxford: Clarendon Press, 1966.
—*The Pickwick Papers.* 1836–7. Ed. Robert L. Patten. Harmondsworth: Penguin, 1972.
—*The Pickwick Papers.* 1836–7. Ed. James Kingsley. Oxford: Clarendon Press, 1986.
—*The Public Readings.* Ed. Philip Collins. Oxford: Clarendon Press, 1975.
—*Sikes and Nancy: a Facsimile of a Privately Printed Annotated Copy, Now in the Dickens House, Presented by Dickens to Adeline Billington.* Ed. Philip Collins. London: Dickens House, 1982.
—*Sketches by Boz.* 1837–9. Ed. Dennis Walder. Harmondsworth: Penguin, 1995.
—*Sketches by Boz and Other Early Papers.* Ed. Michael Slater. London: J. M. Dent, 1994; Columbus: Ohio State University Press, 1994.
—*The Speeches of Charles Dickens.* Ed. K. J. Fielding. Oxford: Clarendon Press, 1960.
Diedrick, James. "Eliot's Debt to Keller: *Silas Marner* and *Die drei gerechten Kammacher." Comparative Literature Studies* 20 (1983): 376–87.
—"George Eliot's Experiments in Fiction: 'Brother Jacob' and the German *Novelle." Studies in Short Fiction* 22 (1985): 461–8.
Disraeli, Benjamin. *The Benjamin Disraeli Letters.* Ed. J. A. W. Gunn et al. 6 vols. to date. Toronto: University of Toronto Press, 1982–.
Dolby, George. *Charles Dickens as I Knew Him: the Story of the Reading Tours in Great Britain and America, 1866–70.* London, 1885.
Duncan, Ian. *Modern Romance and Transformations of the Novel: the Gothic, Scott, Dickens.* Cambridge: Cambridge University Press, 1992.
Durkheim, Emile. *The Elementary Forms of Religious Life.* 1912. Trans. Karen E. Fields. New York: Free Press, 1995.
Eisenstein, Sergei. "Vertical Montage." *Towards a Theory of Montage.* Ed. Michael Glenny and Richard Taylor. *Selected Works.* London: BFI Publishing, 1991. 2: 327–99.
Eliot, George. *Daniel Deronda.* 1876. Ed. Barbara Hardy. Harmondsworth: Penguin, 1974.
—*Essays of George Eliot.* Ed. Thomas Pinney. New York: Columbia University Press, 1963.
—"Evangelical Teaching: Dr. Cumming." *Westminster Review* (Oct. 1855): 436–62. *Selected Essays, Poems and Other Writings.* 38–68.
—*Felix Holt, The Radical.* 1866. Ed. Fred C. Thompson. Oxford: Clarendon Press, 1980.
—*George Eliot: a Writer's Notebook 1854–1879.* Ed. Joseph Wiesenfarth. Charlottesville: University Press of Virginia, 1981.
—*The Journals of George Eliot.* Ed. Margaret Harris and Judith Johnston. Cambridge: Cambridge University Press, 1998.
—*The Letters of George Eliot.* Ed. Gordon S. Haight. 9 vols. New Haven: Yale University Press, 1954–78.
—*Middlemarch: a Study of Provincial Life.* 1871–2. Ed. David Carroll. Oxford: Clarendon Press, 1986.
—*The Mill on the Floss.* 1860. Ed. A. S. Byatt. Harmondsworth: Penguin, 1979.
—"The Natural History of German Life." *Westminster Review* (July 1856): 51–79. *Selected Essays, Poems and Other Writings.* 107–39.

—*Scenes of Clerical Life*. 1858. Ed. Thomas A. Noble. Oxford: Clarendon Press, 1985.
—*Selected Essays, Poems and Other Writings*. Ed. A. S. Byatt and Nicholas Warren. Harmondsworth: Penguin, 1990.
—*Silas Marner, the Weaver of Raveloe*. 1861. Ed. Q. D. Leavis. Harmondsworth: Penguin, 1967.
—"Worldliness and Other-Worldliness: the Poet Young." *Westminster Review* (Jan. 1857): 1–42. *Selected Essays, Poems and Other Writings*. 164–213.
Ellmann, Richard. *Oscar Wilde*. New York: Knopf, 1988.
Engels, Friedrich. *The Origin of Family, Private Property, and the State*. 1884. Reprinted and abridged in *The Marx–Engels Reader*, ed. Robert C. Tucker. 2nd edn. New York: Norton, 1978. 734–59.
Eysteinsson, Astradur. *The Concept of Modernism*. Ithaca: Cornell University Press, 1990.
Farmer, John S. *Slang and its Analogues Past and Present*. 1890. New York: McGraw-Hill, 1958.
Feltes, N. N. "Community and the Limits of Liability in Two Mid-Victorian Novels." *Victorian Studies* 17 (1973–4): 355–69.
—*Modes of Production of Victorian Novels*. Chicago: University of Chicago Press, 1986.
Ferguson, Priscilla. *Paris as Revolution: Writing the Nineteenth-Century City*. Berkeley: University of California Press, 1994.
Feuerbach, Ludwig. *The Essence of Christianity*. Trans. Marian Evans. 1853. New York: Harper, 1957.
Flaubert, Gustave. *The Letters of Gustave Flaubert, 1830–1857*. Ed. and trans. Francis Steegmuller. Cambridge: Harvard University Press, 1979.
Fleishman, Avrom. *Fiction and the Ways of Knowing: Essays on British Novels*. Austin: University of Texas Press, 1978.
[Forman, H. Buxton.] Rev. of *Middlemarch*. *London Quarterly Review* 40 (April 1873): 99–110.
Forster, John. *The Life of Charles Dickens*. Ed. A. J. Hoppé. 2 vols. London: Dent, 1966.
Foucault, Michel. *Discipline and Punish: the Birth of the Prison*. Trans. Alan Sheridan. New York: Vintage, 1979.
Freedgood, Elaine. *Victorian Writing About Risk: Imagining a Safe England in a Dangerous World*. Cambridge: Cambridge University Press, 2000.
Freud, Sigmund. *The Standard Edition of the Complete Psychological Works of Sigmund Freud*. Trans. and ed. James Strachey. 24 vols. London: Hogarth Press, 1953–74.
Gagnier, Regenia. *The Insatiability of Human Wants: Economics and Aesthetics in Market Society*. Chicago: University of Chicago Press, 2000.
Gallagher, Catherine. *The Industrial Reformation of English Fiction: Social Discourse and Narrative Form, 1832–1867*. Chicago: University of Chicago Press, 1985.
Garrett, Peter K. *The Victorian Multiplot Novel: Studies in Dialogical Form*. New Haven: Yale University Press, 1980.
Gauchet, Marcel. *The Disenchantment of the World: a Political History of Religion*. Trans. Oscar Burge. Princeton: Princeton University Press, 1997.
Giddens, Anthony. *Politics and Sociology in the Thought of Max Weber*. London: Macmillan, 1972. Rpr. in *Politics, Sociology and Social Theory: Encounters with*

Classical and Contemporary Social Thought. Stanford: Stanford University Press, 1995. 15–56.

Gilbert, Sandra M. and Susan Gubar. *The Madwoman in the Attic: the Woman Writer and the Nineteenth-Century Literary Imagination*. New Haven: Yale University Press, 1979.

Girard, René. *Violence and the Sacred*. Trans. Patrick Gregory. Baltimore: Johns Hopkins University Press, 1977.

Goffman, Erving. *Interaction Ritual: Essays on Face-to-Face Behavior*. Garden City: Anchor Books, 1967.

Goldberg, Michael. *Carlyle and Dickens*. Athens: University of Georgia Press, 1972.

Goodwin, Gregory. "Keble and Newman: Tractarian Aesthetics and the Romantic Tradition." *Victorian Studies* 30 (1987): 474–94.

Goux, Jean-Joseph. *Oedipus Philosopher*. Stanford: Stanford University Press, 1993.

—*Symbolic Economies: After Marx and Freud*. Trans. Jennifer Curtis Gage. Ithaca: Cornell University Press, 1990.

Graver, Suzanne. *George Eliot and Community: a Study in Social Theory and Fictional Form*. Berkeley: University of California Press, 1984.

Green, Ronald. "Developing *Fear and Trembling*." *The Cambridge Companion to Kierkegaard*. Ed. Alastair Hannay and Gordon D. Marino. Cambridge: Cambridge University Press, 1996.

Gribble, Jennifer. "Introduction." *Scenes of Clerical Life*. By George Eliot. Harmondsworth: Penguin, 1998. ix–xxxvi.

Grillo, Virgil. *Charles Dickens's* Sketches by Boz*: End in the Beginning*. Boulder: Colorado Associated University Press, 1974.

Habermas, Jürgen. *The Structural Transformation of the Public Sphere: an Inquiry into a Category of Bourgeois Society*. Trans. Thomas Burger. Cambridge: MIT Press, 1989.

Haight, Gordon S. *George Eliot: a Biography*. 1968. Harmondsworth: Penguin, 1985.

Halévy, Elie. *England in 1815*. Trans. E. I. Watkin and D. A. Barker. New York: Peter Smith, 1949.

—*Victorian Years: 1841–1852*. Trans. E. I. Watkin. New York: Peter Smith, 1951.

Hamer, Mary. *Writing by Numbers: Trollope's Serial Fiction*. Cambridge: Cambridge University Press, 1987.

Harden, Edgar F. *A Checklist of Contributions by William Makepeace Thackeray to Newspapers, Periodicals, Books, and Serial Part Issues, 1828–1864*. Victoria: University of Victoria Press, 1996.

—"The Discipline and Significance of Form in *Vanity Fair*." *PMLA* 82 (1967): 530–41.

—*The Emergence of Thackeray's Serial Fiction*. Athens: University of Georgia Press, 1979.

Harrison, Brian. *Drink and the Victorians*. London: Faber and Faber, 1971.

Harrison, J. F. C., and Dorothy Thompson. *Bibliography of the Chartist Movement, 1837–1976*. Sussex: Harvester Press, 1978.

Hegel, G. W. F. *Aesthetics: Lectures on the Fine Arts*. Trans. T. M. Knox. 2 vols. Oxford: Clarendon Press, 1975.

—*Early Theological Writings*. Ed. Richard Kroner. Philadelphia: University of Pennsylvania Press, 1971.

—"Introduction to the Philosophy of History." *Reason in History: a General Introduction to the Philosophy of History.* Trans. Robert S. Hartman. Indianapolis: Bobbs Merrill, 1953.

—*Lectures on the History of Philosophy.* Trans. E. S. Haldane and Frances H. Simpson. 3 vols. New York: Humanities Press, 1974.

—*The Phenomenology of Mind.* Trans. J. B. Baillie. New York: Harper & Row, 1967.

Herstein, Sheila R. *A Mid-Victorian Feminist: Barbara Leigh Smith Bodichon.* New Haven: Yale University Press, 1985.

Hertz, Neil. *The End of the Line: Essays in Literature and Psychoanalysis.* Ithaca: Cornell University Press, 1985.

Hewitt, Martin. "Ralph Waldo Emerson, George Dawson, and the Control of the Lecture Platform in Mid-Nineteenth Century Manchester." *Nineteenth-Century Prose* 25(2) (Fall 1998): 1–23.

Heyns, Michiel. *Expulsion and the Nineteenth-Century Novel: the Scapegoat in Realist Fiction.* Oxford: Clarendon Press, 1994.

Hilton, Boyd. *The Age of Atonement: the Influence of Evangelicalism on Nineteenth-Century Social Thought, 1785–1865.* 2nd edn. Oxford: Clarendon Press, 1991.

Hobsbawm, E. J. *On History.* New York: New Press, 1997.

—and George Rudé. *Captain Swing.* New York: Pantheon, 1968.

Hollander, Samuel. *The Economics of J. S. Mill.* 2 vols. Toronto: University of Toronto Press, 1985.

Hollis, Patricia. *The Pauper Press.* New York: Oxford University Press, 1970.

Homans, Margaret. "Dinah's Blush, Maggie's Arm: Class, Gender and Sexuality in George Eliot's Early Novels." *Victorian Studies* 36 (1993): 155–78.

Houghton, Walter E. *The Victorian Frame of Mind, 1830–1870.* New Haven: Yale University Press, 1957.

Howes, Craig. "*Pendennis* and the Controversy on the 'Dignity of Literature.'" *Nineteenth-Century Literature* 41 (1986): 269–98.

Hughes, Kathryn. *George Eliot: the Last Victorian.* New York: Farrar Straus & Giroux, 1999.

Hughes, Linda K., and Michael Lund. *The Victorian Serial.* Charlottesville: University Press of Virginia, 1991.

Hume, David. *A Treatise on Human Nature.* Ed. L. A. Selby-Bigge. Oxford: Clarendon Press, 1978.

[Hutton, R. H.] Rev. of *Middlemarch. Spectator* (3 August 1872): 975–6.

Huysmans, J. K. *Against the Grain* (*A Rebours*). New York: Dover, 1969.

Ingham, Patricia. "'Nobody's Fault': the Scope of the Negative in *Little Dorrit.*" *Dickens Refigured: Bodies, Desires and Other Histories.* Ed. John Schad. Manchester: Manchester University Press, 1996. 98–116.

Inwood, Stephen. *A History of London.* New York: Carroll & Graf, 1998.

Jacobus, Mary. *Reading Woman: Essays in Feminist Criticism.* New York: Columbia University Press, 1986.

Jaffe, Audrey. *Scenes of Sympathy: Identity and Representation in Victorian Fiction.* Ithaca: Cornell University Press, 2000.

—*Vanishing Points: Dickens, Narrative, and the Subject of Omniscience.* Berkeley: University of California Press, 1991.

Jakobson, Roman. "Two Aspects of Language and Two Types of Linguistic Disturbances." 1956. *Language and Literature.* Ed. Krystyna Pomorska and Stephen Rudy. Cambridge: Belknap-Harvard University Press, 1987.

Jameson, Fredric. *Late Marxism: Adorno, or, The Persistence of the Dialectic.* London: Verso, 1990.

—"Marxism and Historicism." 1979. *The Ideologies of Theory: Essays 1971–1986.* Vol. 2. Minneapolis: University of Minnesota Press, 1988. 148–77.

—*The Political Unconscious: Narrative as a Socially Symbolic Act.* Ithaca: Cornell University Press, 1981.

—*Postmodernism, or, The Cultural Logic of Late Capitalism.* Durham: Duke University Press, 1991.

—"The Vanishing Mediator; or, Max Weber as Storyteller." 1973. *The Ideologies of Theory: Essays 1971–1986.* Vol. 2. Minneapolis: University of Minnesota Press, 1988. 3–34.

Jay, Elisabeth. *The Religion of the Heart: Anglican Evangelicalism and the Nineteenth-Century Novel.* Oxford: Clarendon Press, 1979.

Jay, Martin. *The Dialectical Imagination: a History of the Frankfurt School of Social Research, 1923–50.* 1973. Berkeley: University of California Press, 1996.

Jerrold, Walter. *Douglas Jerrold and Punch.* London, 1910.

—*The Life of Douglas Jerrold.* 2 vols. London, n.d.

John, Juliet. *Dickens's Villains: Melodrama, Character, Popular Culture.* Oxford: Oxford University Press, 2001.

Johnson, Edgar. *Charles Dickens: His Tragedy and Triumph.* 2 vols. New York: Simon and Schuster, 1952.

Johnston, Kenneth. *Wordsworth and* The Recluse. New Haven: Yale University Press, 1984.

Jones, Henry. *Browning as a Philosophical and Religious Teacher.* London, 1891.

Jones, Norman. *God and the Moneylenders: Usury and Law in Early Modern England.* London: Basil Blackwell, 1989.

Jordan, John O. and Robert L. Patten, eds. *Literature in the Marketplace: Nineteenth Century British Publishing and Reading Practices.* Cambridge: Cambridge University Press, 1995.

Jump, John D., ed. *Tennyson: the Critical Heritage.* London: Routledge & Kegan Paul, 1967.

Kant, Immanuel. *The Critique of Judgment.* Trans. James Meredith. Oxford: Oxford University Press, 1952.

—*The Critique of Pure Reason.* Trans. N. Kemp Smith. London, 1929.

Kaplan, Fred. *Dickens: a Biography.* New York: William Morrow, 1988.

Kaufmann, Walter. *Nietzsche: Philosopher, Psychologist, Antichrist.* 4th edn. Princeton: Princeton University Press, 1974.

Kay, James Phillips. *The Moral and Physical Conditions of the Working Classes Employed in the Cotton Manufacture in Manchester.* 2nd edn. London: James Ridgeway, 1832.

Kermode, Frank. *The Sense of an Ending: Studies in the Theory of Fiction.* New York: Oxford University Press, 1968.

Kierkegaard, Søren. *Either/Or.* 1843. Ed. and trans. Howard V. Hong and Edna H. Hong. 2 vols. Princeton: Princeton University Press, 1987.

—*Fear and Trembling.* 1843. Ed. and trans. Walter Lowrie. Princeton: Princeton University Press, 1954.

Kincaid, James. *Dickens and the Rhetoric of Laughter.* Oxford: Oxford University Press, 1971.

Kirk, Neville. *Capitalism, Custom and Protest, 1780–1850*. Vol. 1 of *Labour and Society in Britain and the USA*. Aldershot: Scolar Press, 1994.

Kittler, Friedrich A. *Discourse Networks, 1800/1900*. Trans. Michael Metteer and Chris Cullens. Stanford: Stanford University Press, 1990.

Klancher, Jon P. *The Making of English Reading Audiences, 1790–1832*. Madison: University of Wisconsin Press, 1987.

Knoepflmacher, U. C. *George Eliot's Early Novels: the Limits of Realism*. Berkeley: University of California Press, 1968.

—*Religious Humanism and the Victorian Novel: George Eliot, Walter Pater, and Samuel Butler*. Princeton: Princeton University Press, 1965.

Kowaleski-Wallace, Elizabeth. *Their Fathers' Daughters: Hannah More, Maria Edgeworth, and Patriarchal Complicity*. New York: Oxford University Press, 1991.

Kreuger, Christine L. *The Reader's Repentance: Women Preachers, Women Writers, and Nineteenth-Century Social Discourse*. Chicago: University of Chicago Press, 1992.

Kucich, John. *Repression in Victorian Fiction: Charlotte Brontë, George Eliot and Charles Dickens*. Berkeley: University of California Press, 1987.

Kurrik, Maire Jaanus. *Literature and Negation*. New York: Columbia University Press, 1979.

Lacan, Jacques. *Feminine Sexuality: Jacques Lacan and the école freudienne*. Ed. and intro. Juliet Mitchell and Jacqueline Rose. Trans. Jacqueline Rose. New York: Norton, 1982.

Lane, Christopher. *The Burdens of Intimacy: Psychoanalysis and Victorian Masculinity*. Chicago: University of Chicago Press, 1999.

Lane, Robert E. *The Loss of Happiness in Market Democracies*. New Haven: Yale University Press, 2000.

Langbauer, Laurie. *Novels of Everyday Life: the Series in English Fiction, 1850–1930*. Ithaca: Cornell University Press, 1999.

Langbaum, Robert. *The Poetry of Experience*. New York: Random House, 1957.

Laplanche, Jean, and J.-B. Pontalis. *The Language of Psycho-Analysis*. Trans. D. Nicholson-Smith. New York: Norton, 1973.

Larson, Janet. *Dickens and the Broken Scripture*. Athens: University of Georgia Press, 1985.

Law, Graham. *Serializing Fiction in the Victorian Press*. Basingstoke: Palgrave Macmillan, 2000.

Lawrence, Christopher. "The Nervous System and Society in the Scottish Enlightenment." *Natural Order: Historical Studies of Scientific Culture*. Ed. Barry Barnes and Steven Shapin. London: Sage, 1979. 19–40.

Leavis, Q. D. "Introduction." *Silas Marner, the Weaver of Raveloe*. By George Eliot. Harmondsworth: Penguin, 1967. 7–43.

Levine, George. *Darwin and the Novelists*. Cambridge: Harvard University Press, 1988.

—ed. *The Cambridge Companion to George Eliot*. Cambridge: Cambridge University Press, 2001.

Lewes, George Henry. *A Biographical History of Philosophy*. 1845–6. Rev. edn. 2 vols. New York: Appleton, 1857.

Lodge, David. "*Middlemarch* and the Idea of the Classic Realist Text." *New Casebooks: Middlemarch*. Ed. John Peck. New York: St. Martin's Press, 1992. 45–64.

Lukacher, Ned. *Primal Scenes: Literature, Philosophy, Psychoanalysis*. Ithaca: Cornell University Press, 1986.

Lukács, Georg. *The Theory of the Novel*. Trans. Anna Bostock. Cambridge: MIT Press, 1971.

McCann, J. Clinton, Jr. "Disease and Cure in 'Janet's Repentance': George Eliot's Change of Mind." *Literature and Medicine* 9 (1990): 69–78.

McKee, Patricia. *Public and Private: Gender, Class, and the British Novel, 1764–1878*. Minneapolis: University of Minnesota Press, 1997.

McKenzie, K. A. *Edith Simcox and George Eliot*. London: Oxford University Press, 1961.

McKeon, Michael. *The Origins of the English Novel, 1600–1740*. Baltimore: Johns Hopkins University Press, 1987.

McLaughlin, Kevin. *Writing in Parts: Imitation and Exchange in Nineteenth-Century Literature*. Stanford: Stanford University Press, 1995.

McLeod, Hugh. *Religion and Society in England, 1850–1914*. London: Macmillan, 1996.

McMaster, Judith. "Novels by Eminent Hands: Flattery by the Author of *Vanity Fair*." *Dickens Studies Annual* 18 (1989): 309–36.

Machin, G. I. T. *Politics and the Churches in Great Britain, 1832–1868*. Oxford: Clarendon Press, 1977.

Mandler, Peter. *Aristocratic Government in the Age of Reform: Whigs and Liberals 1830–1852*. Oxford: Clarendon Press, 1990.

Mann, Michael. *The Rise of Classes and Nation-States, 1760–1914*. Vol. 2 of *The Sources of Social Power*. Cambridge: Cambridge University Press, 1993.

Manning, Peter. "Wordsworth in the *Keepsake*, 1829." *Literature in the Marketplace*, ed. Jordan and Patten. Cambridge: Cambridge University Press, 1995. 44–73.

Manning, Sylvia. "Social Criticism and Textual Subversion in *Little Dorrit*." *Dickens Studies Annual* 20 (1991): 127–47.

Marcus, Steven. *Dickens From Pickwick to Dombey*. New York: Norton, 1965.

—*Engels, Manchester and the Working Class*. New York: Norton, 1974.

—*Representations: Essays on Literature and Society*. 2nd edn. New York: Columbia University Press, 1990.

Martin, Carol A. *George Eliot's Serial Fiction*. Columbus: Ohio State University Press, 1994.

Martin, Loy D. *Browning's Dramatic Monologues and the Post-Romantic Subject*. Baltimore: Johns Hopkins University Press, 1985.

Marx, Karl. *Capital, Volume One*. 1867. Trans. Ben Fowkes. Harmondsworth: Penguin–New Left Books, 1976.

—*The Economic and Philosophic Manuscripts of 1844*. Trans. Martin Mulligan, ed. Dirk J. Strunk. New York: International, 1964.

—*The Eighteenth Brumaire of Louis Bonaparte*. 1852. New York: International, 1963.

—*The German Ideology, Part One*. Ed. and intro. C. J. Arthur. New York: International, 1970.

—*Theses on Feuerbach*. 1845; 1888. *The Marx–Engels Reader*. Ed. Robert C. Tucker. 2nd edn. New York: Norton, 1978. 143–5.

Mathias, Peter. *The First Industrial Nation: an Economic History of Britain, 1700–1914*. 2nd edn. London: Methuen, 1983.

Matus, Jill L. *Unstable Bodies: Victorian Representations of Sexuality and Maternity*. Manchester: Manchester University Press, 1995.

Maurice, F. D. *Theological Essays*. 1853. New York: Harper, 1953.

Maurice, Frederick. *The Life of Frederick Denison Maurice*. 2 vols. London: Macmillan, 1884.

Meiksins Wood, Ellen. *Democracy Against Capitalism*. Cambridge: Cambridge University Press, 1995.

Meisel, Martin. *Realizations: Narrative, Pictorial, and Theatrical Arts in 19th-Century England*. Princeton: Princeton University Press, 1983.

Micale, Mark S. *Approaching Hysteria: Disease and its Interpretations*. Princeton: Princeton University Press, 1995.

—"Hysteria Male/Hysteria Female: Reflections on Comparative Gender Construction in Nineteenth-Century France and Britain." *Science and Sensibility: Gender and Scientific Inquiry, 1780–1945*. Ed. Marina Benjamin. Oxford: Basil Blackwell, 1991. 200–39.

Mill, James. *Elements of Political Economy*. 3rd edn. 1826. *James Mill: Selected Economic Writings*. Ed. Donald Winch. Edinburgh: Oliver & Boyd, 1966.

Mill, John Stuart. *The Collected Works of John Stuart Mill*. Ed. J. M. Robson. 33 vols. Toronto: University of Toronto Press, 1963–91.

Miller, Andrew. *Novels Behind Glass: Commodity Culture and Victorian Narrative*. Cambridge: Cambridge University Press, 1995.

Miller, D. A. *The Novel and the Police*. Berkeley: University of California Press, 1988.

Miller, J. Hillis. *Charles Dickens: the World of his Novels*. Cambridge: Harvard University Press, 1958.

—"The Fiction of Realism: *Sketches by Boz, Oliver Twist*, and Cruikshank's Illustrations." *Charles Dickens and George Cruikshank*. Ed. Ada A. Nisbet. Los Angeles: William Andrews Clark Memorial Library, 1971. 1–69.

—"Narrative and History." *ELH* 41 (1974): 455–73.

Mintz, Alan. *George Eliot and the Novel of Vocation*. Cambridge: Harvard University Press, 1978.

Mizruchi, Susan. *The Science of Sacrifice: American Literature and Modern Social Theory*. Princeton: Princeton University Press, 1998.

Mommsen, Wolfgang. *The Political and Social Theory of Max Weber*. Chicago: University of Chicago Press, 1989.

Mooney, Edward F. *Knights of Faith and Resignation: Reading Kierkegaard's* Fear and Trembling. Albany: State University of New York Press, 1991.

Moretti, Franco. *Atlas of the European Novel, 1800–1900*. London: Verso, 1998.

—*Modern Epic: the World System from Goethe to Garcia-Marquez*. New York: Verso, 1996.

—*Signs Taken for Wonders*. Rev. edn. London: Verso, 1988.

—*The Way of the World: the Bildungsroman in European Culture*. London: Verso, 1987.

Moses, Michael Valdez. *The Novel and the Globalization of Culture*. New York: Oxford University Press, 1995.

Myers, Frederic W. H. "George Eliot." *Century Illustrated Monthly Magazine* 23 (November 1881): 57–64.

Myers, William. "The Radicalism of *Little Dorrit*." *Literature and Politics in the Nineteenth Century: Essays*. Ed. John Lucas. London: Methuen, 1971. 77–104.

—*The Teaching of George Eliot*. Totowa: Barnes & Noble, 1984.

Nairn, Tom. *The Break-Up of Britain: Crisis and Neo-Nationalism*. London: New Left Books, 1977.

Nayder, Lillian. "The Cannibal, the Nurse and the Cook in Dickens's *The Frozen Deep*." *Victorian Literature and Culture* 19 (1991): 1–24.

—*Unequal Partners: Charles Dickens, Wilkie Collins, and Victorian Authorship*. Ithaca: Cornell University Press, 2000.

Nehamas, Alexander. *Nietzsche: Life as Literature*. Cambridge: Harvard University Press, 1985.

Newman, John Henry. *Apologia Pro Vita Sua*. Ed. A. Dwight Culler. Boston: Houghton Mifflin-Riverside, 1956.

Newsome, David. *Two Classes of Men: Platonism and English Romantic Thought*. London: John Murray, 1972.

Nietzsche, F.W. *Beyond Good and Evil*. Trans. Walter Kaufmann. New York: Vintage, 1966.

—*On the Genealogy of Morals*. Trans. Walter Kaufmann and R. J. Hollingdale. New York: Vintage, 1989.

—*Thus Spoke Zarathustra*. Ed. and trans. Walter Kaufmann. *The Portable Nietzsche*. New York: Viking/Penguin, 1982. 103–439.

—"Über Wahrheit und Lüge im aussermoralischen Sinne." 1873. Trans. Daniel Breazeale as "On Truth and Lies in a Nonmoral Sense." *Philosophy and Truth: Selections from Nietzsche's Notebooks of the early 1870's*. Ed. Daniel Breazeale. Atlantic Highlands: Humanities Press, 1979. 79–97.

Noble, Thomas A. *George Eliot's* Scenes of Clerical Life. New Haven: Yale University Press, 1965.

Norman, Edward R. *The Victorian Christian Socialists*. Cambridge: Cambridge University Press, 1987.

Nunokawa, Jeff. *The Afterlife of Property: Domestic Security and the Victorian Novel*. Princeton: Princeton University Press, 1994.

Oldfield, Derek and Sybil. "*Scenes of Clerical Life*: the Diagram and the Picture." *Critical Essays on George Eliot*. Ed. Barbara Hardy. New York: Barnes & Noble, 1970. 1–18.

Oppenheim, Janet. *"Shattered Nerves": Doctors, Patients, and Depression in Victorian England*. New York: Oxford University Press, 1991.

Orwell, George. "Charles Dickens." *Dickens, Dali and Others*. New York: Reynal and Hitchcock, 1946. 1–75.

Paris, Bernard J. *Experiments in Life: George Eliot's Quest for Values*. Detroit: Wayne State University Press, 1965.

Parossien, David. *Oliver Twist: an Annotated Bibliography*. New York: Garland, 1986.

Patten, Robert L. *Charles Dickens and his Publishers*. Oxford: Clarendon Press, 1978.

—*George Cruikshank: His Life, Times, and Art*. 2 vols. New Brunswick: Rutgers University Press, 1992, 1996.

—"Serialized Retrospection in *The Pickwick Papers*." *Literature in the Marketplace*. Ed. John O. Jordan and Robert L. Patten. 123–42.

Payne, David. "Thackeray v. Dickens in *The Book of Snobs*." *Thackeray Newsletter* 51 (May 2000): 1–6 and 52 (Nov. 2000): 1–2.

Pearson, Richard. *W. M. Thackeray and the Mediated Text: Writing for Periodicals in the Mid-Nineteenth Century*. Aldershot: Ashgate, 2000.

Pelling, Margaret. *Cholera, Fever and English Medicine, 1825–1865*. Oxford: Oxford University Press, 1978.

Peters, Catherine. *The Thackeray Universe: Shifting Worlds of Imagination and Reality*. London: Faber and Faber, 1987.

Philpotts, Trey. "Trevelyan, Treasury and Circumlocution." *Dickens Studies Annual* 22 (1993): 283–301.

Pocock, J. G. A. *The Ancient Constitution and the Feudal Law*. New York: Norton, 1967.

—*Virtue, Commerce, and History*. Cambridge: Cambridge University Press, 1985.

Poovey, Mary. *Making a Social Body: British Cultural Formation, 1830–1864*. Chicago: University of Chicago Press, 1995.

—*Uneven Developments: the Ideological Work of Gender in Mid-Victorian England*. Chicago: University of Chicago Press, 1988.

Price, Leah. *The Anthology and the Rise of the Novel: From Richardson to George Eliot*. Cambridge: Cambridge University Press, 2000.

Prickett, Stephen. *Romanticism and Religion: the Tradition of Coleridge and Wordsworth in the Victorian Church*. Cambridge: Cambridge University Press, 1976.

Pyle, Forrest. *The Ideology of Imagination: Subject and Society in the Discourse of Romanticism*. Stanford: Stanford University Press, 1995.

Qualls, Barry. "George Eliot and Religion." *The Cambridge Companion to George Eliot*. Ed. George Levine. Cambridge: Cambridge University Press, 2001. 119–37.

—*The Secular Pilgrim of Victorian Fiction: the Novel as Book of Life*. Cambridge: Cambridge University Press, 1982.

Ray, Gordon N. *Thackeray: the Uses of Adversity*. New York: McGraw-Hill, 1958.

—"*Vanity Fair*: One Version of the Novelist's Responsibility." *Essays by Divers Hands* 25 (1950): 87–101.

Reed, John. *Dickens and Thackeray: Punishment and Forgiveness*. Athens: Ohio State University Press, 1995.

Richetti, John. *Popular Fiction Before Richardson: Narrative Patterns, 1700–1739*. 2nd edn. Oxford: Clarendon Press, 1992.

Richmond, Legh. "The Dairyman's Daughter." 1810. *Annals of the Poor, or Narratives of* The Dairyman's Daughter, The Negro Servant, *and* The Young Cottager. New York, [1856?].

Ricoeur, Paul. *Lectures on Ideology and Utopia*. Ed. George H. Taylor. New York: Columbia University Press, 1986.

Ritchie, Hester Thackeray, ed. *Thackeray and His Daughter*. New York: Harper, 1924.

Rothfield, Lawrence. *Vital Signs: Medical Realism in Nineteenth-Century Fiction*. Princeton: Princeton University Press, 1992.

Rubinstein, W. D. *Men of Property: the Very Wealthy in Britain since the Industrial Revolution*. New Brunswick: Rutgers University Press, 1981.

Rueschemeyer, Dietrich. *Power and the Division of Labor.* Stanford: Stanford University Press, 1986.

Sanders, Andrew. *Dickens and the Spirit of the Age.* Oxford: Clarendon Press, 1999.

Scaff, Lawrence A. *Fleeing the Iron Cage: Culture, Politics and Modernity in the Thought of Max Weber.* Berkeley: University of California Press, 1989.

Schacht, Richard. *Nietzsche.* London: Routledge & Kegan Paul, 1983.

Schiller, Friedrich von. *Letters on the Aesthetic Education of Man.* 1795. Trans. Elizabeth M. Wilkinson and L. A. Willoughby. Oxford: Oxford University Press, 1967.

Schlicke, Paul. *Dickens and Popular Entertainment.* London: Allen & Unwin, 1985.

Schor, Hilary. *Dickens and the Daughter of the House.* Cambridge: Cambridge University Press, 1999.

—"Fiction." *A Companion to Victorian Literature and Culture.* Ed. Herbert F. Tucker. London: Blackwell, 1999. 323–38.

Schumpeter, Joseph. *History of Economic Analysis.* New York: Oxford University Press, 1994.

Schwartz, Pedro. *The New Political Economy of J. S. Mill.* London: Weidenfeld and Nicolson, 1972.

Schwarzbach, F. S. *Dickens and the City.* London: Athlone Press, 1979.

Screpanti, Ernesto, and Stefano Zamagni. *An Outline of the History of Economic Thought.* Trans. David Field. Oxford: Clarendon Press, 1993.

Sedgwick, Eve Kosofsky. *Between Men: English Literature and Male Homosocial Desire.* New York: Columbia University Press, 1985.

Semmel, Bernard. *George Eliot and the Politics of National Inheritance.* New York: Oxford University Press, 1994.

—*John Stuart Mill and the Pursuit of Virtue.* New Haven: Yale University Press, 1984.

Shaw, Harry. *Narrating Reality: Austen, Scott, Eliot.* Ithaca: Cornell University Press, 1999.

Shell, Marc. *The Economy of Literature.* Baltimore: Johns Hopkins University Press, 1978.

Shillingsburg, Peter L. *Pegasus in Harness: W. M. Thackeray and Victorian Publishing.* Charlottesville: University Press of Virginia, 1992.

Showalter, Elaine. *The Female Malady: Women, Madness, and English Culture, 1830–1980.* New York: Pantheon, 1985.

—"Guilt, Authority and the Shadows of *Little Dorrit.*" *Nineteenth-Century Fiction* 34 (June 1979): 20–40.

Shuger, Debora. *The Renaissance Bible: Scholarship, Sacrifice and Subjectivity.* Berkeley: University of California Press, 1994.

Shuttleworth, Sally. "Fairy Tale or Science? Physiological Psychology in *Silas Marner.*" *Languages of Nature: Critical Essays in Science and Literature.* Ed. L. J. Jordanova. New Brunswick: Rutgers University Press, 1986. 244–88.

—*George Eliot and Nineteenth-Century Science.* Cambridge: Cambridge University Press, 1984.

Silverman, Kaja. *Male Subjectivity at the Margins.* London: Routledge, 1992.

Simcox, Edith J. *A Monument to the Memory of George Eliot: Edith J. Simcox's* Autobiography of a Shirtmaker. Ed. Constance M. Fulmer and Margaret E. Barfield. New York: Garland, 1998.

—*Natural Law: an Essay on Ethics.* London, 1877.

Simmel, Georg. "The Metropolis and Mental Life." *Individuality and Social Forms.* Ed. Donald L. Levine. Chicago: University of Chicago Press, 1971. 324–39.

Simpson, David. *Fetishism and Imagination: Dickens, Melville, Conrad.* Baltimore: Johns Hopkins University Press, 1982.

—*Romanticism, Naturalism and the Revolt against Theory.* Chicago: University of Chicago Press, 1993.

—ed. *The Origins of Modern Critical Thought: German Aesthetic and Literary Criticism from Lessing to Hegel.* Cambridge: Cambridge University Press, 1988.

Smith, Adam. *The Nature and Causes of the Wealth of Nations.* 1776. Ed. R. H. Campbell and A. S. Skinner. Oxford: Clarendon Press, 1976.

—*The Theory of Moral Sentiments.* Ed. D. D. Raphael and A. L. Macfie. Oxford: Clarendon Press, 1976.

Smith-Allen, James. *In the Public Eye: a History of Reading in Modern France, 1800–1940.* Princeton: Princeton University Press, 1991.

Staten, Henry. "Is *Middlemarch* Ahistorical?" *PMLA* 115 (2000): 991–1005.

Stewart, Garrett. *Dickens and the Trials of Imagination.* Cambridge: Harvard University Press, 1976.

Strauss, David Friedrich. *The Life of Jesus, Critically Examined.* Trans. George Eliot. New York: Calvin Blanchard, 1855.

Suchoff, David. *Critical Theory and the Novel: Mass Society and Cultural Criticism in Dickens, Melville, and Kafka.* Madison: University of Wisconsin Press, 1994.

Sutherland, John. *Thackeray at Work.* London: Athlone Press, 1974.

—*Victorian Fiction: Writers, Publishers, Readers.* New York: St. Martin's Press, 1995.

—*Victorian Novelists and Publishers.* Chicago: University of Chicago Press, 1976.

Swanston, Hamish F. G. *Ideas of Order: Anglicans and the Renewal of Theological Method in the Middle Years of the Nineteenth Century.* Assen: Van Gorcum, 1974.

Swartz, David. *Culture and Power: the Sociology of Pierre Bourdieu.* Chicago: University of Chicago Press, 1997.

Tambling, Jeremy. *Dickens, Violence and the Modern State: Dreams of the Scaffold.* London: Macmillan, 1995.

Taylor, Charles. *Hegel.* Cambridge: Cambridge University Press, 1975.

Taylor, D. J. *Thackeray: a Life.* London: Chatto & Windus, 1999.

Thackeray, William Makepeace. *The Book of Snobs.* 1848, 1855. Ed. John Sutherland. New York: St. Martin's Press, 1978.

—"A Box of Novels." *Fraser's Magazine* 29 (Feb. 1844): 153–69.

—"A Brother of the Press on the History of a Literary Man, Laman Blanchard, and the Chances of the Literary Profession." *Fraser's Magazine* 33 (March 1846): 332–42.

—*Catherine.* 1839–40. Ed. Sheldon Goldfarb. Ann Arbor: University of Michigan Press, 1999.

—"Christmas Books – No. 1." *Morning Chronicle* (24 Dec. 1845): 5–6. *W. M. Thackeray's Contributions to the Morning Chronicle.* Ed. Gordon N. Ray. Urbana: University of Illinois Press, 1955. 86–8.

—"Epistles to the Literati – No. XIII." *Fraser's Magazine* 21 (Jan. 1840): 71–80.

—"Going to See a Man Hanged." *Fraser's Magazine* 22 (Aug. 1840): 150–8.

—"Horae Catnachianae." *Fraser's Magazine* 19 (April 1839): 407–24.

—*Letters and Private Papers of William Makepeace Thackeray.* Ed. Gordon N. Ray. 4 vols. Cambridge: Harvard University Press, 1944.

—*The Luck of Barry Lyndon*. Ed. Edgar F. Harden. Ann Arbor: University of Michigan Press, 1999.
—*Notes of a Journey from Cornhill to Grand Cairo*. Vol. 6 of *The Works of William Makepeace Thackeray [Centenary Biographical Edition]*. Intro. Hester Thackeray Ritchie. New York: Harper, 1910. 227–418.
—"The Professor." *Bentley's Miscellany* 2 (Sept. 1837): 277–88.
—"A Shabby Genteel Story." *Fraser's Magazine* 21–22 (1840): 677–89, 90–101, 399–414.
—"Strictures on Pictures: a Letter from Michael Angelo Titmarsh, Esq." *Fraser's Magazine* 17 (June 1838): 758–64.
—*Vanity Fair: a Novel without a Hero*. 1847–8. Ed. Peter L. Shillingsburg. New York: Norton, 1994.
—*The Yellowplush Correspondence*. 1837–8, 1840. Ed. Peter L. Shillingsburg. New York: Garland, 1991.
Thompson, E. P. *The Origins of the English Working Class*. New York: Vintage, 1966.
—*Witness Against the Beast: William Blake and the Moral Law*. New York: New Press, 1993.
Tillotson, Kathleen. *Novels of the Eighteen-Forties*. Oxford: Clarendon Press, 1954.
Tomalin, Claire. *The Invisible Woman: the Story of Nelly Ternan and Charles Dickens*. New York: Alfred A. Knopf, 1991.
Tonna, Charlotte Elizabeth [Charlotte Elizabeth]. *The Works of Charlotte Elizabeth*. 7th edn. Intro. H. B. Stowe. New York: M. W. Dodd, 1849.
Travis, John F. *The Rise of the Devon Seaside Resorts, 1750–1900*. Exeter: University of Exeter Press, 1993.
Trilling, Lionel. *Matthew Arnold*. New York: Columbia University Press, 1949.
—*The Opposing Self: Nine Essays in Criticism*. New York: Viking, 1955.
Trollope, Anthony. *An Illustrated Autobiography*. 1883. Wolfeboro: Alan Sutton, 1989.
Vallone, Lynne. *Becoming Victoria*. New Haven: Yale University Press, 2001.
Viner, Jacob. "Bentham and J. S. Mill: the Utilitarian Background." 1949. *Essays on the Intellectual History of Economics*. Ed. Douglas A. Irwin. Princeton: Princeton University Press, 1991. 154–75.
Viswanathan, Gauri. *Outside the Fold: Conversion, Modernity, and Belief*. Princeton: Princeton University Press, 1998.
Wach, Howard M. "Culture and the Middle Classes: Popular Knowledge in Industrial Manchester." *Journal of British Studies* 27 (1988): 375–404.
Walder, Dennis. *Dickens and Religion*. London: Allen & Unwin, 1981.
Walicki, Andrez. *Marxism and the Leap to the Kingdom of Freedom: the Rise and Fall of the Communist Utopia*. Stanford: Stanford University Press, 1995.
Wallerstein, Immanuel. *The Modern World System: Capitalist Agriculture and the Origins of the European World-Economy in the Sixteenth Century*. San Diego: Academic Press, 1974.
—*The Modern World-System III: the Second Era of Great Expansion of the Capitalist World-Economy, 1730s–1840s*. San Diego: Academic Press, 1989.
Warner, William. *Licensing Entertainment: the Elements of Novel Reading in England, 1694–1750*. Berkeley: University of California Press, 1998.
Webb, R. K. *Harriet Martineau: a Radical Victorian*. New York: Columbia University Press, 1960.

Weber, Marianne. *Max Weber: a Biography*. Trans. and ed. Harry Zohn. New Brunswick: Transaction Books, 1988.
Weber, Max. *Ancient Judaism*. Trans. and ed. H. H. Gerth and Don Martindale. New York: Free Press, 1952.
—*From Max Weber: Essays in Sociology*. Trans. and ed. H. H. Gerth and C. Wright Mills. New York: Oxford University Press, 1946.
—*The Protestant Ethic and the Spirit of Capitalism*. 1904–5. Ed. and trans. Talcott Parsons. Intro. Anthony Giddens. New York: Scribners, 1958.
—"'Objectivity' in the Social Sciences." 1904. *The Methodology of the Social Sciences*. Ed. and trans. E. A. Shils and H. Finch. New York: Free Press, 1949.
—"Politics as a Vocation." 1919. *From Max Weber*, trans. H. H. Gerth and C. Wright Mills, 77–128.
—*The Rational and Social Foundations of Music*. Trans. and ed. Don Martindale, Johannes Riedel and Gertrude Neuwirth. Carbondale: Southern Illinois University Press, 1958.
—"Science as a Vocation." 1919. Trans. H. H. Gerth and C. Wright Mills. *From Max Weber*. 129–56.
—"The Social Psychology of the World Religions." Trans. H. H. Gerth and C. Wright Mills. *From Max Weber*. 267–301.
—"*Zwischenbetrachtung* [Intermediate Reflections]." 1915. Trans. H. H. Gerth and C. Wright Mills as "Religious Rejections of the World and their Directions." *From Max Weber*. 323–59.
Weintraub, Stanley. *Victoria: an Intimate Biography*. New York: E. P. Dutton, 1987.
Welsh, Alexander. *The City of Dickens*. Oxford: Clarendon Press, 1971.
—*George Eliot and Blackmail*. Cambridge: Harvard University Press, 1985.
—"Waverley, Pickwick and Don Quixote." *Nineteenth Century Fiction* 22 (1967–8): 19–30.
Wheeler, Burton M. "The Text and Plan of *Oliver Twist*." *Dickens Studies Annual* 12 (1983): 41–61.
White, Edward M. "Thackeray's Contributions to *Fraser's Magazine*." *Studies in Bibliography* 19 (1966): 67–84.
Wicke, Jennifer. *Advertising Fictions: Literature, Advertisement, and Social Reading*. New York: Columbia University Press, 1988.
Wilberforce, Robert and Samuel. *The Life of William Wilberforce*. 5 vols. London, 1838.
—eds. *The Correspondence of William Wilberforce*. 2 vols. London, 1840.
Wilberforce, William. *A Practical View of Christianity*. London, 1795.
Wilde, Alan. "Mr. F's Aunt and the Analogical Structure of *Little Dorrit*." *Nineteenth Century Fiction* 19 (1964): 33–44.
Wilkins, William Glyde. *Charles Dickens in America*. New York: Scribner, 1911.
Willey, Basil. *Nineteenth Century Studies*. 1949. New York: Harper & Row, 1966.
Williams, Raymond. *The Country and the City*. New York: Oxford University Press, 1964.
—*Culture and Society, 1780–1950*. 2nd edn. New York: Columbia University Press, 1983.
—*Keywords: a Vocabulary of Culture and Society*. Rev. edn. New York: Oxford University Press, 1983.
—*Marxism and Literature*. Oxford: Oxford University Press, 1977.
—*The Politics of Modernism*. London: Verso, 1989.

Wilson, Edmund. "Dickens: the Two Scrooges." *The Wound and the Bow*. Boston: Houghton Mifflin-Riverside, 1941. 1–104.
Wilt, Judith. *Ghosts of the Gothic: Austen, Eliot and Lawrence*. Princeton: Princeton University Press, 1980.
Woodmansee, Martha and Mark Osteen, eds. *The New Economic Criticism: Studies at the Intersection of Literature and Economics*. London: Routledge, 1999.
Wordsworth, William. *The Letters of William and Dorothy Wordsworth*. Ed. Ernest de Selincourt and Mary Moorman. 2nd edn. Oxford: Clarendon Press, 1969.
—*The Prose Works of William Wordsworth*. 3 vols. Ed. W. J. B. Owen and J. W. Smyser. Oxford: Clarendon Press, 1974.
Wynne, Deborah. *The Sensation Novel and the Victorian Family Magazine*. Basingstoke: Palgrave Macmillan, 2001.
Zizek, Slavoj. *The Sublime Object of Ideology*. London: Verso, 1989.

Index

Printed in the United States
71086LV00003B/49-57